Springtime with the Railway Girls

Maisie Thomas was born and brought up in Manchester, which provides the location for her Railway Girls novels. She loves writing stories with strong female characters, set in times when women needed determination and vision to make their mark. The Railway Girls series is inspired by her great-aunt Jessie, who worked as a railway clerk during the First World War.

Maisie now lives on the beautiful North Wales coast with her railway enthusiast husband, Kevin, and their two rescue cats. They often enjoy holidays chugging up and down the UK's heritage steam railways.

T0307503

Also by Maisie Thomas

The Railway Girls
Secrets of the Railway Girls
The Railway Girls in Love
Christmas with the Railway Girls
Hope for the Railway Girls
A Christmas Miracle for the Railway Girls
Courage of the Railway Girls
Christmas Wishes for the Railway Girls

Springtime with the Railway Girls

MAISIE THOMAS

PENGUIN BOOKS

PENGUIN BOOKS

UK | USA | Canada | Ireland | Australia
India | New Zealand | South Africa

Penguin Books is part of the Penguin Random House group of companies whose addresses can be found at global.penguinrandomhouse.com

Penguin Random House UK

Published in Penguin Books 2024
001

Copyright © Maisie Thomas, 2024

The moral right of the author has been asserted

Typeset in 10.4/15pt Palatino LT Pro by Jouve (UK), Milton Keynes
Printed and bound in Great Britain by Clays Ltd, Elcograf S.p.A.

The authorised representative in the EEA is
Penguin Random House Ireland, Morrison Chambers,
32 Nassau Street, Dublin D02 YH68

A CIP catalogue record for this book is available from the British Library

ISBN: 978–1–80494–223–9

www.greenpenguin.co.uk

MIX
Paper | Supporting responsible forestry
FSC® C018179
FSC www.fsc.org

Penguin Random House is committed to a sustainable future for our business, our readers and our planet. This book is made from Forest Stewardship Council® certified paper.

To the old girls of The Hollies FCJ Grammar School,
in particular the year group who started in 1972.

And also to the staff, especially Mrs Jones (Latin),
Mrs Trueman (English) and Miss Smith (History).
It is thanks to Miss Smith's teaching that
I now write books set in the past.

Springtime with the Railway Girls

Chapter One

January 1944

The loud ring woke Persephone and she reached out a hand to bat at the alarm clock on her bedside cabinet, pressing down the button on the top to silence the clamour. She pulled her arm back beneath the covers, sparing a thought for the time when a maid would have crept into her room while she slumbered to get the fire going, returning later with a cup of hot chocolate for Miss Persephone to get her day off to a cosy start. How things had changed. Not just for her; for everyone. But, by crikey, they had changed for her. Matt Franklin had changed her life beyond belief.

She had been at work until two this morning and then had been called upon to do another hour, so she had slept in late today. She swung out of bed, pushing her feet into her slippers, and drew her dressing gown out from inside the bed. It was much nicer to get into a toasty warm gown than a chilly one that had hung up neatly all night on the back of the door.

Going to the window, she pulled open the thick blackout curtains followed by the lavender silk curtains, which matched the lavender satin bows that held back the white muslin drapes falling prettily to the floor on either side of her half-tester bed. Tying her dressing gown more closely around her, Persephone used the flat of her hand to wipe clear a patch of condensation on the inside of the window-pane. There were even patches of frost there too.

Outside, snow lay on the ground, several inches deep. The sky was a soft duck-egg blue with wisps of cloud. The light from the sun, though milky, was sufficient to bring forth a smattering of twinkles from the snow, especially where it smothered the hedges. Persephone sighed and then smiled at her own reaction to the scene below her window. Even after more than four years of war, of anxiety and rationing and the blackout and every single thing one cared to mention being in frightfully short supply – even after all that, nature could still pull something special out of the bag and take one's breath away.

Tugging the lavender curtains closed again, she hurried into the bathroom that stood in between her bedroom and the one on the other side. She'd had the bathroom to herself almost the whole time since she had been shunted off to Darley Court by Pa and Ma at the outbreak of war. That had been a huge luxury to start with, because Meyrick House, the family's ancestral pile down in Sussex, wasn't exactly over-endowed in the bathroom department. Even so, Persephone now reckoned that her favourite times at Darley Court had been when first her friend Colette and later her sister Iphigenia had stayed in the opposite bedroom, and there had been much crossing through the bathroom to sit on one another's beds and talk. Those had been special times, though for very different reasons. Colette had come to

Darley Court in need of sanctuary after she had left her husband, while Iphigenia had been here as an ordinary guest, sprinkling the magic dust of her charm wherever she went.

Next to the porcelain enamelled bath, with its black line around the inside showing precisely how much – or rather, how little – water was permitted for wartime ablutions, was a copper gas-geyser on a wood-and-metal stand. From the top of the geyser, a cylindrical flue reached up almost to the blue-painted ceiling before turning and disappearing through the line of flower-decorated tiles that topped the plain white ones below.

Persephone cleaned her teeth and washed her face and hands, using the tiniest possible quantity of soap. It was essential, of course, to ration all kinds of things and Persephone had discovered that although it was possible to live without many items, there were others that it was a dratted nuisance to do without. Soap was definitely on the 'dratted' list. To be fair, though, she was fortunate to have a job that didn't involve getting mucky – unlike her chum Margaret, who cleaned locomotives in the engine shed for a living, not to mention Miss Brown's land girls.

Persephone returned to her bedroom. Fond as she was of it, she had to admit that the paint on the window frames, picture rail and door could do with a fresh coat, but nobody had been allowed to have paint for decorative purposes for simply yonks. It couldn't be spared. Besides, if there were to be some paint kicking around, she would far rather see it sprucing up the tired-looking stations and waiting rooms that she saw every day in her work as a ticket inspector.

She hurried into her clothes. Over a long-sleeved silk

blouse she wore an olive-green suede top, rather like a long, slimline waistcoat. On top of this went a sweater knitted for her by dear Mrs Grayson. It had padded shoulders and a high round neckline that hugged her throat. Persephone drew on straight-cut wool trousers, fastening the buttons on the side and pushing her hands into the hip-level pockets on the side-seams to make sure they didn't create an unsightly bulge. After putting on two pairs of socks, she stuffed her feet back into her slippers. It was the second full week of January and so far the month had been jolly chilly, with the low temperature expected to continue, though this was nothing compared to the exceptionally hard winter of 1942 when the country had been blanketed by several feet of snow and the birds had died frozen to the branches of trees. Persephone remembered her face being so cold that it had felt as if it was on fire.

She ran downstairs to the cavernous kitchen, where Mrs Mitchell, who had been the housekeeper here since dinosaurs roamed the earth, provided porridge and toast with a scraping of marge. Afterwards Persephone shoved her feet into her wellies and put on her brown-and-tan tweed jacket with flap pockets, wrapping herself up in the scarf knitted for her by Nanny Trehearn-Hobbs, who had unravelled an old sweater belonging to Persephone's brother Giles, thus making the scarf doubly precious. Pulling on a pair of shabby old gloves, she headed outside to be given a job by Mr Hattatt, the head gardener, a sweet old boy with oodles of knowledge about the land.

Outside, Persephone's breath fogged in the sharp air. Unsurprisingly, there was snow to be shovelled from the stable yard and then – a great honour – she was permitted to help sort through the potting shed, sharpening and oiling the tools, readying everything for the new season. The tools were always in good nick because of Mr Hattatt's rule that nothing could be put away after a day's work without first being cleaned, dried and then wiped with an oily rag.

Later, Persephone went to Miss Brown's office, where Darley Court's elderly owner spent much of her time. Around the walls, the shelves held books and military helmets from wars of yesteryear. Miss Brown's magnificent desk stood facing the windows while much of the floor was taken up by a vast table covered by a detailed map of the grounds, showing how they had been arranged for crop rotation for wartime. All the various vegetables and salad produce were put into three groups called A, B and C, which were then grown at different times of the year. This year was a B, C, A year. Last year had been C, A, B.

But it wasn't just the land that Miss Brown oversaw. Together, she and Persephone worked their way through the lists of forthcoming training events Darley Court would be hosting. They checked the dates and put everything in the diary, together with notes about the necessary catering. Even before the war began, back when air-raid shelters were being delivered to houses and sandbags were appearing everywhere, Miss Brown had volunteered Darley Court as a place for meetings and training for all local Civil Defence services, such as the ARP, First Aid and other casualty services, the engineering services, the Auxiliary Fire Service and the WVS.

Miss Brown might be in her seventies, but woe betide

anyone who made the mistake of imagining that meant she was frail and in need of guidance. She was a strong character with a shrewd mind and sharp eyes. Persephone thought the world of her.

Then, after a helping of Mrs Mitchell's rabbit hotpot, Persephone prepared to set off for work. She was proud to wear her smart uniform, not least because she wore on her lapel the London Midland & Scottish badge, showing its linked emblems of a thistle for Scotland and a rose for England, both of them beneath a wing with the cross of St George. Another reason for loving her uniform and all it represented was that she had her job on the railways to thank for introducing her to Matt. The thought of her handsome boyfriend brought a spontaneous smile to her lips.

Matt was a fireman on the railways and it was his job to keep his train running smoothly. He had to keep the fire stoked inside the engine's massive fire-box, shovelling the coal into the right spot at any given moment, always aware of the terrain and the driving conditions and how much energy was being taken from the fire. On top of this, he had to keep an eye on the water gauges and ensure the water never ran low as well as use his hammer to break up huge lumps of coal and spray water on the footplate to dampen down the dust.

After working at Victoria Station as a ticket collector, Persephone had met Matt once she was promoted to the post of ticket inspector, which required her to travel on the trains. Matt worked very long hours. Everyone did these days, of course, but the engine drivers and their firemen worked longer shifts than anyone. Their shifts might last eighteen or twenty hours. The trains kept running day and night, regardless of weather conditions or air raids. The railway infrastructure was also a target for Jerry – tracks, bridges, stations, sidings, marshalling yards. The engine drivers and firemen did highly skilled, dangerous jobs that called for years of experience.

Persephone had heard of one driver who had worked solidly for twenty-two hours, only to go home and find his house had been destroyed by the Luftwaffe and his wife and children had all copped it. She thanked heaven that her lovely Matt had never suffered such a terrible calamity. He still had all his family. He lived with his mother and father, who was a police sergeant, and he had two sisters. Peggy, who, in her thirties, was a similar age to her brother, was married and had her own home – an empty one these days, her children having been evacuated at the outbreak of war. She worked in a home for old soldiers. The other sister, Jill, the youngest by some years, lived with her parents and had a job in a munitions factory.

Persephone was fond of the two girls and Sergeant Franklin, but she had never forgotten what Matt's mother had once said to her.

'I don't want you toying with my son's affections.'

As if she would! But she could see Mrs Franklin's point of view. The Honourable Miss Trehearn-Hobbs and Matt Franklin, railwayman. It wasn't a conventional combination by any stretch of the imagination.

Persephone's family weren't pleased about it either. Pa had given her the most awful wigging. Persephone had been staying at Meyrick House last spring and Pa had ordered her to come to London to see him specifically so he could give her a carpeting she would never forget.

'You've shown that the pressure of war work has made you lose your respect for your upbringing and everything you've ever learned. Not only have you brought shame on your mother and me and the whole family, but you've also shown that doing a man's job has addled your brains. You've let down every right-minded woman in the country.'

How that had hurt. She had known, of course, that Pa would take grave exception on behalf of the family honour, but to be told she had let down all women had taken Persephone's breath away. She had nothing but respect for the hundreds of thousands of women and girls from all walks of life who were engaged in war work. She didn't believe her father was right in his assessment of her situation, but it had injured her to be told it all the same.

On the other hand, Iphigenia had positively encouraged her to get together with Matt – though only to indulge in a wartime fling.

'The war has given all you single girls this marvellous opportunity to enjoy yourselves. What's wrong with that? Grab it with both hands, little sister, that's what I say. You'll have years and years to be a respectable married lady afterwards. And I promise not to tell tales on you.'

Persephone and Matt were all too aware of the complications their relationship had brought swirling to the surface, yet neither of them had backed away. Their closeness had grown out of true friendship. In spite of the social barrier between them, they had much in common, not least the way they had both striven to follow their dreams. Matt had given up a grammar school education in order to join the railways while Persephone had for years wanted to be a journalist. Although her desire to work full-time for a newspaper had no chance of being realised, she had throughout the war produced a steady stream of articles for the local press and women's magazines, in particular *Vera's Voice*. There was a particular knack to writing the sort of thing that the magazines currently wanted and Persephone had worked hard to produce the right mixture of encouragement, compassion and common sense.

Hers and Matt's was a steady, loving relationship. It ought to have everything going for it . . . but not when the social ramifications were taken into account.

Persephone arrived at Victoria Station to find the concourse busy, as always. She knew the station inside out from her days as a ticket collector: the large clock with Roman numerals hanging from the metal gantry underneath the vast overarching glass canopy; the noticeboards in between the platform entrances; the long line of little windows where passengers queued for tickets; and the small, pale-yellow-tiled buildings grouped together, each with its name above the entrance in elegant capital letters against a background of deep blue – GRILL ROOM, BOOKSTALL, RESTAURANT, BUFFET.

It was towards the buffet that Persephone now headed. She had been there so often that her feet would probably take her there even if she didn't intend to go. This was where she and her friends met up whenever they could, shifts permitting. They couldn't all attend every time, which meant that a full house was extra special.

There was a strict rule that, even if they were off duty, employees in uniform mustn't be seen in public sitting in the buffet, smoking and chatting, in case it looked as if they were slacking. Over her uniform Persephone wore her caramel-coloured wool coat with its oversized collar and buckle belt, together with a hat that had a rather snazzy curled brim. Her uniform peaked cap was in a bag dangling from her wrist.

A couple of soldiers darted forward, vying with one another to open the door for her. Persephone thanked them with a smile, then insisted they go ahead of her in the queue. Most people gave way to the lads who were fighting to save the country. Indeed, as soon as the people in the queue realised there were Tommies present, they immediately sent the boys to the front, where Mrs Jessop, in common with buffet staff the country over, gave them tea and scones, waving aside their offer of payment.

When her turn came, Persephone purchased a cup of tea, stirring it with the teaspoon that was fastened by a thin chain to a small block of wood. With the shortage of crockery and cutlery, it was a long time since Mrs Jessop had taken any chances with her spoons. She was careful with her crockery too and only handed out the good cups and saucers to her regulars, with strangers having to make do with mugs, old sugar basins or even jam jars.

Making her way between the tables, Persephone approached the one her chums had bagged. When the buffet wasn't too busy, Mrs Jessop didn't mind if they pushed two together, but at this time of day they had to squeeze round a single table. Emily and Fay shared a chair, as did Margaret and Colette.

Persephone looked at her friends one by one, mentally ticking them off, her heart filling with affection for them. Cordelia, the grey-eyed, ash-blonde wife of a well-to-do solicitor, had a cool gravity that belied her warm heart. The other mature member of their group was working-class Dot Green whose keen hazel eyes missed nothing, though not in a mean way. Generous and eminently sensible, Dot was the sort who would do anything for anyone. She sometimes referred to the younger members of their group as her 'daughters for the duration'.

One of these 'daughters' was dark-haired Alison, who was newly married. They had all attended her Christmas Eve wedding. Cordelia and Dot had been guests while Colette and Joan had acted as matrons of honour and Persephone, Emily and Margaret had been bridesmaids alongside Alison's sister Lydia.

Next to Alison sat lovely Joan, who had returned to work some weeks ago after being at home with her precious son Max. He would be two this coming spring. Joan had previously been a station porter but now she was a clerk in the new PAYE tax office. She had appeared a bit anxious about this role at first but seemed to be settling in now. It was no secret among the friends that Joan would dearly have loved to return to her former role as a porter, but that would have involved shifts and the PAYE work meant office hours, which was what fitted in best with her family life. There were many women up and down the country who would have given their eye teeth for the privilege of working office hours.

Cordelia's daughter, Emily, was a strikingly pretty girl with eyes the colour of cornflowers and dark hair with a natural curl. The youngest member of their group by some years, she was now a lad porter. All young porters, regardless of sex, were 'lads'. Colette, dear Colette, was the quietest of them, though the shyness they had all associated with her when they first knew her had long since slipped away. Colette had endured a perfectly vile time with her husband, but he was well and truly out of the picture now, thank goodness.

Margaret, dark-haired and hazel-eyed, had the physically demanding job of engine cleaner. And then there was Fay, the newest recruit to their ranks. Confident and good-looking with gorgeous dark-red hair, she worked in women's welfare.

Joan shifted sideways on her seat. 'Plonk yourself here with me,' she invited Persephone. 'I'll have to go in a few minutes anyway, so then you can have the chair to yourself.'

Persephone smiled. 'Got to get home to Max?'

Joan's blue eyes softened at the mention of her little son. 'Yes. Having the chance to see you all is a real treat and I wouldn't miss it for anything, but I can't be late for Max.'

'What about you, Alison?' asked Cordelia. 'Have you got to hurry home to make Joel's tea?'

Alison looked pleased, her brown eyes sparkling. Each time Persephone had seen her since the day of her December wedding, her skin had been radiant, a clear outward sign of her happiness.

'No, as a matter of fact,' said Alison. 'He's working late today. Our hours won't coincide again until next week, worse luck.'

'Are you enjoying being an old married lady?' asked Fay.

'I've never been happier,' Alison said simply.

'It does me good to see my daughters for the duration settling down in good marriages,' Dot declared. 'Alison and Joel, Joan and Bob.'

'Mabel and Harry,' Joan added.

'I wasn't forgetting them,' said Dot.

She looked at Persephone and Persephone's shoulders tightened, the hairs lifting on her arms. Please don't let Dot say she and Matt would be next.

But Dot merely said, 'And you, love – you're happy with your Matt an' all, aren't you?'

Persephone relaxed. 'Yes, very.' She hesitated. She had never shared this with anyone before, but she could trust these dearest of friends to understand and support her – and quite honestly, some support wouldn't come amiss. 'It's . . . different for us.' Heaven help her, she had almost said *difficult*. 'You know, because of the social side of it.'

'The Honourable and the fireman,' said Alison.

Persephone nodded. 'You and Joel, and Joan and Bob, have got your happy ever afters. So have Mabel and Harry.'

Emily sat up straighter. 'But you seem so happy.'

'Oh, I am. We are,' Persephone assured her. 'It's just that we can't have the happy-ever-after part.' She looked around at her friends. Nobody demurred. Of course not. 'It's not like that for us. As Alison says – the Honourable and the fireman.'

'Oh, chick,' Dot said sympathetically.

'The war brought us together,' said Persephone, 'and I'm grateful for that, but I also know – we both know – that once the war is over . . .'

'Which it will be in the foreseeable future,' said Margaret, 'after the advances the Allies have made.'

'Precisely.' Although her heart felt as though it was cracking open, Persephone kept her tone light and steady. 'We don't have happy ever after to look forward to. What we have is happy for now. When you think about it, that's as much as anyone can truly rely on in wartime.'

Happy for now.

It sounded so simple – so sensible. But it also placed an extra barrier between her and her clever, interesting, kind Matt, because what they had now was all there was and all there could ever be.

Happy for now.

Unsettled for now.

Chapter Two

Persephone wished with all her heart she could see more of Matt. It wasn't easy having a happy-for-now relationship, especially when the times they could be together often felt few and far between, thanks to the excessively long shifts Matt worked plus Persephone's job and her overtime, not to mention her duties at Darley Court. The knock-on effect of this was that the times they did spend together felt snatched and unspeakably precious.

Did Matt experience the same need that Persephone did to make these times as special and perfect as possible? And the knock-on effect of *that* was that they avoided the difficult things – such as talking about the future. But then, they didn't have a future, did they? They were both well aware of that. So what was there to talk about? Nothing.

Persephone felt impatient with herself. Why must she keep on and on thinking about it? All she was doing was hurting herself.

Today Matt had the whole day off. His mother had nabbed him for the morning to do some jobs at his sister Peggy's house. A means of keeping him away from his toffee-nosed girlfriend? Persephone honestly didn't know. All she knew was that Matt was good-natured and generous, a staunch family man who was always happy to lend a hand. It was one of the reasons she thought so highly of him.

They were to spend this afternoon together for the first time since before Alison's wedding, which in this context felt like a devil of a long time ago even though less than three weeks had gone by. Persephone dressed in her herringbone skirt and wore a silk blouse beneath a warm jumper. Clothes-wise, it was easier to see Matt in the daytime because her day clothes looked – well, more ordinary. Perfectly tailored, yes, but not as far removed in quality and style from the norm as her evening garments were. Mind you, after more than four years at war, four long years of shortages and making do, everyone's clobber was looking pretty tired these days, no matter what their social background.

Persephone pulled on her boots and slipped her arms into the sleeves of her caramel-coloured wool overcoat. She wrapped a scarf around her neck, put on a hat, then reached for her gloves. She was going to meet Matt outside the cinema. They had agreed to see *Girl Crazy* but quite honestly they were every bit as keen to watch the Pathé news as they were to see Mickey Rooney and Judy Garland. Everybody sat up straighter these days during the newsreel. There was a fresh feeling of anticipation in the air, a keen sense of expectation. Was this going to be the year of victory? After the considerable successes the Allies had scored over the past year and a half, could the civilian population now look forward to a massive assault on Europe? The time felt ripe.

When Persephone arrived outside the cinema, Matt was already there. She saw him before he saw her, pleasure fizzing through her as she took in his lean, strong lines. Maybe he sensed her gaze upon him because he turned and looked her way, a warm smile lighting up his face. Persephone smiled in return or quite possibly beamed with pure happiness. He was so very important to her.

She darted between the pedestrians on the pavement, hurrying towards Matt to be enfolded in his arms. It was something she would never have dreamed of doing before the war, but these days it was common to see girls showing their affection in public. The urgency of the 'live for today' feeling had infected everyone.

Soon they were inside the auditorium, holding hands in the tobacco-smoky atmosphere. There was barely time to say anything before the lights went down and the voices around them subsided as the audience's attention focused on the screen. In recent weeks the newsreel had provided welcome information about the Soviet forces driving back the Germans and re-taking Kiev, as well as the meeting in Tehran between Mr Churchill, President Roosevelt and Stalin, and the sinking of the German battleship, the *Scharnhorst*.

There had been reports of matters at home too: that awful Mr Mosley's release from prison, for one, something that, according to Persephone's sister Iphigenia, had got their father, the General, thoroughly steamed up, even though Mosley had to live under house arrest. The announcement on New Year's Day of an extra ounce of tea for people aged seventy and over had been welcomed, but the sad news just before Christmas of the death of dear Beatrix Potter had filled Persephone with nostalgia for the set of books on the nursery shelf back at Meyrick House.

As enjoyable as *Girl Crazy* was, it was less absorbing than it might have been had Persephone and Matt been able to go out together on a more regular basis. Being in Matt's company was a distraction, to say the least. It was one of the problems of not seeing all that much of one another. It created a feeling of having to squeeze everything in.

When they came out of the cinema, the afternoon temperature was dropping. Swirls of frost coated the windowpanes, adding extra patterns on top of the anti-blast tape inside the glass. In the busy streets, everyone was bundled up in scarves and gloves with hats pulled down and collars turned up. The snow had long since turned to slush. Persephone and Matt dived into a café for tea and buns and a good long chat.

'I want to hear all about Alison and Joel's wedding,' said Matt. 'I hate to think how long it's been since I've seen you.'

'It can't be helped.' Persephone kept her tone light, though really she often felt heartsore. She gave an edited account of Alison's big day, reckoning that Matt would be about as interested in the dress and the flowers as her brothers would have been. 'I wish you could have been there,' she added. For her, this was the most important detail.

'I would have been proud to escort the most beautiful bridesmaid.' Matt's eyes crinkled as he smiled at her.

'I know you had to work over Christmas, but I hope you were able to spend some time with your family.'

'It isn't just me working long hours,' said Matt. 'The girls do too, and Dad. And Mum has her WVS duties. We were all in and out at various times, but we did manage to have a while together.'

Persephone smiled. 'That's quite a feat.'

'Peggy was a bit fed up, though she tried not to let it show. For her it was yet another Christmas of being separated from her children. She desperately hopes this will be the last one.'

'We're all hoping for that,' Persephone concurred. 'Surely this has to be the year the war is won.'

'Let's hope so,' Matt said soberly before asking cheerfully, 'How about you? Did you hear from your family over Christmas?'

'Ma telephoned Darley Court on Christmas afternoon and my sister rang in the evening.'

She didn't say so to Matt but Ma had asked bluntly if she would be seeing 'that fireman' during the festive period.

'No?' Ma had said. 'Good.'

Good. Good? Persephone was missing her beloved boyfriend and being brave about not being able to see him at this special time of year – and her mother's reaction was, 'Good.'

Iphigenia had also asked if Persephone would be seeing Matt, but her response to the answer has been, 'Rotten luck, darling, but maybe for the best.' In the spring of last year, Iphigenia had encouraged Persephone to indulge in a little wartime fling – not that Persephone would ever have done such a thing – but Iphigenia had seen it as a way of having fun. She was deeply concerned at the way Persephone's relationship with Matt had become serious.

Now Persephone felt a sudden urge to ask Matt about the future – about *their* future. But they had agreed to be happy for now – and that meant that asking was forbidden.

Chapter Three

At home after work, Alison was busy cooking so-called fillets of pork. It was a recipe in a home-made cookery book her friends had given to her as a wedding present. All of them had written recipes in a notebook – and not just her friends either. They had invited other special people to contribute as well, not least Alison's mother and sister. Then there was dear Mrs Jessop in the buffet at Victoria Station who, ever since early in the war, had let Alison and her chums leave messages for one another in a notebook that was kept under the counter so they could make arrangements to meet up. Mrs Jessop said they were her most regular customers. Mrs Mitchell, the housekeeper at Darley Court, had also written some recipes, as had Joan's grandmother. Her friends had even pasted in a recipe from Mabel, so that even though she had moved away when she got married, she was still included.

Alison was glad that Mabel had married the man of her dreams, but she knew full well that the dashing Harry Knatchbull would never have suited her. With his film-star good looks, his dazzling smile and easy charm, he was the sort to set hearts fluttering wherever he went, but in Alison's eyes he wasn't a patch on her Joel, with his blue eyes and his cheery good humour. Best of all, Joel was kind and thoughtful. The two of them had gone through huge emotional upheaval in the weeks before their marriage, but they had weathered the turmoil and had emerged from it with a deeper appreciation of one another.

This recipe Alison had selected from her cookery book was one that had been included by Mrs Grayson whom Alison had lived with in Wilton Close. Mrs Grayson wasn't the landlady even though she did all the catering. The landlady was Mrs Cooper, who was taking care of the house for the owners, Mr and Mrs Morgan, who had gone to live on the North Wales coast for the duration to be close to their son. He worked for the Inland Revenue and their HQ had been relocated to Llandudno.

Alison studied the recipe. The fillets were made of flaked pork sausagemeat, breadcrumbs and mashed potato, with added seasoning. Alison hummed to herself as she worked. She loved cooking for Joel. Sometimes she felt a bit embarrassed by how much, because it seemed rather like the way she used to feel back in the old days, the pre-Joel days, when she'd had a boyfriend called Paul and all she had wanted in the whole wide world was to get engaged, get married and spend the rest of her days taking care of him. She hadn't minded one way or the other about going out to work in those days. Having a job was just what she did while she waited to get married.

But now – oh, how different life was now! How different *she* was. She loved working for the railways. In the autumn of 1941 she had been singled out to gain experience in a variety of railway jobs. She hadn't known why at the time, but now she knew it had been to provide her with a strong understanding of life on the railways in order to give her the best possible foundation for her role as— she caught her breath at the mere thought of it. Imagine it. She, Alison Lambert-as-was, the new Mrs Joel Maitland, was going to be involved in work so vital and secret that she couldn't even tell her husband even though he was a doctor and therefore totally trustworthy.

The doorbell rang. It was rent day. Joel had been here on the previous occasions when the rent man had called and Alison had let Joel deal with the matter. Now she felt grown-up and, yes, it might be daft but it made her feel married to fetch the money and the rent book from the sideboard drawer and go to answer the door. She turned off the light in the hall before she opened it, so as not to break the blackout.

Just outside stood a middle-aged man. He was tall and, even wrapped up in overcoat and scarf, he looked rather lean. Beneath his trilby was a wide-browed face and a square jaw.

'Good God,' he said in a voice that mixed surprise with disdain. 'Then it's true.'

Alison stared. 'What is?'

'She's moved another couple into Tony's house.'

The man's attitude made Alison bridle. This wasn't the sort of thing you expected from the rent man. 'You know that. We've been here since Christmas. My husband has been paying you the rent.'

'What are you talking about?' the man exclaimed testily. 'Of course he hasn't. This is the first time I've been here. Where is she?' he demanded.

Alison's heart sank so hard it seemed to clout the pit of her stomach. 'You're not the rent man.'

'Of course I'm not. I'll tell you who I am, madam. I am Mr Anthony Naylor and this is my son's house. Where is Colette?'

'She's away caring for a sick relative,' said Alison. This was the story they had agreed upon.

'She's what? Balderdash!' Mr Naylor retorted. 'This property is in my son's name and his wife ought to be residing here. I demand to know where I can find her.'

Alison worked in the onward travel office, which ensured smooth timetabling for passengers changing trains to complete long journeys or joining one of LMS's steamship services. The office had always done important work but never more so than in wartime. Part of its war work was to organise complicated journeys in such a way that precedence on the lines was given to troop trains and trains carrying food, fuel and munitions. This meant that ordinary passengers had to put up with all sorts of delays, which they did mostly without complaint, because everybody knew the importance of transporting soldiers, weapons, food and other essentials. Passengers still made the most of the train service. Parents wanted to visit their evacuated children when they could, which wasn't often, and parcels were sent all over the country. Having a nationwide network of railways to rely on helped to provide a sense of life going on as normal.

Alison was the newest recruit to the office. She was getting to know her colleagues. There was Miss Marchant, the middle-aged daughter of an elderly mother whom she lived with. She wore her hair in an old-fashioned bun, which made her look older. Miss Marchant was never anything other than loyal when she mentioned her mother, but her younger colleagues were of the opinion that she was well and truly under the thumb.

Then there was Mrs Deane, who in her early thirties was a few years older than Alison. She was blue-eyed, her blonde hair always beautifully styled with never a wisp out of place. Alison suspected sugar-water and that Mrs Deane's sumptuous waves might crack clean in two if they were touched.

Mr Snape was an older gentleman. Word had it that he had retired on the first Friday of 1939 only to return to his desk the following Monday, war having been declared on the Sunday. There was nothing he didn't know about the best places to shunt trains onto alternative tracks or into sidings to let an important train go steaming past. Alison had silently vowed to learn all she could from him.

Alison's family and friends all knew where she worked but they had no idea of what lay ahead for her. Sometimes she wished she could discuss her forthcoming responsibilities with her colleagues but she had no way of knowing which of them, if any, would be working on a similar task to her own. Or maybe they were all to be involved, every single one of them having been sworn to secrecy and all of them casting occasional glances at their colleagues in onward travel, wondering the same thing that Alison so often wondered.

When she finished work and caught the bus, Alison didn't get off at Seymour Grove to go to her new home but stayed aboard until she reached the terminus at Chorlton so she could call in at her old home in Wilton Close near the rec. She had come to live here when she was going through a time of deep despair. Heartbroken at being dumped for another girl by Paul, and then having to brace herself to play the part of bridesmaid to her sister Lydia, she had badly needed a bolt-hole and where better than Wilton Close? Mrs Cooper had a reputation among Alison's friends for providing a secure and happy home for her young lodgers.

To start with Alison had occupied the little box room at the far end of the landing, which Mrs Cooper had turned into a bedroom. There were two steps down into it and it had a small window. On the far wall, the ceiling sloped down to about four feet from the floor. A narrow bed had been pushed into the corner and there was a cupboard and a chest of drawers. At the time, the double room had belonged to Margaret and Mabel. Mabel had left to get married in June of last year and gone down south to live near Bomber Command, and at that point Alison had moved into the double room with Margaret.

It was Margaret she had come to see this evening.

'She's having a strip-wash,' said Mrs Cooper.

Alison grinned. 'A good scrub-down, you mean.'

As well as being physically demanding, cleaning the locomotives was grubby work, to say the least. All the girls wore their hair tucked away inside turbans but even so, there were times when Mrs Cooper had to lay a cloth over Margaret's pillowcase.

'Is it all right if I pop upstairs and wait in the bedroom?' Alison asked.

She went up to what had previously been her room. The Morgans had slept in single beds, a small cupboard standing beside each one. There was a chest of drawers, a dressing table with a triple mirror, and a wardrobe with a long mirror inset in one of the doors. The furniture was old and was a handsome matching set. The room boasted a fireplace, but this far into the war, and with fuel so scarce, it was a long time since it had been used. What coal they had was burned downstairs.

Alison glanced round the room, smiling to herself. She lived such a different life now. She loved living with Joel and having a home of her own to take care of – well, she had until Mr Naylor had appeared on the doorstep. That had been deeply unsettling but she wasn't going to let it spoil the way she viewed her new home. Mr Naylor had no reason ever to turn up again now that he knew Colette no longer lived there.

Margaret walked in, clad in a dressing gown, her wet hair wrapped in a towel. She gave a little start of surprise when she saw Alison but then she smiled.

'You made me jump.'

'Sorry. Here, let me help you dry your hair. Sit down.'

'Have you come to the wrong house by mistake?' Margaret teased.

'Very funny. Joel won't be home until later so I thought I'd drop round.'

Alison towel-dried Margaret's hair until it was damp, then put it in rollers for her. She knew the style Margaret preferred, with her waves scooped away from her face and her fringe also swept to the sides and worn in tiny crinkles. It was a simple style that many girls favoured.

'Is there any news about Sally?' Alison asked, sitting on the bed when she'd finished.

Sally was Margaret's chum from the engine shed. Last year she had been led well and truly up the garden path by a boyfriend who, when she had found out she was expecting a baby, had turned out to be rather more married than he had led her to believe. Margaret had stood by Sally from the start, though Alison had had a real down on her to begin with before she learned to be less judgemental and more compassionate. She was ashamed of that now. She had done a lot of growing up in the few months before she got married.

The house in Wilton Close had proved to be a safe haven for Sally, just as it had for others before her, though Mrs Cooper had made it clear that Sally must leave before her condition started to make itself obvious to the world so that in years to come the house wasn't known as the one where the pregnant girl had taken refuge. Mrs Morgan, the owner's wife, had been made aware of Sally's situation but Mr Morgan had been left in the dark. He would have been outraged had he known.

Sally had left to enter a mother and baby home in nearby Sale, where her baby had been born in December, some weeks early. She'd had a bad time and Miss Emery, the assistant welfare supervisor for women and girls on the LMS railway, had arranged for her to be taken care of in a convalescent home afterwards.

'She's still in the convalescent home,' Margaret told Alison. 'She was only expecting to stay for a month, but they're letting her stay until the end of January because that's when the baby would have been due. Also, they want to keep her there to give her some protection from this awful flu that's doing the rounds. But whether she'll stick it out to the end of the month, I don't know. She's got her strength back now.'

'That's good,' Alison said warmly.

'Yes, it is,' Margaret agreed, 'but she's been feeling very down. It's something that happens to some women when they've had a baby, apparently, though in Sally's case it could be because of . . . you know.'

Alison nodded. Sally had had to face the trauma of surrendering her baby to be adopted and knowing she would never see him again.

'Maybe she'd be better off back at work,' said Alison. 'I don't want to sound unfeeling,' she added gently, very aware of how extremely unfeeling she had been towards Sally at one point, 'but she needs to put this behind her and move on. I know she'll never forget the baby, but she has to make a life for herself.'

Margaret tilted her head to one side and then the other as if weighing Alison's words. 'She knows that, but I think it's easier said than done.' She gave Alison a smile. 'Not that it isn't lovely to see you, but you didn't come here to talk about Sally, did you?'

'Well, no – though I do want to keep abreast of what happens to her. I need to speak to Colette, but I've got something to say to you as well.'

Alison took a moment to choose her words. Things between her and Margaret had been difficult – and that was putting it mildly – during the weeks running up to Alison's wedding because of an old relationship between Margaret and Joel. Although everything had been sorted out and had ended on a good note, Alison had more that she wanted to say.

'I want you to know how very happy I am now. My life has never been better. I love living in Colette's old house and I love being married to Joel. What I mean is: there are absolutely no lingering questions or ill-feeling on my part. I wanted you to know that.'

'Thank you,' Margaret whispered.

'And I hope you end up with the same kind of happiness as I have,' Alison added.

'As long as you don't try your hand at fixing me up with a chap again.'

They both laughed.

'No matchmaking,' Alison promised. She could see now, looking back, how very strange and inappropriate her attempt at playing Cupid must have felt to Margaret at the time.

Hearing the front door open, Alison left Margaret to get dressed and went downstairs, where Colette was removing her double-breasted blue wool overcoat and cream-coloured scarf. She took off her hat and gave her buttermilk-fair hair a little shake. Looking up, she smiled as she saw Alison on the stairs.

'Hello, stranger. What are you doing here?'

Aware of tension in her muscles, Alison drew in a deep breath. She hated to spoil things for Colette, who truly didn't deserve to have any more bad things happen to her. Something must have shown in her expression because Colette's face changed.

'What is it?' she asked.

'Can I have a word?' Alison asked. Coming down the final stairs, she led the way into the dining room.

Colette shut the door behind them and looked at her.

There was nothing to be gained by trying to pave the way. 'Tony's father came to the house. He'd heard that a couple had moved in and he was – well, indignant about it.'

'He would be,' Colette said quietly.

'He thought you were still living there. I thought I was talking to the rent man at first but I soon realised my mistake. He wanted to know where you were, so I said you were away looking after a sick relative.'

'What did he say to that?'

'The actual word was "Balderdash!" I'm sorry, Colette.'

'It's not your fault.'

'He wanted to know where you'd gone.'

'And you didn't tell him.' There was no suggestion of a question in Colette's voice.

'Of course not, but – well, he knows now that you've moved out. I hope it isn't going to cause problems for you. He wasn't happy.'

Colette huffed out a short sigh. 'He's keeping tabs on me for Tony's benefit, no doubt. I wonder who it was that spread the word about you and Joel moving in.'

Alison experienced a niggly little feeling inside. 'I don't like the thought of your private business being talked about.'

'Being talked about is part and parcel of being a separated wife.' Colette's tone was light but that didn't mean she didn't care. 'I just hope it doesn't rebound on you for living in that house.'

'People wouldn't be so petty,' Alison exclaimed.

'I hope not.' Colette smiled and the expression in her blue eyes softened. 'I'm very happy here in Wilton Close. I hope you and Joel are as happy in my old house as I am here.'

Chapter Four

Although Colette kept it to herself, she felt prickly and unsettled at the idea of Tony's father turning up at her old house, demanding answers to his impertinent questions. Except that the questions weren't impertinent, were they? Not entirely. The house was in Tony's name and folk would say that his father was entitled to keep an eye on it. What upset Colette the most was what Alison *hadn't* said. She hadn't uttered a word about Mr Naylor being rude or loud, but there had been something in her manner, a suggestion of feeling ill-at-ease, that had left Colette in no doubt that Alison had found the encounter deeply unpleasant, even disturbing.

Colette gave a little shudder. She couldn't help it. She remembered Mr Naylor all too well. As an eighteen-year-old bride who hadn't known any better, she had admired and respected him. It wasn't until five years later that she had started to see him for what he truly was. But at the start, Tony and his mother had seemed in awe of his father, something that Colette's mother had found reassuring.

'It means he's a good, strong head of the family. Just what everyone needs.'

Colette had known that Mother had been referring to her own late husband every bit as much as to Tony's father. Dad had passed away unexpectedly, which had come as a horrible blow for Colette and Mother. Just as unexpected had been the debts of which they had previously been unaware. They had found themselves in terrible financial straits.

Another reason why Mother had been so keen for Colette to marry Tony was his position with the Water Board. Everybody knew that was a job for life, with a proper pension. A widow's pension as well, should the worst happen. Mother had told everyone she was friendly with at church and they had all been deeply impressed.

It had taken a long time for Colette to see the real Tony, partly because of her own naïvety and her tendency to see the best in people, partly because she was surrounded by people telling her what a marvellous husband she had and partly because . . . well, when someone loved you as much as Tony loved her – and he was always telling her how much – that meant they had your best interests at heart, didn't it? It meant they only wanted the very best for you.

That was why, when he had criticised her, often adding, 'I'm telling you for your own good,' she had believed him and she'd known it was silly to feel upset. Tony was helping her to be a better person, a better wife. He was helping her not to make a fool of herself in public. She had even been grateful to him in the early days for paying such close attention to every aspect of their lives together. Some husbands barely noticed domestic details, but Tony noticed everything and Colette had tied herself in knots in her efforts to make everything perfect, wanting him to smile and praise her, vaguely dreading that his eyes would flicker in displeasure.

Somewhere along the line, the vague feeling of dread had become less obscure, more defined . . . less easy to ignore or explain away. It became something she lived with, day in, day out, and nobody else had the faintest idea what she was going through.

No one knows what goes on behind closed doors.

Nobody else knew that what Tony praised her for this time might draw forth a barb of criticism next time. She never knew where she stood. It took her a long time to realise that unkindness could be hiding beneath that 'I'm telling you for your own good.'

And then there was the face Tony presented to the world, always genial and smiling. It added to the impression he gave of being the perfect husband. But it also masked the anger he would feel towards someone who got on his wrong side . . . anger that would remain concealed until he reached home and took his ill-humour out on Colette.

No one knows what goes on behind closed doors.

All the while, Colette had felt stupid and inadequate, scared of doing the wrong thing, of making a mistake, spoiling things. It was horrible that everything was her fault – not just feeling it but *knowing* it, believing it, living in a state of fear and uncertainty because of it.

And Tony had honestly expected her to be grateful. Grateful for his love and support, grateful for the close interest he took.

Grateful he didn't hit her.

She would never forget the first time Tony had expected her to be thankful for this. She had overheard a pair of housewives talking in the fishmonger's, lowering their voices in shock as they discussed a local man who had thumped his wife when he'd had a skinful.

Later, at the tea table, Colette had mentioned it. Tony had curled his lip in disgust.

'Disgraceful,' he declared.

'The women said it only happens when he's drunk.'

'Drink is no excuse,' said Tony. Then he said earnestly, 'I'd never hit you, no matter what. You know that, don't you? You have nothing to fear from me. You're lucky to have such a principled man as your husband.'

Colette was astounded. Of course she had nothing to fear. It had never occurred to her for a single moment that she might have. It had never occurred to her that an ordinary man who treated his wife decently would let the thought of violence cross his mind, still less that he would point out to his wife that he would never inflict it on her. Were other wives of decent men grateful not to be knocked about? Had she been wrong to take it for granted?

In any case, Tony did seem to believe that Colette was fortunate in this respect and clearly required her to think so too. After that it became something that popped into the conversation now and again, the fact that Tony would never lay a finger on her and that she was a fortunate wife and ought to be grateful.

And it was true. He never did lay a finger on her.

Until the day he did. And the time after that when he knocked her practically into the middle of next week.

'You've got something on your mind,' Mrs Cooper said, sounding concerned.

Colette looked at her lovely landlady, who was also a dear friend. She was a small, thin woman with faded fair hair and her eyebrows owed more to pencil than to natural growth. Her hands were work-roughened but her eyes showed the generosity of her heart. She always had time for others. Losing Lizzie, her beloved only child, hadn't embittered her, no matter how deep her sorrow ran. In spite of her shattering bereavement, which had come just months after the death of her husband, Mrs Cooper had displayed simple, unassuming courage, knuckling down and getting on with her life as best she could and that included keeping a caring eye on other people.

It had been no hardship at all to Colette to leave her matrimonial home and the greatest possible pleasure to move into Mrs Cooper's house. There had been a question as to whether Colette would have the old box room all to herself or whether she would share the big room with Margaret. From last summer until November, Margaret's friend Sally had stayed in Wilton Close and she'd had the box room. Then Sally had to go away to look after a sick relative for some weeks and she might return to Wilton Close at the end of the month.

'Wouldn't Sally and Margaret like to share with one another?' Colette had asked, wanting to do the right thing. She didn't mind which room she had.

'I'm sure Sally would be happy with either arrangement,' said Mrs Cooper. 'When she came here, it was a temporary thing and quite honestly I don't know what plans she has for the future.'

Colette had opted to share with Margaret. She had

appreciated her privacy in recent months, but in Wilton Close she wanted to feel she was part of the household and that meant sharing. Besides, she didn't want to give Margaret the impression she was stand-offish, which was the last thing she was. After leaving her marriage, Colette had been invited to move into Darley Court for as long as she needed and she'd been given a bedroom close to Persephone's, with a shared bathroom in between. How Colette had liked being with Persephone. It came as a revelation what a pleasure it was to enjoy company in the home environment after the strain of living with Tony.

It had brought her closer to Persephone, who had been sorry when Colette chose to leave. Colette was sorry as well, but returning to her matrimonial home had been the right thing to do. After the magistrate had taken Tony's side in spite of his guilt, and even given him the option of joining the army instead of going to prison, Colette had felt a deep need to go back home and hold her head up. She wasn't the wrongdoer. She also wanted to do it for the sake of any local women who were unfortunate enough to live with a Tony of their own. She wanted them to see that it was possible to survive an abusive marriage.

Now, Colette and Mrs Cooper were in the kitchen together, washing up after an evening meal of vegetable stew followed by steamed date pudding, expertly made by Mrs Grayson. Margaret had been excused clearing-up duty because she was going out dancing with Persephone and Fay. Colette liked Fay who, in her previous job with the Corporation, had been a big help to Mabel when she was setting up the Lizzie Cooper Nursery. Now Fay worked in a welfare post on the railways and Colette suspected her kindly competence and calm intelligence would make her good at the work.

'You don't have to say anything if you'd rather not,' said Mrs Cooper, 'but I'm always here to listen if you need it. You know that, chuck.'

Colette filled with an inner warmth. Yes, she did know. It was Mrs Cooper who had overheard Tony being sharp and unkind to Colette at a dance. She had shrewdly put two and two together and realised that this wasn't the first time. Colette had been unable at first to confide her troubles. Indeed, she could hardly bear to admit them to herself. But Mrs Cooper was nothing if not patient. She hadn't pushed and that, in the end, had helped Colette to reach out for the support she hadn't previously known she needed.

'It's Tony's father,' Colette said now and went on to describe how he had turned up at her old house and attempted to browbeat Alison.

'Poor girl. How nasty,' said Mrs Cooper. 'But I'm sure she coped. She didn't give him your new address, did she?'

'No. I hope he isn't going to make a habit of turning up there. Do you think I ought to go round to his house and see him?'

'What would that achieve?' Mrs Cooper asked, alarmed.

'It would get him out of Alison's hair. He'd know there would be no point in going there again.'

'Presumably he already knows that if Alison refused to say where you're living now.'

'True,' Colette conceded.

Even so, now that the idea was in her head, she kept thinking about it. She wanted to keep well away from Mr

Naylor – she couldn't think of him as Father any longer – but if she did, would she always be half-expecting him to pounce on her? He was definitely keeping his eyes open for her, she was in no doubt about that. That being the case, wasn't it cowardly to steer clear of him?

Besides, she would like to see her mother-in-law again. She had always been fond of Bunty. Bunty! It was such a jolly-hockey-sticks sort of name and Bunty was a real mouse. Colette had always called her Mother because that was what she'd been told to do, but really she hadn't wanted to. She would have preferred to call her Mum or Ma or anything other than Mother, which was the name she had been brought up to use for her own mother. But both Tony and his father wanted her to say 'Mother' and that was that.

If it had taken Colette a long time to understand that Tony's behaviour towards her stemmed not from kindness or affection but from a deep determination to control her, then it had taken her longer still to appreciate where Tony's actions had come from. Now she firmly believed he had learned his behaviour from growing up watching the way his father treated his mother.

Bunty, dear Bunty, scarcely breathed a word in her husband's company. She spent her life scurrying around trying to anticipate his every wish and requirement. Colette would never forget the occasion when her eyes had been opened to what the real Bunty could be like when she was freed from her husband's presence. She could be friendly, interesting – amusing, even. That had happened when Colette and Bunty had gone on a shopping expedition together and had bumped into Dot.

Seeing the real, hidden Bunty had made Colette realise she was herself a long way down the path towards being totally under Tony's thumb. Looking at the downtrodden, obedient Bunty, she had glimpsed what lay in store for herself if she didn't find the strength to break free.

The chance to see Bunty again would be another reason to call on her parents-in-law. She would dearly like to provide Bunty with some moral support – or was she kidding herself? Was such a thing even possible?

This coming Saturday was going to be the four-week anniversary of Alison and Joel's wedding. Alison popped round to Wilton Close one evening after work during the week. She was very fond of both Mrs Cooper and Mrs Grayson and didn't want them to feel as if she'd forgotten them. She had gone round to their house last week, but that had only been because of Mr Naylor turning up on her doorstep. The two ladies had been good to her at a time when she had needed it most, welcoming her into their home and treating her with kindness. She had loved living in Wilton Close, not least because it had been her first taste of living away from her parents.

It would have been nice to see Colette too, but she was still out at work. She was a railway chaperone, which meant she accompanied passengers who needed assistance.

'I thought that chaperoning meant working the kind of desirable hours that the rest of us can only dream of,' Alison said with a smile.

'She has to fit in with the times that suit whoever she's taking care of,' said Mrs Grayson. 'She'll be home in an hour or so.'

'Meanwhile, we should have someone else for you to see,' said Mrs Cooper; and was that a twinkle in her eye? 'We're expecting Sally any minute now.'

'Sally?' Alison asked. 'Is she moving back in?'

'If she wants to,' said Mrs Cooper, 'she'll be welcome.'

'No offence to Colette,' said Margaret, 'but it's better for her not to be here when Sally comes. That way we can talk freely.'

Alison nodded. Sally's pregnancy had been kept secret so that not just her personal reputation but also that of the household could emerge unblemished.

'If she comes back,' said Alison, 'you'll have a full house again, Mrs C.'

Shortly after that the doorbell rang and Margaret went to admit her chum. The others looked round as Sally walked in. Alison hadn't seen her since before she left here to enter the mother and baby home last November and she couldn't help looking for changes. Although none were discernible, Alison knew that there could well be deep changes on the inside.

Sally had brought some Cadbury's chocolate. 'I've been saving my sweetie ration so I could bring you a little something,' she said to Mrs Cooper and Mrs Grayson. 'It isn't much compared to everything you did for me, but it comes with gratitude.'

'There was no need to bring us anything,' said Mrs Cooper, 'but it's lovely of you to think of it.'

'You were so good to take me in,' Sally said with feeling. 'Most people would have turned me away. My old landlady couldn't throw me out fast enough. You'll never know how much of a difference it made to me, being able to come here and be treated with kindness and respect.'

Alison bit her lip. There had been precious little of those from her when she had first found out about Sally's condition, though she had subsequently come to see matters in a more compassionate light. She had apologised to Sally, and to the other three as well, for her initial attitude. She had done her best to make it up to Sally by asking Joel to use his professional contacts for a recommendation for a good mother and baby home for Sally to go to.

'Margaret told us you had permission to stay in the convalescent hospital until the end of the month,' Mrs Cooper said to Sally. 'I want you to know that you are welcome to come back here, if that's what you would like.'

'Now that there's no danger of me bringing the house into ill-repute, you mean,' said Sally, immediately followed by, 'I'm sorry. That didn't come out right. What I mean is, you took a risk letting me stay here before.'

'Yes, we did,' said Mrs Grayson, 'and we got away with it – you included.'

'But all of that is behind you now,' said Mrs Cooper, 'and your old room is waiting.'

Sally's blue eyes filled and she brushed away a tear or two. 'You're so kind. Thank you. But,' and she paused to take a deep breath, 'I won't be coming back.'

'Sally!' Margaret exclaimed.

'Are you sure?' asked Alison.

Sally nodded. 'Positive. I've had a lot of time to think. There's precious little else to do when you're convalescing.

It isn't just that I won't be coming back to Wilton Close. I'm going to leave the railways as well. I know I'm supposed to go back to my old life and carry on as if nothing ever happened. That's what the unmarried girls used to talk about at Rookery House. They seemed to be looking forward to it, but I've decided that's not the right thing for me. It would feel too strange. It was very hard giving up my son . . .' Her voice trailed away and she bent her head, sniffing and swiping with her hanky.

Margaret laid a gentle hand on her arm. 'I know,' she whispered.

Sally raised her tear-stained face. 'I just can't go back to how it was as if nothing has happened. I – I feel as if I deserve something better than having to face that. I know that unmarried mothers aren't meant to deserve anything good, but—'

She didn't get any further before Alison waded in. She didn't know quite what she was going to say, only that she wanted to say something and she wanted it to be the right thing.

'Don't say that, Sally. You *do* deserve good things. There was a time when I would have been one of the people looking down their nose and believing that you were no better than you should be, but I know differently now. I know that you're a decent, worthwhile person. You've been through a tough experience and if moving away and starting again is what you have to do, then do it and make the best of it – because you deserve the best, you really do. But for what it's worth, I'll be sorry to see you go.'

'We all will,' said Mrs Cooper.

'Miss Emery has helped me to apply to be a land girl,' said Sally.

'Do you know where yet?' asked Mrs Grayson.

Sally smiled. 'I heard this morning. They're sending me up to Cumberland. I'm going in the third week of February. 'It's going to be completely different to railway work. It'll be long hours and exhausting.'

'It sounds like working in the engine sheds so far,' Margaret said with a watery smile.

'What I mean is I'll be so busy working I won't have time to think,' said Sally, 'and when I finally do have time to think, maybe things won't hurt so much.'

Chapter Five

Crystals of frost coated the bare stems of the wild plants along the sides of the railway tracks and a haze of February mist slid across the landscape as the steam engine hauled its long line of coaches into the sidings for an unscheduled stop. It was normal for passenger trains to give way to those carrying troops or munitions, fuel or food. It had been going on since the beginning of the war and everyone was used to it. Persephone regarded what might possibly be a considerable wait as a good opportunity to squeeze her way through the crowded corridors and into compartments that were bursting at the seams so she could get everybody's ticket checked.

She loved working as a ticket inspector. It was far more interesting than her previous position as a ticket collector, though she had tackled that role cheerfully and made the most of it, as was her duty. Besides, it was in her nature to make the best of things.

Something else that was second nature to her was seeing opportunities for writing articles. She'd recently been thinking about the retirement home for old soldiers where Matt's sister Peggy worked. That would make an interesting subject, wouldn't it? Today was going to be a buffet evening and she looked forward to sharing the idea with her friends.

After she clocked off, she made her way along the concourse. It was always busy at this time of day with a mixture of people wending their way purposefully through the crowd, intent upon getting to their train in good time to bag a seat, and those who were waiting. There was no space on any of the benches and a glance through the waiting-room window showed that that was full as well. Many people stood, smoking, reading the newspaper or chatting to their companions. The sounds of voices, footsteps and railway announcements echoed around the huge space.

The buffet was crowded as well. Fay, Joan and Cordelia sat around a table. Emily was about to join them. She had removed her porter's jacket and cap and wore her own clothes so that she looked like a member of the public. Emily's nut-brown coat with a tie belt and slight flare from the waist suited her trim figure. As for that pale pink felt hat trimmed with magenta, that brought a smile to Persephone's lips. The hat had originally belonged to Cordelia, but Emily had borrowed it so many times that there could be little doubt as to which of them it now really belonged to.

Persephone queued up and bought her cup of tea, exchanging a few words with Mrs Jessop, who must be on her feet all day every day behind the counter, but she never complained. If anything, she seemed to thrive on it.

Persephone wound her way between the tables, keeping an eye open for bags and luggage on the floor. Greeting her chums, she sat down. It wasn't long before they had all arrived.

'Is everyone here?' Persephone glanced around. 'Good. I need you all to put your thinking caps on, please, ladies. I'm thinking of seeking permission to base an article around the old soldiers' home where Matt's sister works, but first I need to have a particular way of looking at it.'

She had learned from experience that it wasn't enough simply to describe something, no matter how well or amusingly one did it. What was required was a way of presenting it so as to give the readers something to think about.

'The old boys' memories of the last war,' suggested Dot, 'and some comparisons.'

'The tactics for getting all the residents out into the shelter during an air raid,' said Margaret. 'That can't be all that easy. I imagine some of the men are infirm.'

'That's old hat,' said Alison. 'We haven't had any air raids for ages.'

'Don't tempt fate, Alison,' Dot chimed in. 'Just look at what's happening in London now.' She gave a shudder, and she wasn't the only one. Jerry had resumed his bombing of the capital last month and it didn't look like stopping any time soon.

'I gather that the high explosives are even more powerful this time around,' said Joan.

'And have you heard about the anti-personnel explosives?' Colette asked. 'They detonate when they're disturbed by the rescue teams. It doesn't bear thinking about.'

They all looked at one another.

'Let's get back to Persephone's article,' Cordelia suggested.

'Good idea,' said Alison.

Fay spoke up. 'Why not base a piece around wartime songs? "Keep the Home Fires Burning" and "Goodbyeee" and "I'm Forever Blowing Bubbles" from the Great War. The memories they evoke for the residents and how they feel about a new set of wartime songs such a short time later, especially after they were all told at the time that they were fighting the war to end all wars.'

There was a moment's profound silence as everyone digested this.

'That's a beautiful idea,' said Persephone. 'Very poignant. Do you mind if I pinch it?'

'You're not pinching it,' Fay said with a smile. 'I'm giving it to you.'

The conversation moved on. It wasn't long before it turned to the major assault on Europe that everyone was certain the Allies were building up to.

'I read in the newspaper,' said Cordelia, 'that there are now one million four hundred thousand non-British troops here in Britain. That has to mean something.'

'The war has been going our way for some time now,' Dot added. 'Look at the Anzio landings a week or so back. Surely it can't be long now before we invade Europe.'

Dear Dot. Was she thinking of her sons, Archie and Harry? They had fought in the North Africa campaign. For Dot, the end of the war would mean having her family reunited. Everyone in the country must feel the same. At the same time, the end of the war and the gradual return of the men would hammer home to all the bereaved families just what they had lost – and that those losses would last through all the coming years of peace.

It turned out it wasn't just her sons Dot had in mind.

'Our Jimmy and Jenny will be leaving school this summer,' she said. 'I remember the excitement of the day they were born, Archie's daughter and Harry's son, cousins born on the same day. I don't think I've ever known such joy as that.'

'Babies fill you with happiness and you entertain such hopes for them,' Cordelia observed.

'Aye, you do,' said Dot, 'and then real life comes along, complete with its own ideas.'

'Like the war,' Emily put in.

'Exactly,' said Dot. 'Jenny and Jimmy are about to leave school. So much of their childhood has been swallowed up by wartime.'

'I know there's talk of the school leaving age being raised to fifteen,' said Alison.

'Imagine stopping on at school to fifteen,' Dot said wonderingly. 'What will they do in that extra year? It's only grammar school pupils who stop on until they're fifteen.'

'Presumably those pupils will stay until they're sixteen instead,' said Cordelia.

'Crikey.' Dot grinned. 'I finished school at thirteen.'

'Times change,' said Fay.

'Not everything does,' said Dot. 'Here we are in the middle of another ruddy war.'

'Not "in the middle", I hope,' Cordelia replied.

'Coming towards the end of,' Emily added.

'Let's hope so,' said Colette.

When they all got up to leave, Persephone made a moment to have a word with Fay.

'Thanks for your idea about the songs. It's exactly what I needed.'

'You're welcome,' said Fay. 'I hope you can get a good article out of it.' She paused before adding, 'My mother writes articles too. She's been a regular contributor to *Vera's Voice* since before the last war.'

'Really? What's her name?'

'She writes as Fay Randall.'

Persephone smiled. 'Which explains where your name comes from. My pen-name is Stephanie Fraser.'

Fay returned her smile. 'Much less of a mouthful than Persephone Trehearn-Hobbs.'

As they went their separate ways, Persephone thought about Fay's mother having such a long relationship with *Vera's Voice*. Personally, Persephone would give her eye teeth to know that a similar future lay before her. One step at a time, she told herself. And the next step on her professional road was the article about the old soldiers' home.

Matt had arranged for Persephone to visit his sister Peggy at home so she could seek Peggy's opinion about the likelihood of being permitted to write about the old soldiers' home. Normally Persephone would have taken her idea straight to the home's owners since they were the ones with the power to say yea or nay, but she welcomed the opportunity to become friendlier with Peggy whom so far she had seen only under Sergeant and Mrs Franklin's roof. Going to Peggy's house felt like a chummy thing to do. Matt and Peggy were of similar ages and had been great friends as children, always playing together, according to their mother. They remained close now.

It was a grey afternoon with moisture hanging in the air. Persephone wrapped up warmly in her caramel-coloured coat, her gauntlet-style gloves and the scarf Mrs Cooper had knitted for her. Mrs Mitchell lent her an umbrella.

'Do you think I'll need it?' Persephone asked, looking out of the window. 'It's not raining as such, just trying to drizzle.'

'It's up to you,' Mrs Mitchell replied, 'but if you don't take it, it'll probably pour down.'

Persephone laughed. 'And if I do take it, the sun will break through. I think I'd better borrow it just in case.'

Peggy lived in Ordsall, not far from her parents. Persephone was well acquainted with the bus route and Matt had provided directions from the bus stop to Peggy's house. Sergeant and Mrs Franklin lived in a road of terraced houses with side roads after every block of six or eight houses. Each building had a small front garden and a big window, criss-crossed with anti-blast tape, next to the door. Where Peggy lived, the homes were smaller and had no front gardens. Curls of smoke rose from some of the chimney-pots.

Lifting the knocker, Persephone gave it a cheery rat-tat, smiling as she waited. When there was no answer, her smile turned to a frown. Should she knock again?

'Persephone!'

Hearing Peggy's voice, Persephone turned. Dressed in a headscarf and overcoat, Peggy came hurrying along the pavement with a basket over her arm.

'Sorry,' said Persephone. 'Am I early?' She wasn't but it was polite to say so.

'No, it's me,' said Peggy. 'I thought I'd be back before now.'

'Stuck in a queue?'

Peggy slotted her key into the lock, looking over her shoulder at Persephone. 'Sort of. I heard that Benson's the grocer's had a consignment of tins of tuna delivered just as they shut for dinner, so of course I had to be there the moment they opened again at two o'clock.'

'Along with half the neighbourhood,' said Persephone.

'Three quarters, at least. But they didn't open, and they didn't open, and everyone was wondering and grumbling. Then a woman came along and tried to push her way to the front of the queue. Well, you can imagine the response to that. Then she said, "I'm Mr Benson's sister and I'm opening the shop. If you don't let me through, no one will get any tuna." She was most indignant.' Pushing open the door, Peggy stepped inside. 'I shouldn't keep you talking on the step. Come in.'

Persephone followed her into a narrow hallway. 'Did you get your tuna?'

Peggy hung up her coat on a peg on the wall. 'Yes, thank goodness. It was one tin per customer and I got one of the last ones. Hang up your things here and come on through. I'll put the kettle on.'

The parlour was small, with what looked like hand-me-down furniture. The room was chilly.

'Don't start the fire for my benefit,' Persephone said quickly as Peggy went to kneel in front of the hearth.

'I always start it about now and make it last,' Peggy told her. 'I put fire-bricks in the sides and at the back, which saves fuel.'

'And you never add another lump of coal after eight in

the evening,' Persephone finished with a smile. It was what everyone was urged to do. A box containing a mixture of fabrics caught her eye. 'Are you making toys?'

'Slippers for the children. Their foster mother sent me cut-outs of their feet. It takes three or four layers of wool for each sole and I make the uppers from more or less anything – tapestry, curtaining, even old carpet.'

'You must miss your children,' Persephone said sympathetically. 'I'm sorry. It seems such an inadequate thing to say.'

'I miss them dreadfully,' Peggy admitted, 'and it never gets any easier. I visit them once a year. Once! They've been with their foster parents for so long that I'm worried they won't want to come home again.'

'I'm sure they will,' said Persephone. 'I expect all the children are dying to return home.'

'Do you think this will be the year the war ends?' Peggy asked. 'Lord, I hope so.' She gave herself a shake. 'Tea,' she announced and left the room, returning shortly with a tray, which she placed on a small table between them. 'Now then, Matt said something about an article.'

Persephone explained her ideas and Peggy was pleased to be consulted.

'The home is run by Mr and Mrs Kerslake,' said Peggy. 'I'll have a word with them and see what they think. I hope they agree. I'm sure the old fellows would be delighted.'

As she spoke, she got to her feet in response to a knock at the front door. She left the room and Persephone heard voices in the hall. After a moment or two, Mrs Franklin walked in. She wore her hair rolled neatly at the back of her neck and her dark eyes were observant. Her dress, with narrow stripes of plain dark brown and brown floral with a brown belt, was one Persephone had seen before. Over the top she wore a warm cardigan knitted in cable stitch.

'Good afternoon, Mrs Franklin,' Persephone greeted her.

Mrs Franklin nodded. 'How do.'

'I'll fetch another cup,' said Peggy.

'I gather you're here about another one of your articles,' Mrs Franklin said when Peggy left the room. 'Jill told me.'

'That's right,' said Persephone. 'Peggy has kindly offered to help me.'

'Oh, aye?' Mrs Franklin's eyes narrowed. 'Going to use us again, are you?'

'I didn't use you on that other occasion,' Persephone said, polite but firm. Last year she had found inspiration when she first met Matt's family and had written a highly successful piece about good manners oiling the wheels of meetings between the different social classes. She had written in general terms and not specifically about anyone of her acquaintance, but Mrs Franklin had been deeply offended. 'I'd never do such a thing.'

'Aye, well, you'd better not,' said Mrs Franklin. 'That's all I can say.'

Compulsory overtime meant that Persephone's Saturday-night shift extended throughout Sunday morning. Alison was due to work on Sunday too, and since Persephone's clocking-off time coincided with Alison's dinner break, they met up for a quick cuppa in the buffet before Persephone headed for home.

Alison plonked herself down in a chair, putting her plate

and cup on the table. 'Meat-paste with carrot chutney,' she announced, nodding towards the sandwich. 'And a potato scone to follow.'

'Hearty fare for the onward travel organiser,' Persephone said with a smile. 'Did Mrs Jessop save them for you?'

'Yes. I nipped in first thing and asked her.'

'She's been such a brick all the way through the war,' said Persephone. 'What would we have done without her?'

'It wouldn't have been so easy for all of us to meet up as much as we do, that's for certain,' said Alison.

'And that would have meant we wouldn't have become such friends,' Persephone added. 'We owe her a great deal.'

Alison bit into her sandwich and shut her eyes for a moment. 'I needed that. Are you and Matt doing anything for Valentine's Day?'

Persephone shook her head. 'Different shifts. That seems to be the story of our lives.' She spoke lightly even though the thought of it weighed on her heart. Since she and Matt didn't have a future to look forward to, surely the least they deserved was an easier present? 'What about you and Joel?' she asked.

'We've both got the evening off,' said Alison. 'Lucky us. Joel is taking me out for a meal at the Midland, where we got engaged.'

'Very romantic,' Persephone said approvingly.

'I wish you and Matt could have time together as well.'

Persephone shrugged lightly. 'It's the way it is.'

Putting down her sandwich, Alison leaned forward. 'The build-up to Valentine's Day used to drive me half-crazy back when I was going out with Paul. All I could think about was the proposal I was sure I was going to get, which of course I never did. I'm so glad now that it never happened. Joel is absolutely the right husband for me.'

Persephone smiled. 'I imagine there are a lot of girls who are hoping that by the time tomorrow evening comes to an end, they'll have a ring on their finger.'

'But not you,' Alison said softly. 'Tell me to mind my own business, but . . . it can't be easy for you – for either of you.'

'It's the way it is,' Persephone said again. 'We both know that. But if you want the truth, I shall be bracing myself when I come to work on Tuesday morning, because there are going to be a lot of engagement rings being flashed about.'

'Oh, Persephone,' said Alison.

'I know I keep on saying it, but it's how it is.' Persephone hoped her smile looked natural. 'And as if Valentine's Day weren't enough of a trial, we have leap year as well.'

'Yet more proposals,' said Alison. 'Speaking of which,' she added with a cheeky grin, 'I don't think I ever showed you my engagement ring, did I?'

'Do you know, I don't think you did,' Persephone replied, playing along. She seized Alison's hand so she could look at the emerald. 'It's beautiful,' she said sincerely.

'I wish I knew what to say to you,' said Alison. 'You're my friend and I care about you and want you to be happy, but I know you and Matt can't be together for ever. What am I supposed to say?'

Persephone's heart melted. 'You just said it. I'm your friend and you care. That means everything. I know that when the war ends, things are going to be tough for me emotionally, but I'll have my friends and that will be enough.'

It would have to be. She would make sure it was. She wouldn't let herself crumble. Not outwardly, at any rate.

The stiff, chilly breeze made Persephone's face prickle as she alighted from the bus but setting off at a brisk walk for Darley Court soon warmed her up. She planned her afternoon. First: letter-writing. Then she would lend a hand outdoors. Mr Hattatt had put *Rhubarb – divide old roots* on the list for February and it hadn't been crossed off yet, so she might get started on that.

As she walked between the two big stone gateposts to go past the gatekeeper's lodge, where the land girls now lived, the door opened and the land girls spilled out, chuckling and all greeting her at once.

'Hello! Nippy, isn't it?'

'Got to dash or Mr Hattatt will have our guts for garters – and if he doesn't, Miss Brown will.'

'Drat. We didn't bank the fire down. Be a love and do it for us, Persephone.'

And they were on their way, hurrying away up the drive. Persephone laughed. It wasn't like them to be disorganised, but sorting out the fire wouldn't take a minute. She pushed open the door— and stopped on the threshold.

'Hello, Persephone,' said Matt.

There he was, tall and handsome, his build slim but strong, his eyes crinkling as he smiled. Persephone felt a tiny tug at the skin around her eyes as they widened in surprise, then her pulse started to race and she – the writer, the wordsmith – had the oddest feeling of being tongue-tied.

Matt laughed. 'Shall I close the door?'

He moved behind her and did so. Persephone turned to face him.

'What are you doing here?' she asked.

'Apart from taking you by surprise?'

'Apart from that,' said Persephone, lifting her face to his.

He dipped his head down and kissed the tip of her nose. 'Come and sit by the fire. It would be a terrible shame to waste it after the land girls left it burning.'

Matt helped her off with her coat, beneath which she wore her uniform. Persephone dropped her hat on the shelf and Matt hung her coat on one of the pegs on the wall before holding the parlour door for her to go through. With its handsome chairs and the vast fire surround with a three-shelved overmantel alongside the wireless and the standard lamp with the fringed shade, the room was a cosy mixture of the old and the new.

They sat on the hearthrug, opposite each other, each leaning back against an armchair. Well, that was a waste of an opportunity, wasn't it? Persephone moved position, settling herself next to Matt. He draped an arm around her shoulders, hooking her closer.

'Why didn't you tell me?' she asked.

'This is your Valentine's surprise. We can't have any time together tomorrow so we've got this instead.'

'It's better than a Valentine's Day thing because it really did come as a complete surprise.'

'Good,' he said. 'I wanted to please you.'

Persephone laid her head against him, enjoying the scent of the coal fire but more than anything enjoying being with Matt.

'How was work?' he asked.

'The trains weren't too crowded today, for a wonder. Certainly no fare-dodgers to deal with,' she added, referring to how she and Matt had first become friendly.

'I'm pleased to hear it,' he answered in a mock-stern voice. 'I don't want another chap thinking he can help you out in a tricky situation.'

Persephone put on a serious voice. 'That's very true. That last fellow who weighed in to help has ended up hanging around all the time.'

'Poor you,' Matt murmured. He lifted her chin with the tips of his fingers and angled his head for a sweet kiss. 'Mm. That was nice. Again?'

After another kiss, Persephone snuggled against him once more, releasing a gentle sigh of pure happiness.

'This is perfect,' said Matt. 'The two of us by the fire on a cold day, with the wireless for company. Do you mind it being on?'

'Of course not.' Persephone cocked her head to listen, recognising *In Your Garden*. 'What's on after this?'

'A symphony concert from Edinburgh,' said Matt, 'and after that, a saxophone quartet.'

'Oh, are you stopping there?' teased Persephone. 'I thought you were going to announce the programmes up to *Children's Hour*.'

'Unfortunately, I have to be gone by then. Sorry,' Matt added.

'Don't be sorry. Having this time together is unexpected and wonderful. Let's not spoil it by thinking about when it has to end. That'll happen soon enough without us dwelling on it.'

After a moment Matt said quietly, 'We're experts at that, aren't we? Making the most of now.'

Persephone's heartbeat slowed. 'So is everyone. It's a wartime thing. But that isn't what you mean, is it?'

'I just want this afternoon to be perfect. Something special to remember. Tell you what. Let's switch off the wireless and see what records the girls have got. They said we could use the gramophone if we wanted.'

It was a wrench to leave the comfort, excitement and gentle strength of being in the circle of Matt's arm, but Persephone rose and went to look through the records in their paper sleeves while Matt turned off the radio concert. After a moment he came to look over her shoulder.

'They've got a recording of Scottish country dances,' he said. 'We could do "The Gay Gordons" up and down the drive. Or – look at this. *Victor Sylvester and His Ballroom Orchestra*.'

'Let's see the label,' said Persephone. 'Oh, look. "You're Dancing on My Heart". That's his signature tune.'

'Let's dance to it,' said Matt.

Persephone glanced around the room. 'I don't want to be a wet blanket but there isn't space for a quickstep.'

'We don't need a dance floor.' Matt placed the record on the turntable and lifted the arm into position. The record crackled before the music started. 'Not when there's a perfectly good hearthrug. We'll just hold one another and sway.' He offered her his hand. 'Will you do me the honour?'

Persephone gave him her hand and they skirted the furniture as they headed for the hearthrug. Matt took her in ballroom hold and she gazed up into his eyes as they swayed from side to side. Persephone didn't know which one of them made it happen – perhaps they both did it at the same moment – but their extended arms gently folded against them and the dance hold became more of an embrace as the music swirled around them. 'You're Dancing on My Heart'. Persephone laid her head against Matt's chest and tried not to weep.

In those moments, they weren't the Honourable and the fireman. They were the ticket inspector and the fireman. They were two people dancing. They were wartime sweethearts.

It was perfect and it was heart-rending.

Chapter Six

They were more than halfway through February and the days were drawing out. The weather couldn't seem to make up its mind. There were days when the gutters gurgled as rain or sleet filled them and buses churned up sloppy sprays onto pavements and unfortunate pedestrians. But there were also days of sudden brightness that added a welcome glimmer to the fresh green of early growth and made colours more vivid.

Alison, Joan and Margaret accompanied Sally to the station when she embarked on her new life in the Land Army. They arrived at Victoria hurrying through a sheet of drizzle.

'I can think of things I'd rather be doing than working on the land in this weather,' Alison joked.

They found the right platform. The train was already there.

'Thank you all for coming to see me off,' said Sally. 'I wanted you here because of how much you did for me when I had my troubles.'

'That was Margaret,' said Alison.

'Yes, it was,' Joan agreed.

'Mainly it was, yes,' Sally agreed with an affectionate look at the friend who had stood by her from the start. 'But you two helped as well, especially you, Joan, with all the information you gave me. And Alison found out about Rookery House for me.'

'That was Joel really,' said Alison. 'I just passed the details on.'

Sally shook her head in mock exasperation. 'I'm trying to say thank you and it's not easy when someone keeps trying to duck out of having done anything helpful.' Then in a serious voice she added, 'I'll tell you what you did that was helpful, Alison. You changed your mind about me. You started off seeing me as a fallen girl who was in the worst sort of disgrace, but then you revised that opinion and saw me for what I was, a decent girl who had been taken in by a rotter.'

'I'm sorry I was horrid to begin with,' said Alison.

'Your original attitude was normal and only what I expected, what anyone would say I deserved,' said Sally. 'But it meant the world to me when you changed your mind and wanted to help me. You've no idea how good that made me feel. It helped give me the strength to carry on.'

Alison didn't know what to say to that. Sally hugged her, then Joan and last of all Margaret before they helped her onto the train with her luggage.

'Don't wait for the train to pull out,' said Sally, 'or I shall start blubbing and I don't want to do that.'

So, with a final wave through the window, the three of them walked back down the platform towards the barrier.

'Are you all right?' Joan asked Margaret. 'You'll miss her.'

'I'm glad she's going off to a new life,' said Margaret. 'I'd have loved it if she'd stayed here and gone back to her old job in the engine sheds, but that would have been too difficult for her and I can understand that.' She smiled. 'I wish her all the best.'

'So do we all,' said Alison. 'She deserves it.'

After an early breakfast on Saturday, having seen Joel off to work, Alison flicked through the recipe book her friends had given her. It was quite possibly the most special present she had ever received. She loved being married and feeling she was looking after Joel and their home, though she was still sometimes finding it a bit of a struggle to fit everything in. Joan had warned her about this.

'You have to do everything you'd have had to do as a wife before the war – cooking, cleaning, shopping – but you have to do it on top of working full-time plus compulsory overtime. And the shopping takes for ever because of having to queue.' Then Joan had grinned. 'But aside from that, it's a doddle.'

Alison had always been organised so it had been somewhat disconcerting not to get to grips with her new responsibilities right away, but she knew it was only a matter of time. All over the country, female war-workers were putting in long hours and then going home to clean their houses and put meals on the table, and now Alison was one of them. It was something to be proud of, an extra contribution to the war effort.

According to Dot, 'The powers that be couldn't manage without us doing all the jobs we've moved into, but it never occurs to them that there's any effort involved in also running our homes and taking care of our families. It's just taken for granted that all the domestic stuff gets done. We don't get any credit for it.'

'They probably think the pixies do it in the night,' Cordelia had said drily.

Dot had laughed at that. 'I wouldn't say no if a few pixies turned up at my house to lend a hand.'

As she looked through her cookery book, recalling Dot's words brought a smile to Alison's lips. She was aware of one household task that had vanished from the list – thank heaven. Back in the days of nightly air raids, whenever a bomb landed, the interiors of all the houses in the vicinity of about a mile, no matter how clean they were, ended up covered with a film of dust and soot. That was how Mrs Cooper's little cleaning business, Magic Mop, had started. She had offered her service to perform a post air-raid clean. The business had soon developed into a traditional cleaning service and Mrs Cooper was highly valued by her regular ladies.

Opening a page with one of Mrs Grayson's recipes, Alison settled on potato piglets to have that evening with Joel. It would give her a chance to use the apple-corer that had been a wedding present from Auntie Stella. Before the war, an apple-corer would probably have seemed a very stingy gift, but these days it was like being given gold dust.

Potato piglets involved removing the lengthways core of each potato, stuffing it with sausagemeat and then baking it. It sounded delicious. At the bottom of the recipe, Mrs Grayson had added a note to remind Alison that in wartime there was no such thing as leftovers and the potato cores could be used to thicken soup.

Alison quickly wrote her shopping list. There shouldn't be a problem getting sausagemeat, though she would have to see what the butcher had in stock before she decided what to have for Sunday lunch tomorrow. Then she would need veg from the greengrocer. Winter cabbage would go nicely with the potato piglets, and she could make a baked jam sponge for pudding, which she and Joel could finish off tomorrow.

Singing one of her favourites, '(We're Gonna Hang Out) The Washing on the Siegfried Line', to herself and feeling very much the busy housewife, she put on her outdoor things, fastening her moss-green coat and putting on her hat before winding her long red scarf around her neck and picking up her shopping bag. It was a cold morning with dull skies and cloud cover lending a grey cast to the light. Making her way to the butcher's, Alison joined the queue. Mrs Cooper had told her it was a good way to meet the locals and this was true. Alison very much wanted to be part of her new community. She loved the idea of herself as the happy young wife going about her domestic duties and part of that was discussing the price of cod with the neighbours and knowing whose little one had got ten out of ten for spelling.

She was pleased to join the queue behind Mrs Nuttall, who lived across the road. She was in her thirties and her war work was in a factory. The two of them chatted. When more women tacked on behind them, the conversation widened to include the newcomers.

Presently a middle-aged woman in a cavalry twill overcoat and an old felt hat stopped beside Mrs Nuttall.

'Hey,' said one of the women behind Alison. 'I hope you

aren't trying to worm your way into the queue, Mavis Summers.' Her tone was rude but in a good-natured way, a mock-jibe between friends.

'Charming,' Mrs Summers replied in the same tone. 'I stop for a word with our Becky and get accused of shoving my way in.'

'This is my mum, Mrs Summers,' Mrs Nuttall said to Alison. 'Mum, this is Mrs Maitland. She and her husband have moved in over the road into the Naylors' old house.'

'How do,' said Mrs Summers. 'Your husband's at home with you, is he? Reserved occupation?'

'He's a doctor,' Alison said with pride.

Mrs Summers nodded her approval. 'I'll be glad to have a respectable family in that house.'

'Respectable?' Alison felt a chill that had nothing to do with the bite in the air.

'Oh aye. That Mrs Naylor was a very quiet girl. She wouldn't say boo to a goose, but it didn't stop her walking out on her marriage,' Mrs Summers declared. 'I'll be much happier knowing our Becky has a doctor and his wife over the road. That Mrs Naylor lowered the tone.'

Alison bristled as the breath caught in her throat. What a thing to say! But then she remembered the occasions when Colette had mentioned that folk weren't shy of saying bad things about her. Alison recalled her own mother's reservations when Alison wanted Colette as one of her matrons of honour. Yes, and she remembered too how she had stood up to Mum.

But somehow, in the time it took to acknowledge those

memories, the talk around her had moved on – and Alison hadn't spoken up in defence of her friend.

With Joel out at work all day, Alison had promised to visit her parents that afternoon. Lydia was going to be there too. Alison prepared the potato piglets and popped them in the meat safe ready to bake when she got home, then she set off. She and Joel lived in Seymour Grove on the south side of Manchester and Mum and Dad lived to the north, so she had to go into the middle of Manchester and then out again. It was a bit of a hike but more than worth it to see her family.

Dad was a builder and he said he had never been busier. Mum gave her time to the WVS. In the early part of the war she had been involved in the local rest centre, the place where people went when they were bombed out and in need of just about everything – clothes, food, toiletries, new ration books, somewhere to stay.

'You name it and the WVS provides it,' Mum used to say. 'If we can't provide it, we know an organisation that can.'

These days Mum did welfare work and helped run the clothes exchange, the make-do-and-mend class and the mobile library. She also devoted one afternoon each week to volunteering at a café where soldiers from overseas could find help and advice and, if they were homesick, a sympathetic ear.

While she'd been organising Alison's wedding, Mum had still worked for the WVS but she had attached great importance to her daughter's big day and so had been less of an officer and more of a foot soldier for a few weeks. Alison's lips now twitched into a smile as she remembered something Lydia had said after Alison's Christmas Eve wedding. Well, she hadn't said it as such. She had whispered it with a cheeky twinkle in her eye.

'Now that your wedding is over, Mum can channel her energy into bossing the WVS again.'

Whereupon Mum had inserted her head in between Alison's and Lydia's to say, 'I do not boss, Lydia. I organise.'

'I know, Mum.' Alison had hugged her. 'You've given me a wonderful wedding.'

She had, too. It had been Mum's idea to borrow the neighbours' Christmas trees to line the walls of the church hall and she had organised an excellent spread despite the lack of resources. Mum had made some compromises too, such as when Alison had put her foot down about inviting Colette to be one of her attendants. Mum had ended up applauding Alison's staunch support of her friend and had found out for herself that Colette was a likeable person. That had meant a lot to Alison.

Nevertheless she had no intention of mentioning the disparaging words uttered by Mrs Summers that morning. How very judgemental Mrs Summers had been. The bizarre thing was that everybody knew what Tony Naylor had been like, because it had been reported in the *Manchester Evening News*, yet most folk criticised the young wife whose confidence he had systematically sapped.

Dad and his men were out working on repairs, a never-ending job in wartime. Mum, Alison and Lydia sat together, drinking tea and enjoying Mum's carrot cake.

'How is married life?' Mum asked Alison.

'I still feel as if I never stop, but I'm getting used to

leaving the dusting halfway through to dash off to work, and I've realised that, no matter how much time you allow for it, queuing at the shops always takes twice as long as that.'

'And when you reach the front, they've sold out,' Mum added.

Alison laughed. 'And just when I'm about to make myself a cup of tea, I remember I haven't finished the ironing or laid the table for breakfast or sewn that button back on Joel's shirt.'

'A woman's work is never done,' said Mum.

'I'm tired of hearing you moan about it,' Lydia said tetchily to Alison.

'What?' Alison asked, startled.

'Some of us have husbands who are away fighting for their country,' Lydia pointed out as she had many times before. 'Some of us would give anything to be sewing on our husband's buttons.'

'I didn't mean to upset you,' said Alison, 'and I wasn't moaning.' She had intended to be light-hearted about it, even amusing.

'I know.' Lydia looked shamefaced. 'I just – I miss Alec so much.'

'I know you do, darling,' Mum said sympathetically.

'I shouldn't take it out on you,' Lydia said to Alison. 'You deserve better. It just gets me down sometimes. I bought some braid a day or two ago to trim our cushion-covers and I was so pleased with myself for finding something pretty. Then I said to myself, is this all I've got to show for being married? New braid for the cushions? Let's face it. It's not as though Alec will see it until goodness knows when.'

'But he will see it one day,' Mum said firmly. 'It's your job to make sure he has an attractive, comfortable home to come back to.'

'I know how lucky I am to have Joel in a reserved occupation,' Alison said softly.

'And in such an important job as well,' Mum said admiringly. 'It's quite something to have a doctor in the family.'

Alison glanced at Lydia. Would she take umbrage because Alec was 'only' a warehouseman? Mind you, the army had trained him as a mechanic and there was talk of his carrying on as a motor mechanic after the war. Mum was dubious but Dad said there would be a lot more motor cars on the roads in years to come. He said the price of them would come down and more men would be able to afford them.

Lydia smiled. 'Having Joel around will be useful if one of us is poorly.' Then she added in a serious voice, 'Do you think they really will introduce this new health service after the war?'

'It's a wonderful idea,' said Mum, 'but how will they ever afford it? Nobody having to pay for medical treatment. What does Joel think of it?'

'He's keen for it to happen,' said Alison. 'You know he's a paediatrician at heart. He can't bear to think of children missing out on treatment because their parents can't afford to send for the doctor.'

'That's always been a problem,' Mum agreed. 'As a young mother, I counted myself lucky that your father could afford what we needed. I could get the doctor round if one of you girls was poorly and your father has always paid into the Hospital Saturday Fund as well.' She started to get up.

'I'll clear away these things and then I'll show you what I've started knitting.'

Alison rose. 'You stay put, Mum. Lydia and I will wash up.'

Once they were in the kitchen, Lydia said, 'I'm glad to get you on your own. I wondered if . . .'

'If what?' Alison asked but she didn't really need to.

'You know,' said Lydia. 'If you're late with your monthly.'

'I already told you,' Alison said in a low voice. 'We've decided not to have children immediately. We want to enjoy being together first.'

'It's all right for you,' said Lydia. 'You have the luxury of making that choice. I haven't seen Alec since our honeymoon – and that was in 1942.'

Alison gave her sister a hug. She loved Lydia and wanted to support her, but secretly she was tired of having this conversation. Yes, it was a huge shame that Lydia hadn't had the honeymoon baby she had wanted so much, but it was as if she couldn't think of anything else. If only Alec could get some leave and come home just for the purpose of putting Lydia in the pudding club! That would give Lydia what she longed for and stop her moaning to her sister. Alison couldn't think of anything better.

Then she felt guilty. She had so much. Her husband was at home and they were lucky enough to have had a house handed to them on a plate.

'Are you doing anything tomorrow?' Alison asked.

'No, not really.'

'Why don't you come over to our house? Come in time for dinner. I'll add more veg to eke things out. Please say yes.'

'Thanks,' said Lydia. 'I'd like that – and I promise there won't be any baby talk.'

Alison gave her another hug.

The potato piglets were a success, as were the lentil cutlets Alison made for Sunday dinner. There hadn't been anything other than sausagemeat left when she reached the head of the butcher's queue yesterday, but that had turned out to be a good thing because she had plenty of lentils to make an extra cutlet for Lydia. In the afternoon the three of them went for a walk. Alison slid her gloved hand in the crook of Joel's arm and he offered his other arm to Lydia. It was a raw day. Everyone they saw was wrapped up inside warm coats and scarves. The sky was streaked with grey clouds bloated with rain and the air was heavy with moisture.

'It feels as if it's going to chuck it down later,' Lydia commented. 'I'm glad I brought my umbrella. I'll probably need it on my way home.'

'I've had enough of winter,' said Alison.

'If you look at the flower patches people have kept in their gardens,' said Joel, 'you can see new shoots appearing. That's a good sign. It isn't all bare trees with bony branches.'

'Very poetic,' Alison replied with a laugh.

But Joel was right. There were indeed long-awaited signs of fresh growth. One house they passed had a pot of snowdrops beside the doorstep.

'I remember my grandmother calling them February fair maids,' Joel remarked.

'That's a pretty name,' said Lydia.

'I wonder if I could get hold of some bulbs for next year,'

said Alison. 'I'd like to have our own little clump of February fair maids in our garden.'

'Our garden.' Joel squeezed her hand within his arm. 'Doesn't that sound good? I'm still bowled over by Colette's generosity in giving us the house.'

That reminded Alison. She told Lydia and Joel what Mrs Summers had said in the butcher's queue yesterday.

'And what did you say?' Lydia asked.

'I didn't,' Alison admitted. 'I'm ashamed of myself now but at the time, it took my breath away to hear Colette being criticised so openly. I wish I'd stood up for her.'

'You were taken aback,' said Joel and Alison was grateful to him for recognising it and not blaming her.

'Besides,' Lydia added, 'if you had answered back, you'd have got yourself talked about and that wouldn't have helped anyone, least of all Colette.'

'That's true,' said Alison, 'but I still feel bad about it.'

'I'll tell you what you could do,' said Joel. 'You said Mrs Summers is Mrs Nuttall's mother. Have a quiet word with Mrs Nuttall. Don't make a big thing out of it, but make it clear that Colette is our friend and we're grateful to her for giving up her home.'

Alison liked the sound of that. Should she add something about the terrible time Colette had endured with Tony? No. She didn't want Mrs Nuttall to feel like piggy-in-the-middle between her mother and Alison.

They walked briskly, enjoying exploring their new neighbourhood with Lydia. Alison was always proud to be seen with Joel and she liked nodding and saying, 'How do,' to people they now recognised.

'We're so lucky to have Colette's house,' she said. 'I hate the reasons why Colette wanted to leave, but I love the way things have turned out for us.'

'And Colette seems happy at Wilton Close,' Joel added.

'Yes,' Alison agreed sincerely. 'She and Mrs Cooper have a special closeness and I can't think of anything nicer than the two of them being able to live together.'

'Really?' Beneath the brim of his faithful old trilby, Joel's eyebrows climbed. 'Even nicer than the two of us living together? Wash your mouth out, Mrs Maitland.'

Alison laughed. 'There's nothing in the whole wide world better than us being together.'

'I could have told you that practically the first time we met,' said Joel. Looking at Lydia, he added, 'But it took your sister a devil of a long time to work it out. Whenever we arranged to meet, I never knew whether she was going to appear.'

'I was keeping you guessing,' Alison teased.

'You even let me think you were Olivia de Havilland,' Joel said.

Alison gave his arm a slap. 'I did no such thing. It was you who started that nonsense.'

She smiled, remembering how Joel had joked about them being Errol Flynn and Olivia de Havilland after they had helped to chase a man who had seemed to be a Jerry saboteur, though he had turned out to be nothing of the kind. Afterwards Joel had used the beautiful film star's name for Alison after she avoided introducing herself.

They walked up the front steps into the Seymour Hotel for a cup of tea before heading for home, quickening their pace as it started to drizzle. They were laughing as the house came in sight.

'There's your mum and dad,' said Joel.

'Did you invite them to come for tea?' Lydia asked.

Dad turned to look at them. Alison saw his face – and her pulse began to race. Mum walked briskly towards them, her face white as she stretched out her arms towards them – no, not towards all of them but towards Lydia. Fear streamed through Alison. The three of them picked up speed, the girls dropping Joel's arms. Then Lydia stopped dead.

'No,' she said, her voice flat. 'No.'

She tried to turn away but Mum reached them and wrapped her arms around her.

'Leave her be, Janet,' said Dad. 'Let's all go indoors.'

As if that would make any difference. Alison knew what was coming, but as long as nobody said it, as long as nobody uttered the actual words, she could hope against hope that she was wrong, mistaken, wide of the mark.

Joel unlocked the front door and ushered them all inside. Nobody took off their outdoor things. They trooped into the parlour and stood looking at one another. Lydia breathed slowly, her chest rising and falling.

'I think you should sit down, Lydia,' said Dad, but she didn't move, just stared at him. He heaved a sigh. 'I'm so sorry, love. This arrived.' He took one of the dreaded telegrams from his pocket. 'The boy went to your address and you weren't there, so one of the neighbours sent him round to ours.'

Instead of taking the telegram, Lydia stood utterly still.

Then she seemed to rear up, her whole body jerking in rejection of the moment, her chin jolting upwards and to the side.

'Do you want Dad to open it?' Mum asked gently.

Lydia's jaw tightened. Her eyes suddenly filled with fire that drained away just as abruptly, leaving her expression bleak.

'He could just be missing in action,' said Mum.

Just. *Just.* Being MIA was the good outcome when a telegram arrived. MIA was something that left hope alive.

Alison put an arm around Lydia's shoulders, shocked by how different she felt. In Mum's kitchen yesterday, although slim, she had been soft and supple to the touch. Today she was brittle.

'Shall I read it?' Dad asked.

Lydia took it from him and opened it. She lowered her head to read it and a second later she sagged, doubling over, knees crumpling. The room was suddenly full of movement as the rest of them surged forward to grab her, to support her, keep her up, transfer her to the sofa. Mum plumped down beside her, trying to hold her, but Lydia, with a shake of her shoulders, freed herself.

'Put the kettle on,' Joel said quietly to Alison. 'I'll stir up the fire and get everyone's coats off.'

In the kitchen Alison went through the motions. Alec, she thought. Alec, she kept on thinking over and over.

Alec Alec Alec.

Gone.

Chapter Seven

Colette approached Victoria Station, taking a moment as she often did to appreciate the sight of the handsome building with the clock tower at the top of the curved front corner. Once she was inside, the sound of a train starting to pull out echoed around the concourse and the long lines of platforms, reaching high above into the arched canopy of metal-framed glass.

Dressed in her blue coat and cream wool scarf with tassels at the ends, together with her hat and gloves, Colette might give the impression of being an ordinary passenger, but she was just as much a railway employee as the uniformed porters and ticket-collectors. Her role – her official role – was that of chaperone and it was her job to assist vulnerable passengers by travelling with them. Wearing her own clothes meant that other passengers didn't approach her, so she could concentrate solely on the person or people she was looking after that day. It also meant, as far as Colette was concerned – though she didn't think it had ever occurred to the railway company – that the person in her charge had the feeling of being treated with respect because they had her full attention.

She might be required to accompany a blind or frail person or a mother with a handicapped child. More than once she had travelled with an elderly passenger with senile decay, ensuring they alighted at the correct station and helping them to find the person who was there to meet them. Colette loved her official job. It was rewarding and worthwhile and she would have been more than happy for it to be her real job, just as everyone else believed it to be, including her friends. She didn't like misleading them, but it was essential to keep her real role a secret.

Now she threaded her way between the people on the busy concourse, passing the long ticket office with its line of windows where passengers queued to purchase their tickets. Tucked away round the side was a door the general public weren't even aware of. It was kept locked from the inside. Colette knocked and waited to be admitted. Within the large ticket office was an office-within-an-office in one corner. She had been here many times when she had to see Mr Gordon.

He was a handsome man in his forties, with a high forehead and thinning golden-brown hair above a serious, clever face and thoughtful eyes. He sometimes looked shrewd but not in an unkind way. He was quietly spoken and Colette had never heard him raise his voice. She had never seen him agitated either, no matter what he'd had to deal with. He was a stickler for the rules, not because he was pernickety but because it was an important aspect of his work. Colette was willing to bet he was utterly honest and trustworthy in his personal life as well as at work. She couldn't have been specific about why she thought this, but it made sense to her. He had integrity and she liked that. She admired it. It represented everything that was the exact opposite to the way her life had been with Tony.

Mr Gordon's secretary was a pleasant, middle-aged woman called Mrs Lister. She favoured a shaped, nipped-in jacket, which was a shame because it made her look top-heavy. A less form-fitting garment would have been much more flattering. She greeted Colette with a polite smile and showed her into Mr Gordon's office. That was something Colette had noticed about her. She had never simply waved Colette in.

Mr Gordon rose politely. Colette liked that about him. Plenty of bosses wouldn't show that courtesy.

'Should I . . . ?' asked Mrs Lister.

'Yes, please,' said Mr Gordon. To Colette he explained, 'It's eleven o'clock, which means it's time for a cup of tea. "Should I?" and "Yes, please" is our not-so-subtle secret code for whether Mrs Lister should bring in two cups or defer tea until after you've gone.'

He smiled and his habitually serious expression softened. Colette smiled back. She liked him in a professional sort of way. He always explained to her exactly what she had to do and that had given her confidence in the early days of doing this job.

Although she did genuinely chaperone vulnerable passengers, her real role was to gather evidence of misdemeanours carried out by railway employees or passengers. Obviously this needed to be done secretly, which was why this post ran alongside her public post of chaperone. No one, not even Mrs Cooper, knew about her other responsibilities. Truth be told, she did a lot more chaperoning than she did investigating, so it wasn't as much of a lie as it might have been.

And wasn't 'investigating' an overblown word! It made

her sound like a detective and she most certainly wasn't that. She did things like purchase tickets from employees who looked as though they were doing everything above board but who were really on the fiddle.

Mr Gordon was the person who issued her with these assignments and every time she was instructed to come here to his office, she knew this was the reason.

Mrs Lister brought in a tray of tea.

'Saucer or handle?' the secretary asked her.

It was a common enough question these days, the choice between having a proper cup but no saucer or a handle-less cup with a saucer. Colette, who was innately courteous and always wanted the other person to have what was more desirable, still hadn't worked out which was the politer choice to make.

'Please give Mrs Naylor the handle,' said Mr Gordon.

Colette thanked them both with a smile. Mrs Lister left the office and Colette turned her full attention to Mr Gordon as he explained her latest job. It didn't take long and Colette was all too aware of not having finished her tea. Ought she to knock it back and leave? But Mr Gordon was nothing if not a gentleman and he chatted about this and that before taking Colette by surprise by referring to the occasion when she had brought Emily to see him. That had been in the spring of last year when Emily had been disturbed to find that there was pilfering going on in the stores by a number of the porters.

'That was ages ago,' Colette exclaimed.

'It has stayed with me,' Mr Gordon told her. 'I remember you saying, "There are times when someone does the wrong thing, but they do it with the best of intentions." That made me see things in a different light – though, of course, it was still a very serious matter. It made me think what a kind person you must be.'

Colette's cheeks felt warm. 'Thank you.' She finished her tea and stood up.

Mr Gordon thanked her for coming and politely half-rose from his seat as she left.

As she left the ticket office and returned to the concourse, Colette smiled to herself.

Five days had passed since Lydia had received the telegram that everyone dreaded. Alec was gone – for ever. He was never going to come home. Alison found it hard to take in, so goodness knew how much worse it must be for Lydia. His in-laws, not to mention his own family, hadn't seen him since the weekend of the wedding and now they were never going to see him again. His absence, which had been an ordinary part of their wartime lives, now felt like the biggest and most important part. Whichever way they turned, there it was. Alison couldn't think about it without feeling cold deep inside.

She had been given the Monday off on compassionate grounds and had taken the Tuesday as well from her holiday allowance, spending both days with her shocked family.

On the Tuesday evening she had tentatively asked Lydia, 'Would you mind awfully if I went back to work tomorrow?'

Lydia had shrugged. As her shoulders lifted, the sides of her mouth turned down. She didn't look at Alison, though

Alison sensed her sister wasn't avoiding her eyes as such. It was more that she didn't have the energy to focus.

'Why not?' Lydia replied in a voice that managed to be dull and offhand at the same time. 'I'm going to.'

Alison was taken aback. 'Lydia! You can't.'

'Why not?' Lydia asked again and now she did look at Alison. 'It's not as though there's a funeral to organise. The best I can hope for is a war grave. Oh, God, Alison . . .'

But just when Alison had thought Lydia would collapse in distress, she had drawn herself upright and taken a deep breath. When the telegram had arrived, she had gone from slender and creamy-complexioned to thin and dull-eyed overnight. The change in her was startling, scary even.

'You have to take care of yourself,' Alison had urged, anxious to say the right thing. 'Alec wouldn't want to see you like that.'

Lydia had said, 'Alec won't see me ever again,' and that was that. Subject closed.

Now, on Friday evening, Alison's friends were due to meet up in the buffet, an arrangement that had been put in place before Alec died. That was how Alison measured time now. Before Alec died. Since Alec died.

'Should I go to the buffet?' she had asked Joel that morning. Normally a decisive person, in this instance she seemed unable to make up her mind. 'Would it look . . . I don't know – frivolous?'

'No, it wouldn't,' Joel said firmly. 'It will look exactly what it is, a chance for your closest friends to support you.'

So, after she clocked off, Alison went to the buffet. She of all people knew the value of letting others show their concern. When her long-time boyfriend Paul had ditched her, she had isolated herself and borne her heartbreak alone, but she had realised in the end what she had missed by turning away from her friends. They would help her now. They would make her feel cared for and she could say anything to them.

As she entered the buffet, all her feelings came rushing to the surface, clogging her throat. Immediately she saw her friends' concerned faces turning towards her. It was too much. She had to direct her gaze elsewhere, taking in the fireplace with the clock on the wall above, the curved counter with its wood-panelled front, the people seated at the tables, their bags on the floor, the couple in the corner holding hands. Lydia and Alec would never again do that.

'Go and sit down,' said a soft voice by her side and Persephone inserted herself into Alison's place in the queue.

'Park yourself next to me,' Dot invited as Alison reached the table. 'We were just talking about this here plan to let women teachers carry on teaching after they get married.'

'It's always seemed barmy to me that married women aren't allowed to teach,' said Fay.

There were one or two other comments. Alison wasn't fooled. She knew perfectly well they had been talking about Lydia. They were just giving her a minute to dampen down her feelings and get them under control.

Persephone put a cup of tea in front of her. Dot immediately produced a small bottle from her handbag and poured something into Alison's tea.

'There you go,' said Dot. 'That'll help.'

'What is it?' Alison asked.

'Cooking sherry,' said Dot. 'I've been hoarding it since before war broke out, so you've got to drink it. Waste not, want not.'

Obediently Alison lifted the cup to her lips. She took a sip and coughed.

'It's supposed to be brandy for shock,' said Cordelia, 'but needs must.'

'We're all so very sorry about Lydia's husband,' said Colette.

Alison nodded. 'Thanks. I know you are.'

'How is she getting on?' asked Emily. 'I'm sorry. That must sound like a stupid question.'

Alison's sigh was filled with all her worries for her sister. 'She's gone back to work.'

'Already?' asked Joan.

'That's brave of her,' said Margaret.

'Bravery has nothing to do with it,' said Alison. 'She said, "What's the point of staying at home?" She's right, I suppose.'

'The poor love,' said Dot. 'It's not as though work is going to take her mind off it.'

'She'll be miserable wherever she is,' said Emily.

Alison looked at Emily. 'I imagine you're remembering your own experience after Raymond.'

Colour appeared in Emily's cheeks. Raymond was the boy she had been in love with and he had loved her too . . . until his feelings for her had worn off. It had been a bad time for the young girl.

'I know Lydia's loss is far worse than mine was,' Emily

said with simple dignity, 'but I remember how hard it was for me and I feel sorry for her.'

'My thoughts are flying in a dozen different directions all at once,' said Alison. 'All I want is to help Lydia, but . . . it can't be done, can it?'

'Listen, chick,' said Dot. 'You caring about her is what she needs. You being by her side is what she needs.'

'It doesn't sound like much,' Alison whispered.

'It's everything,' Dot assured her.

'And don't forget,' Cordelia added, 'that we're here whenever you need us.'

'You look after Lydia,' said Margaret, 'and we'll look after you.'

When she got home, Alison had a good old weep for Lydia and Alec. She'd been fond of Alec but she knew she hadn't valued him as she should have done. Back when she had been going out with Paul, she had secretly looked down on Alec because Paul had a better job, which meant he would be the better provider in years to come. Alison had viewed the whole world through the prism of being Paul Dunaway's girlfriend in those days. It had made her very self-satisfied and she was ashamed of that now. She could only hope that other people hadn't realised.

She thought back over her conversation with her friends. She was keen to tell Joel about it.

She waited until they were at the table, eating the curried cod she'd made. Joel had praised her for making something so tasty but Alison had to concentrate to taste anything at all. It was as if her entire self was focused on Lydia's tragedy.

'They were all so kind and understanding, just as I knew they would be,' she told Joel.

He nodded. 'I've said it before and I'll say it again. You have a good set of friends.'

'The very best.' Alison found herself blinking away tears. She cleared her throat, pretending she wasn't fighting with her emotions, though she knew Joel wasn't fooled. 'Margaret said, "You look after Lydia and we'll look after you." Isn't that wonderful? It's made me remember that I'm not the only one who needs support. Do you recall what Mrs Summers said about Colette in the butcher's queue? And you suggested I might let Mrs Nuttall know that we consider Colette a good friend and we're grateful to her?'

'That's not top priority at the moment,' said Joel.

'Compared to Alec's death, of course it isn't,' said Alison, 'but my friends want to support me and I want to support them too. It would be all too easy in the circumstances not to bother speaking to Mrs Nuttall about Colette, but it's one of those situations where, if you don't say something quickly, you miss your chance for ever.'

'And that might not seem to matter in the aftermath of family bereavement,' said Joel, 'but later you might be sorry and wish you'd said something.'

'Exactly. I knew you'd understand.' It was one of the things Alison loved about him, his sensitivity to others.

'I'll pop over the road and have a word,' said Joel. 'There's no need for you to do it.'

'No, I'd like to. I'm the one who stood there like an idiot and let Mrs Summers have her say. Besides, it would be better coming from me.'

'Woman to woman, you mean.'

'If you say something,' said Alison, 'it will seem like I've told tales, but if I do it, I can keep it friendly.' She found herself smiling even though in recent days that had been the last thing she'd felt like doing. 'It's a bit soon to be falling out with the neighbours.'

As it turned out, there was no need for Alison to go over the road because, after she had cleared the table and washed up and she and Joel were listening to a concert on the wireless, there was a knock at the door. Joel went to answer it, returning moments later ushering Mrs Nuttall into the sitting room ahead of him. She was holding a small flowerpot containing snowdrops.

'I'll leave you ladies to it,' Joel said and disappeared.

'Please, sit down,' said Alison.

Mrs Nuttall held out the snowdrops. 'These are for you. It isn't much, just a token to say how sorry I was to hear about your family's troubles. Your poor sister.'

Alison's chest hitched. She remembered the snowdrops she and Joel had seen on their Sunday walk before they'd come home and found Mum and Dad waiting on the doorstep. Alison had fancied having her own little clump of February fair maids and now she had it. She would never see snowdrops again without thinking of Alec.

'Oh, I'm sorry, love,' said Mrs Nuttall. 'I've made you cry.'

'I'm all right, really,' said Alison. 'Well, I'm not, but . . .'

'I know. It has to come out sometimes and when it does, there's no stopping it. My cousin Beattie got the telegram last year so I know what your family is going through. It's not easy on anybody. How is your sister doing?'

'She's coping by going back to work.'

'Already? That's quick. You just have to let her get on with it and be there when she needs you. Anyroad, I'd best be going.' She started to stand up.

'Oh, please don't go quite yet,' said Alison. 'I was intending to come and see you.'

Mrs Nuttall sat back down. 'That's nice. Why?'

They weren't on dropping-in terms. Quite honestly, they were both too busy with their demanding, time-consuming jobs.

'It's what your mother said about Mrs Naylor letting down the tone of the neighbourhood,' said Alison. 'I know it was your mum and not you, but I want you to know that Mrs Naylor is a good friend of mine – of both of us, me and my husband. The house we were supposed to have fell through and she gave up her house for us instead. I wanted you to know that.'

'Fair enough,' said Mrs Nuttall. 'And you're right: it was Mum and not me. Actually, I always felt I might have liked Mrs Naylor if only I'd been allowed to get close enough to make friends, but she kept herself very much to herself.'

'That was her husband, not her,' said Alison. 'She's a good person who was married to a bad man, but he presented a different face to the world.'

Mrs Nuttall nodded, eyes thoughtful. 'I used to think the same as my mum. Well, you can imagine all the gossip that went flying around when she left here, can't you? But d'you know what made me start to think differently? It was when she came back again. Most folk called it brazen but I thought it took real courage.'

'It did.' Alison was pleased that her neighbour had recognised it.

'You aren't going to hold what Mum said against me, are you?'

'Of course not,' Alison assured her.

'And you don't expect me to ask her to keep her trap shut?'

'Even more of course not. If it helps,' said Alison, 'my own mother had plenty of reservations concerning Mrs Naylor until recently. I just wanted you to know she's my friend.'

'And you don't like hearing gossip about her.' Mrs Nuttall nodded again. 'Well, I'm sorry to tell you that you've come to live in the wrong place in that case, but you've already discovered that.'

'With bells on,' said Alison.

'If I hear gossip in future,' said Mrs Nuttall, 'do you want me to pass on that Mrs Naylor gave up her house for your benefit?'

'Yes, please,' said Alison. 'Do you think it will make a difference?'

Mrs Nuttall gave her a pitying look. 'Not really, but it'll give folk something else to think about and that's as much as you can hope for.'

Chapter Eight

Persephone sat on a bench tucked away in a corner of Leeds Central Station, waiting for Matt. It was a place where, her routes permitting, they met up occasionally during Matt's long shifts. He worked alongside Mr Gibson, an engine driver with many years of experience under his belt. Persephone considered them to be well suited. Matt thought highly of his colleague from whom he said he had learned a great deal. Whenever Persephone saw the two of them together, she was always impressed by their obvious liking and regard for one another.

'Like an old married couple,' Matt had teased her when she remarked on this to him.

But she knew she was right. She had heard Mr Gibson call Matt 'Byron'. It was a jokey way of referring to Matt's love of poetry, but the nickname was spoken with fondness and respect, never in a disparaging way.

Through Matt, Persephone had come to know Mr Gibson. He always called her 'miss' in deference to her rank in life. Once he had taken her aside and told her to be careful with Matt's heart. He hadn't expressed it quite like that, but that was what he meant.

'He's a good chap, is young Franklin,' Mr Gibson had told her, 'and he thinks a lot of you.'

'I think a lot of him too.'

'You know what I'm getting at,' said Mr Gibson. 'I wouldn't want to see him hurt.'

'Believe me, Mr Gibson, that's the very last thing I want to do,' Persephone assured him.

'I don't doubt your good intentions for a minute, miss,' Mr Gibson replied, 'but you're out of one drawer and Matt Franklin is out of another. It seems to me that you'll have more to console yourself with after the war than he will.'

Persephone imagined her mother's fury if a member of the lower orders had dared to speak to her so openly, but Persephone took it in good part. She knew Mr Gibson had Matt's best interests at heart and she respected that.

'I understand your meaning, Mr Gibson,' she had told him.

How tempting it had been to add, 'But I can't give him up,' but she had stopped herself because that would have sounded dramatic. Moreover, what if Mr Gibson were to repeat it to Matt? 'I can't give him up' hardly fitted in with the happy-for-now attitude they had agreed to apply to their wartime romance.

Remembering that conversation now as she sat on the bench waiting for Matt to join her, Persephone smothered a sigh. Mr Gibson had only been expressing the same reservation that everyone felt – and he'd certainly expressed it more kindly than her parents had done. Everybody regarded their relationship as doomed to fail.

'That's because they don't understand that you and Matt see it as a wartime thing,' Dot had said reassuringly.

'Oh.' Persephone was startled. 'For a moment there, I thought you said "fling". That's the word my sister uses.'

'All right. Romance, then,' Dot corrected herself, not taking offence.

'Sorry,' Persephone had said. 'I didn't mean to sound sharp.'

She was sure that their unconventional relationship must make it tricky for her friends to talk about her and Matt. It was easy to discuss couples who looked as though they had a future. Everyone knew what to say, what to expect. But a couple who took it one day at a time – what were their friends supposed to say about that? It just wasn't the done thing.

'You have to do what feels right for the two of you,' Margaret had told her and the others had murmured their agreement. While Persephone had silently blessed them for it, she'd also tingled all over with the knowledge that 'one day at a time' wasn't what she truly wanted, though she could never admit it. It was harmful even to admit it to herself.

Matt now appeared in front of her and handed her a mug while keeping for himself the jam jar of tea that spoke of wartime shortages. Persephone smiled at him, her heart executing a funny little flip. Beneath the brim of his fireman's cap, his face was grimy. His job had built up his muscles, but best of all he had a good heart. The heart of a family man.

It was the first time they had seen one another since Alison had shared the news of Lydia's bereavement. It was also the first time since Persephone's visit to the old soldiers' home where Peggy worked, but talking about that would feel selfish just now. She told Matt about Lydia's husband.

'I'm sorry to hear it,' he said.

'They got married a little over two years ago and haven't seen one another since,' said Persephone. 'And now this.'

'The cruelty of it,' Matt remarked.

'Apparently, Lydia went back to work almost immediately.'

'People have to find their own way to cope,' said Matt. 'I don't want to sound unfeeling towards Alison's family, but hearing about her brother-in-law immediately makes me think of my own brother-in-law.'

'Peggy's husband,' said Persephone.

'I hope he comes home safe.'

'I wish they all could,' Persephone said with feeling. 'Too many have been lost already.'

'It must have brought your brothers to mind as well,' said Matt.

Persephone nodded. She loved Roddy and Giles dearly. 'When Pa first told me I was to be sent to Manchester for the duration, I raided the boys' chests of drawers and brought a sweater belonging to each of them with me. I wear them for comfort and for luck – theirs, not mine.'

'I wonder if Lydia is wearing Alec's sweaters now,' said Matt. 'That's the closest she'll get to him for the rest of her life.'

Persephone scooted along the bench to be closer to him. 'It doesn't bear thinking about.'

'We must think about it,' said Matt. 'People die. We hope and pray it won't happen to those we know and love. We feel shaken when it happens to people on the edge of our lives, like Lydia's husband, and we're grateful it didn't happen to someone closer.'

'And then we feel guilty for being grateful,' said Persephone. 'It seems so complicated sometimes.'

'It is in some ways. In others it's blindingly straightforward.'

'We have to make the most of what we've got,' said Persephone.

'Live for the moment,' said Matt.

'Like you and I do,' said Persephone.

'Like we do,' Matt echoed.

But how good could the moment be if it didn't lead to a hoped-for future?

It was the end of February. Colette noticed folk bending over their window-boxes – planting something for the table or indulging in some pretty annuals to lift their spirits through the summer? It was more than time for her to call on her parents-in-law. She had let the time slip through her fingers and she knew it was because she was scared of facing up to Mr Naylor. Her father-in-law was such a strong character. No, that wasn't the right word. It was possible to be strong but also kind and gentle. Tony's father was forceful and could hector anybody into submission. Qualms rippled through Colette at the thought, but she wasn't going to be hectored into anything.

Work commitments meant that she ended up going on leap year's day. She felt anxious as she approached their house – no, not *their* house. Mr Naylor's house. Colette had never heard him refer to it as 'our house', only ever as 'my house', which technically was true since he earned the money that paid all the bills, including the rent, and it was his name on the rent-book. But a kind husband, a loving and respectful husband, wouldn't have said 'my house'.

It wasn't too late to change her mind and go scuttling off in the opposite direction, but she couldn't do that. She mustn't. It would be cowardly. She didn't feel brave but she couldn't live with herself if she acted like a coward.

The front door had a lion's-head knocker. When Bunty answered Colette's knock, her face flushed in surprise, then she paled.

'Who is it?' called Mr Naylor from inside the house.

Bunty glanced over her shoulder. 'It's Colette.'

Mr Naylor erupted from the parlour. He stood in front of Bunty. 'If you've come to inform me that you've left home, I already know – no thanks to you.'

'May I come in?' Colette asked.

Mr Naylor looked over her head as if checking for eavesdroppers. Then he turned and went back into the parlour, Bunty quickly stepping out of his way.

As Colette entered the house, her shoulders tightened and her heart pitter-pattered, but she had nothing to fear – had she?

'Let me take your coat,' Bunty offered.

Colette was reluctant to remove it. She slipped her gloves into the flap pockets and handed the coat and her scarf to her mother-in-law.

'It's good to see you,' Bunty said softly.

Colette wanted to say, 'It's good to see you too,' but Bunty was already leading her into the parlour. Superficially nothing had changed – and yet there were the same changes that existed in everybody's homes these days. It wasn't as warm as it would have been before the war; the cushion covers had thinned; and the wireless enjoyed a prominent position.

Mr Naylor remained on his feet until the two women sat down. Colette was reminded of the warm courtesy when Mr Gordon had risen to his feet for her. Mr Naylor's courtesy was of a different breed. There was something commanding and tetchy in it.

Bunty took her usual armchair. Colette looked at the seat that had always been hers when she came here with Tony. She didn't want to sit there but the alternative was to take Tony's usual chair and she had no wish to do that, so she took her old place, fighting a sensation of defeat.

Mr Naylor sat down in his armchair. He had his own table beside it, with his own ashtray.

'It's nice to see Colette again, isn't it?' said Bunty. She didn't say it confidently or defiantly; she didn't lift her chin. But at least she said it. Said it? Whispered it, more like.

'Nice, you call it?' snapped Mr Naylor. 'That shows how much you know.' Thus dismissing his wife with casual scorn, he focused his attention on Colette. 'I take it you've come to explain yourself. Well, go ahead. This should be interesting.'

Colette felt chilly inside. She pressed her lips together to prevent them from wobbling. Then she took a breath to steady herself. She wasn't going to give in and let fear take over, no matter how much her old memories came storming back.

'I haven't come to explain myself, as you put it, because that suggests you're entitled to an explanation.'

Mr Naylor surged to his feet. 'What?' he roared. 'How dare you speak to me in that way!'

'But with hindsight,' Colette continued, 'I can see that I ought to have told you I was moving.'

'Aha! *Now* we're getting somewhere.' Mr Naylor plumped down into his armchair again. He nodded crisply and jutted out his chin. How complacent he appeared. 'I'm willing to listen to your apology.'

'The reason I should have told you—'

'—is because I am your father-in-law and as such, Tony's representative.'

Colette began again. 'The reason I ought to have told you is so that you wouldn't have turned up on the doorstep, demanding information from Mrs Maitland, the new tenant.'

Mr Naylor stared at her – as well he might. She had never answered him back before. Bunty gazed at the carpet. Would Mr Naylor take it out on her later? Colette wanted to make amends, but how could she without prostrating herself? And that would do her cause no good at all.

'I'm here to ask you not to go to the house again,' she said. 'There's no need now that I've left.'

She used a conciliatory tone, hoping to keep the lid on Mr Naylor's temper. That might – might – make things easier for Bunty afterwards. The tone seemed to work. Mr Naylor's complacency increased and Colette sagged inwardly with relief, but then Mr Naylor's eyes hardened.

'When you say "the house", I take it you mean Tony's house, my son's house – your matrimonial home. The house that by rights you should be living in, awaiting your husband's return from the war. That's what any decent wife would do.'

Colette's breath snagged in her throat. 'Do you mean that after what Tony did to me—?'

Mr Naylor banged his fist down hard on the arm of his chair. 'One mistake! One! It shook me to the core when Tony hurt you like that, but now that you've come round here, pretending to be all meek and mild, when really you're trying to lay the law down, I'm starting to see what made him lose his rag like that.'

Colette stood up. 'I think I should leave.'

Mr Naylor rose too. 'Aye, you do that. And don't come back until you're ready to issue a proper apology.'

Chapter Nine

Colette loved living in Wilton Close and felt completely settled in. She adored Mrs Cooper and Mrs Grayson, especially Mrs Cooper, who had given her so much help when living with Tony had reduced her to a state of fear and despair every single day of her life. Mrs Cooper had even handed over her darling Lizzie's identity in the form of her birth and baptism certificates together with, of all things, a swimming certificate to enable Colette to make a fresh start as Betsy Cooper.

Colette was increasingly fond of Margaret too and enjoyed sharing a room with her. It added to her new sense of herself and the person she was. Like most young women, Colette had gone from her mother's house to her husband's with nothing in between. Colette hated the war, of course, but it made her glad to think of all those girls who were billeted away from home. If this taught them to be confident and independent, maybe they wouldn't be so susceptible when they met a charmer. She certainly hoped so.

Margaret was friendly and considerate, which made her easy to share with. She thought the world of her family too, and, an only child herself, that was something Colette loved to see. Moreover, after her unhappiness with Tony, it was reassuring. Margaret wrote regularly to her brother William overseas and her sister Anna in Shropshire and she took pleasure in sharing their letters. Margaret wasn't the only person in Wilton Close whom Anna wrote to. She also corresponded with Mrs Grayson. The two of them had never met but Mrs Grayson had provided the encouragement – and the recipes – for Anna to set up a small baking business to earn a bit of pin-money, and they had become firm friends.

Back when Colette used to come to Wilton Close every weekend to visit Mrs Cooper and Mrs Grayson, Tony came too. He had taken care of the garden and the ladies had been delighted to receive his help, but Colette had known his real reason for coming had been to keep tabs on her. Now she was one of the workers in the garden.

Margaret had a list of jobs that needed doing month by month. She looked at the list for March.

'We need to plant shallot and onion sets, and sow new potatoes, leeks, sprouts, peas and lettuces.'

Margaret seemed to be a keen gardener. Sometimes her father came round and lent a hand. Colette had seen real happiness in Margaret's eyes at the sight of him. Margaret might have changed her surname to Thomas in honour of her late mother, but she was still very much Mr Darrell's daughter. Colette liked Mr Darrell, who was kindly and civil. He and Margaret had been estranged earlier in the war, though Colette didn't know why and frankly didn't want to know. She knew what it felt like to have folk talking about her behind her back and made it a rule not to nose her way into other people's private lives.

Colette appreciated the general lifting of spirits that she found wherever she went. It was as if the very air everyone breathed was different, brighter. From being bone-tired after more than four years of war, people seemed refreshed, newly focused . . . more hopeful. The USAAF and the RAF were bombing German aircraft factories and munitions factories in what were said on the Pathé news to be the largest raids of the war so far.

They must be heading towards the end of the war now. Colette was sure that must be the thought in every mind, the hope in every single heart.

Today Colette was to accompany a teacher and her class to a countryside destination some miles from Chester. This was where the children's school had been evacuated to at the outbreak of war and the children Colette would be accompanying were those whose parents had fetched them home to Manchester when the dreaded bombing had not immediately commenced. Their teacher had had the bright idea of reuniting these youngsters with their old classmates who had stayed behind in the countryside and had lived as evacuees.

'How successful the outing will be, I'm not sure,' Miss Stidson told Colette when they met on the platform. The teacher was in her late twenties, with mousy hair and a humorous mouth. 'I thought it such a good idea to start with, but others in the staffroom aren't so sure. They say the children were too young when they were separated to remember one another now.'

'How old were they?' Colette asked.

'Six rising seven, and now they're ten rising eleven. That's a long time for children.'

Colette smiled. 'We'll do our best to have a good day out.'

'Thank you,' said Miss Stidson. 'And thank you for not saying it will all be fine. That's what my mother said before I left home this morning. I find you saying, "We'll do our best," much easier to believe. Excuse me while I count heads.'

Colette glanced at her wristwatch. The other chaperone, Mrs Makepeace, a comfortable, middle-aged lady with a motherly manner, should be here any moment. She was cutting it fine, which definitely wasn't what Colette expected of her.

Then, to Colette's surprise, Mr Gordon appeared.

'Good morning, Mrs Naylor. Mrs Makepeace missed her footing on the kerb outside the station and has twisted her ankle, I'm afraid, so you've got me instead.'

'I'm sorry to hear that,' said Colette. 'Sorry about Mrs Makepeace, I mean, not about you.'

'I'll make myself known to Miss Stidson,' said Mr Gordon, 'and then we can get the children on the train.'

There were thirty-five children all together and the train guard had been asked to keep seats for them so they could stay together even if they had to sit on one another's knees to make room for adults. Miss Stidson did a final head count before they set off. The guard walked past the window, slamming doors along the length of the train. He blew his whistle and the train whistle answered after which the engine slowly pulled out of the station, chuffing as it picked up speed.

The journey didn't last all that long, but the children seemed to think it went on for hours on end. Colette spent much of her time taking children to and from the WC. When it was time to alight, Mr Gordon held the door open while Miss Stidson performed another head count on the platform.

'There's one missing,' she said.

'It's Tim Breslaw,' a freckled lad piped up. 'He's going to run away and join up.'

Colette looked at Mr Gordon, expecting to see vexation since he was an important man standing in for a lowly chaperone, but instead he grinned, looking surprisingly boyish. A moment later the smile vanished and he looked suitably serious as befitted an adult in charge of children, but Colette was glad to have glimpsed that smile.

Mr Gordon jumped aboard, hauled young Breslaw out from beneath a seat and deposited him on the platform, where Miss Stidson proceeded to administer a dressing-down.

Mr Gordon said quietly to Colette, 'We're chaperones for the railway journey. It's not in our remit to accompany the class on the visit, but we might as well – if you don't mind?'

'Let's,' said Colette. It was a lot of children for one person to be in charge of.

They waited for the train to pull out and the children waved it off.

'Hey,' said one of the boys. 'There's only one track. How are we meant to get home again if all the trains can only go that way?'

The children immediately surged to the edge of the platform to peer down at the single set of tracks and Miss Stidson had to call them to order.

'Not to worry,' said Mr Gordon. 'It's because this is a small country station. Trains travel in both directions but they have to take turns to pull in because there is only one single track. Can you see the signal-box down the line that way?' He waited for the children to crane their necks and peer along the railway track towards the signal-box. 'See how the box is on top of another structure? That's for two reasons. The box has to be high up so the signalman has a good view of the line, and the structure underneath, the locking room, contains all the mechanics for the levers he works.'

'What are the levers for?' asked one of the boys.

'To work the points, of course,' replied a girl. 'Don't you know anything?'

Mr Gordon smiled. 'The signalman works the signals and the points. The signals tell the train drivers when to stop and when to go. The points are a way of moving a train from one set of tracks to another. If you look down that way to the side of the signal box, you can see where the single track becomes two.'

'I'm sure we all found that very interesting,' put in Miss Stidson, forestalling more eager questions, 'but now we really must press on.'

The children formed a crocodile and she led the way out of the station, with Colette at the back of the line. They walked through the village to the school, which was a Victorian building with a bell-tower.

Miss Stidson raised her voice to address the children before they went indoors.

'You're going to see friends you haven't seen since the beginning of the war. It will be very exciting to be reunited. I expect you all to be on your best behaviour.'

'I'm not sure that "exciting" and "best behaviour" go particularly well together,' Mr Gordon murmured to Colette, 'but we'll see.'

The visitors were taken into the school hall, all bare floorboards and high windows. The children sat on the floor and their former school-fellows, led by Miss Ramsden, the teacher who had been evacuated with them, filed in and sat cross-legged. There was some fidgeting and pointing as the children picked out faces they remembered and a couple of the visitors cried because they didn't recognise anybody, but with a little encouragement the children soon sorted themselves out and the atmosphere lightened, especially during the dinner-hour. The visitors had brought sandwiches, which the resident evacuees were far more interested in than their school dinner of baked vegetable rolls.

Afterwards Miss Stidson explained to her class that because the village school wasn't large enough, the evacuees had lessons in the mornings and local children in the afternoons.

'Cor, so you only go to school part-time,' Tim Breslaw said enviously. 'I wish I could be an evacuee.'

'This means we can all spend the afternoon with our old friends,' said Miss Stidson in a jolly voice. 'Miss Ramsden says you may play on the school field or go into the woods or nearby fields.'

'If the visitors leave the school field,' said Miss Ramsden, 'they must be in company with evacuee children, because they know their way around. You must all listen for the bell at half past three and you must come running as soon as you hear it.'

Some children dispersed eagerly while others hung back, including some of the boys, which surprised Colette. She had expected them to be more adventurous.

'It might be because of your presence, Mr Gordon,' said Miss Ramsden. 'The only men the evacuees are accustomed to seeing tend to be elderly.'

Mr Gordon nodded. He raised his voice to speak to the remaining children. 'Come on, you lot. Who wants to have a race?'

After several races, including a relay and a walking-backwards, Tim Breslaw came pelting across the field.

'It's Reggie, miss,' he blurted out to Miss Stidson. 'He's hanged himself.'

'He's what?'

'He's got caught on some barbed wire and he's hanging upside down.'

'Tell us exactly what happened,' said Miss Ramsden.

'We were climbing over this barbed-wire fence,' said Tim, 'and he sort of fell over the top and his foot got tangled up in the top two wires and they're wrapped round his ankle. There's blood everywhere and his foot's going to come off if we don't save him.'

'We'd best cut along and save him, then,' said Mr Gordon. 'Miss Ramsden, please could you ask the local doctor to come to the school. The lad might be in need of stitches.'

Colette darted indoors and held her clean hanky under the tap, then she ran after Mr Gordon and Tim. They found Reggie flat on his back with his foot stuck in the air. Blood trickled from his ankle down his leg and inside his grey shorts.

'We'll soon have you out of this pickle, old man,' Mr Gordon said.

Removing his jacket, he pushed his hands inside the arms as if putting it on back to front, but without letting his hands stick out. He grasped the barbed wire and forced it apart while Colette carefully removed Reggie's trapped foot. She tried not to wince when Reggie whimpered in pain and distress as his flesh was pulled away from the barbs. Colette then used her wet hanky to clean up as much blood as she could before Mr Gordon swung Reggie up into his arms and set off for the school. There, after a perfunctory examination, the doctor applied iodine and advised sending a note home to Reggie's mother telling her to watch for signs of infection.

Reggie had a fine old time telling the dramatic tale of being trapped in the barbed wire and Tim made the most of describing his part in the rescue. The afternoon continued with no further untoward incidents and when the school bell clanged at half past three, the children came running from all directions back to the school field.

At last they were on the train going home. Colette breathed a silent sigh of relief. Then, when the child opposite started to wriggle, she got to her feet to make the first of many trips to the WC.

Everyone alighted safely at the other end. Miss Stidson did yet another head count before Mr Gordon and Colette accompanied the crocodile through the ticket barrier and watched them on their way.

'Good work, Mrs Naylor,' said Mr Gordon. 'I couldn't have managed that barbed-wire business without you.'

'I'm glad to have helped,' she replied.

'Well, goodbye, then.'

He gave her a farewell nod. Although he smiled, his face was set in its usual serious lines and Colette couldn't help recalling that boyish grin from earlier on.

Chapter Ten

Which wartime songs mean the most to you personally? And which war are they from? I visited a retirement home for old soldiers recently . . .

Persephone read through the piece she had typed up. She had thought hard about the tone she wanted to evoke, a mixture of the uplifting and the nostalgic that she hoped would appeal to readers of *Vera's Voice*. She had loved visiting the home and had found the residents charming. Having learned from Peggy before her visit that there was a piano, she had practised a number of Great War songs as well as popular tunes from the music hall so she could lead a good old singsong before she started chatting to the elderly residents.

She had chosen to write the piece as herself. Sometimes she adopted the voice of a middle-aged auntie, opening with something like: *The other day, a young friend asked me . . .* or *How times have changed! Do you remember when a lady would never have smoked a cigarette in public, but these days . . .*

Producing publishable articles wasn't just about having something interesting, useful or amusing to say. It was also about how it was presented. It had been a real pleasure to write as herself this time, a girl of the current wartime generation interacting with those who had not simply lived through the last war but served in it. The residents had loved through it, too. Several of the men were widowers and they had shared their romantic stories with her. Persephone, seeing the light in their eyes and the glow in their cheeks, had glimpsed their younger selves and had warmed to them all the more.

She folded the article and the covering letter and slid them inside an envelope that had already been used twice. She addressed it to Mrs Newbold, the editor at *Vera's Voice*. It was an address she knew by heart. She hoped Mrs Newbold would be pleased to hear from her again.

After that, having finished her work, it was time for her reward, namely to enjoy the letters that had arrived for her that day. She came from a family of energetic letter-writers. As well as corresponding with family and chums, Persephone also wrote to a number of chaps in the services, not just her brothers but also the dashing young blades she had danced with in London before the war. She thought of them with great affection. As well as the ones she was simply chummy with, there were a couple who'd been serious about her – Algy, who would have made her a viscountess, and dear, devoted Monty who had sent her orchids every day.

She could have had either of them, had she so chosen, but there had never been any question of it, not while Forbes Winterton lived and breathed. Oh, Forbes, with his intriguing smoky-grey eyes! How she had worshipped him. They had spent quite a lot of time together because he was pals with Roddy and Giles and also because, truth be told, Persephone had made darned sure they did, so a considerable amount of her worshipping had taken place from close up.

Not that Forbes had ever entertained the smallest idea. What a prize idiot she had been.

In the end, unbeknownst to Persephone, her mother had written to Forbes when he'd been laid up in a military hospital in Hertfordshire last year. Persephone had been thrilled to bits to hear from him, not least because he hoped for a visit. By crikey, at the time it had felt like the most important letter she'd ever received. She had gone racing down to Hertfordshire, in so far as one could race anywhere by train these days, certain that Forbes had undergone a change of heart and that he longed to see her as much as she longed to see him . . . only for it to turn out that he saw her the same way he always had, as his chums' little sister, which made her as good as a little sister to him too.

Persephone had been heartbroken. It hadn't occurred to her that she might one day meet someone else, even though she had seen this very thing happen to Alison. Then Matt had come along and now Forbes Winterton of the smoky-grey eyes was little more than a fond memory.

Out of the various letters that had arrived for her that day, the one Persephone saved until last was from her sister. In it, Iphigenia included a description of the return of the air raids to London, which Jerry had started off again at the beginning of the year. It was nowhere near as bad as it had been first time round, according to Iphigenia, but it was jolly unpleasant all the same.

I'd forgotten the way the house sways when the bombs land nearby, she wrote, *and all the doors swing open as if by magic. It's horrid to see all the fresh damage the next morning – garden paths torn up and chucked into the middle of the road, the fronts of buildings ripped off to leave everything inside on display, and broken glass all over the show. I swear the soles of my shoes are encrusted with glass these days. But we must all take a deep breath and get on as best we can, knowing that however bad it is here, they are on the receiving end of a lot worse in Germany.*

At the end of all that, Iphigenia had added, *Having made London sound so very appealing, I have an invitation to offer you* and Persephone couldn't wait to tell her friends the next time she met them in the buffet.

When she got there, she saw they had pushed two tables together which meant that for once they weren't practically sitting on one another's knees. As she joined them, they were talking about the latest Salute the Soldier Week.

'All the offices in Hunts Bank have set targets for the amounts they hope to raise,' said Joan, 'and that includes the PAYE office, of course.'

The PAYE office, where Joan worked, was housed in a building beside the railway tracks instead of in the administration building.

'All the streets round our way are setting targets too,' said Alison.

'The Civil Defence groups that come to Darley Court for training have all got fundraising plans,' said Persephone. 'They're determined to outdo one another.'

'The schools are in competition an' all,' said Dot.

'Mummy's bridge group is holding a raffle, aren't they, Mummy?' said Emily. 'They've got their hands on some good prizes. A full set of curlers, for one. Real curlers!'

'Now that is a good prize,' Dot agreed. 'I'm tired of having to use pipe-cleaners.'

'There's a raffle at our local church as well,' said Fay. 'The booby prize is a toilet roll.'

The others looked at her in astonishment.

'That's the *booby* prize?' Margaret asked.

'It should be the top prize,' declared Dot. 'I'd rather win that than anything else they have on offer.'

'Miss Brown got me to dig out one of Darley Court's china tea sets to donate to a raffle,' said Persephone.

'A whole tea set!' Alison exclaimed. 'To be won for the price of a ticket?'

'No, it's going to be split up,' Persephone explained. 'There will be twelve prizes of a cup, saucer and tea plate, and two others of the milk-jug and sugar-bowl together, and the teapot on its own.'

'That's very generous of Miss Brown,' said Colette.

'I'm sure loads of people will buy tickets in the hope of winning a cup and saucer,' Margaret added.

Cordelia laughed. 'It reminds me of a cartoon in *Punch*. It shows two elegant ladies about to have tea and one is offering a choice of mugs to the other. "Will you have shaving or coronation?" You can imagine it happening, can't you?' she added as the others chuckled.

'That's priceless,' said Fay.

When they had finished discussing the various dances, quizzes, sponsored runs, concerts and other events being held to support the Salute the Soldier Week, Dot asked, 'Has anyone got any news?'

Persephone was delighted to share hers. 'Iphigenia has suggested I join her in London in April if I can swing the annual leave.'

'You must go if you can,' Colette said at once.

'I'd love to,' said Persephone.

She glanced at Alison and Margaret, certain that her mention of Iphigenia must have brought their own sisters to mind. Margaret's older sister Anna had been evacuated in 1939 because she was in the family way. She and her little twins, Tommy and Anne-Marie, were spending the war in Shropshire. As for Lydia—

But what Alison said was, 'I'll never forget what your sister did for me. Packing up all those dresses and sending them to Darley Court so I could have a choice of wedding dress. That was so very generous.' Then, her voice suddenly sounding fierce, she added, 'You must go. It's a privilege to be able to see the ones we love.' Her voice caught on the final words and she blinked back tears.

'It's a wicked thing to say and I know I shouldn't even think it, let alone say it,' Cordelia said quietly, 'but it would have been far better all round if Tony had been killed instead of Lydia's husband.'

'It's jolly unfair,' said Margaret.

'Life isn't fair,' Colette said softly. 'I learned that a long time ago.'

It was Mrs Cooper and Mrs Grayson's night for the knitting circle at St Clement's. Mrs Grayson, as well as being a talented and resourceful cook, was an accomplished knitter. Colette had never seen her matrimonial home, which Mrs Grayson's estranged husband had required her to quit at short notice so he could move in with his bit on the side, but apparently it had been stuffed to the rafters with knitted articles – quilts, blankets, antimacassars, cushion covers, coasters, tea-cosies, not to mention the covers on coat-hangers, hot-water bottles, waste-paper baskets and draught excluders. Since the beginning of the war Mrs Grayson had focused her considerable skills on knitting for the war effort and goodness alone knew how many cot-blankets and items of clothing she had provided for families in need as well as knitting for the troops.

Colette had intended to go to the knitting circle too, but Mrs Cooper encouraged her to go to the pictures with Margaret and Persephone instead.

'I know you must feel a lot older than other girls your age after everything you've been through,' said Mrs Cooper, 'but the fact is you're young and you should be out enjoying yourself.'

'I enjoy going to the knitting circle,' Colette said mildly.

'You know what I mean,' said Mrs Cooper. 'Go to the pictures,' she said with a smile. 'At least behave as if you're young even if you're older inside your head.'

Colette allowed herself to be persuaded. The girls chose to see the drama *Yellow Canary* because it starred the matinée idol Richard Greene. According to something Margaret had read in a film magazine, he had been given leave from the services to appear in the film.

The evening began as always with the Pathé newsreel. It was the middle of March now and the news included British advances in Burma, the taking of Kherson by Soviet troops and the destruction of the ancient monastery of Monte Cassino. Colette's gaze was transfixed. What if the next item, or the one after that, gave her a glimpse of Tony? The thought was scary. What if her seeing him on the screen would somehow make him aware of her? Yes, she was completely daft to imagine any such thing, but years of being under his control had left her with a deep-seated fear. At the same time, though, part of her would welcome seeing him on the screen, just so she could confirm with her own eyes that he was hundreds of miles away across the sea.

When they got home, Margaret went up to bed as she had an early start. Colette took her a mug of Ovaltine to sip before she went to sleep, then stayed up to make bedtime drinks for the ladies when they got home.

While the three of them sat in the front room, Colette decided to share something that she'd had on her mind.

'Do you think I ought to go and see Tony's mother?'

'It's a kind thought,' said Mrs Cooper.

'It's taking kindness a step too far, if you ask me,' said Mrs Grayson. 'After what Tony did to you—'

'That's not his mother's fault,' said Colette. 'She's as ground down by his father as I was by Tony – more so. Much more so. She's been under the thumb for thirty years. Thirty! I had it for five and that was bad enough.'

'And what do you hope to achieve?' Mrs Grayson asked. 'If it stirs things up, it could be worse for her.'

'I know,' sighed Colette. 'I thought of that when I saw them last month. But I still feel I'd like to contact her.'

'Well, be careful, that's all I can say,' said Mrs Cooper. 'Remember: any contact you have with her may well be reported back to Tony by his father.'

'There's no "may well be" about it,' said Mrs Grayson. 'I'd say it's a certainty. The poor lady won't have a choice in the matter.'

Colette shivered. 'I hate the idea of Mr Naylor passing on information about me to Tony.'

They left it at that. Colette decided to give the matter more thought. If she were to see Bunty, they would have a pretty bland conversation if Colette could only say things that she wouldn't mind being passed on to Mr Naylor and then to Tony.

What she really wanted was to rescue Bunty. Wouldn't that be wonderful! But what would happen if she did? She couldn't bring her to live in Wilton Close because Mr Naylor would come banging on the door. He didn't know – so far – where Colette was living, or she assumed he didn't, but it would be another matter altogether to keep his wife's whereabouts a secret from him.

Besides, would Bunty even want to be rescued? Early on in her marriage Colette had tried to befriend her mother-in-law, but Bunty hadn't let her get close. Was she too scared? Or was she silently pleading for help? Colette knew how that felt.

And any contact she initiated with Bunty ran the risk of giving Tony a peep-hole into her life. Dread rolled in her stomach. She couldn't let that happen. She just couldn't.

Colette checked the time on the station clock, then presented herself at the ticket-office window. It was a cool, breezy day filled with the fresh green scents of spring.

'A single to Manchester Victoria, please,' she said.

She slipped the ticket inside her purse. She wouldn't take it out again until she was in Mr Gordon's presence. The return ticket he had given her this morning was in a separate zipped pocket inside her handbag. She sat on the bench to wait. The ticket she had purchased would go towards providing Mr Gordon with the evidence he needed to prove that an employee was on the fiddle.

Colette looked up at the sound of the chuffing that heralded the approach of the train as it rounded the gentle curve and came towards the station, white clouds puffing from the funnel. The train coasted to a halt, brakes shrieking. The doors banged open and passengers jumped out.

Colette joined those climbing aboard. The train was crowded and she didn't get a seat, but she didn't mind. At least she was standing beside a window and could watch the world go by. As the line of coaches trundled along behind the loco, she saw a group of four women standing beside the tracks. They were dressed in trousers and heavy jackets, their hands resting on the handles of pickaxes and shovels. Colette immediately thought of Mabel. This was the job she used to do. As a lengthman, she had been one of a gang of four who had lifted sleepers to resettle the ballast underneath.

When she returned to Victoria, Colette was already digging inside her handbag to remove the suspect ticket as she knocked on the side door to the ticket office. As she entered, she was disappointed to see that Mr Gordon's office was empty.

'Good afternoon, Mrs Naylor,' said Mrs Lister, pausing in her typing. 'Mr Gordon isn't here at present. Would you like to leave the ticket with me? At what precise time did you make the purchase?'

Colette handed it over, gave Mrs Lister the information

and left her making a note of it. Colette lowered her head with a small sigh. It made her realise that she had been looking forward to seeing Mr Gordon again even if it was only for two minutes. Now that she knew him a little better after the children's day trip, she was more sure than ever of his integrity. She had sensed it previously but now she knew it for certain. Moreover, he was good-humoured and surprisingly flexible for a man she had previously associated with sticking religiously to the rules at work. It was silly of her, she knew. Just because he followed the rules at work and sought out those who broke them for their own personal gain, didn't mean he was bound to be rigid in all situations.

It was a buffet evening and when Colette walked in, Emily was the only one already there. Colette was pleased to have the chance for a chat, just the two of them. She was fond of Emily and thought highly of her.

She asked Emily about the pilfering that had been going on this time last year. 'Is it still happening?'

'I don't think so – and I'm sure I'd have got wind of it if it were still going on. Mr Gordon handled the matter really well last year – very firmly. Everyone knew exactly where they stood afterwards.'

'I can imagine that,' Colette agreed. She felt pleased. It was daft but she liked to hear Mr Gordon being praised.

'What made you bring it up?' Emily asked.

In that moment Colette realised for the first time that it was because she'd wanted to talk about Mr Gordon. But she couldn't possibly say so.

Chapter Eleven

The next day Colette was back to being a chaperone. She escorted an elderly gentleman to Fleetwood. He was civil, friendly and chatty but he couldn't retain anything that was said to him and if he asked Colette once where they were going, he asked her a hundred times. All Colette could do was smile sweetly and say the same things over and over again, understanding that for Mr Philpott, each time was the first time.

On her way back from Fleetwood, Colette took out her knitting. When she had started out as an investigator-cum-chaperone, she had asked if she was allowed to knit or read when she was alone and the answer was an emphatic yes.

'Bring your knitting,' Miss Emery had said. 'Bring a book. What matters is that you look like an ordinary passenger.'

When she was engaged in investigation work, she could pass the time as she pleased on days like yesterday when she simply had to test someone at another station. On other occasions, she might have to watch somebody, either a passenger or a member of staff, and knitting was a way of hiding in plain sight while she kept an eye on them. When she was chaperoning, she gave her full attention to the person or people in her charge, but once her duty to them was discharged, out came the needles or her book.

Back at Victoria, as she negotiated her way along the crowded concourse, she heard her name being called.

'Mrs Naylor, what a pleasant surprise.' Mr Gordon's serious face softened as he smiled. 'How are you?'

'Very well, thank you. And you?'

'Fine, thanks. Busy day?'

She told him about Mr Philpott.

'Poor fellow,' said Mr Gordon. 'It must be a great strain for his family. Mrs Naylor, do you have to rush off? I have to be back here in an hour or so to meet someone but I was just about to pop over to the Worker Bee – do you know it?'

'The little café on Deansgate. Yes.'

'I wonder if you'd care to join me, just for a bit of a chin-wag, if you aren't . . .'

The rest of the sentence faded away. Colette experienced a flutter of pleasure. She had felt friendly towards Mr Gordon since the children's day trip and would enjoy spending some time with him. Besides, he had to be back here in an hour or so, which made her feel she wasn't getting into anything tricky.

When they entered the little café, they negotiated the small compartment just inside the door. Early on in the war, the café's owner had been fined for breaking the blackout, so he had made a wooden frame from which hung lengths of black cloth, so that once someone came through the door, they were inside a black-lined cubicle. This meant that no matter how many customers came and went, there was no danger of the blackout being broken. It being daylight when Colette and Mr Gordon arrived, the blackout curtains were drawn back and all they had to do was step over the foot of the frame.

With a cheerful 'My treat,' Mr Gordon paid for beans on toast and a pot of tea for them both. They sat at a table next to the wall, which felt private as they chatted about the day out they'd had with Miss Stidson's class.

'You'll be pleased to know,' said Mr Gordon, 'that young Reggie is none the worse for his adventure with the barbed wire. I went round to the school to ask after him,' he added in answer to Colette's enquiring look.

Colette was impressed. 'That was a kind thing to do.'

'I've a young daughter of my own,' he told her, 'and I'd like to think that if she needed a helping hand, someone would provide it.'

Colette considered that his visit to the school went above and beyond providing a helping hand, but she didn't feel it was her place to say so. 'What's your daughter's name?' she asked instead.

'Evie.'

'Evelyn?' Colette asked.

Mr Gordon smiled. 'Evalina.'

'How pretty,' Colette commented, meaning it.

'A pretty name for a pretty girl, though I do say so myself.'

'I'm sure she's a sweetheart,' said Colette. 'Was she evacuated?'

'No, she lives at home with me.'

'That's nice for you and her mother.'

Mr Gordon's face clouded. 'For me and her aunt, actually. Evie's mother passed away some years ago.'

'I'm sorry to hear that,' Colette murmured.

'Thank you. It was a difficult time. Fortunately, my wife's sister, who is unmarried, came to live with us to act as housekeeper. I'm grateful to her, not just for taking care of the domestic side of things but also because she has enabled me to keep Evie at home with me.'

'I'm sure she must be an important part of your life – and Evie's.'

'It was hard on Evie losing her mother so young,' said Mr Gordon.

'And you do hear of men who lose their wives and then they have to send their children off to live with relatives,' said Colette.

'Yes, indeed. Poor blighters. In the early days, whenever I felt particularly wretched over Lilian's death, I would remind myself how lucky I am to have an understanding sister-in-law who is as keen as I am for Evie to have the best possible home life.'

'She has obviously made a significant difference to both your lives,' said Colette.

'Here I am blathering on about myself,' said Mr Gordon. 'What about you, Mrs Naylor? Forgive me if this sounds impertinent – it isn't intended to be – but I am aware of the difficulties you faced before Mr Naylor joined up.'

Colette seriously doubted that anybody outside her closest circle could possibly be fully aware of what she had endured, but she knew her companion meant well. There was real sympathy in his eyes and no sign of the snooping sort of curiosity she sometimes had to evade.

'I assume you read about the court case in the paper,' she said.

'Yes, I did. I hope that doesn't sound tasteless,' said Mr Gordon. 'And – again, forgive me if I'm speaking out of turn – I think what your husband did to you, putting you in hospital like that, was a rotten disgrace.'

'Thank you,' Colette said quietly.

'Let's change the subject, shall we?' Mr Gordon suggested with a kind smile.

The conversation flowed easily and Colette was glad she had accepted the invitation. She kept an eye on the clock on the wall, which was positioned such that she could glance across at it but Mr Gordon would have to turn round.

'Should we be going back?' she asked. 'You said you only had an hour or so.'

'What? Yes.' Mr Gordon shot his cuff and looked at his wristwatch. 'I'd quite lost track.' He smiled at her. 'Are you ready?'

He held her chair for her as she got up. Colette fastened her coat and picked up her handbag. Where had the time gone? She had never felt so comfortable in anyone's company before.

There was a meeting in the buffet a day or two later and Colette wondered whether to mention her beans on toast with Mr Gordon. She felt shy of doing so but that didn't stop her wanting to confide. She admitted to herself that she did want to talk about him and wanted to hear what her friends had to say.

The others had heard of him because he had helped Persephone last year when she had first been promoted to the position of ticket inspector and had faced a situation with fare-dodgers. He had also, of course, sorted out the matter of the porters' pilfering after Colette had persuaded

Emily to turn to him, though the others didn't know about that because it was confidential.

When Colette brought up the subject of going to the Worker Bee, her friends clearly attached no significance to it. Well, they wouldn't, would they? They probably thought that after her experience with Tony, she would never look at another man as long as she lived. Besides, she was married.

So it was up to Colette to steer the conversation the way she wanted it to go – and she definitely wanted it to go that way.

'The thing is . . . well, I rather like him,' she said and tried to look as if she hadn't noticed more than one of her friends sit up straighter.

'You like him?' said Emily. 'As in, you *like* him, not just ordinary like him?' Before Colette could answer, she added, 'But he's so *old*.'

That made Colette laugh. 'He's probably a similar age to your mother, maybe a little older.'

'Oh yes, positively ancient,' Cordelia murmured wryly.

'He's too old for you, at any rate,' Emily informed Colette decisively.

'Actually,' Colette answered, 'that's one of the things I like.' Aiming for a lighter note, she went on, 'I had a young husband and he was a brute who controlled my every waking moment. Mr Gordon is . . . tried and true, you might say.'

'And do you think he likes you too?' Joan asked gently.

Colette hesitated. 'This isn't like when I met Tony and we liked one another right away. Mr Gordon and I have known one another since I started in my chaperone job, but it's only recently that we've got to know each other on a more personal level.' She frowned. 'That makes it sound as if something has happened between us, something emotional, something shared, and it hasn't been like that. We had the day out with the children, and after that he invited me to have a chat with him while he wasn't busy, and I've seen a different side of him.'

'A side you find attractive,' said Fay.

Colette nodded. 'It's early days, of course, but we really seemed to get along and I think – I hope – he sees me as more than a colleague.'

Her friends looked at one another.

'I can honestly say I've never heard a word against him,' Persephone remarked, 'and I know that he's very good at his job. People respect him.'

'Let's get down to brass tacks,' said Dot. 'Is he a bachelor?'

'He's a family man,' said Colette. 'He's a widower with a daughter.'

'How old is she?' Alison asked.

'I'm not sure, but she sounds quite young. Her aunt lives with them as housekeeper. Mr Gordon said that having his sister-in-law there was what enabled him to keep Evie at home.'

'Talking of brass tacks,' said Joan with an apologetic glance around the table. 'He might be single but you're not. Sorry, but someone had to say it.'

'Don't feel bad about it,' said Colette. 'I've been thinking the same thing myself. I don't want to make any assumptions about Mr Gordon and me, but obviously Tony has been very much on my mind.'

'You could divorce him,' said Fay.

'There's a terrible stigma attached to being divorced,' Margaret pointed out.

'Better the stigma than having Tony breathing down your neck,' said Dot.

'There might not be the same stigma in years to come,' Cordelia said thoughtfully. 'Divorce is going to be far more common after the war.'

'All those hasty weddings,' Fay said with a sigh, 'and all those irregular babies.'

'What are irregular babies?' Emily asked.

'Babies born out of wedlock,' said Alison.

'Or babies born to married ladies,' said Fay, 'but the husband is away in the services and can't possibly be the father.'

'Anyway,' said Colette, 'I can't imagine Tony agreeing to divorce.'

'He might not have a choice,' said Fay. 'His violence towards you is on record, thanks to the court case.'

'We're all getting somewhat ahead of ourselves,' said Colette, a tingle of embarrassment rising up the back of her neck and sweeping across her face. 'I only said I liked Mr Gordon, that's all.'

Even so . . . could she have a future with him?

Chapter Twelve

The days lengthened and the weather was kinder as March went on. Yes, it was often windy but the trees filled out with young leaves and the air was tangy with the rich scent of newly turned soil in gardens and on allotments.

Alison had been going regularly to Lydia's and also to Mum's to talk about Lydia, who had gone through a phase of wondering whether Alec really was dead. She speculated that maybe his identity had got mixed up with that of another soldier. It wasn't as though they could go to the funeral parlour to visit the deceased.

'I told her, "Of course he's dead." What else was I to say?' Mum explained to Alison. 'She looked at me as if I'd committed the most terrible betrayal.' She gave Alison a pained stare.

'Lydia knows he's gone,' Alison tried to reassure her. 'It's just so hard to believe.'

'It's hard for all of us.' Mum sighed deeply. 'Just when we were all so happy because of you marrying Joel.'

It was Joel whom Alison clung to for strength during this dark time for Lydia. He held her when she wept and listened with understanding when she wanted to talk.

'Spend as much time with your family as you think you should,' he urged her. 'They need you. Your sister needs you.'

Alison felt a pain in the back of her throat and recognised it as guilt. She wanted to support Lydia, of course she did, but she also wanted to be at home with her new husband. Their shifts gave them precious little time together as it was.

Of all people, it was Lydia who recognised this.

'You shouldn't keep coming over here to see me,' she told Alison. 'I know how inconvenient it must be.'

'I don't care about that,' Alison declared.

'You should be at home with Joel,' Lydia replied. 'I mean it, Alison. Grab every single moment you can.' She rubbed her arms, her voice tightening as she added, 'Alec never had a single leave after our wedding weekend.'

Yet more guilt washed through Alison. She remembered with distressing clarity her own ungracious wish that Alec could come home for long enough to get Lydia pregnant.

And then the choice of how much time to devote to her sister was removed from her hands. In the last weekend of the month, Alison was on duty. On the Sunday morning, Mr Samuels walked into the onward travel office, looking grave. Without the need for him to say a single word, everyone turned and looked at him. A frisson ran around the room and the hairs stood up on Alison's arms.

'Good morning, ladies and gentlemen,' he said. 'Your attention, please. This morning, the chief operating officers of all the railway companies received a telephone call with the order "Go!" This means that the country's railways must now transport all the troops, equipment and ammunition to the marshalling centres ready for the invasion of Europe. We have a number of weeks in which to achieve this, but make no mistake. The number of weeks is not an invitation for complacency. Rather, it is a sign of the scale of the operation the railways are to undertake. It is estimated that around twenty-five thousand special trains will run – and they must do so without the general public becoming aware. Fortunately,' he added wryly, 'passengers are accustomed by this time to having their services interrupted.' He took a moment to look searchingly around the long room, allowing his gaze to rest upon every face. 'I know I can depend upon each and every one of you to perform your duty to the very best of your ability. I need not add that you may speak of this to nobody.'

Alison felt fired up with patriotism and resolve as she set off for work every day after Mr Samuels made his announcement. Part of her also boggled at the knowledge of what she was involved in, what she had been chosen to do. But that was part and parcel of wartime, wasn't it? Everyone had to do whatever was required of them and sometimes that meant taking on a task that was of extra significance. Alison felt proud and humble at the same time.

She found herself taking an even keener interest in the war news and listened avidly when Persephone talked about a letter she'd had from Iphigenia. Alison was always interested in anything Iphigenia had to say because she was grateful to her for providing her with a glamorous wedding dress and the most heavenly of veils, but this time Alison was extra interested because of events in London. There had been a huge display in Trafalgar Square of field guns and anti-aircraft guns alongside many other essential things such as a mechanical repair shop and an amphibious vehicle.

Allied troops had chatted with the admiring public. Iphigenia had attended that event on the day before Mr Samuels had appeared in the onward travel office. Then, on the Monday, there had been marching bands and the King had taken the salute from a dais outside Buckingham Palace.

But if Alison's mind was elsewhere, Mum certainly wasn't impressed.

'You aren't spending as much time here now,' she complained to Alison. 'Lydia's widowhood hasn't magically gone away. I know you're newly married and you want to save your annual leave to be with Joel, and that's fair enough, but honestly, Alison, can't you spare your own sister a bit more time?'

That made Alison feel awful. She went to see Lydia as soon as she could. It was early April and buds and blossom were forming on the trees alongside the fresh leaves. Short showers left the air sparkling and smelling bright and damp. Spring was here. Lydia's loss seemed even more cruel.

Alison was especially glad that she had come round to see Lydia, because her sister was down in the dumps.

'I keep thinking how much I wanted to have a honeymoon baby,' she said with a deep sigh. 'If I'd got in the family way, at least I'd have something of Alec left with me now.' She glanced at Alison, a surprisingly sharp look. 'You mustn't leave it too long, you know. It's . . . it's arrogant to think you've got the choice, to think you can pick and choose when you have your family. Anything could happen and all your plans could go up in smoke. It's vile being widowed.'

'I know,' Alison whispered.

'No, you don't,' Lydia shot back at her. 'No one does who

hasn't been through it. You lose everything. You don't just lose your husband. You lose your entire future. All the things you imagined and dreamed about and looked forward to – gone!'

Gathering her courage together, Alison said softly, 'I know life is pretty bad now and that it will be for a long time, but . . .'

'But what? I'm young? I'll meet someone else?'

'Well, you might. You're a lovely girl and I'd hate to think of you going through the rest of your life alone.'

'How could you?' Lydia demanded. 'How could you be so . . . unfeeling? Telling me to forget Alec and move on.'

'I didn't say that – and I'm not unfeeling. It's what happened to me. I felt as if the world had come to an end when Paul left me. Then along came Joel.'

'Oh aye, you got together with him pretty quickly, didn't you?' There was a taunt in Lydia's voice.

Alison was shocked. 'That was just the way it happened.'

'Maybe you didn't love Paul as much as you thought you did,' said Lydia, 'since you were able to replace him so soon.'

'It wasn't like that,' Alison insisted.

'Wasn't it? Then what was it like? You're the expert, telling me I'll find another husband.'

'I didn't say that. I didn't mean that.'

'Didn't you?' Lydia raised an eyebrow.

'I just wanted to show you that there is still hope, that you can still have a future.'

'Well, it doesn't feel like it,' said Lydia, but her anger was abating now. She looked worn down and wretched, though she still had the spirit to say crisply, 'You got dumped by one man so you went and found another. I'm not that sort. Alec was my one and only.'

Alison was hurt and angry but she knew she must give Lydia leeway to vent her feelings. At least Lydia was talking – which was more than Alison had done when Paul had left her heartbroken.

'I'm sorry if I said the wrong thing,' said Alison. 'I never intended to make light of your relationship with Alec or your love for one another. I just wanted to give you hope, that's all.'

There was a heavy silence and it seemed that Lydia wouldn't speak.

Then she said, 'Things turned out well for you and I'm happy about that, I truly am. I'm sorry for what I said about you finding another man. That was horrid. I know you want to make me feel better because you're my sister and you want to help, but it doesn't work like that. Telling me I'll meet someone else is like saying I didn't think much of Alec.'

'I never meant that at all,' Alison said quietly.

'I know that.' Lydia took Alison's hand. 'But it's important that you never say it again.'

Finally Alison understood that this situation wasn't about what she wanted to say. It was about what Lydia needed to hear. That was how to make her feel loved and supported. She needed to feel listened to.

'You're my sister and I love you,' Alison said. 'It breaks my heart that this has happened to you. I know how much you loved Alec and I know he adored you too. I promise that in future I will fully respect your grief.'

Lydia nodded. 'Thank you,' she said in a stiff, formal little voice.

'And I promise not to try to make you feel better.'

Tears filled Lydia's eyes. 'You have made me feel better.'

Alison held her as she succumbed to a storm of weeping.

Colette was looking forward to seeing Mr Gordon again, perhaps even spending some time together. Who was she trying to kid? There was no 'perhaps' about it. She very much hoped for more time together, but she didn't see him around the station and she couldn't go into the ticket office without a proper reason to do so.

At home she told Mrs Cooper and Mrs Grayson about him. She couldn't tell her friends and leave these two dear ladies out. Besides, she valued their opinions. As long as she lived she would never forget how Mrs Cooper had helped her to break free from Tony.

'Oh, my lovely girl!' Mrs Cooper exclaimed. 'There is part of me that is glad and grateful to know that Tony didn't damage you to the point where you could never look at another man – but the other part says this is too soon. You mustn't rush into anything.'

'Believe me, I'm in no hurry,' Colette said. 'I didn't go seeking this. It just happened. If you'd told me as recently as a few weeks ago that I'd be interested in Mr Gordon in this way, I'd have thought you were mad.'

'What's he like?' asked Mrs Grayson.

'He's rather serious but he also has a sense of humour,' Colette began. 'A sense of fun,' she expanded, picturing him running races with the children on their day trip. 'He's clever and he has an eye for detail, which must make him good at his job.' She thought of Persephone and Emily, who had both faced troubles at work that Mr Gordon had dealt with. 'He's the sort you can turn to. You can rely on him.'

'He sounds a good man,' said Mrs Cooper.

'He does,' Mrs Grayson agreed, 'but don't forget you're a married woman. Don't forget the way your old neighbours in Seymour Grove looked sideways at you, and that was just for being separated. There will be much greater censure if you start seeing another man. I know what folk will say. They'll wonder if this Mr Gordon is the reason Tony battered you. Believe me, once the gossip starts, it's a small step from asking a question about something to stating it as if it's a fact.'

'When I met Tony,' said Colette, 'I was an innocent girl from a sheltered upbringing. I've learned a lot of lessons since then and I can see what a decent, worthwhile man Mr Gordon is. After all that time with Tony, all that time of being afraid, here is a man I can trust. And I know I'm still married, but . . .' Her throat seemed to close over.

'This answers one question, anyway,' said Mrs Grayson. 'You've been agonising over seeing Tony's mother. This means you definitely can't, not while you've got Mr Gordon in your thoughts. That really would be playing with fire.'

'I hadn't thought of it that way,' said Colette.

It was something new to think about. She knew Mrs Grayson was right. If she hoped for any sort of friendship with Mr Gordon – and she did – then she couldn't visit Bunty. It would be too complicated.

She was due to collect train tickets from Mr Gordon the next day. Smiling to herself, she deliberately went to the ticket office just before eleven o'clock, remembering the occasion when he had given the nod to Mrs Lister to provide tea for two.

She wiped the smile from her face before she knocked on the side door and waited to be admitted. As she approached Mr Gordon's office, she could see through the window that he was seated behind his desk. Mrs Lister glanced up from her typewriter and gave Colette a small smile.

'Good morning, Mrs Lister. I've come to collect tickets from Mr Gordon.'

'Yes, of course,' said the secretary. She stood up and inserted herself in the open doorway. 'Mrs Naylor is here, Mr Gordon.'

She stepped aside and Colette went in, feeling happy and a little breathless. But then – then Mr Gordon glanced over her shoulder. Nobody else would have noticed what happened next, but Colette did. Instead of the nod she had hoped for, the nod she had taken for granted, the nod that had brought her here just before the magic time of eleven o'clock – instead of that he gave an almost imperceptible shake of his head.

Colette's legs felt weak and her heartbeat was sluggish. She had come here specifically to enjoy a cup of tea with Mr Gordon, had been looking forward to it, but now she wanted to sink through the floor. If he thought of her in any way other than the professional, if she meant anything at all to him, wouldn't he have said, 'I'm sorry not to offer you a cup of tea'? But he hadn't said anything – and that told Colette all she needed to know.

Chapter Thirteen

The more Alison thought about it, the more remarkable it seemed. She recalled Mr Samuels saying last year that the British and the Americans had been planning the invasion of Europe for three years. The contribution of the British railways was an essential part of their plans. It wasn't simply a matter of transporting troops, ammo and heavy equipment such as tanks down to the south coast. All trains, having disgorged their cargo, then had to return, empty, before setting out on another run. And while these trains, hundreds of them, thousands of them, were travelling north to south, south to north, north to south again, the passenger network had to be maintained, as did the regular supplies of food and fuel to the four corners of the kingdom.

Not only that, but all this had to be achieved – and 'had to' were the important words: failure could not be countenanced – using rolling stock that was increasingly old and tired. Alison knew that all the railway companies were running locomotives that in peacetime would have been retired long since. Moreover, passenger travel was reckoned to have increased by more than half, thanks to the war having dispersed families and given many people longer journeys to work.

Although Alison was afire with dedication to her work,

Lydia was never far from her thoughts. Joel worried about Lydia too.

'Why don't you two sisters have a few days away together?' he suggested when he and Alison were at her parents' house for tea. Lydia wasn't there. 'It might help to lift Lydia's spirits a little. A change of scenery, you know, a change of routine. You wouldn't have to go far.'

Mum pounced at once. 'You hardly took any time off when Lydia was widowed,' she said to Alison, 'but surely now you can see the necessity of booking a little holiday for her sake. Joel wants you to.'

Alison pressed her lips together. It was out of the question now that the railways had been mobilised, but she couldn't say that. But if she refused, what would her family think of her? She tried to fudge her way around the subject.

'I don't know. You know leave has to be booked well in advance.'

She felt mealy-mouthed saying it and caught Joel's look of surprise, but he didn't say anything, thank goodness. Alison contrived to move the conversation along by asking Mum how she thought Lydia was coping with being back at work.

Later on, Alison went into the kitchen to help Mum to clear up.

'I'm surprised at you, Alison,' Mum said stiffly. 'I expected better of you than that. I thought you'd jump at the idea of going away with Lydia. It need only be for a day or two. Is that so much to ask? You've got everything and Lydia has lost her husband.'

'I can't just book a holiday,' said Alison. 'There's my job.'

Mum made a sound that was part-laugh and part-scorn, mostly scorn. 'What are you talking about? It's just another one of your placements.'

'No, it isn't. This is the real thing.'

'Is it?' Mum was put out. 'All those different jobs you've had: I thought you were building up to something special, something important – and they were just building up to *this*? All you're doing is working out which trains to shunt into which sidings while troop trains go past. I realise it has to be done, but you can hardly call it special work, can you?'

After some days of chaperoning, Colette had to go and see Mr Gordon again to be given a new assignment. She didn't relish the thought of seeing him, but that was her own fault for having been so silly, for putting two and two together and coming up with a wildly improbable answer. One thing was for certain: she definitely wasn't going to go to his office at eleven o'clock. She might be stupid but she wasn't *that* stupid.

She was surprised therefore when, after giving her instructions and tickets, he mentioned their previous trip to the Worker Bee.

'I wondered if you might be free at some point to go somewhere for a cup of tea and a chat, perhaps. I thought maybe later today or tomorrow.' He glanced away from her and then looked back at her again, which made him appear . . . well, shy or uncertain, perhaps, but Colette couldn't afford to weaken.

'I'm not free, I'm afraid, but thank you for asking.'

What had made her add those final words? That was

what her mother had taught her to say when she was a little girl and now she had trotted out the phrase all over again.

Mr Gordon looked taken aback and his eyes clouded, then his expression turned to a polite mask.

'Of course,' he said. 'I apologise if I spoke out of turn.'

She wanted to tell him he hadn't. She wanted to ask him to explain himself. But her resolve to return to a purely professional relationship held good and she left his office, not putting her tickets into her handbag until she was about to leave the ticket office and return to the concourse. She felt fluttery and upset and it took her a moment to compose herself.

She didn't know what game Mr Gordon was playing – if indeed that was what he was doing. He probably wasn't, she conceded. He was too honest and straightforward for that. He had too much integrity. It seemed more likely that she had somehow blundered. After all, what did she know of relationships? She had been taken in by a good-looking charmer who, once she had a ring on her finger, had set out to control every aspect of her life. She wished now that she had refrained from opening her heart to her friends as she had, but at the time she'd been unable to stop herself. She hadn't wanted to.

Dear Mrs Cooper realised something was wrong, much to Colette's dismay.

'Is it obvious?' she asked. 'I don't want to make a show of myself.'

'You aren't,' Mrs Cooper reassured her with a smile. 'I can see it because you bring out my mother-hen tendencies.'

Colette smiled too, acknowledging the special bond

between them. It was a short step from there to confiding her woes.

'It's Mr Gordon. I think I've made the most awful twerp of myself, seeing something that wasn't there. I thought – I let myself think that he might be interested in me and now it turns out I was mistaken.'

'Oh, my dear lass,' said Mrs Cooper.

'There's no call for sympathy,' said Colette. 'I don't deserve it. What I deserve is a good talking-to for having made a prize chump of myself. I'd rather not mention it to the others quite yet. I want to get used to it first.'

'I won't breathe a word, I promise.'

'I know you won't,' said Colette.

'I admit I was in two minds as to whether a new relationship was the right thing for you,' said Mrs Cooper, 'or rather, whether it was the right thing just now. I love the thought of you finding true happiness in due course.'

'So do I,' said Colette. 'Maybe I should be grateful that this has happened – my silly crush, I mean. At least it has shown me that Tony didn't kill my heart stone dead.'

'Don't say that,' Mrs Cooper exclaimed. 'Of course he didn't. He couldn't.'

'This made me feel as if my life was opening up in a new way, allowing me a glimpse of what might lie ahead,' said Colette. 'That in turn made me see how very guarded I had to be after I married Tony. I walked on eggshells the whole time. I tried so hard to do the right thing and be the wife he wanted me to be, but it was as if he kept changing the rules.'

'It was very hard for you,' said Mrs Cooper. 'It took great courage for you to leave him.'

'I didn't exactly leave him,' Colette corrected her. 'I ran away and made a new life. I'll never forget how you helped me become Betsy Cooper.'

'I don't want you to spend your whole life looking back at your marriage, chuck,' said Mrs Cooper.

'Coming to admire and think highly of Mr Gordon,' said Colette, choosing her words with care, 'brought warmth and – and a feeling of freshness into my life, together with a feeling I can only describe as . . . freedom. Well, so much for freedom,' she added drily. 'It made me lose my head good and proper and that's not like me at all. As for Mr Gordon, we seemed to get along well – but what of it? We talked about his family – but again, so what? He might tell everyone he ever meets about his late wife and the sister-in-law he's grateful to because her presence in his home enables him to keep his little girl with him.' Deep down, though, Colette didn't really believe that. She looked squarely at Mrs Cooper. 'It's far more likely that he talked about his domestic situation because in me he found a sympathetic listener – in the same way as I found a sympathetic listener in him. That's the truth of the matter. We were just two people carrying different burdens of sorrow.'

It was the middle of April and Easter had come and gone. Along with everyone else in the cinema, Persephone saw on the Pathé newsreel that the Russians had captured Odessa and were closing in on Sebastopol. At Darley Court, she helped thin out the seedlings and hoed the ground around the young crops. She was looking forward to visiting Iphigenia in London, the continuing air raids notwithstanding. Ma had written to say she would come up from Sussex to see her in London. Did this mean Persephone would be expected to stay in the family's town house with her parents? But her invitation to stay with Iphigenia held good.

She couldn't wait to see her sister again. Persephone was aware that other people admired her own looks but personally she had always felt that Iphigenia's were far more alluring. Those blue-grey eyes and that silver-blonde hair made her a real stunner. She could have had her pick of the aristocratic crop in her London Season and Hugo was lucky to have married her, all the more so considering he was plain Mr McLean Grey.

It wasn't just sisterly love and admiration that accounted for Persephone's eagerness to be reunited with Iphigenia. She would also value the opportunity to talk to her sister about her relationship with Matt. Much to Persephone's astonishment, even before she and Matt had got together, Iphigenia had encouraged her to get to know the handsome fireman – only for it to transpire that Iphigenia meant for her younger sister to indulge in a fling.

'This is wartime. You said yourself one should make the most of every moment. Why not let your fireman help you feel better about yourself? Where's the harm? He'll enjoy it too,' Iphigenia had said blithely. 'I'm not suggesting you marry him, for pity's sake. Sweetie, I know girls who are going through men like a dose of salts, but after the war, they'll know exactly whom to marry and live happily ever after with. We all know whom we can and can't marry. War doesn't change that. It's just that before marriage comes along, the war has given all you single girls this marvellous opportunity to enjoy yourselves. What's wrong with that? Grab it with both hands, little sister, that's what I say. You'll have years and years to be a respectable married lady afterwards. And I promise not to tell tales on you.'

Persephone had never felt comfortable about that. Now, a year on, she wanted to have a heart-to-heart with her sister and be honest about how much Matt had come to mean to her.

Her friends were all happy on her behalf that she was going on a trip and would see her family.

'Though we do appreciate it won't be all plain sailing for you,' Cordelia said one evening in the buffet.

'The last time I saw my family was when that dratted piece appeared in the society column,' said Persephone, wincing at the memory.

She couldn't suppress a sigh. Clarinda, which was the name allotted to a newspaper writer of high-society gossip, had informed the world and his wife of the Honourable Persephone Trehearn-Hobbs's association with a humble railwayman. Before the war, Persephone had herself enjoyed being Clarinda and she was well aware that the column's most important rule was to write in flattering terms. Certainly there had been no hint of censure in Clarinda's words, but in revealing Persephone and Matt's relationship, the new Clarinda had caused trouble for Persephone within the ranks of her family. When Persephone had found out by chance who had taken over as Clarinda, she'd realised to her deep dismay that her successor in the role had acted with calculated malice, knowing what a stink it would cause.

Persephone said now to her chums, 'I had a letter from my mother yesterday. She said, and I quote, "It won't do you any harm to be seen in public with your father and me." In other words, my lowly boyfriend is a wartime aberration and my parents haven't disowned me.'

'Ouch,' said Alison.

'Ouch with bells on,' added Joan.

'I hope it isn't going to cast a shadow over your trip,' said Dot.

'Fingers crossed,' Persephone said brightly, 'but honestly I don't know what to expect.'

Matt was pleased she was going to see her family.

'I couldn't imagine being so many miles away from mine,' he said.

Matt's love for his family was one of the things Persephone valued most in him. She loved her family too but knew that it was being miles away from them that had enabled her to become involved with Matt. Had she been in Sussex with Ma or Grandmama, or in London with Iphigenia or Pa, she would never have been permitted to have a serious relationship with a man from the lower orders.

It said a lot for Matt's strength of character that he wasn't worried at the prospect of her returning to her old social world. Or did it? Persephone didn't want him to be upset, but there was a part of her that wished he didn't want her to go. No, not really, she corrected herself. She would hate it if he was jealous. Nonetheless, she couldn't prevent the question from appearing inside her head: did Matt's cheerful acceptance of her forthcoming trip suggest that she cared for him more than he did for her?

With Allied troops streaming into Britain, many of them via the Mersey, the organisation of transport around the clock created an atmosphere of intense concentration in the onward travel office. Getting trains and their crews into the required places time after time took knowledge, precision and an unwavering eye for detail. In common with her colleagues, Alison routinely ended each long shift tired and yet with her brain buzzing. The hardest part was leaving the office behind and walking back into her real life where her husband, her family and friends all thought she was handling railway traffic in the normal way and nobody guessed the true nature of her work.

She was proud and excited to be involved. Determined, too. Focused. The future of her country was at stake. The future of Europe was at stake and she, Alison Maitland, was playing a tiny but essential role in a crucial endeavour.

The next time she met up with her friends in the buffet, the conversation turned to work.

'How are you getting on in the PAYE office?' Persephone asked Joan. It was no secret that Joan had taken a while to settle in.

'I'm feeling more confident,' said Joan, smiling. 'There was a time when I thought I'd never feel that way.'

'Do you miss being a porter?' asked Emily.

'Yes, but I need to work office hours.' Joan shrugged.

'You can't have everything. I know how lucky I am compared to most mums, being able to go home to my little boy every evening.'

'You've got two professions under your belt,' said Margaret. 'Tax clerk and sewing-machinist. You'll have a choice of what to do after the war.'

Joan smiled. 'After the war I'll be a housewife and mother. I promised Bob and it's what we both want.'

'There might be another little Hubble by then,' said Dot.

'Neither of us wants Max to be an only child,' said Joan.

'You're quiet, Alison,' said Fay. 'How is your job coming along?'

'Oh, fine,' Alison answered. 'It suits me.'

'How is Lydia getting along at work?' asked Cordelia.

'She's coping, I think.' Then Alison sighed. 'That's an easy thing to say, but what does it really mean? She's getting through the days. That's as much as can be said. She's lost weight; she's gone thin. Mum and Dad are so worried about her.'

'They must be,' said Fay. 'What job does she do?'

'She's a clerk in a shipping office in one of the warehouses on the banks of the River Irwell. She's worked there for years.'

'At least going out to work gives some structure to her days,' said Dot. 'It seems like small comfort but in its own way, it must help. I hope so, anyroad.'

'It's still early days,' Cordelia added.

'There's a girl called Alice in the engine shed,' said Margaret. 'Her brother was killed in action last year and when she came back to work, she threw herself into it like never before, as if she was dead set on winning the war single-handed. Not that I'm criticising Lydia if she's not the same,' she added.

'Grief takes everyone differently,' said Colette. 'No one can possibly know how they will react in a certain situation until it actually happens to them.'

Alison shook her head. 'I'd do anything to help Lydia, but I just don't know how. I remember when an elderly lady who lives near my mum was widowed after sixty years of marriage. She turned into a shadow of her old self and my gran said, "She's lost heart." That's what I can't help thinking now about Lydia. She's lost heart.'

Alison went to visit Lydia at her flat – though she felt a twinge of guilt for thinking of it as Lydia's. It used to be *their* flat when anyone mentioned it. Now it was just Lydia's. It was in a house near the local cricket pitch. Around twenty years ago it had been converted into two decent-sized flats and Lydia and Alec had been lucky enough to get the downstairs one. Dad had done a bit of work to improve the kitchen, providing new cupboard doors and a Belfast sink. In the sitting room the curtains and cushion-covers were second-hand.

Alison's glance fell on Lydia's tapestried sewing-bag propped up against the side of the armchair. The bag gaped open and an empty cushion-cover could be seen together with a length of braid, some of it attached to the top seam with pins while the rest dangled loosely. Alison recalled that Lydia had bought that braid to jolly up her cushion-covers. That had been just before—

Lydia caught her looking.

'All right,' she said tetchily. 'I know I haven't done the braid.'

'I didn't say a word.' Alison spoke in a gentle voice. It was all too easy to get on Lydia's wrong side these days.

'You didn't need to,' said Lydia. 'It's only a bit of braid. It doesn't matter.'

Wondering how best to respond, Alison settled for an offhand 'Better hide it away so Mum doesn't see it, then.'

'She's already seen it,' Lydia answered. 'I thought she was going to tell me to get the job finished.' Her voice trailed away.

'But she didn't? It would have been just like her if she had.'

'Actually,' said Lydia, 'she offered to take the braid and the covers and do the trimming for me, but I said I'd get round to it.'

'And will you?' Alison asked.

Lydia shrugged. 'Not the way I'm feeling at the moment.'

'Then why not let Mum do it? She'd be glad to help.'

'Oh aye?' There was a gleam of challenge in Lydia's eyes. 'You think a few tarted-up cushions will make me feel better?'

'Of course not.'

'I don't need help,' Lydia insisted. 'I don't want it. You of all people should understand that.'

'Me?' Alison asked, confused.

'Yes, you. Don't you remember what you were like after Paul left you? You turned your back on everyone.'

Alison was surprised and unsettled at having her own

behaviour thrown in her face after all this time. 'That doesn't mean it was the right thing to do. In fact, it definitely wasn't, I can promise you that.'

'So what should I do, then?' Lydia asked in a brisk voice. 'Weep and wail all over the place? This is wartime and we're meant to be getting on with whatever life throws at us. I'm sorry if I'm not grieving in the way everybody wants me to, but it's all I can do to remember to breathe in and out.'

'Oh, Lydia—'

'This is the way things are for me now,' Lydia ploughed on. 'There isn't a single thing anybody else can do about it. I've just got to . . . get on with it.'

Chapter Fourteen

'It's not quite the walk in the park I could have taken you for before the war,' Matt said with a rueful smile.

Persephone smiled back. As long as she was in Matt's company, she didn't mind where she was. So what if the park no longer had lawns and a bowling green and pretty flowerbeds? As the two of them walked along hand in hand, some people broke off from their work to pass the time of day. It was lovely to be accepted as a couple, to be seen by these friendly strangers as belonging together.

They stopped for a few minutes to chat to an elderly gentleman who was sticking twigs in the ground to support his young pea plants.

'Well, I mustn't keep you,' he said after a while. 'I'm sure your time together is precious.'

Persephone and Matt said goodbye and walked on.

'I've got something to tell you,' said Matt. 'Something to offer you, to be precise, if you're interested.'

'That sounds mysterious.'

'Well, there is secrecy involved,' said Matt. 'I've been told I have to make that clear. You see, as well as driving passenger trains during the day, Mr Gibson and I often drive munitions trains at night.'

'I had no idea,' Persephone exclaimed.

Matt grinned. 'I have got permission for you to come with us on a munitions run. You'd have to stay in the guard's van the whole time, which means you wouldn't see much, but then there isn't really anything to see. It's just another train journey, to all intents and purposes. What d'you think? Would you like to?'

Persephone's breath caught on a gasp. Would she like to? Would she *like* to?

'It's a marvellous opportunity,' she burbled. 'I'd love to, I really would. You organised this specially for me?'

Matt laughed. 'Well, I can't think of anyone else who'd want to do it.' Then he was serious. 'You wouldn't be allowed to use the information in an article until you received permission to do so, which wouldn't be until after the war.'

'I understand. You know you can rely on me.' Persephone danced around to stand in front of him, bringing him to a standstill so she could hug him. 'Thank you, thank you. This means the world to me.'

'It's not every fellow who has a girl who thinks that travelling on a munitions train is such a good present.'

Standing on tiptoe, Persephone planted a light kiss on his mouth. 'Best present ever,' she whispered.

It was, too. She had always longed to be taken seriously as a journalist. She enjoyed writing for *Vera's Voice* and other publications, but her original ambition had been to report for a daily newspaper. Back in '39 when war was imminent and she had been Clarinda, the society columnist, she had done her best to persuade Mr Bunting, the newspaper editor, to give her the chance she yearned for, but he had declined.

His precise words had been, 'Great Scott, you really mean it, don't you? You actually imagine you can do this. You think you can be a reporter in London when war comes,' and his astonishment had been hard to swallow. Persephone had done her best to persuade him differently but he wouldn't be swayed.

But this opportunity that Matt had laid in front of her was something special. It might not be the write-it-today, read-it-tomorrow reporting she used to dream of, but it was an important wartime story, something to be told after the war when it was safe to share such details. It would be an honour to write it.

And it was thanks to Matt that she had been offered this chance. There couldn't be a better man in the world than Matt Franklin and she counted herself deeply fortunate that they were a couple. She was so proud of him. Those fighting on the front line were hailed as heroes, and rightly so, but there was also heroism in working on the railways. The endless stamina and sheer doggedness it took to keep the railways running, to transport coal and food and supplies around the country . . . to transport explosives and detonators, weapons and spare parts for armed vehicles . . . all at the same time as taking Mrs Smith to visit little Johnny who'd been evacuated to Wales. That was what the railways did. They were helping to keep the country running and they were helping to win the war.

Just think. When the time came that her article about the munitions train could be published, she and Matt wouldn't be a couple any longer. The war had brought them together and peace would force them apart.

Persephone couldn't tell her friends about the munitions-train piece she was going to write, which made her feel unusually isolated. She had no qualms about keeping a war-time secret because she had been brought up to put duty first. What bothered her was knowing that peacetime would see the end of her and Matt. She had known this all along, of course, but the munitions train brought it home to her in a more meaningful way than she had previously allowed herself to glimpse. Her heart quaked but she knew there was no alternative.

Was this one of the reasons why her mother was keen for her to visit London? As a timely reminder of her true place in society?

It seemed certain now that the war was entering its final phase and Matt's munitions train felt symbolic of it. Of course the war would go on for months yet and Persephone longed for it to be over as much as anyone, but . . . *but*.

She concealed her thoughts, presenting her customary sunny face to the world. Determined not to sink into the doldrums, she made a point of paying attention to her friends, asking after Lydia, checking that Emily was happy in her job and complimenting Mrs Jessop so that she knew her hard work in the buffet was appreciated.

To her delight, Persephone had the chance of a chinwag with Colette. Persephone was at Southport Station waiting to return to Manchester Victoria in her capacity as ticket inspector when she spied Colette fussing the station cat.

Colette wore a beige-and-brown checked coat with a slight flare of fabric below the softly nipped-in waist that suited her buttermilk-fair hair and gentle demeanour.

Persephone went across to her. 'Hello! Fancy seeing you here.'

Colette straightened up. 'I accompanied an elderly couple here so I'll be on my way back soon.' She glanced at the station clock. 'On the three-thirty.'

'Snap!' Persephone was pleased. 'All we need now is for Dot to be the parcels porter and we'll have a full house.'

Colette smiled. 'A full set would be if Matt was the fireman.'

'We've got time for a cuppa,' said Persephone.

They headed for the buffet, where they bagged a small table in the corner.

'Tell me to mind my own bizney,' said Persephone, 'but have you seen Mr Gordon again?'

Distress flickered across Colette's face but her voice was steady as she answered. 'No. As a matter of fact, I wish I'd never said anything to the rest of you.'

'I'm sorry to hear that,' said Persephone. 'Why?'

'Oh, I think I read too much into it.' Colette shook her head and smiled but Persephone couldn't help noticing the bleakness in her eyes. 'Silly of me.'

'Are you sure?' Persephone asked. 'Only you seemed happy when you talked about him.'

'Don't rub it in.'

'I'm not – not on purpose. I'm sorry.'

'He paid me some kind attention,' said Colette, 'and I

read something into it that I shouldn't have. It's understandable when you think about it. After all the time I spent tippy-toeing around Tony, having a man being honest-to-goodness kind to me turned my head. I can see now what a twit I was. D'you mind if we talk about something else?'

Persephone immediately changed the subject but afterwards she couldn't stop thinking about Colette's disappointment. If anybody deserved some happiness, it was Colette. Persephone hadn't been taken in by her apparent acceptance of the situation. There had been real hurt in her blue eyes and Persephone had wanted to fuss her and give her a hug.

She had always been fond of Colette and once the truth had emerged about Tony, had come to admire her as well. After she had finally left Tony, Colette had moved temporarily into Darley Court, the one place her friends were sure Tony wouldn't dare to come banging on the door. Living side by side had given Persephone and Colette the chance to get to know one another more closely and they had held long conversations about Colette's situation and everything that had led her to escape from Tony and start a new life in London as Betsy Cooper, until he had tracked her down and forced her to return to Manchester with him. It had shaken Persephone – it had shaken all the girls – to realise just how much Colette had lived through without any of them having the first idea of it.

Persephone's shift ended shortly after the train returned to Manchester Victoria, as did Colette's, so the two of them went together to catch the bus. On their way out of the station, they paused beside the Great War memorial. It filled an entire wall. Much of it comprised a huge map made of tiles that showed the routes of the old Lancashire and Yorkshire Railway network. Below stretched a row of seven bronze panels with the names of the fallen engraved in long lists upon them, men who had all left their railway jobs to fight for King and country. At one end was a panel showing St George slaying the dragon and at the other end stood St Michael the Archangel, sword aloft, with his foot on Lucifer's neck. The panels with the saints were each flanked by two smaller panels with flaming torches. Each of these four bore a single word: UNITY, STRENGTH, COURAGE, SACRIFICE.

'All those men who never came home,' Colette murmured.

'So many widows and fatherless children,' said Persephone.

'So many unmarried girls who are now middle-aged spinsters because they lost their sweethearts.'

'It's a dreadful cliché,' said Persephone, 'but there can be no denying the truth of it: war is a cruel business, not just because of the men who die or who are maimed for life, but because of the lasting effects on all the families for so many years to come.'

Leaving the memorial, they headed for the bus stop and travelled to Chorlton together, where they went their separate ways. Colette was still in Persephone's thoughts when she arrived home to Darley Court. She'd had an early start that day and it was teatime when she got there. After the delight of bumping into Colette at Southport Station, she now had the pleasure of finding Mrs Cooper and Mrs

Grayson with Mrs Mitchell, the housekeeper. She and Mrs Grayson had been friends for years and early on in the war Mrs Mitchell had arranged for Mabel to become Mrs Grayson's lodger, which, down the line, had led to Mrs Grayson becoming so dear to the railway friends.

When Mrs Mitchell bore Mrs Grayson away to talk about jam-making, Persephone chatted to Mrs Cooper.

'It's lovely to see Mrs Grayson here,' said Persephone.

'Which is your polite way of asking how she got here,' said Mrs Cooper.

Persephone chuckled. 'You've rumbled me.'

In spite of her laughter, Persephone recognised what a big thing it was for Mrs Grayson to be here. Lack of support at the time of a long-ago bereavement had made the poor lady cling to her home to the extent that eventually she had become unable to leave it. That was one of the reasons Mrs Mitchell had sent Mabel to live there – to do the shopping. After years of being confined within her own four walls, Mrs Grayson had gradually found the courage to make short journeys accompanied by a friend. Although she now often went to St Clement's church and church hall and to the shops and the hairdresser's in Chorlton, Darley Court was a long way for her to go. On previous occasions Cordelia or her husband had kindly paid for a taxi, but Mrs Cooper couldn't run to such a luxury.

'I thought we'd practise walking here, going a bit further each time while Mrs Grayson got used to it,' Mrs Cooper explained. 'It's not that far if you cut through Chorltonville. She has far more confidence these days. This is only our second practice run and she didn't want to wait any longer. She was determined to get all the way here today, so here we are. I'm very proud of her.'

'I hope we'll see more of her here in future,' said Persephone. 'Mrs Mitchell would enjoy that – and so would I. Talking of seeing people, I saw Colette today on Southport Station of all places.'

'She said at the breakfast table that she'd be escorting somebody to Southport,' said Mrs Cooper. 'How did she seem to you?'

'How d'you mean?'

Persephone used a casual voice but it took more than that to outfox Mrs Cooper.

'Since you didn't say she seemed fine, should I assume you have a reason for concern?' Mrs Cooper asked. 'I'm not playing games. Colette is upset and I'm worried about her.'

'You mean because of Mr Gordon?' replied Persephone.

'That's exactly what I mean. I promised Colette I wouldn't talk to anyone about it, but since you've obviously noticed it, I'm going to break my word because I do so want Colette to be happy. I wasn't at all sure about her starting a new relationship, but now he appears to have gone off the boil and I don't like seeing her upset.'

'But has he gone off the boil?' Persephone asked. 'Or did Colette misunderstand in the first place? That's more or less what she said to me.'

'And to me, but I don't see it that way. Not that I said as much to her.'

'How do you see it?' asked Persephone.

'I can't imagine Colette getting hold of the wrong end of the stick like that,' said Mrs Cooper. 'She's such a sensible girl. She's been through more than any of us can imagine and she's hardly likely to blunder into a new mistake, no matter how different the situation.'

'She's shy at heart too,' said Persephone.

'She's blaming herself now for misinterpreting Mr Gordon's courtesy and kindness,' said Mrs Cooper.

'Do you think there has been some sort of misunderstanding between them?'

'Who knows?' Mrs Cooper answered sadly.

Persephone gave her a hug. 'It makes me want to jump in feet first and do something to help.'

'I feel the same,' said Mrs Cooper, 'but we mustn't interfere. Colette wouldn't thank us for that. Even though she's confided her troubles, at heart she's a private person. She has to cope with this in her own way.' She sighed. 'And the rest of us will have to wait and see.'

Chapter Fifteen

Alison joined her friends in the buffet. She had prepared the vegetables and left them in a pan of water before she set off for work that morning. She was going to make tuna croquettes that evening, a dish from the treasured cookery book her chums had presented her with.

'Excuse us. Can we squeeze past you?'

The girls on the other side of the table shuffled their chairs forwards to let a couple of young women get by. Both of them had defined cheekbones, perfectly arched eyebrows and curled-under fringes worn high on their foreheads.

'Joan Crawford lookalikes,' Dot whispered. 'Not that I'm criticising. Far from it. Joan Crawford is a beauty.'

'And we all know how important it is for girls to look their best these days,' Fay added, 'not just for their own morale but also to lift the spirits of those who look at them.'

'It's like that Yardley advertisement about the subtle bond between good looks and good morale,' said Emily.

'Oh aye,' said Dot. 'I've seen those advertisements. "Put your best face forward." Isn't that one of them?'

'Beauty is all very well,' Cordelia remarked with a sigh, 'but I think I'd kill for a cake of really good soap like we used to have before the war.'

'That's only available to girls with a Yank for a boyfriend,' said Alison.

'And to her friends,' said Persephone. 'One of Miss Brown's land girls is engaged to an American and she keeps the other land girls in soap, nylons and sweets.'

Dot gave Margaret a nudge. 'That's what you need to do, love. Get engaged to a Yank and the rest of us will reap the benefits.'

'As it is, we're all making do with less and less,' observed Colette. 'What we do have is smaller than it used to be.' She laughed. 'Even bus tickets are smaller and thinner.'

'And men's ties,' added Cordelia.

'I had to cut the tails off Bob's good shirt to make a new collar and cuffs,' said Joan.

'My friend Lucy made herself a brassiere out of cheesecloth,' said Emily.

'Our Pammy made French knickers fastened at the side with buttons,' said Dot, 'because she couldn't find knicker elastic anywhere.' Then she laughed. 'And our Sheila has been using gravy browning to paint her legs to look like she's got stockings on, but the local lads yelled, "Hello, Oxo legs!" when they saw her.'

'Wearing trousers is a way to avoid bare legs,' said Margaret.

Cordelia pretended to be shocked. 'Remember how scandalous it was to wear trousers before the war.'

'There was one occasion when my brother took me for a spin on the back of his motorcycle,' said Persephone. 'I wore trousers and when we stopped at a café, we were refused service.'

'But now trousers are a badge of honour,' said Emily, giving her mother a glance loaded with significance.

'There's no need to look at me like that, Emily,' said Cordelia. 'It's your father you have to convince, not me.'

'I'll wait until I'm twenty-one if I have to,' said Emily.

'I sincerely hope the war will be well and truly over long before then,' replied Cordelia.

As the others discussed the possibility of the war finally coming to an end, Alison kept quiet. She wished she could reassure her friends but she couldn't utter a word about the supposedly peaceful stations that in reality had been developed into vast hubs with miles of additional sidings able to accommodate hundreds upon hundreds of wagons. Nor could she mention the ambulance trains that were being prepared, the thought of which sent a profound chill into her core, making her think of Alec and of the many thousands of deaths that were still expected to happen.

Dot laid a hand on Alison's arm. 'Are you all right, chick? You look stricken.'

Alison couldn't talk about the certainty of the coming invasion of Europe but she could talk about matters closer to home. 'Alec,' she said. 'Lydia. Everyone who has already given their lives. Everyone who is still going to get killed.'

'Now then, that's enough of that.' Dot's voice was gentle, not bracing, but it held a firm note too. 'The people who have given their lives did it for the rest of us so we can be free. That's what this war is about. Freedom.'

'I looked at the words on the station's war memorial recently,' said Persephone. 'Unity, strength, courage and sacrifice. It's so sad and sobering to think that the Great War didn't put a stop to all wars as it was supposed to, but maybe ours will. That's what we have to hope for.'

'Our freedom is what Lydia's Alec gave his life for,' said Emily.

'And Letitia,' said Joan, looking wounded at the thought of her late sister.

'And Lizzie,' said Dot. 'We'll never forget any of them.'

Joel was on duty all weekend so Alison decided to go to Lydia's on Saturday afternoon, calling in at Mum's first. Dad opened the door to her but Alison barely had time to kiss him hello before Mum practically bowled him aside and faced Alison, shoulders squared and eyes snapping.

'Did you know about this?' she demanded in an angry challenge.

'About what?' Alison asked in surprise.

'Did she tell you?'

'Now then, Janet,' said Dad. 'Let Alison get across the threshold, can't you? Come in, Alison. We've had a bit of an upset, as you can see.'

'Rather more than a bit,' Mum muttered.

'Whatever is it?' Alison asked as she entered the house. 'Is Lydia all right?'

'She's fine—' said Dad, and 'She's not thinking straight—' said Mum at the same moment, leaving Alison looking from one to the other in bewilderment.

'Will one of you please tell me what's going on?' She was starting to feel scared.

'She's joined up.' All at once, Mum was fighting tears. Her voice thickened. 'As if it isn't bad enough that she's lost Alec, now we might lose her as well. I can't bear to think of it.'

Now the tears flowed freely and Dad put his arms around her, looking across at Alison.

'Why don't you go round to Lydia's?' he suggested. 'She'd probably appreciate an opportunity to talk about it. She didn't get much of a chance when she came here to tell us.'

Alison nodded. She felt all quivery inside. She could understand why Mum was distraught but it was important to support her sister even though the thought of Lydia joining up and being put in harm's way made a sour taste fill her mouth.

She walked to Lydia's flat near the cricket pitch. Alec had been an ace bowler. Alison knocked and waited to be let in.

The door opened and Lydia eyed her watchfully. 'If Mum's sent you to talk me out of it, you're too late. It's all arranged.'

Alison didn't say a word. She stepped inside, put her arms around Lydia and held her for a moment. Alison could feel her bones.

'Let's go and sit down and you can tell me all about it,' Alison said softly.

Lydia led the way into the sitting room. 'You mean Mum and Dad haven't done that already?'

'All I know is that you've joined up.'

Lydia sat rigidly upright, shoulders sharp. 'Are you going to give me a hard time too?'

'I wouldn't dare,' Alison replied with a smile. 'Besides, what could I say or do that would compare with facing the wrath of Mum?'

Lydia's shoulders relaxed. 'That's true. Did she have a go at you too?'

'In your absence, yes. Thanks very much for letting me walk into the storm unprepared.'

Lydia grinned. 'At least you could honestly say you had no idea. Just imagine if I'd told you beforehand.'

'That's true. So you've joined up, then? But you're in a reserved occupation.'

'The war has dragged on for so long that the government is trawling through the reserved lists to find out who can be spared for the services. I'm joining the WAAF.'

Alison was impressed. The Women's Auxiliary Air Force were the girls who, among other things, had jobs in aircraft maintenance as mechanics, engineers and fitters, interpreted aerial photographs and worked in wireless operation.

'Alec would be proud of you,' said Alison and could see from Lydia's expression that this was the right thing to say.

'It's because of him that I'm doing it. It feels as if I'm taking over where he left off even if I won't be in the army like he was.'

'What job will you do?' Alison asked.

'I hope I don't end up being a clerk just because I've been one since I left school,' said Lydia. 'I'd like to do something different. Maybe a wireless operator or a barrage balloon operator.'

'Barrage balloons are very heavy to control, I believe,' said Alison.

'You have to learn about wind changes and how to fill the balloons and get them in the air,' said Lydia. 'But I don't know what job I'll be given until after I'm there.'

'It's a lot to take in,' said Alison.

'I don't see why,' said Lydia. 'Alec being killed – that was a lot to take in. This, me joining up, is nothing by comparison. It feels as if the rest of my life is going to be nothing by comparison.'

Chapter Sixteen

Walking home to Wilton Close from the bus terminus, Colette glanced over garden walls on Beech Road. There were vegetable patches a-plenty but what she was really looking for was flowerbeds. She had always loved flowers. One householder had kept a sunny corner for pasque flowers, their rich purple petals surrounding their golden centres. The neighbour's wall boasted a blanket of pretty aubretia in pale pink and violet while in another garden a splash of bright yellow delighted Colette's eye. She didn't know the real name for these tiny flowers that smothered their stems, but her mother used to call them egg-yolk flowers.

Colette experienced a pang of sorrow for poor Mother, who had died relatively young. She was only in her forties, but at least she had died believing that Colette was happily married to a man who would take care of her and wouldn't saddle her with the debts Colette's late father had left behind. Mother had never known the truth of her only child's marriage.

As Colette opened the front door, she inhaled the delicious scent of onion. Mrs Grayson had promised rabbit pudding for tea. Colette had always loved cooking, though it had taken Tony's absence to prove it. Before that, part of liking cooking had been being able to hide away in the kitchen. After Tony had joined up, though, Colette had discovered she really did enjoy it. It was said that preparing meals for one felt as though it wasn't worth the bother, but Colette had never thought that.

Even so, she enjoyed having meals provided for her. It was lovely to feel looked after. Not pretend-looked after, not controlled-looked after, the way Tony had treated her. What she received from Mrs Cooper and Mrs Grayson was warm-hearted, honest looking after that made her feel liked, appreciated and safe.

Mrs Grayson looked out of the kitchen as Colette took off her jacket and hat. 'Hello, dear. Good day?'

'Yes, thanks,' Colette answered. 'I escorted a mother whose two children were both in calipers.'

'Polio, was it? The poor lady. Poor children, too. Some folk have a lot to cope with. Are you hungry? Tea will be ready in twenty minutes.'

'Shall I set the table?' Colette offered.

'Margaret's already done it, but thank you for offering.'

Soon Colette, Margaret, Mrs Cooper and Mrs Grayson were seated round the table, where Mrs Cooper said grace.

'God bless the farmers and the land girls and especially the brave merchant seamen, who all work hard to keep the country fed. Amen.'

They chatted as they ate. For afters, Mrs Grayson had made bread-and-marmalade pud.

'I hope you put this recipe in Alison's cookery book, Mrs G,' said Margaret. 'It's delicious.'

That evening Colette and Margaret were to go to the pictures in Chorlton with Persephone and Miss Brown's land girls, whom they were going to meet up with outside. Shortly before they were due to set off, the doorbell rang. Colette opened the front door – and there was Mr Gordon. Colette caught her breath. Then her gaze went to the bunch of honesty he held, its white flowers shimmering against the grey-green foliage.

Mr Gordon cleared his throat. 'Mrs Naylor, I hope you don't mind, but I took the liberty of checking the records at work for your address. I, er – these are for you.'

He held out the flowers and Colette took them automatically. Behind her, the door to the front room opened.

'Who's at the door?' came Mrs Cooper's voice.

Colette looked round. 'It's Mr Gordon.'

'Well, don't keep him standing on the step, dear. Do come in, Mr Gordon.'

Colette moved to let him past. She shut the door behind him, feeling fluttery and caught out and ridiculously happy.

'Take your visitor into the front room, Colette, and introduce him to Mrs Grayson,' said Mrs Cooper. 'I'll just pop upstairs and tell Margaret you shan't be going with her to the pictures, shall I?'

As Mrs Cooper trotted upstairs, Colette pulled herself together and showed her unexpected guest into the front room to meet Mrs Grayson whose eyes gleamed with interest. Colette devoutly hoped Mr Gordon wasn't about to get the third degree.

Mrs Cooper reappeared. 'Colette, dear, why don't you two go into the other room so you can chat privately? And I'll put these in water for you.'

She tweaked the flowers from Colette's unresisting fingers

and gave her a secret push to get her moving. Before she knew it, Colette was in the dining room with Mr Gordon. With Mr Gordon! And he had brought her flowers. She could hardly string two thoughts together.

She sat down at the table but instead of sitting opposite her, Mr Gordon moved a chair to the end of the table so they faced one another across the corner. He couldn't have got any closer to her unless he had sat beside her and the fact that he had moved the chair felt very intimate.

'Mrs Naylor,' he said, 'I owe you an explanation and an apology.'

Oh. So that was it. He'd come to make sure she knew she'd been deluded to imagine he might like her. Being a gentleman, he was going to apologise as if it was his fault even though it was hers.

The door opened and in came Mrs Cooper, beaming, carrying a vase with the honesty. She produced a crocheted doily that she placed in the centre of the table and stood the vase on it.

'There,' she said. 'Don't they look pretty?'

Colette made an effort. 'They're lovely. Thank you, Mr Gordon. You shouldn't have.'

'I know what Mabel would say if she was here,' said Mrs Cooper. 'She'd say you must never tell a man he shouldn't have brought you flowers.'

As she left, closing the door behind her, Mr Gordon leaned towards Colette. Was he about to take her hand? Of course not. Stupid idea.

'To get back to that apology,' he said.

'There's really no need,' said Colette. 'If anyone should

apologise, it ought to be me. I've clearly put you in a bit of a spot. It's very generous of you to take the blame.'

'I'm not sure what you mean by that, but please let me say my piece. I've been planning it for some days. I want to get this right. It matters, you see. It matters very much.' Mr Gordon paused before adding quietly, 'You matter very much.'

Surprise flushed through Colette's body. Mr Gordon's words were so completely different to what she had braced herself for.

'That time when I asked you to go to the Worker Bee with me, I said I had to get back in an hour or so to meet someone,' said Mr Gordon. 'That wasn't true. I said it because I hoped it would make it easier for you to come with me. Being asked along for an hour isn't the same as an invitation with no specific ending. I thought – I hoped – that it would give you the confidence to accompany me. I thought it would seem as though you were simply helping me to fill a little time. I'm over-explaining. Nerves.'

Nerves? Now Colette really was confused. She couldn't imagine Mr Gordon feeling nervous. He was such a steady sort of man with a quiet assurance about him.

'The thing is,' he continued, 'asking you the way I did was a way of getting you to come with me without my having the fear of asking you properly and possibly being refused. It was a rotten thing to do and I'm ashamed of it. It was a way of taking advantage. It wasn't the act of a gentleman and I apologise.'

Colette's insides quivered. 'You wanted to ask me to go out with you?'

'Yes.'

When he didn't say anything else, Colette said simply, 'I enjoyed it.'

'Did you? So did I – very much.'

'But I thought you couldn't have enjoyed my company, because when I came to your office . . .' She swallowed, gulped more like, before admitting, 'I deliberately arrived at eleven o'clock so you would ask Mrs Lister for tea for two, only you didn't. You looked at her and I saw you shake your head, so then I knew. You'd only taken me to the Worker Bee because you had time to kill and I was making a fool of myself for hoping otherwise.'

'No,' Mr Gordon replied at once. 'It was my fault. I thought I was the one being a fool. A man my age . . .'

'What's age got to do with it?' Colette asked.

'I think anybody looking at the two of us would supply an answer to that.'

'You took me to the Worker Bee because you didn't feel comfortable asking me out properly and then you decided you were too old for me anyway. Now you intend to apologise and walk away. Is that it?'

'No,' said Mr Gordon. 'Far from it. I'm here to apologise and . . .'

'And what?' Colette prompted softly.

Mr Gordon glanced away, then looked at her and began to speak. 'You're a very kind person and I know from working with you that you're sensible and reliable.' He shook his head. 'Listen to me – sensible, reliable! I'm making a hash of this. What I really want to say is that on the trip with the children, and then when we went to the Worker Bee, we got along in a more personal kind of way. At least, it seemed to me that we did.'

'I thought so too,' Colette said quietly.

'Did you?' His expression brightened. 'Mrs Naylor, I like you very much. Do you think . . . ? That is to say, I hope . . .'

Colette tingled all over with a mixture of happiness and astonishment. Her original instincts hadn't played her false after all. 'Yes,' she whispered. 'I like you too.'

Mr Gordon bowed his head. When he lifted it, his eyes were shining. 'I've been hoping that we might – well – see something of one another, get to know each other.'

'I'd like that too,' Colette told him. 'Only . . . I'm married. I don't think of myself as married in any real sense after the way Tony treated me, but . . .' Something squeezed painfully inside her chest.

'But on paper, and in the eyes of the law, you are still his wife,' said Mr Gordon. 'I know that. Believe me, I've agonised over it. I don't want to put myself in the wrong. Nor do I want to let down my family. I don't want to place you in a difficult position either.'

'I'm already in a difficult position,' said Colette. 'I wouldn't want to drag you into it with me.' Her heart creaked, the happiness of moments ago swamped by cruel reality.

'And yet I do want to get to know you.' Mr Gordon spoke softly. He gave a light shrug. 'It might turn out that we're completely wrong for one another, though I seriously doubt it.'

'The last thing I want is to put you in a difficult position with your family,' Colette assured him. 'If your sister-in-law knew you were seeing a married woman . . .' She shut her eyes. This was far worse than being talked about in the street in Seymour Grove. 'I wouldn't want anyone to think ill of you.'

'And I wouldn't wish to compromise you in any way,' he replied. 'You were the innocent party in the breakdown of your marriage, but I'm sure you've been on the receiving end of the lion's share of the gossip.'

Colette nodded. The more she thought about it, the more obvious it became that they hadn't a hope of forming a relationship. She braced herself for the moment when Mr Gordon got up and walked away for good.

But he said, 'It doesn't matter how much I tell myself that we ought to go our separate ways. Something deep inside me refuses to do that. I have no right to ask you if you will spend time with me, but I'm going to ask you all the same. Will you give us the chance to get to know one another?'

She shared all his reservations and she hated the thought of putting their personal reputations at risk. Moreover, she desperately didn't want to hurt his family, especially Evie.

And yet – and yet –

'I'd like that,' she said softly, 'very much.'

Chapter Seventeen

It felt good to be back in Iphigenia's London house – though it had changed somewhat since Persephone's last visit. They were in Iphigenia's sitting room, where the central feature was the grand piano and one of the chintz armchairs was evidently the cat's favourite scratching-post. The furniture had been shunted around and one wall was now taken up by masses of boxes of fabric for bandages. Tomorrow the WVS ladies were due to descend on the house to measure and cut bandages for various types of injury.

Iphigenia had started with the Red Cross at the onset of war and had subsequently joined the War Organisation, which was based in Grosvenor Crescent and joined together the Red Cross and St John Ambulance. Iphigenia had taken to referring to her house as 'the stores' because it provided temporary accommodation for first-aid equipment. She had some girls living with her too. They were FANYs who, in spite of belonging to the First Aid Nursing Yeomanry, were actually attached to the Motor Transport Corps.

Iphigenia was as beautiful as ever. She wore her unusual silver-blonde hair scooped away from her face, which emphasised her elegant cheekbones, and the fitted bodice of her dinner dress showed off her figure. When she tilted her chin a fraction to blow out a stream of smoke, it was impossible not to admire the graceful line of her throat. Persephone too had dressed for the evening. She had always loved dressing up, and never more so than after spending a long train journey in a tweed jacket and rayon crêpe dress so as to have a sporting chance of arriving at Iphigenia's house uncrumpled. She'd had it drummed into her years ago that it was disrespectful to arrive at one's destination travel-stained.

She hadn't stayed here with her sister since before the war.

'That's how our lives are always going to be measured, isn't it?' she remarked. 'Such-a-thing happened before the war. I haven't seen So-and-So since before the war. Do you think we'll be saying it for years to come?'

'Bound to be,' said Iphigenia. 'For the rest of our lives, I shouldn't wonder. Undoubtedly it's what Ivor Novello will be saying. Poor fellow.'

'Foolish fellow,' Persephone corrected her. 'He must have known he had no business using those petrol coupons, so honestly, what did he expect?'

'Well, he's paying the price for it now,' said Iphigenia. 'How many weeks did he get?'

'Long enough to cool his heels.'

'And no privacy about it, either,' Iphigenia commented. 'Everyone knows what he did and it'll hang over him for the rest of his life. It just goes to show one should aim to live a blameless life. And if that isn't possible,' she added archly, 'then one should take care not to get caught.'

'Is that aimed at me?' Persephone kept her voice light and free of accusation.

Iphigenia tapped her cigarette on the edge of a marble ashtray. 'It wasn't, actually, but since you've brought it up, how is your handsome fireman?'

'He has a name, you know,' said Persephone.

'Of course he does. Forgive me,' said Iphigenia. 'Matthew Franklin.'

'Matt.'

'You never mention him in your letters,' said Iphigenia.

'I don't want to fan the flames. No pun intended.'

'You don't want me blabbing to Ma, more like.'

Persephone smiled. She couldn't help it. 'After the revelation in Clarinda's society column last spring, it's difficult to see how anything could possibly make the situation worse for Ma and Pa.'

Iphigenia's blue-grey eyes became serious. 'Things weren't easy for them after that – or for me, for that matter. The whispers, the knowing smiles. Worst of all, the friends who were positive that Clarinda must have got it all wrong. Darling, when I said you might indulge in a little fling, it should have gone without saying that I meant for you to be discretion itself.'

'It was never my intention to be written about in the newspaper,' Persephone replied with a touch of tartness.

'We just have to hope it won't be held against you for evermore,' said Iphigenia. 'It won't be forgotten, of course, but with luck, people will see it for what it is.'

'And what is that, exactly?' asked Persephone.

'A harmless wartime dalliance,' said Iphigenia. 'Lord knows, there are enough of them going on,' she added when Persephone was silent. 'I could tell you one or two tales about ladies of our acquaintance that would make your hair curl.'

Persephone was startled. 'You don't mean—?'

'Myself? Certainly not. I'm a respectable married woman. But I know of one titled young lady who could have her pick of the officers' mess but she has eyes only for a certain good-looking young private. After the war, she will naturally make an entirely proper marriage and nobody will be any the wiser.'

'Apart from the good-looking young private,' said Persephone.

'He'll return to his real life and never speak of it again,' said Iphigenia. 'It wouldn't be respectful.'

'It sounds as though you know exactly what is going to happen.'

Iphigenia nodded. 'I do, little sister. A wartime fling is like anything else. It comes with rules attached. One rule is that when the fling comes to an end, it is never referred to again.' She sat back, looking comfortable and serene. 'It becomes nothing more than a nostalgic memory.'

'And is that what you foresee for Matt and me?'

Iphigenia sighed softly, her serenity giving way to concern. 'It's going to be hard for you because everybody knows. One has to hope it won't be held against you.' She shook her head. 'One also has to hope your husband can shrug it off.'

Persephone couldn't tolerate it a moment longer. 'You've made it clear how you see things. Now let me describe how I see them. Matt is not a wartime fling. Do you understand me?'

Frowning, Iphigenia uttered a short, nervous laugh. 'Of course he is. What else could he possibly be?' Her expression altered and Persephone braced herself for anger or disdain, but Iphigenia's features softened. 'Persephone, darling, I know you have feelings for him but please don't misunderstand them. You're a good person and you have a warm heart, but don't let it run away with you. Don't let it fool you into believing that what you feel for your Matt is real and lasting. It can't be. It simply can't. You know that as well as anyone does.' Now disdain did enter Iphigenia's blue-grey eyes. 'If Matt Franklin has attempted to persuade you of anything different—'

'No, he hasn't,' Persephone cut in. 'Our relationship is purely something for wartime as far as he is concerned.'

'And what about as far as you are concerned?' Iphigenia asked.

'Oh, I know the rules. I'm well aware that we can't continue as we are – but that's what I'd like to do.' Persephone's voice dropped. 'More than anything else in the world, that's what I'd like to do.'

After a short silence Iphigenia asked, 'Have you said this to him?'

'No,' said Persephone.

'Good. Then don't. You mustn't give him ideas.'

'What is that intended to mean?' Persephone challenged her sister. 'I hope you aren't suggesting that Matt is with me because he intends to use the connection for his own benefit.'

'Well, really, how should I know what his intentions are? Pa would cut off your allowance on the spot, but you'd still have your godmother's money. That would be a fortune to a railway fireman.'

'Stop it!' Persephone exclaimed. 'Don't say such things. Matt is a decent man with morals and standards. For your information, he takes a certain amount of flack for being with me. There are comments about being with an upper-class girl, about his being my bit of rough.' Heat poured into her face, scorching her cheekbones. 'Is that how you think of him? As my bit of rough?'

'I'm positive that's the last thing he is,' said Iphigenia. 'I trust your judgement and I'm quite sure you wouldn't have stuck with him this long if there wasn't a lot more to him.'

'There is,' Persephone said with conviction. 'He won a grammar school scholarship but he ended up leaving there to join the railways. He had something called a privileged apprenticeship, which meant he was given two days off each week to go to technical college. Don't you see? He followed his heart.'

'What I see is that he surrendered the chance of grammar school qualifications and a respectable job,' answered Iphigenia. 'And before you say anything,' she added, quickly forestalling Persephone, 'I'm not implying that being a railway fireman isn't respectable. I'm sure he's as honest and hard-working as the day is long, but you can't tell me that by choosing to work on the railways he was putting his future wife and children first. You call it following his heart, but if you were to ask the family or indeed anyone of our acquaintance, they'd all tell you that he gave up the opportunity to gain academic qualifications and the possibility of a future in a professional position. He had the chance to go up in the world through his own academic ability, but he opted not to.'

'I admire him for it,' said Persephone. 'I know what it is to have a dream.'

'Oh, sweetie, you and your writing. It's not the same thing at all.'

'It's exactly the same,' Persephone replied.

'Now you're being ridiculous,' said Iphigenia. 'I'm sorry but it's true. You were born into an ancient family and you've grown up with every possible advantage. If it hadn't been for the war, you'd never have done a day's work in your life.'

'But I always wanted to,' said Persephone. 'I wanted to be a journalist.'

'But you didn't need to. That's the point, darling. You've never needed to earn your daily crust. If anyone had printed something you'd written, it would probably have been to curry favour with Pa.'

'Believe me, it wouldn't have curried any favour at all,' said Persephone. 'Pa was always against my writing.'

'Only because you insisted upon taking it so seriously. He wouldn't have minded if you'd treated it as a little amusement.'

They stared at one another. Persephone remembered when this visit had first been planned and how she had wanted to have a heart-to-heart with her sister. Well, here she was having it, only it didn't feel like much of a heart-to-heart. It was more of a battle.

'I owe you an apology,' said Iphigenia.

Tears of relief welled up behind Persephone's eyes. Had her words swept aside Iphigenia's preconceptions?

'I wish I had never encouraged you to have your fling with Matt,' said Iphigenia. 'You obviously have the wrong temperament for it and you've got yourself in too deep. I'm sorry for putting ideas in your head.'

'Oh.' It felt as though she had been dashed with cold water. 'That's not what I hoped you were about to say. I thought that maybe you were going to come down on my side.'

'Darling, I'm always on your side. Why do you think I'm saying these things? I'm trying to help you.'

'Trying to help me see sense, you mean.'

'Yes,' said Iphigenia. 'I don't deny it. Your feelings have run away with you and the last thing I want is for you to get hurt.'

'For the record,' said Persephone, 'Matt Franklin is not and never was a fling. I have never viewed him that way. We started out as friends and that grew into an attraction on both sides. If my family doesn't care for it, I have to tell you his family isn't exactly turning cartwheels either. Matt and I are both fully aware of the impossibility of a future together and we know that all we have is wartime.'

'The war will end,' Iphigenia said gently. 'Some people hope it might even happen this year, but Pa says it will be next year at the earliest.'

'I know,' said Persephone. 'And I do want the war to end – but I don't know where I'll find the strength to say goodbye to Matt.'

In a single graceful movement Iphigenia discarded her cigarette in the ashtray, rose to her feet and crossed to sit on the arm of Persephone's chair, slipping an arm around her shoulders.

'Darling, I know it's brutal for you,' Iphigenia said, 'and I wish to heaven I'd never encouraged you.'

'It's not your fault,' said Persephone. 'All you suggested was a fling and I knew I wasn't the sort for that. I could never get involved just for fun.'

'I can see that now,' Iphigenia said quietly.

'And I didn't get together with him because of anything you said. It was something that grew from our friendship. Our feelings for one another developed and strengthened until we realised how right we are for one another.'

Iphigenia pressed her lips together, her eyes dewy with concern. 'Don't bite my head off but wouldn't it be better to part company now? The sooner the better and all that.'

'Oh, but I can't,' Persephone exclaimed without needing to think about it. 'I don't want to. I want to cling on until the last possible moment.'

After a second Iphigenia said, 'I think I may regret asking this, but do you love him? I mean, truly love him?'

Persephone nodded.

'Does he know?'

'I don't know,' said Persephone. 'We never talk about things like that. One can't when the relationship is purely temporary.'

'Does he love you?' was Iphigenia's next question, still in the same soft voice. 'I know he can't say so, but you must sense if he does.'

'I honestly don't know for certain,' Persephone answered. 'Part of me wants him to, but another part doesn't want to put him through the misery.'

'You do understand that you can't see him again after the war?'

'Isn't that what I've just been telling you?' said Persephone.

'I know, but you might be entertaining mad thoughts.' Iphigenia spoke in a kind voice. 'That wouldn't do at all.'

'You won't tell Ma, will you?' said Persephone. 'She'd be appalled.'

'I won't breathe a word.'

'I'll know if you do because she'll lock me in the cellar and chuck the key in the Thames.'

'She would, too,' Iphigenia said with a smile. 'Oh, Persephone, what a rotten mess.'

'That's one way of putting it.'

'You shall have to be very brave when the time comes,' said Iphigenia.

'Don't worry,' said Persephone. 'I shan't let the side down.'

Chapter Eighteen

Wherever she went in London, Persephone thought of the descriptions she might have written had she been able to spend the war here as a reporter. The parks and squares had all long since surrendered their railings to be melted down for the war effort. Doorways were protected by sandbags and even if one ignored the rubble and signs of destruction, those buildings still proudly standing were tired and shabby beneath a coating of soot and grime.

'It's not as bad as it was,' Iphigenia said cheerfully. 'Plenty of repairs are under way these days, which makes it easier to cycle around in the blackout.'

'Don't tell me you've still got a battery for your bicycle-lamp,' said Persephone. It hardly seemed possible in these times of dire shortages. 'I can't recall the last time I set eyes on one of those. I've been steering with one hand and aiming a torch with the other.'

'Shame on you.' Iphigenia chuckled. 'I thought you were supposed to be the one with the imagination. A chum of Hugo's fixed me up with a small paraffin lamp that he clamped to the front of the old boneshaker.'

'No – really?' Persephone breathed.

'Absolutely,' Iphigenia confirmed. 'I leave a trail of smoke wherever I go.'

'I'm impressed.'

'You'd be surprised at some of the things I've had a go at since war broke out and I started doing my bit,' Iphigenia said airily. 'Providing shelter from air raids for the population of a city this size was a job and a half, I can tell you. The fleas had a field day. Would you care to know how to remove them from bedding? One simply pops in a hot-water bottle. That attracts them all to the warm spot whereupon one pats the area with damp soap to pick them up. Of course,' she added, 'that wouldn't work these days with soap rationing. No one would dream of using up their precious soap in that way.'

Persephone slept with Iphigenia in her double bed because every other available space in the house was occupied, including under the dining table. Persephone soon got to know the girls who bunked in the house. One of them had just come back from a few days' leave, bringing with her a bad case of what the others called 'Irish tummy.'

'It's because the food over there is so much richer,' Iphigenia explained to Persephone. 'They don't have rationing and shortages, so the food is more full-bodied, you might say.'

Another of the girls, Penny, was the younger sister of Caroline Reid-Rothers whom Persephone had been pally with during her first London Season. Caroline had married well from that Season while Persephone had spent the entire time dreaming hopeless dreams of Forbes Winterton and his smoky-grey eyes.

Penny was in the Motor Transport Corps.

'Mummy and Daddy are perfectly happy for me to be a

driver,' she said, 'because it's the officers who get ferried around.'

When they weren't driving or dancing until dawn, the Motor Corps girls worked in Iphigenia's ballroom, packing boxes of necessities to send out to POWs. They all adored Iphigenia for putting them up.

'It must be handy for your work,' said Persephone.

'It's handy for going to nightclubs,' said Penny.

That made Persephone look back at her own life. She had never been footloose like these girls. She had fallen deeply in love as a youngster and after that no one but Forbes Winterton would do. Yes, she had enjoyed London and the round of country-house parties, but for her there had never been any romantic thrill attached to any of it, only the desperation of longing to be seen by Forbes as something other than a little sister.

When she had finally been forced to accept that Forbes was never going to view her in a romantic light, she had surprised herself by becoming strongly attracted to Matt. He was the other half of herself. Knowing him, luxuriating in their closeness, had made Persephone see how empty the years had been when she had focused on Forbes. He had been a dream, nothing more.

In Matt she had a true friend, someone with whom to hold a serious conversation or to mess about with. They followed the war news together, enjoyed films and dancing, and were utterly comfortable in each other's company . . . except for the knowledge that their time together was temporary.

Persephone had been heartbroken once before when she

had accepted that she had to put Forbes behind her. In due course she would have to face up to losing Matt. How on earth was she to bear it?

Honestly, only Ma would arrive in London with a heap of wonderful evening gowns and two pounds of sausages.

'They're from the home farm,' she said, handing the packet to Persephone, 'for you to send to your friend Mrs Cooper.'

Persephone laughed in sheer surprise. 'Sausages!'

'Why not? They travel better through the post than liver does. And all the dresses are so you can have a good time while you're here.'

'Let's get them unpacked and have a look,' Iphigenia said at once.

The three of them spread out a couple of layers of evening gowns across Iphigenia's bed.

'All my lovely dresses from before the war,' sighed Persephone, running her fingers over the array of silk, velvet and crêpe-de-chine, a pearl-edged neckline here, a spotted-net overskirt there.

'And my cast-offs,' said Iphigenia. 'Oh, look at this silk taffeta with the waterfall frills down the side. I wore this again and again in '39. Do you remember what a scorcher that summer was?'

'I remember you giving this to me,' said Persephone, picking up a finely-striped silk dress with a high waistline, 'but I don't think I ever got the chance to wear it because of toddling off to Darley Court.'

'This one always suited you.' Ma lifted up a dress of

royal blue with a sunray-pleated skirt that flowed and flared as she showed it off.

'It's gorgeous,' said Iphigenia.

'Heavenly,' Persephone agreed, 'but I couldn't possibly wear it now, not with all those teeny-tiny pleats.'

'I suppose not,' Ma conceded. 'They're not exactly patriotic when new skirts aren't allowed to have any pleats at all. Still, there are plenty of other things you can wear. I assume you have some invitations lined up, Iphigenia?'

'A whole row of them on the mantelpiece,' said Iphigenia. 'I want Persephone to have the best time possible.'

'The war has lasted a long time,' said Ma. 'It's important to have the chance to wear a pretty dress and have a good time. It boosts the morale.'

Iphigenia was as good as her word. During the day Persephone either looked up old chums or helped Iphigenia with her war work, often breaking off to attend one of the popular lunchtime concerts held at the National Gallery. The admission fee of only one shilling meant that people from all walks of life could attend. Matt would approve, she knew.

In the evenings, the two sisters were taken out and about by Hugo's friends or his brother David to dinner or to a dance or the theatre. Persephone felt herself relaxing into her old way of life, enjoying the fun, the banter and the familiarity of having so much in common with her companions even if she hadn't met them before. They all hailed from the same sort of background.

Of course, it wasn't all fun in the evenings. There was this new round of ghastly air raids to contend with as well.

'You have to forget everything you remember about the old air raids,' Iphigenia warned. 'Do you remember how we used to talk about a bomber's moon?'

'It meant that the night sky was bright enough to attract Jerry over because he'd be able to see,' said her brother-in-law, David. He worked in the War Office. 'This time round, Jerry prefers the thickest darkness he can get, because our anti-aircraft guns are more effective now than they used to be.'

It was surprising how quickly Persephone adjusted to the sounds of explosions and gunfire while shrapnel fell like hailstones.

'Perhaps it's like riding a bicycle,' she suggested after a busy couple of hours in which the occupants of Iphigenia's house had all grabbed buckets of sand and water and rushed across the square to tackle incendiaries. 'Once one knows what to do, one simply never forgets.'

But there was something one absolutely could never get used to, no matter how many times it happened, as Persephone discovered the following morning when she went out to examine the damage from last night and found that in the road parallel to Iphigenia's, four houses on one side and five on the other had been squashed like pancakes.

'Probably thanks to a parachute-mine of large calibre,' said David.

Persephone shivered. This so-called 'little Blitz' was pretty awful. Please don't let the same thing happen in Manchester.

Ma came to Iphigenia's house one morning when Iphigenia was out at a meeting.

'I hope you're making the most of your stay in London, Persephone.'

'I'm having a fine old time, thanks,' said Persephone.

'I'm pleased to hear it,' said Ma. 'It's gratifying to see how easily you have fitted back in.'

'What do you mean by that?' Persephone asked. She employed a civil, good-natured voice but she felt a sudden need to take care.

Ma arched an eyebrow. 'You tell me,' she challenged.

'Very well. You meant it as an indirect way of criticising me for my relationship with Matt.'

'Precisely,' said Ma. 'Your father and I are never going to approve of it. One day you'll regret it. It will become the skeleton in your personal cupboard, the ill-advised dalliance that you couldn't resist during the war.'

'Ma . . .' Persephone started to say.

'You'll never escape from it, child,' Ma went on. 'It will always be there. In years to come, when you meet new people, whether it's at a garden party or a hunt ball or at supper after the theatre, there will always be somebody who'll look at you in a certain way and murmur to their partner, "Isn't she the one who . . . ?" How shall you feel about that? And how do you imagine your husband will feel?'

'If it's so very disgraceful,' said Persephone, 'maybe I won't have a husband. Maybe no one will take me on.'

'Don't speak to me in that way,' snapped Ma. 'I don't care for defiance.'

'I wasn't being defiant,' Persephone said. 'I was merely following on from your own remarks.'

'I suggest you consider your future carefully,' Ma advised. 'Life can be hard for spinsters, no matter what their rank in life. If you fail to marry, you'll end up one day having to live with Iphigenia or one of the boys. Is that what you want? And please don't tell me that you intend to support yourself by writing, because that certainly won't keep you in the manner you've been brought up to expect.'

'I have to say you don't paint a very rosy picture of my future, Ma.'

'You could have a rosy future if you so choose,' Ma replied. She said nothing more, just waited.

Knowing she was being manipulated but too intrigued to resist, Persephone said, 'Go on.'

'It's very simple,' said Ma. 'For years now, the old families have had to marry money in order to keep their houses and their estates going. Your father and grandmama and I have been talking. Grandmama has always intended to leave her money to you and Iphigenia, but she will leave the lot to you on condition that it goes into your marriage.'

Persephone stared. She could hardly believe what she was hearing. 'Like a dowry?'

'If you wish to call it that. After the war, there will be more families than ever in need of a financial boost.'

'To do up the house and put in central heating, you mean,' said Persephone.

'It's better to do it by bringing in a bride with money,' said Ma, 'than by flogging off the family portraits.'

'This is madness,' Persephone exclaimed. 'Quite apart from any other consideration, I wouldn't dream of grabbing Iphigenia's inheritance.'

'She's already agreed to it,' said Ma. 'You look shocked. Good. I wondered what it would take. And please don't take issue with Iphigenia for not telling you. She was sworn to secrecy. We all want the best for you, Persephone. This liaison with your railway fireman is beyond the pale and we are determined that you should not suffer because of it in the long term. Grandmama and Iphigenia are offering you a future that is appropriate and secure. Familiar as well, a continuation of the life you have always led.'

'But—'

'Don't refuse, child,' said Ma, speaking over her. 'Don't say anything. Give some serious thought to what you owe to the Trehearn-Hobbs name. Consider also the manner in which you wish to conduct the rest of your life. After all, I can't imagine you being content to live in a two-up-two-down in a Manchester back street – can you?'

Chapter Nineteen

As April merged into early May, the flowerbeds in which Colette had previously admired handsome pasque flowers and jolly egg-yolk flowers now housed elegant columbines in a range of pretty hues.

'My mother used to call them granny's bonnets,' said Mrs Grayson when Colette mentioned the columbines at home.

'The forget-me-nots are starting to appear,' said Mrs Cooper. Sadness flickered across her face. Was she thinking of Lizzie? But then she smiled once more. 'What can we expect in the garden this month, Margaret?'

'The seedlings have to be thinned out,' said Margaret, 'and Dad says the potatoes need to be covered over with earth in case of late frost. He'll be along regularly to lend a hand.'

'He's a good man,' said Mrs Grayson.

Colette nodded in agreement. A little thrill ran through her at the thought that she had her own good man now. They had been out together a couple of times, first to the pictures and then to a piano recital that was being held to raise money for a Salute the Soldier fundraising drive. There were a good many of those going on at the moment.

Mr Gordon had told her openly, 'I'd like to see you at every opportunity and sweep you off your feet, but I don't think that's right for either of us. We both have to be completely sure and in due course I will need my daughter and Dorcas – that's my sister-in-law – to see that I haven't rushed into anything.'

'I can understand that,' Colette had assured him. 'The last thing we want to do is upset any apple-carts.'

'I think it's better for you too if we take things steadily,' Mr Gordon said. 'Forgive me if I seem to be making your decisions for you.'

'I think you're right,' said Colette. 'This feels special and precious and I want to take my time.'

Mr Gordon had raised her hand to his lips.

'One day at a time,' he had murmured. 'We'll manage somehow. In the meantime, let's simply enjoy getting to know one another. I think we ought to move on to first names, don't you? I know you're Colette.'

'I'm not sure I'll ever be able to think of you as anything other than Mr Gordon,' Colette said with a smile.

'I hope you'll give Nathan a try at least.'

'Nathan,' said Colette, testing it.

'But only in private, of course,' he warned her. 'At work we'll still be Mr Gordon and Mrs Naylor to one another.'

Colette was happy with that. It was important to behave in a professional manner in the workplace. She also wanted to keep their fledgling relationship between the two of them. Not out of shame or anything of the kind but simply because she was a private person and she'd had more than enough of being pointed out and talked about after the court case against Tony.

She was happy to tell her friends, though. She knew how

much they cared about her and any questions they asked would be born of concern for her well-being, not out of grubby interest in the intricacies of her life.

In the buffet she took great delight in sharing Nathan's first name. Her friends' reaction was much the same as her own had been.

'I'm sure he'll always be Mr Gordon to me,' Dot said with a chuckle.

The others laughed too, echoing her words.

'Using first names sounds very promising,' Fay observed.

Colette blushed and smiled at the same time. 'We're taking things slowly but yes, it does feel promising. Actually, there is something I wanted to ask you all, if you don't mind.'

'Of course' and 'What is it?' were the replies as the others leaned forward, concentrating their attention on her. Colette looked around, seeing the concern in their eyes. She tipped her head back for a moment, closing her own eyes as gratitude filled her. How lucky she was to have friends like these.

'It's going to sound silly,' she began, 'but Mr Gordon – Nathan – asked if I'd care to go dancing one evening and I said no. I think I said it automatically, without even thinking.'

'Why?' asked Emily.

'Because I'm separated and separated wives don't go out dancing, not unless they want to earn themselves a certain reputation.' Colette looked at her friends, anxious to hear their thoughts.

'It sounds rather daring,' agreed Alison. 'It's one thing to attend a fundraising concert together. A pair of colleagues might do that quite innocently, but going to a dance has certain connotations.'

'Do you think I shouldn't?' Colette asked at once.

'I didn't say that,' Alison replied. 'I'm just warning you to be careful, though I'm sure you don't need to be warned.' She looked around the table. 'Sorry. I didn't intend to shut the subject down.'

'Nay, love,' said Dot. 'It's right to say what you think. That's what Colette wants – isn't it, chick?'

'Yes,' Colette confirmed.

'There are two things to consider here,' said Cordelia. 'One is, would you actually like to go to a dance? The other is . . . well, we all know what the other is.'

'Dancing first,' said Fay. 'Would you like to?'

'If I'm honest, I'd love to,' said Colette. 'I haven't been to a dance since before I ran away to London. I never really enjoyed going out dancing with Tony because I was always scared of doing something wrong. It always seemed that if I relaxed and took pleasure in the evening, Tony would pull me back into line.'

'He sounds a brute,' said Fay.

'Aye, love,' said Dot. 'He was a brute, but a very clever one, and none of us had the first idea what he was truly like and what our lovely Colette was suffering day after day.'

'I have a couple of suggestions if you'd like to go dancing,' said Fay. 'Or you could just tell me to mind my own business.'

'No, please,' said Colette, 'I'd like to hear them.'

'How about a tea-dance?' said Fay. 'That's a quiet sort of thing to do, not at all like going to a busy dance hall. Or we could all go out together to a dance, complete with husbands and boyfriends, and all dance with one another's partners.'

'That's a good idea,' said Alison. 'In fact, two good ideas.'

'All of us going out together might be like throwing Mr Gordon – Nathan – into the lions' den,' said Persephone.

'I'm not sure either of us is ready for that,' said Colette. 'It would – well, it would make us more official, if you get my meaning.'

'I can see that,' said Joan. 'You've kept yourself to yourself since Tony went away and you've hardly gone out at all other than to the pictures and the knitting circle.'

'That's true,' said Margaret. 'The simple fact that you're embarking on this new relationship is proof of how much it matters.'

'I've never been the sort to take relationships lightly,' said Colette. 'When I left school, my first job was in a factory where I was a packer. Most of the women were older than me by some years but there was another girl just a year older and she was always chopping and changing boyfriends. My mother used to say she got through them like a dose of salts.'

'That's a good one.' Dot laughed. 'I must remember that.'

'In a way I admired her,' Colette recalled, 'because she was so much more confident than I was, though at the same time I knew I would never want to be like her. I didn't want a string of boyfriends. I dreamed of meeting the right man and getting married.'

'And you ended up with Tony,' said Emily.

'More fool me,' Colette said ruefully.

'But now you have another chance,' Cordelia said. 'You're older. You've suffered. You've also shown great courage. If anyone had told me before the war that I would be comfortable for my daughter to associate with a separated wife, I would have laughed at them. But I am happy for Emily to know you, Colette, because I think you set a sterling example of moral strength. I admire you. We all do. Mrs Cooper thinks the world of you and I set a high value on her opinion.'

'Hear, hear,' echoed Alison.

Warmth crept into Colette's cheeks, but although she was embarrassed, she was delighted too, despite feeling sure she didn't deserve the fulsome praise Cordelia had heaped upon her.

'You said you used to dream of meeting the right man and getting wed,' said Dot. 'Might Mr Nathan Gordon be the right man? It's a blunt question but it has to be asked.'

'Is he the man for me?' Colette lifted her chin. 'I'd like the chance to find out,' she said, though in her heart she already knew the answer.

'If he is, chick,' said Dot, 'what about the future? There's still Tony.'

Dread touched Colette with cold fingers. 'Oh yes, there's still Tony. He might be away fighting overseas, but he is still very much here and a part of my life, no matter how much I try to tell myself otherwise. And I know the end of the war is coming. Everyone is hoping for it and I promise you I don't want it to drag on, but . . .'

'But Tony will come home,' Margaret said quietly.

'I won't go back to him,' Colette declared, 'no matter what he says or does to try to force me and no matter how he makes me appear in other people's eyes.'

'He could never make you look bad,' Emily said loyally. 'It isn't possible. You're a good person.'

'Bless you, but it isn't that simple,' said Colette. 'He was the one who was violent, but with his solicitor's help, he made it sound as if I deserved it. That's the thing about Tony. He always appears so reasonable, so plausible.'

Joan glanced around to make sure she couldn't be overheard by anyone at the neighbouring tables, then lowered her voice to ask, 'Will you seek a divorce?'

'Yes – and that has got nothing to do with Nathan and me,' Colette told her friends. 'It's what I need in order to feel safe, though how straightforward it will be, I don't know.'

'Tony's violence is on record,' said Cordelia. 'He can't worm his way out of that. The magistrate gave him the choice between going to prison or joining the army.'

'Aye, but this is Tony we're talking about,' said Dot. 'He won't make a divorce easy.'

A small shudder passed through Colette's shoulders. Dot was right. Colette remembered sitting in court and listening in horror as Tony had wrapped the magistrate around his little finger when he was in the dock for having beaten her up. Might he be able to employ the same cleverness to get the divorce refused?

Chapter Twenty

Alison and Joel met Mum, Dad and Lydia at London Road Station to see Lydia off. Mum was pale but determined, though the way she kept looking down at her gloved hands showed her nerves. Dad set Lydia's suitcase on the platform, then made a fuss of lighting his pipe while they all said their goodbyes.

'What time is the train due to leave?' Alison asked.

'Eleven-forty,' said Lydia.

'Perhaps you should get aboard and nab a seat.'

'Alison!' Mum exclaimed.

But Lydia didn't mind. 'Trying to get rid of me?'

'Of course not,' said Alison, 'but you know how the trains fill up.'

Joel peered through the window of a Ladies Only carriage. 'There are spaces in here. I'll take your case on board and ask someone to keep a seat for you.'

In spite of the sorrow and strain of the occasion, Alison felt a glow of pride. Joel's good-natured civility held its own special charm and whoever he asked would be happy to agree to his request.

'Have you got everything?' Mum asked Lydia.

'It's a bit late if I haven't,' Lydia answered with a grin.

Dad took his pipe out of his mouth. 'I would say, "Don't fuss, Janet," but I know there's no point.'

'I'm not fussing,' said Mum. 'I'm just—'

'Fussing,' Alison suggested.

Joel stepped out of the train onto the platform. 'All sorted.'

They all chatted for a while. It felt odd, pretending to hold a normal conversation when there was nothing remotely normal about this situation. Alison felt torn. Lydia wanted this and therefore Alison wanted it for her, but at the same time she hated the thought of her sister going away for no one knew how long. Damn this war. Not only had it wrenched Alec from them, but also it was taking Lydia away.

'Thanks for coming to see me off,' Lydia said to Alison. 'Joel too. I know you only get a day off together once in a blue moon and I'm sorry you had to spend it doing this. I hope you're going to do something nice afterwards.'

'We are, actually,' said Alison. 'We're off to the pictures this afternoon and then we're going to a tea-shop. Joel's good at making things special.' She stopped. Was that tactless?

But Lydia said in a normal voice, 'He's always considerate, isn't he? You're lucky.'

'I sometimes come home to find a bar of Cadbury's waiting for me or a pretty flower in the bud-vase you gave us as a wedding present.'

'The perfect husband,' Lydia replied with a smile. 'What else does he do for you?'

'He might bring me a cup of tea in bed. He's even been known to choose books for me if my shifts mean I can't get to the library.'

'He doesn't!'

'He does. He's good at choosing books I'll enjoy.' Alison's voice trailed away. Why had Lydia got her talking like this? The last thing she wanted to do was rub her sister's nose in it.

But Lydia pulled her close to whisper in her ear, 'Don't ever shy away from talking to me about your husband. Understand?'

'Yes,' Alison whispered back.

As the platform clock neared twenty to twelve, Lydia hugged Dad and had a few words with him, then she put her arms around Mum. After that it was Alison's turn for a final goodbye and they shared a tearful hug. Joel kissed Lydia's cheek and she climbed aboard to find her seat, squeezing between the passengers who were standing.

They waved through the window as the train got ready to go, then stepped back as it pulled away.

'Oh, my little girl,' said Mum.

'She'll be fine,' said Dad.

'I know,' said Mum. 'This is what she needs. I just wish that what she needed was to stay here.'

After they left the station, Alison and Joel went to the pictures, choosing *The Dancing Masters* in preference to *Northern Pursuit* because Joel liked Laurel and Hardy. First they watched the Pathé news, which included an upbeat report on the show that had opened the previous weekend on the last day of April, featuring the prefabricated houses that were intended to help solve the housing crisis the country faced after so much bombing. Alison watched in fascination.

Homes built not from bricks but from concrete panels bolted together! What would Dad think of that? Each one was a two-bedroomed bungalow, with a kitchen and bathroom next to each other so that all the pipes were in the same place. In the tobacco-scented darkness, Alison heard around her a few intakes of breath as people saw the bathroom complete with an adult-sized bath and a flushing toilet. A far cry from the outside lav and the tin bath hanging from a sturdy nail outside the coal shed.

When Alison and Joel left the cinema, Alison said, 'I know there's a huge need for more houses. So many people have been displaced and these prefabs are much quicker to put up than real houses, but do you really think this is what the future is going to look like? Prefab bungalows and Utility furniture.'

'The war has cost a fortune,' said Joel, 'and the country is deeply in debt. People need somewhere to live.'

'Of course they do,' Alison agreed, 'but how strange to live in a place like that instead of a proper house that has taken time to build by skilled craftsmen – bricklayers, plasterers, glaziers, plumbers.'

'There speaks the builder's daughter,' Joel said with a smile.

They went to a tea-shop near the Seymour Hotel. It was pretty tired-looking, but where wasn't these days? It was spotless and the middle-aged sisters who ran it were always pleasant. A lady in the queue at the fishmonger's had told Alison that the tea-shop had been a thriving concern before the war. Now the sisters made a couple of trays of rock cakes, carrot scones and eggless boiled cake each day and closed when they ran out.

Over tea and a scone each, Alison and Joel talked for a while about Lydia, expressing their hope that she would find peace of mind, then they moved on to Colette's situation.

'She says the age difference doesn't matter,' said Alison, 'and I suppose it doesn't as long as he's kind to her.'

'Trust is always going to be the most important thing for her from now on,' said Joel, 'after everything she went through.'

'Maybe his age makes her feel safe,' Alison suggested.

Joel laughed and his blue eyes twinkled, making him look boyishly handsome. 'You make him sound like Methuselah.'

'There must be twenty years between them,' Alison pointed out. 'And he has a daughter.'

'How old?' Joel asked.

'I'm not sure.'

'What I mean is, child or adult?'

'Child,' said Alison. 'His late wife's sister lives with them and looks after her.'

'Better than a grown-up daughter the same age as Colette,' said Joel. 'Her life is complicated enough without that.'

'She's hoping for a divorce but is worried Tony will put the kibosh on it.'

'But Tony was found guilty of assaulting her,' said Joel.

'He and his solicitor made it sound like she had driven him to the end of his tether.'

'Regardless of how Tony tries to manipulate the system in his own favour,' said Joel, 'the fact is there's going to be an explosion in the divorce rate when the war is over. All those marriages that would never have taken place in peacetime.'

'Like ours?' Alison teased him.

Joel shook his head at her. 'You know what I mean, you

wretched girl. All those marriages that seemed right at the time but weren't built on a firm foundation.'

Emotion rose in Alison. She and Joel had been severely tested before their wedding. It had been a difficult time, to say the least, but the result was that neither of them had any doubt about the solid basis on which their lives together were built.

'And then there are all the servicemen who are going to come home to find an extra child in the family,' said Joel. 'They'll have to make a decision: divorce the wife for infidelity or take on the child as their own.'

'Not an easy choice,' said Alison, recognising that in the past she would have been quick to pass judgement in such matters, but now she was more broad-minded and compassionate.

'The point being,' said Joel, 'that in a climate where divorce is suddenly much more common than it once was, Tony may well find it harder to get his own way. Even if he does manage to block a divorce, what will it achieve? Colette will never go back to him.'

'True,' Alison said thoughtfully, 'but it would stop her marrying someone else.'

'You think it's that serious with this new chap?'

'I don't think she's the sort for light-hearted dalliance,' said Alison. 'It breaks my heart to think of Colette not being free to marry again because Tony won't allow it. It makes my blood boil too.'

'She's lucky to have you on her side,' said Joel.

'I'm very fond of her and I admire her enormously,' said Alison. 'There was a time when I was horribly jealous of her because she appeared to have everything I longed for. I was desperate for Paul to propose and every time I looked at Colette I saw a happily married girl with an adoring husband. I couldn't have been more wrong. We were all wrong, but that was what we honestly believed at the time. We used to say how lucky she was to have such a devoted husband. If only we'd known.'

'She didn't want you to know,' Joel said quietly.

'The hardest part to think about is that she was so ground down that she believed everything Tony said to her. She thought she wasn't good enough. She thought she needed him to set her straight.'

'She's well and truly beyond all that now,' said Joel. 'She's her own person. Even if Tony causes trouble and heartache in the future, she'll always have her friends to support her. That counts for a lot.'

'Strong friendships make all the difference,' agreed Alison. 'That's why I had all those attendants at our wedding even though Mum was iffy about it to start with. The friends I've made in wartime have come to mean everything to me. Lydia worked mainly with women of Mum's age. There were other girls in the shipping office and she got on with them but she was never close to them the way I am to my work-friends.'

'Let's hope she makes some good pals in the WAAF,' said Joel.

'Fingers crossed,' said Alison.

If Lydia could build some staunch female friendships in her new life, that would help her to get through this dark time. Alison knew how much her own friends meant to her.

For Lydia to have friends who would become every bit as important was Alison's dearest wish for her sister.

Persephone couldn't make up her mind. Should she tell Matt what her mother had proposed? To do so would rub in the vast difference in their respective social positions and she wouldn't feel comfortable doing that. The last thing she wanted was to make Matt feel he wasn't good enough, even though he knew full well that this was the way her family viewed him. On the other hand, if she didn't tell him, that would make her uncomfortable too because she would be keeping a secret and that didn't sit right with her.

She didn't want to undermine their relationship in any way. What they had was all the more precious for being a temporary arrangement. Her family were appalled and now proposed to purchase her future respectability by dangling her in front of an ancient family who were in need of updated plumbing, fresh gilt on the family portrait frames and a new roof. Matt's family were also unhappy that he had embarked upon a relationship that by its very nature could have no future. True, it was only his mother who had said so outright to Persephone, but Persephone didn't fool herself. She knew that while Sergeant Franklin, Peggy and Jill were all perfectly sweet to her, they must be tearing their hair out at the thought of the sorrow Matt would face when she and he were finally obliged to separate.

Then there was the way in which many of their colleagues viewed their relationship. Persephone had never quite grown used to the knowing glances, the interest laced with a touch of scorn, the jokey remarks that didn't quite conceal criticism. She tried to rise above them because what else could she do? If she hadn't had the affection and support of her friends, life would have been much harder, though she knew that plenty of people would consider that her chums were doing her a serious disservice by lending her their support. They were helping her to live in a bubble – but so what if they were? Persephone's relationship with Matt meant the world to her and she wanted to make the most of it while she still could. That she was storing up deep unhappiness for herself in the future was something she was aware of but tried not to dwell on.

Happy for now.

It was more than many people had. Look at Lydia, losing the husband she hadn't seen since the weekend of their wedding back in 1941. In a state of utter despair, she had joined the WAAF.

Look at Dot, who hadn't set eyes on her sons since their brief leave after Dunkirk. Their wives hadn't had them at home since the spring of 1940 and Jimmy and Jenny were growing up without their fathers.

It was the same for Matt's sister Peggy whose husband was away serving his country, but in her case her children were away too. They had been evacuated back in '39. So had the sons of Joel's sister Venetia. So had the sons and daughters and grandchildren of tens of thousands of families.

When she pictured the difficulties in other people's lives, when she thought of their lengthy separations, Persephone knew how lucky she was to have Matt and she felt guilty for wanting more. She longed to ask him if he felt the same. When they had hit upon their happy-for-now arrangement, they had both known it was all they could hope for. Since then, had Matt grown used to it? Was it now all he wanted? Did happy-for-now suit him? Would it make him uncomfortable to know that their arrangement didn't make her happy the way it should?

The last thing she wanted was to make him uncomfortable – which brought her full circle back to the question of what Ma had suggested for her future. Should she share it with Matt?

The first time Persephone saw him after she came home, he didn't exactly greet her with open arms and she felt an internal quiver.

'Is something the matter?' she asked at once. 'You don't seem bowled over to see me.'

'I wasn't sure what to expect.'

'I don't understand,' Persephone said.

'You've been back in London, living the high life in a grand house, seeing your old friends.'

'Matthew Franklin,' said Persephone, 'I hope you're not suggesting what I think you're suggesting.'

Matt shrugged, which might have looked casual but his expression was earnest. 'I don't want to take anything for granted. I don't want to take *you* for granted. If you said that you've realised the time has come for us to part company, I'd understand.'

Persephone had to pause for a moment while she caught her breath. 'Why on earth would you think that? As a matter of fact, I had a lovely time and shan't pretend otherwise. I loved being with my sister in particular. And yes, I loved gadding about and having the chance to wear some posh dresses, but I'm glad to be back here and I'm glad to be back with you.'

Matt's smile lightened his serious expression. Persephone hooked her hand through the crook of his arm. She was dying to ask if it had been his mother who had sowed doubts in his mind but she refrained. After all, if Mrs Franklin had, then her action wasn't so very different from what Persephone's family had done in offering to provide her with a marriage safety-net after the war.

And that was the moment when she knew she wasn't going to tell Matt. There was nothing to be gained by it, but there was a lot to lose. It would create uncertainty and friction, bringing to the surface all the aspects of their relationship that had made them settle for their happy-for-now arrangement.

It would spoil things – and Persephone couldn't bear the thought of that.

Chapter Twenty-One

Alison dashed out at dinnertime to meet Mum, who had come into town to do some shopping. Not that Alison had time to go into Ingleby's and Lewis's with her. They were meeting for a swift meal before Alison would have to hurry back to work. It was worth it to spend a little time with Mum, who was still fretting over Lydia.

Alison entered the British Restaurant where Mum already had a table and had ordered for them both to save time. The British Restaurants were popular, offering as they did tasty and nutritious meals at reasonable prices. At the start of the war they'd been known as Community Feeding Centres, which had made them sound like charitable institutions. Then Mr Churchill himself had renamed them.

Wartime etiquette said that you could have two courses, either a starter and a main course or a main course and a pudding.

Alison kissed Mum and sat down.

'I've ordered fish cakes for one of us and corned beef hash with onion sauce for the other, followed by baked fruit pie and elderberry roly-poly,' said Mum. 'I'm happy with either combination so the choice is yours.'

Mum was dressed in the WVS uniform of two-piece herringbone tweed suit, hat and handbag. She looked smart but there was no disguising the tiredness around her eyes. She was obviously having disturbed nights because of Lydia. Even so, she did look better than Alison had seen her for a while.

'I've had a letter from Lydia,' said Mum. 'She wants me to share it with you so she doesn't have to write the same things all over again.'

Ah, so that was why Mum looked brighter. 'How's she getting on?'

'She sounds busy,' said Mum. 'Here, read it for yourself.'

Alison took the letter eagerly. Lydia was now in the WAAF camp near Gloucester, having been taken there in the back of a lorry with a load of other recruits. She described big wooden huts around the edges of a parade ground and being woken up by a tannoy early every morning. All the new girls had had a medical examination upon arrival.

'I don't like the sound of the nit nurse,' said Alison.

'I suppose they get all kinds of girls,' said Mum.

'They've all had an intelligence test as well,' said Alison. 'Lydia will have done well in that.' Then she laughed as she read about the kit which included two pairs of corsets.

'They aren't allowed off the camp at all,' said Mum. 'Their only contact with the outside world is letters.'

'Or by telephone,' said Alison, getting to the relevant bit. 'There are several telephone boxes by the camp entrance.' She read on. 'They have to go on route marches the same as the men and they'll have a passing-out parade.' When she came to the end, she looked at Mum. 'It all sounds promising, don't you think? Has it made you feel better?'

'Yes, it has, though I'd rather she had stayed at home, of course.'

'This is what she needs, Mum,' said Alison. 'It will give her a new purpose. I don't like the thought of her being away from home any more than you do, but she has to do what's right for her and we must respect that. Goodness knows how I would cope if anything happened to Joel. I admire Lydia for doing this.'

'But where will it lead?' asked Mum with worry in her eyes. 'She joined the WAAF, for pity's sake. Who knows what danger lies ahead?'

Alison longed to allay Mum's fears by telling her about the coming invasion of Europe, which she devoutly hoped meant that Lydia wouldn't be put in harm's way, or if she was, that it wouldn't be for all that long. But she couldn't say a word.

Persephone felt a swell of anticipation as she got ready to set off. Today was the day, or rather tonight would be the night, when she was to travel aboard the munitions train. She would be with it for the first stage of its journey, from Manchester to Leeds. After that, another crew of driver, fireman and guard would take over and the bombs would be taken from Leeds down to Peterborough and then into East Anglia for distribution to the American air force bases.

Persephone was deeply grateful to Matt for organising this for her. She knew he must have had to jump through a lot of hoops and also that someone would have looked carefully into her background before giving permission. The simple fact that she had been permitted to know the eventual destination of the munitions showed how much she was being trusted.

Something inside her wanted to tell her parents. Of course, it was completely out of the question, but if they could know of this, it would show them that her ambition wasn't a silly, half-baked, attention-seeking fad but a serious vocation to which she was truly committed.

She intended to get as much as she could out of tonight's expedition. Yes, it was important to write about the munition train's journey, but that article couldn't be published until she received permission. In the meantime she could write a rather romantic piece – not lovey-dovey romantic, but romantic in the nostalgic, whimsical sense – about night-time on the station concourse.

She arrived early at Victoria Station. The station never slept. Even in the gap between the last train and the milk train, there were always porters ferrying goods to and fro, cleaners sweeping up and Royal Mail bags being dropped off and picked up.

Persephone was going to mention some of that as the background to her article, but mainly she intended to concentrate on the night-time passengers. She spent a while walking around, observing carefully. She peeped into the waiting-room, where some soldiers lay stretched out sound asleep on the long wooden benches or else sat at the table with their heads on their arms like little children putting their heads down for a nap after dinner. How young the lads looked – and what lay ahead for them?

Then there was the young woman sitting on one of the benches on the concourse. She was good-looking and wore a blue-grey two-piece suit with a dainty hat trimmed with an organdie flower. A cardboard suitcase stood beside her.

She held a Penguin paperback in her hands, its green and white cover showing it to be a crime novel, but she clearly wasn't concentrating on it. She kept looking up and glancing around as if waiting for somebody. Who? A man? The girl was well-dressed. Were they going to elope?

Persephone smiled to herself. Nanny Trehearn-Hobbs always used to say that her imagination would get her into trouble one day, but there was no harm in this sort of speculation. If *Vera's Voice* or another magazine picked it up, this would be an easy, enjoyable piece that would make readers feel comfortable and intrigued at the same time. Everybody had looked at strangers and wondered about them at one time or another and this article would invite readers to do just that.

Persephone transferred her attention to a tall man in a rainproofed overcoat with wide lapels, button-trim on the cuffs and flaps on the pockets, all signs of pre-war fashion. Beneath his brown felt trilby, his features were narrow and severe and he wore a moustache. He was smoking, inhaling hard and blowing out smoke in an energetic stream. His cigarette wouldn't last long at this rate. Judging by the spent stubs gathered around his feet, he had already made serious inroads into his packet. His gaze darted hither and thither, sometimes resting intently on the information board at the head of platform 6, as if he could conjure up fresh information through sheer force of will.

What was the reason behind his concentration? It was tempting to make up a line or two about his having nefarious intentions, but that wouldn't be conducive to the atmosphere Persephone wanted to create for her article.

She shifted her attention to a tired-looking woman of thirty or so, who sat with a girl of six or seven asleep on her lap. Now and then the woman dropped a kiss on the child's head and hugged her more closely.

Over by the ticket office, a haggard man with haunted eyes and a twitch ducked his head and tried not to engage with a pair of kindly WVS ladies who were trying to persuade him to let them accompany him to a hostel.

Persephone's heart reached out to the man, who was clearly deeply troubled if not damaged. What had he experienced that had left him this way? And how many others were in the same boat? Stiff upper lips were important and it was one's duty to be brave and to cope with whatever was thrown at one, but that didn't mean that those who eventually crumbled under the strain were cowards. It meant that after years at war, they had reached their personal limit.

Persephone fiercely hoped that such people would be dealt with compassionately and that they would receive the support they deserved. The Great War might not have been the war to end all wars, but it had led to a better understanding of the emotional and psychological impact of war on the mind. All those poor blighters with shell shock.

Persephone respectfully removed her gaze from the troubled individual and the WVS ladies. There wasn't a place for the man in her nostalgic article and she felt guilty for wanting to write such a piece. It suddenly seemed inappropriate. She thought for a few moments before reassuring herself that her article, should it be published, would have its own tiny part to play in entertaining the nation's readers. With the war having gone on for so long, everyone needed to be able to escape into a world of fiction now and then. And her article, anchored as it would be in real life accompanied by some harmless speculation suggestive of personal stories, would be easy for people to relate to. Who could say? Maybe in its own way, it might even provide a little solace.

Colette and Nathan sat in the cinema's tobacco-smoky atmosphere. They had watched the newsreel and the supporting film, then the lights had gone up for the interval. The aisles were packed with people queuing up to reach the front and buy cigarettes or tubs of ice-cream from the usherettes who wore trays of goods around their necks.

When Nathan had offered to buy ice-cream, Colette had declined.

'I'd much rather sit here with you and talk.'

'That's nice to know,' he replied.

In front of them, a young man in a naval uniform lifted his girl's hand to his lips and kissed it. Colette and Nathan glanced at one another.

Colette smiled. 'Sweet,' she murmured.

'Very,' he agreed.

'It makes me realise how much I'd like us to be free to do that in public.' Colette's voice was barely above a whisper. She couldn't have spoken any more quietly had she been sharing a war secret.

'I know,' Nathan said equally quietly. 'I wish it too.'

'It's all right,' Colette reassured him. 'I know we can't. Just in case.'

'I liked holding you in my arms when we danced at that

tea-dance.' Nathan gave a wry smile. 'But then we had to dance with all those other people as well. Just in case.'

'It was worth it.'

'Bless you for saying so. I sometimes feel scared that you'll decide I'm not worth the trouble.'

'I'd never think that,' said Colette. 'I worry sometimes that you might think it.'

'Never,' Nathan declared.

They smiled at one another. Seeing the warmth in Nathan's eyes, Colette felt her anxiety slide away – for the time being, at least. The truth of her situation hit her, as it did sometimes. She found such pleasure in Nathan's company, yet she was aware the whole time of her status as a married woman and his as a respectable family man. They both knew all too well the importance of treading with care. They were keen to be together and get to know each other, but they could never forget the intricacies of their position. Colette was married and that could rebound on them both.

It was important to give themselves time to decide if they definitely wanted a future with one another. If it turned out that they didn't – and this didn't seem at all likely to Colette – then the discretion of their current arrangement would enable them to ease away from one another with no harm done to either their own reputations or to Nathan's family.

The main thing when they were together was to enjoy each and every moment. Nathan was everything Colette could have wished for in a man. He treated her with kindness, thoughtfulness and respect. She trusted him, knowing he would never play games with her as Tony had.

He had told her about his late wife, Lilian, who had died of cancer, far too young.

'She was a lively character, great fun,' he'd said, 'and she adored being a mother. Before Evie was old enough to go to school, Lilian used to spend all day playing with her and then do her housework in the evening after Evie had gone to bed.'

'She sounds like a wonderful mother,' Colette had remarked, impressed.

'She was,' said Nathan. 'It was a great loss for Evie. Well, it's a major loss when any child loses a parent, but especially so for Evie because of all the time and attention Lilian had always lavished on her.'

But when Colette had asked about Dorcas, Lilian's sister, who now acted as Nathan's housekeeper, he had drawn back.

'I don't mean to be mysterious, but I'd prefer not to discuss her. It wouldn't sit right with me, not when she doesn't yet know about you.'

Colette accepted that. It supported her belief that Nathan would always do what was right. The loving and humorous way he spoke of Lilian, and his respectful attitude towards Dorcas, made her believe that she herself would always be safe in his care.

'Miss Trehearn-Hobbs? I'm Jeanette Westwood. Fireman Franklin sent me to get you. I'm the train guard.'

'How do you do?' Persephone greeted her. She glanced at Jeanette Westwood's left hand. 'Mrs Westwood.'

Jeanette Westwood was in her thirties, with a narrow

face, pointed chin and blonde hair that had been curled a bit too tightly frothing out from beneath her smart peaked cap with GUARD on the front. Her railway buttons gleamed on her jacket and she wore trousers, which almost all the lady-guards did from choice. It was more practical.

Mrs Westwood gave Persephone a nod. 'This way.'

As they approached the entrance to the platform, a gentleman stopped them.

'Excuse me, but that's the platform for Leeds, isn't it? I've got a ticket but I missed the last train.' He smiled, inviting their understanding. 'I couldn't get on with you, could I?'

'I'm sorry, sir,' said Mrs Westwood. 'It isn't a passenger train.'

'There's space in the guard's van, surely? And you're taking this lady with you.'

He indicated Persephone, who, dressed in a skirt and blouse with a linen jacket and a beret, didn't look like a member of staff.

'Go on,' the man encouraged Mrs Westwood. 'You'd be getting me out of a frightful hole.'

'I'm sorry, sir,' Mrs Westwood said again. 'No can do.'

She set off purposefully, leading Persephone through the barrier without a backward glance. Victoria Station's platforms were all beneath its vast canopy and as a rule dim lighting was permitted at the end of each platform closest to the concourse but on this occasion even that wasn't allowed.

'So that it's difficult for anyone on the concourse to make out our train in detail,' Mrs Westwood explained. 'Mind you, if they've got half a brain, they'll know what we're carrying.'

Persephone looked at the long line of wagons with the loco at the front. Every wagon was covered by a tarpaulin, the items beneath creating flat shapes in some cases, humped in others.

'Is there time for me to walk along the platform?' Persephone asked.

'Your boyfriend's getting the train ready, love,' Mrs Westwood replied briskly. 'He hasn't got time to talk to you.'

'I know that,' said Persephone. 'I only meant that I'd like to count the wagons.'

'Twenty-seven, loaded with two hundred tons of bombs and associated pieces – detonators and what have you.'

Persephone was surprised. 'You're allowed to know the details of the cargo? When it's munitions, I mean.'

'I'm the guard. It's my job to know everything about the train.' Mrs Westwood's eyes twinkled. 'Mr Gibson and Mr Franklin might think the train belongs to them, but I know it belongs to me.'

'Would you like me to get straight aboard?' Persephone asked as the two of them came to the guard's van, which was situated to the rear of all the wagons. She knew Mrs Westwood had to see the driver, Mr Gibson, before they set off. Persephone didn't want to make a nuisance of herself, especially after Mrs Westwood's remark about Matt being busy.

'No, you can come with me.' Having made her point, Mrs Westwood was apparently happy to unbend.

Persephone walked alongside her up the platform. She was acutely conscious of the contents of all the wagons. Here she was calmly walking past bombs that were going to flatten parts of Germany. Even after four and a half years at war, it was still a lot to take in.

When they drew level with the loco, Persephone stood back while Mrs Westwood climbed onto the footplate and spoke to Mr Gibson. After a minute she descended, giving Persephone a nod that suggested she approved of the manner in which Persephone hadn't attempted to push herself forward. Persephone smiled to herself. As if she'd come here to ogle Matt!

They climbed aboard the guard's van. Mrs Westwood produced a large pocket watch, which she consulted a couple of times in between writing in her logbook.

'I have to record the driver's name and other details about the train,' she explained.

One more glance at the pocket watch and she descended onto the platform, where she blew her whistle to gain Mr Gibson's attention. Then she stepped back up into the guard's van once more, leaning out to wave her green flag. In reply Mr Gibson blew the train's whistle, after which Persephone heard the loud hissing sound that meant clouds of steam were being pushed out of the lower part of the front of the engine. Then came a great rushing sound and Persephone pictured the huge puff of steam bursting forth from the funnel. The instantly recognisable *puh . . . puh . . .* sound started, slowly at first, and the couplings between the wagons creaked and protested as they stretched. The train gained momentum and pulled out of the station.

Chapter Twenty-Two

They were half an hour or so into the journey. Persephone and Mrs Westwood had talked for a while but Persephone sensed that her companion wasn't really the chatty sort so she fell silent. After all, Mrs Westwood was doing her a massive favour by permitting her to travel in the guard's van. She was also conscious that Mrs Westwood probably hadn't been given a choice in the matter.

Presently Mrs Westwood said, 'I don't really understand how you're supposed to write about this. Being stuck in the guard's van with the blackout blinds pulled down doesn't seem as though it'll make an exciting article.'

'I'll write about it in terms of the driver's and fireman's jobs,' Persephone explained. 'How they have to know their route inside out even in the pitch dark. How they have to know the location of every bend in the track and where every gradient begins and how steep it is. And tonight all this is being done while hauling twenty-seven wagons loaded with two hundred tons of explosives.'

Mrs Westwood nodded. 'It's a big responsibility.'

'It is,' Persephone agreed.

After a while Mrs Westwood offered, 'If you like, you can raise one of the blinds and pull down the window so you can stick your head out. Then at least you'll be able to say you saw the loco pulling the wagons.'

'Oh, that would be wizard,' said Persephone. 'Thanks! Not that there'll be much to see in the blackout,' she added with a laugh.

She jumped up. Mrs Westwood extinguished the dim lighting inside the van and Persephone released the blind over the door. The guard's van had two doors, a set of double-doors through which all the luggage and parcels were brought aboard, and an ordinary door with a window in its top half. The blind rolled upwards and Persephone drew the window down.

Air rushed in, snatching her breath. Tossing her beret behind her rather than have it whisked from her head, she leaned out only to pull herself back with an exclamation as sparks shot past her face. Aside from the surprise, she thought nothing of it, assuming they must come from the loco's fire-box.

Placing her hands on top of the lowered window, she leaned out as far as she could, turning her face towards the front end of the long train. This time when her breath caught, it had nothing to do with sticking her head out of the window. It was pure shock. Her breathing stopped dead, clogging her throat.

Several of the wagons in the centre of the procession were on fire. Flames surged forth and streamed backwards in the powerful current of air, putting the wagons behind in danger. Persephone's heartbeat raced as she pulled her head back inside the guard's van and stared at Mrs Westwood.

'The train's on fire.'

'What? Let me see.'

Mrs Westwood thrust her aside, leaned out, swore, then stepped backwards. Her mouth had dropped open and her eyes were wide, almost bulging.

'What do we do?' Persephone asked.

Mrs Westwood snapped her mouth shut. Her jaw set and she nodded curtly. 'I think they've realised on the footplate. The train is starting to slow down.'

The train whistle sounded.

'That's to alert me,' said Mrs Westwood.

Gradually the train slowed.

'They'll need to take it very steady,' said Mrs Westwood. 'Any sudden jarring could cause an explosion.'

Persephone stuck her head out of the window once more. The smell of flames and smoke whipped past her. As the train's speed decreased, she screwed up her eyes, peering intently.

'I think we're coming to a village,' she said, making out a large expanse of deeper darkness.

Dear heaven, if the munitions load went up now . . .

The train drew alongside a station platform and eased to a halt. Persephone knew it was essential to do so without the familiar jolt at the moment of stopping. She held her breath, her heart beating hard, beating so loudly that it was all she could hear. But she was still alive after the jolt so the train hadn't exploded.

Persephone threw open the door but before she could jump out, Mrs Westwood hauled her back.

'Always look first,' said the guard.

She was right. The train was too long for the platform and Persephone would have launched herself into thin air and probably broken her ankle when she landed. Instead of jumping out, she turned round and climbed down, holding on tightly. Mrs Westwood followed and the two of them ran alongside the safe wagons towards the platform, hurrying up its slope. It wasn't what Persephone thought of as a proper platform but an old-fashioned one with wooden planks.

Matt and Mr Gibson were already out of the loco and were working to uncouple the wagons behind those which were ablaze. Close beside them, the fire roared as it stretched up into the dark night.

Persephone and Mrs Westwood ran towards the men.

'That's it.' Matt stepped back, rubbing the back of his hand across his brow, his cap getting shoved askew in the process. He was breathing hard and his face was streaked with grime but he exuded determination and focus.

'We're going to tow the burning wagons away,' said Mr Gibson.

'You can't!' Mrs Westwood exclaimed.

'Well, we're not leaving them here to blow this place to kingdom come,' Mr Gibson retorted.

Matt caught hold of Persephone's hand for one moment, just one single moment, then he let go, leaving it suspended in mid-air as he ran with Mr Gibson back to the footplate. Persephone felt as if she was weighted to the spot. A chilly sensation started high up inside her chest and trickled inexorably all the way down through her torso, reaching into every corner, and then down through her legs to her feet.

'They'll take the wagons into the countryside and abandon ship,' said Mrs Westwood. 'Come on! That must be the stationmaster's house over there.'

Before they could move, a man with an overcoat over his striped pyjamas came running along the platform.

'Good God, what a thing to happen. This is my station. I've telephoned through to the line controller to warn him – and I've sent for the fire brigade.'

Persephone's gaze was glued to the flames leaping upwards towards the sky as the train drew away. Then it rounded the gentle curve at the foot of a low hill and vanished from sight.

'If they can get the train half a mile further . . .' said the stationmaster.

A colossal explosion rent the night. The earth vibrated and the waiting room's windowpanes fell out and shattered a split-second before the front wall collapsed. In the same moment the planks beneath Persephone's feet rippled, pitching her and her two companions forwards. A reverberation started in Persephone's ankle-bones and raced upwards through each bone in her body as if every single one of them wanted to disintegrate. Her ears were crammed solid with a vast blankness, then they popped painfully.

Hauling herself upright, she dragged one foot in front of the other along the ruined platform. Planks gave way beneath her feet and she staggered and hurled herself forwards. As she fell she seemed to move in slow motion like in a dream, but the hard slap with which she landed was real enough. By the time she reached the end of the platform, her limbs had loosened.

She ran.

Persephone stumbled along as fast as she could beside the railway line. The earth around her was all churned up and she seemed to breathe in flakes of grit and soil. She floundered her way around the bend of what had previously been the hill behind which the train had disappeared a minute ago . . . an age ago. Now the hill was a giant splatter of earth against a backdrop of flames.

Lurching and staggering, gasping for breath, Persephone went on. Her arms and legs were pumping as hard as they could while her mind was frozen with horror. The scene opened up before her and her knees crumbled like Lancashire cheese, bringing her sinking to the ground.

The earth had turned itself inside out. The massive loco was on its side, all its motionwork on display, bringing forth a thought in Persephone's shocked brain: she had never realised before how much elbow grease Margaret must have to put in. The coal-tender, in spite of its heftiness, was deeply buckled and coal had spilled everywhere. The wagons, some on their sides and some end-up, were scattered. Shredded tarpaulin, lengths of metal, buckled couplings and uprooted trees completed the picture.

Adrenaline swooshed through Persephone's system, bringing her to her feet in a fluid movement. She plunged forwards. Only one thing mattered now. Only one. Only one.

She had to find Matt.

In the other bed, Margaret slumbered soundly, but Colette lay awake. She had slept earlier but then she'd woken up and had been lying here ever since. One moment she would snuggle down, feeling all happy and warm at the memory of being in Nathan's company; then in the next moment, she would find herself stiffening as she pictured the path that lay ahead of her.

Tony.

Everything came back to Tony. The prevalent belief was that the war was now entering its final stages. Sooner or later Tony would come home for good. What then?

Divorce. It had to be divorce. Colette had known that for some time. Even if she hadn't started to feel attracted to Nathan, she would still want to get divorced. She needed to be free from Tony, to remove herself from his power, and divorce was the only way. Faking her own death hadn't done it; nor had running away and starting a new life in London under an assumed name. Even taking him to court for his brutal attack on her hadn't provided her with freedom, despite Tony's having been found guilty.

It was said there were going to be many applications for divorce when the war was over. Would the courts show leniency and understanding towards all those couples who had rushed into marriages that would never have taken place in peacetime? Presumably a great many of those couples would have made a joint decision to end their union, which would make it harder for the courts to hold out against them by denying the divorces. Perhaps there would be so many such applications that it simply wouldn't be worth the law's while to drag every couple through drawn-out proceedings.

But that was the couples who jointly wished to separate, which was far from being the case with Tony. For the Naylors, the wish for divorce was going to be entirely one-sided. Colette knew that Tony would fight her every step of the way. What if the judge applauded Tony for his efforts to save his marriage and refused to entertain Colette's request? The mere thought brought the sour taste of dread into her mouth.

All the same, she had to do it, she had to face it, no matter how hard it was. She couldn't remain married to Tony. Even separation wouldn't be enough. She needed the legal protection of being divorced. She had to shake off Tony's hold over her.

Lying in the darkness, she thought back to how Tony and his clever snake of a solicitor had manipulated matters when he had been up before the magistrate for assaulting her. He'd been charming and plausible, full of sorrow for what he'd done to her, and the magistrate had swallowed every word.

What if Tony brought that plausibility to their divorce proceedings?

In the meantime, what of her and Nathan? Would they have to keep their relationship a secret until after the divorce? How long would that take? How long was it before soldiers were sent home after a war ended? Colette had no idea, but there were hundreds of thousands of men involved and it wouldn't happen overnight. And after Tony came home, how long would it take for the divorce to come before the court?

One thing was certain: Tony would never willingly let her go.

Along with everybody else who worked on the railways, Alison was profoundly shocked by the tragedy of the munitions train while at the same time sharing the deepest sense of pride and admiration for the bravery of the two men who had put themselves at such risk in order to drive the burning train away from the village. Mr Gibson had paid with his life while Matt had survived even though he had been hurled two hundred yards by the force of the blast.

Two days after the explosion, Alison and the others converged on Darley Court to be with Persephone, who had now returned. Mrs Mitchell showed them into a sitting room – the same one where Alison had found Mum and Lydia waiting for her when she had arrived at Darley Court, not knowing she was about to be presented with a choice of wedding dresses. It was an attractive room with pale-green walls and a large chimney-piece of white marble and blue hearth-tiles. The velvet curtains were deep red with cream fringes and cream lining and on the chairs and the sofa, the cushions had colourful, beaded covers that made Alison think of the braid Lydia had never got around to sewing on.

'The last time I was here,' she said, 'it was to try on wedding dresses.'

'Typical Persephone,' said Joan. 'So considerate of other people.'

As the others added their own words of agreement, Alison remembered how one of the things that had made her wedding-dress day so very special had been that Persephone had invited Mum and Lydia along to share it with her. Now Lydia was a war widow and had left the family fold. How things changed. How the war had changed everything.

'How is she?' Cordelia asked Mrs Mitchell.

'As you'd expect,' said Mrs Mitchell.

Dot nodded understandingly. 'Being strong. Doing what needs doing.'

'We've all had to face a lot of that in recent years,' said Mrs Mitchell. 'I'll fetch her for you.'

When Persephone entered the room, she looked pale and exhausted but determined, with a new resolution in her violet eyes.

Dot gave her a big hug. 'That's from all of us. How are you, chick?'

'I'm fine, thanks. There's nothing wrong with me.'

'Aye, love, I know,' said Dot. 'You don't care about yourself at the minute, do you? You just care about your Matt and Driver Gibson. We care about them too, and their families, but we care about you an' all.'

Persephone nodded. She glanced away for a moment, clearly concealing a swell of emotion. Then she gave them all a ghost of a smile.

'Thank you,' she said. 'Thank you all for coming.'

'Of course we came,' said Emily.

'You don't have to talk about it if you'd rather not,' said Margaret.

'It might be too soon,' added Cordelia.

'When I stayed here at Darley Court after Tony beat me black and blue,' Colette said quietly, 'sometimes I wanted to talk and sometimes I didn't. You always fitted in with what I needed. You were always so kind and understanding. We want to offer you that same kindness and understanding now.' She didn't take her eyes off Persephone. It was as if they were the only two present. 'If all you want is for us to be here with you, without you having to say a word, that's fine. But if you want to talk,' and here Colette smiled, 'I can assure you from personal experience that it really does help.'

'I'm not sure I can talk about it just yet,' said Persephone. 'It's funny. I've spent several years as a writer, certain I could find the words to express whatever was needed, but now, with this . . . It's too much.'

'Have you seen Matt?' Fay asked.

Persephone nodded. 'He's in hospital outside Huddersfield. They weren't sure he'd pull through, but he has and he's . . . he's doing well. He's got broken bones and his lungs are damaged, though not permanently, I'm happy to say. He had . . . When I found him, he had pieces of glass and shrapnel sticking out of him—'

'Oh, Persephone,' Alison whispered, hearing small gasps of shock from the others.

'Apparently, there are more of them inside him, but the X-rays showed that they aren't in life-threatening places.'

'Poor fellow,' said Dot.

'Which bones are broken?' Cordelia asked.

Persephone closed her eyes for a moment, then took a breath and opened them. 'Some ribs. Both legs.' She carried on speaking over the murmurs of sympathy. 'One leg has a straightforward fracture. The other needed an operation, but it's expected to mend well. And there's damage to one of his shoulders.' Her eyes filled but instead of crumpling, she lifted her chin. 'But he's all right. He's alive and he's going to recover. He's all right.'

They all sat in deep silence, their gratitude for Matt's condition tempered by a profound sorrow.

'Driver Gibson gave his life to save that village,' Cordelia said solemnly.

'And Matt might easily have done the same,' Emily added.

'They knew what they were doing, the pair of them,' said Dot, 'when they uncoupled the safe wagons and drove the train and the burning wagons out of the station. They knew; they must have known. They must have expected to die, both of them.'

'Such courage,' Fay murmured.

'If they hadn't uncoupled the safe wagons,' said Joan, 'the whole trainload would have gone up and the damage would have been much worse.'

'As it was, walls and roofs and windows all around the vicinity were damaged,' said Colette.

'Mr Gibson and Matt saved a great many lives that night,' said Alison, stirred by the thought of it.

'They were heroes,' said Fay.

'They were just ordinary men doing their job and then this happened,' said Dot. 'They could have stopped the train and run for their lives, but they didn't. They stuck with it.'

'Ordinary men doing the extraordinary,' said Cordelia.

'Ordinary men doing what needed to be done,' said Margaret. 'That's the very highest sort of heroism.'

'I feel so sorry for Mr Gibson's family,' Persephone whispered.

'We all do,' said Joan. 'It must have been a massive shock for Matt's family as well, but they've still got him, which they must be overwhelmingly grateful for.' After a pause she added, 'Do you know what sort of recovery he can expect?'

'We aren't being nosy,' Cordelia added. 'Just concerned.'

'And hoping for the best,' Alison added.

Persephone drew in a deep breath and blew it out again. 'It will take time, but he is going to make a good recovery. His lungs and the fractures will heal. They've removed everything that was sticking out of him and patched him up. He'll be immobile until he mends, but . . . he'll mend.'

Chapter Twenty-Three

Colette was deeply grateful that Matt was going to recover. He might so easily have been killed outright, like poor Driver Gibson. Colette's heart reached out to Mr Gibson's family. He had left a wife, two grown-up daughters and three grandchildren. Colette wrote a short but heartfelt letter to the new widow.

I was shocked and sorry to learn of the tragic death of Driver Gibson. It is so very hard to lose a loved one and face life without them. I am sure this must have come as a brutal shock to all the family.

I did not know Driver Gibson personally but I work for LMS and am a friend of Fireman Franklin's girlfriend, so I heard his name mentioned sometimes.

What Driver Gibson did that night was unimaginably brave. He put the lives of others before his own even though he cannot have expected to survive. He was a true hero and I hope that in time this will bring solace to you.

Yours sincerely,
Colette Naylor (Mrs)

She wrote *Mrs Gibson* on the envelope and stuck on a stamp, then handed the letter to Miss Emery to write the address and put it in the post.

Miss Emery smiled sadly. 'I'll add it to all the rest.'

Colette was warmed by the thought of there being many letters of condolence. The railway family was large and caring and the sense of loss was common to all, as was that of profound admiration for the brave and selfless actions of Mr Gibson and Matt.

Colette was due to escort an infirm couple to Wigan Wallgate later that morning. But first she had been asked to see Nathan in his office. She knew it would be work-related. He wasn't the sort to use his professional position for personal purposes.

She knocked on the ticket office's side door and was admitted when she said she had come to see Mr Gordon. She could see through his window that he was on the telephone. When he hung up, she waited for Mrs Lister to announce her. Mrs Lister smiled at her but there was no speculation in her eyes. Colette and Nathan had been very discreet about their new relationship.

Nathan politely rose to his feet as she entered his office. 'Thank you for coming. Please have a seat.' He was perfectly professional but the warmth in his eyes made her feel an answering glow. 'Do you remember Miss Stidson, the teacher? She has been in touch again.'

Colette laughed. 'I'm hardly likely to forget that lad – what was his name? Tim Breslaw, that's it – hiding in the coach when everyone got off, because he wanted to run away and join the army. Not to mention Reggie hanging upside down from the barbed-wire fence.'

Nathan's eyes crinkled when he smiled. 'It was quite a day, wasn't it? Miss Stidson's children and their old chums at the village school have been writing to one another since that visit and now Miss Stidson would like to take her children there again.'

'It's nice to know the first visit was such a success,' Colette commented.

'Miss Stidson has asked if you and I can be the chaperones again,' Nathan told her. 'Strictly speaking, I ought to hand over my place to an official railway chaperone.'

'And shall you?' Colette asked, adding with a rueful smile, 'I was thinking just a few minutes ago that you're not the type to take advantage of your position for personal reasons.'

'Thank you for the vote of confidence,' Nathan replied, 'but in this instance . . . well, Miss Stidson has asked for me by name.' He smiled.

'And you often hear people saying how children are missing out on adult male company,' Colette said innocently, 'especially the boys.'

'That's true,' Nathan replied, deadpan.

'So you'll be going on the trip.' Then Colette added, teasing him, 'Which chaperone will be going with you?'

'The same one as last time. I've checked her work commitments and she's available that day.'

Colette shook her head. 'Hard luck. I've heard she's a nightmare to work with.'

'I've heard that too,' said Nathan, 'but not to worry. I'll keep an eye on her.'

On the day of the outing with the children Colette dressed comfortably in a pretty, knitted twinset and a skirt with a pattern of tiny flowers which Mrs Cooper had encouraged her to choose at the WVS's clothes exchange. It had been a little roomy in the waist and they had altered it together rather than ask Joan, who often helped her friends by sewing for them.

Colette topped off her outfit with a lightweight jacket and straw hat with a narrow brim and a band around the crown. Mrs Grayson had used some oddments of wool to make three daisies which she had then sewn in a cluster onto the band. To the lapel of her jacket, Colette attached her LMS badge.

When she arrived at Victoria Station, she made her way onto the platform, pausing as she went through the ticket barrier to have a word with Mr Thirkle, the ticket collector. He was a dear soul with a kindly manner and he looked smart in his peaked cap and gleaming buttons.

The train stood alongside the platform, its door open to welcome passengers aboard. Some of the coaches were official LMS stock, as shown by their deep-red colour, but other coaches bore the liveries of different companies because rolling stock ended up all over the place these days. The double-doors of the guard's van were also open and the parcels porter was moving the luggage and parcels aboard from a fully-loaded flatbed trolley. Colette breathed in the aromas of steam and smoke, enjoying the way they mingled.

There was no sign as yet of Miss Stidson and her young charges. Colette waited, watching passengers and porters going about their business. Then she had the oddest feeling, the tiniest of prickles at the back of her neck. She turned around – and there were Miss Stidson and an excited crocodile of children coming towards her. Colette smiled with real pleasure. Her sixth sense had indeed known she was being watched, and by a whole host of bright eyes.

She greeted the teacher and said hello to the children.

'And what do we say to Mrs Naylor?' Miss Stidson asked them.

'Good mor-ning, Mrs Nay-lor,' the children sing-songed obediently.

Nathan soon joined them and after the children had greeted him in the same manner, they all climbed aboard. Nathan had arranged for seats to be reserved for them as long as they weren't needed by adults. Soon everybody was settled except for Miss Stidson, who predictably was busy counting heads.

Colette sat with some of the girls and chatted with them on the journey. They admired the daisies on her hat-band and she took her hat off so they could have a closer look, which resulted in the girls vowing to knit daisies of their own.

When they arrived at their destination, the children lined up on the platform, watched over by Colette and Nathan while Miss Stidson again counted heads. Then the adults smiled at the children's fascination as the doors were slammed and the train prepared to leave. Beyond the end of the platform, the signal raised, giving permission to proceed. The guard blew his whistle from the platform, then stepped up into his van and leaned out to wave his green flag. The driver blew the train's whistle and the train started to pull away. Nathan explained the process to the children he was nearest to.

After the train vanished, the group remained on the platform for a few minutes while the children used the WCs. Colette joined Miss Stidson in chivvying the children while Nathan chatted with the stationmaster.

When the children had finished, Nathan said, 'Before we head off, the stationmaster says a train of goods wagons is due in a minute and the points will change to send it off onto a different track – down there, see, where this single track splits and another track comes out of it. The boys might be interested in seeing it.'

Colette was pretty sure Miss Stidson would much rather go straight to the village school but the boys were already clamouring to be allowed to watch the goods train. Nathan once more indicated the position of the points further along the track between the platform and the signal box.

'The signalman has a big bank of levers. Each one opens and closes a different set of points. The points are special pieces of railway track that move across and direct the train from one track to another without stopping.'

Sure enough the loco appeared, hauling a long line of wagons behind it. Some of the wagons had simple roofs, others were covered by tarpaulin. Colette felt shivery, thinking of the goods wagons behind Driver Gibson's engine, though a munitions train wouldn't be travelling in broad daylight . . . would it?

When the train snaked onto the other line thanks to the

operation of the points, the boys cheered. They all waited until the train had vanished and the points moved back to their original position.

'That means the next train that comes this way will go straight ahead, like our train did,' said Tim Breslaw.

'That's right,' said Nathan. 'Clever boy.'

It was more than time to set off for the school. They walked through the village, the children in their neat crocodile, and as on the previous occasion they went into the school hall and sat on the floor to await their hosts. Last time there had been nerves and curiosity and shyness, but this time when the evacuees filed in, there were smiles and waves, the atmosphere a mixture of ease and excitement. Miss Stidson and Miss Ramsden sent the children straight out to play and took cups of tea outside, where they perched together on a low wall, watching the children and chatting to one another.

Nathan smiled at Colette. 'It isn't just the children who are pleased to see one another again.'

Last time he and Colette had stayed with the children all day but this time Nathan had made sure it was all right with the teachers if they disappeared briefly for something to eat.

'Good heavens, yes,' Miss Stidson had said at once. 'You're only meant to escort us on our train journeys. I'm so very grateful for all your extra attention. As for slipping away for a bite to eat, I don't blame you,' she'd added with a smile. 'I'd do it myself if I wasn't duty bound to stick like glue to my class.'

They had passed a tea-shop on their way from the station and that was where they headed now.

'The last time we were in this village, we were Mr Gordon

and Mrs Naylor,' said Colette. 'Now we're Nathan and Colette.'

'A big improvement,' said Nathan.

He opened the tea-shop door for her and a little bell jingled overhead. The waitress offered them a table in the pretty bow window and they read the short menu. They both opted for baked tomato on toast, then Nathan had a lardy cake and Colette had baked custard, which was lovely in spite of being made with dried egg.

'Mrs Grayson says that dried egg is better than people give it credit for,' she said. 'It's a matter of knowing how to make the best use of it.'

Nathan paid for their meals and dropped a donation into the Red Cross collecting box, then they left the tea-shop. Taking Colette's hand, Nathan slipped it into the crook of his arm. Just before they reached the corner that would bring them into sight of the school, he quickly raised her hand to his lips to brush a swift kiss on it before releasing it. They walked side by side back to the school. They didn't touch at all, not so much as a brush of the arm, but Colette was very aware of their nearness, and not just their physical proximity but their emotional closeness and the way that being together felt so right.

She stopped and glanced behind them.

'What is it?' Nathan asked, looking behind also.

'I'm not sure,' said Colette. 'Nothing.'

Nathan smiled. 'A guilty conscience, perhaps, because of walking arm in arm from the tea-shop.'

Colette smiled in return. 'Do you think we've set the net curtains twitching?'

'I don't mind so much about the nets,' said Nathan, 'as long as the children don't see us. I don't fancy travelling home fielding questions about whether you're my girlfriend.'

'No, that would be uncomfortable,' Colette agreed but she felt a little thrill of delight all the same.

Nathan's girlfriend. She was Nathan Gordon's girlfriend.

Colette and Nathan spent the afternoon with the children. This second visit seemed to be as much of a success as the first, possibly even more so.

'I'm delighted,' Miss Stidson confided in Colette. 'I was worried it might fall flat.'

At the end of the day, the two sets of children said goodbye to one another. Although there were a few tears, the farewells were mostly cheerful, not least because they were accompanied by enthusiastic exclamations of 'See you next time!'

'See what you've started,' Nathan murmured to Miss Stidson, who rolled her eyes, but Colette could see how pleased she was.

The crocodile wound its way through the village streets and returned to the station. There was some excitement as the children peered down the track in the direction from which the train home would appear. There was a train already along there, standing next to the signal box. Nathan consulted the stationmaster, then spoke to the children.

'That train you can see waiting beside the signal box is ours, but it can't come into the station yet because this is a small single-track line and the trains have to take turns. Our train down there is waiting for something coming the other way.'

'Is a troop train coming?' piped up Tim Breslaw.

'No,' said Nathan. 'The stationmaster says it will be a goods train. The train drivers have to obey the signals. If the signalman changes the signal to say a train can go, that's called releasing the line and the train then "owns" the line.' He turned to Miss Stidson and Colette. 'Why don't you two ladies sit in the waiting room for a spell? I'll stay here with the children.'

'Thanks,' Miss Stidson said gratefully. 'It's tiring being in charge of a class. You don't stop concentrating all day.'

'I can imagine,' said Nathan.

Colette thought the teacher looked a bit strained around the eyes and could do with taking the weight off her feet.

'I'm just going to nip into the Ladies first,' Miss Stidson said quietly to Colette. 'I won't be a minute.'

The waiting room was down at the other end of the platform. Colette opened the door and went inside. It was a small room, clean but tired-looking with its once brightly-coloured pictures of attractive holiday destinations now faded. Colette sat on a smooth wooden bench. She closed her eyes, relishing the peace after the children's company. Hearing a soft click, she opened her eyes, ready to smile at Miss Stidson.

With the sunshine behind the figure, Colette couldn't immediately see his face but she recognised him instantly, his slim build, the tilt of his head. Her hands went clammy and dizziness swirled inside her mind.

'Hello, Colette,' said Tony. 'Hello, *wife*.'

Chapter Twenty-Four

Colette stared in disbelief. He was here. Tony was here. *Tony.* The man who had controlled her until she hardly dared allow herself an independent thought. The man she had faked her own death to escape from. The man the magistrate had permitted to join the army instead of sending him to prison. Her hands trembled as dread rolled in her stomach.

Without removing his gaze from her, Tony shut the door and stepped further into the room. Colette was used to seeing him in civilian clothes. Now he was in uniform. She felt a fresh thrill of fear as a thought flashed into her head.

No one will believe me. They'll believe him because he's in uniform and everyone thinks the world of our boys in the forces.

'You're here with your boyfriend, I see,' Tony said in the old conversational tone that Colette remembered only too well. He would sound ordinary but really he was positioning himself – yes, and positioning her too – ready to strike. 'What's gone wrong? A lovers' tiff, was it? Have you flounced off down this end of the platform to have a sulk? Some things don't change.'

'I'm not sulking,' Colette responded at once.

It wasn't the first time she'd said it. It was appalling to realise how easily she had slipped back into the old conversation. But it was true. She had never been moody. Her silences had stemmed from being too upset to know what to say. She hadn't seen it at the time but she felt sure now that when Tony called her a sulker, he knew it wasn't true. It was just another way for him to undermine her confidence and make her doubt herself.

And here she was feeling undermined all over again. What had happened to the confidence that had grown since Tony had joined up and gone away at the end of last year?

Colette stood up. Her knees were like blancmange but she curled her fingers tightly into fists that she hid in the folds of her skirt. It wouldn't do to let Tony see this mark of defiance. But why not? She moved her fists out of hiding. Tony gave no sign of noticing. His eyes were intent, his jaw-line taut.

Colette said quietly, 'You've been following me all day.'

'And a good thing too,' said Tony. 'My father told me. He saw you out with your fancy-man and he wrote to me immediately to let me know. I'm on pre-embarkation leave and they've given me an extra day on compassionate grounds because my wife is having it away with a new bloke. "Ruddy disgrace." That's what my CO said. "There's a lot of it about." I didn't believe it when I read Father's letter – couldn't believe it. But it's true. I've seen you with him.'

'We're at work,' Colette said. Above all else she wanted to protect Nathan. 'You remember my job as a chaperone. Mr Gordon and I are acting as chaperones to this class of children.'

'Of course you are.' Tony's voice dripped with honey. 'It's purely professional. There's nothing in it.' Before Colette could move, he was right in front of her, his face bent to hers, his eyes fixed and glaring at her from six inches away. 'Pull the other one. It's got bells on.'

Colette stepped backwards, only for Tony to follow, crowding closer.

'Tony, don't!' she exclaimed. 'Leave me alone. I told you before you joined the army. You want things to go back to how they used to be and they can't.'

'And I told you: you are my wife and that will never change.'

'What's this? Who are you?'

A new voice – Miss Stidson's. She stood in the doorway. Distracted, Tony spun around. Taking advantage, Colette tried to dodge past him but he caught her arm and yanked her back hard enough to force a cry from her.

'What's going on?' Miss Stidson demanded. 'Leave this lady alone or I'll call for the stationmaster.'

'You do that, love,' Tony jeered. 'Tell him that Private Naylor is here having a loving reunion with Mrs Naylor.'

'Oh.' Miss Stidson sounded both startled and taken aback.

Colette tried to pull free. 'Let go of me.' She pulled harder. 'Let *go* of me.'

Miss Stidson darted forwards and tugged at Tony's other arm. 'Let go!'

Tony shook her off, sending her stumbling backwards, exclaiming loudly. Tony's grip on Colette's arm tightening, he hauled her through the door and she staggered into the sunshine.

'That's another thing,' Tony snarled. 'I was about to say, "You're coming home with me," but that's something else

Father told me. You've upped sticks and left, haven't you? I was overseas when I heard that and they wouldn't let me come back and deal with it. It's still my name on the rent book. My father asked the rent man. So what we're going to do now, you and me, is go home – to my home, where my name is on the rent book, to our home, our matrimonial home, the home I provided for you, for my wife, the home you should go down on your knees and be grateful for. We're going to go home and you're going to be my wife, Colette. Do you understand what I'm saying?'

He tugged her closer. It didn't matter how much she resisted. His strength was far superior. All at once Colette's fear vanished. She had been frightened of Tony the whole time they had lived under the same roof, for all the good it had done her. Now was the moment to fight back. He had hold of her left arm and she was right-handed. Tightening the muscles in her free arm, she clenched her fist and thumped Tony in the face as hard as she could. He let go, stepping back, his expression the very picture of surprise, but then the widened eyes narrowed and the slack jaw went rigid.

Colette was thrown back into the past. The time Tony had picked up her dinner plate and hurled it at the wall hard enough to break it. The time he had walloped her and she had paraded her bruises around the local shops for all to see. The time he had hit her and carried on hitting her while her head swam and her vision darkened . . . until in the end she woke up in hospital.

And all those times, the many times, before all that when he had complacently pointed out to her that he had never hit her. Other husbands might deliver a quick slap but he, Tony Naylor, never would. As if she was supposed to be grateful to have a husband who didn't raise a hand to her.

But in the end he had hit her and it had been more than a quick slap. It had been a brutal and sustained assault.

If he could do that once, he could do it again. She could see it in his face.

Tony lunged and grabbed her, his hands grasping her slender shoulders as if he intended to crack the bones and leave her damaged for ever. His right hand let go. It lifted. His whole arm lifted. The elbow bent. The hand formed a fist. The knuckles went white.

Colette knew she had to pull away, had to duck, but the hand on her shoulder made it impossible to move. As Tony drew back his arm, Colette experienced a sickening sense of the certainty of what was coming – and then her brain rushed to catch up as Tony suddenly staggered backwards, dragging her with him before he let go, and she had to scramble to keep her footing.

Nathan was there. He had pulled Tony away and now Tony was rounding on him, squaring up to him. Tony lashed out but Nathan managed to block the blow.

'Run!' Nathan shouted to Colette even as Tony launched himself at him. Nathan seemed about to tumble but kept upright and the two men wrestled.

Colette hesitated. She didn't want to leave Nathan like this, but Tony was younger and had months of army experience under his belt. If she ran, she might draw Tony away. She was the one he wanted. She couldn't lead him down the platform towards the children. Instead she turned and ran in the other direction, down the slope at the end of the platform. At the bottom the ground was covered with small stones, one of which instantly found its way into one of her shoes. Beyond the stony area, where the trackside gave way to turf, Colette hobbled to a standstill long enough to wrench her shoe off, shake the stone out and shove her shoe back on.

She looked back at the two men still struggling on the platform and was just in time to see Tony knock Nathan to the ground. Tony didn't wait. Swinging himself around, he looked straight at her, their gazes locking. There was a moment of utter stillness, then Tony sprang forward into a run at the same time as Colette turned and dashed away. The signal box was thirty-five or forty yards ahead of her. If she could reach there first and run up the flight of steps to the door, the signalman could lock Tony out and she would be safe. Then the military police could be sent for to take Tony away.

Lungs burning, Colette ran as hard as she could but she knew she was no match for Tony. She needed to look over her shoulder to see how quickly he was gaining on her, but she was scared it would slow her down. She couldn't afford that. Was he just inches in her wake, his hand all set to clamp on her shoulder? Fear meant she had to know. She glanced over her shoulder to see Tony was indeed gaining on her – and Nathan was coming after him.

Flinging herself forwards, Colette made a final desperate attempt to reach the foot of the signal-box steps, though she seriously doubted that her legs would carry her all the way to the top. She grabbed hold of the handrail and heaved herself up the first few treads before looking back.

Nathan had caught up with Tony and the two of them were struggling again, exchanging blows. Tony hit Nathan hard and Nathan tottered backwards but immediately threw himself at Tony once more. Apparently taken by surprise, Tony stumbled backwards, catching his foot on the edge of the railway track. He quickly regained his footing by stepping onto the line. Once more the two of them grappled. They were close to the points. Running alongside the tracks towards them came the stationmaster and a policeman.

Tearing her gaze away, Colette hurried up the remaining steps and threw open the door. The signalman was in front of the bank of levers, tugging one of them.

'Hey, you can't come in here.' He turned an angry expression on her.

Colette struggled for breath. 'I work for the railways. Please – you have to help me. I'm being chased by – by a violent man. Can you lock this door?'

'I most certainly can. I'm not having a violent man barging in here. This is a signal box, not a wrestling ring. There's important equipment in here. I can't have it put in peril.'

'Thank you.' Relief flooded through Colette. 'And then can you inform the line controller that we need the military police?'

As she turned to shut the door behind her, she saw the goods train coming down the track towards the station. Like the one that had passed through this morning, it would veer off onto the other track, guided on its way by the points, thus allowing the waiting passenger train to pull forwards to enter the station.

Colette craned her neck to see Tony and Nathan. She had

to go down a couple of steps because the waiting passenger train obscured her view. Her brow furrowed as she took in the sight of the two men. They were still locked together but not in combat. Nathan was – it looked like – good heavens, Nathan was trying to pull Tony free.

Colette sucked in a great gasp of shock. 'Tony's foot is caught in the points – and the goods train is coming.'

The signalman appeared behind her. 'What? Good God!'

He darted back inside. Colette heard the clunk as he pulled the lever and the points opened up, allowing Nathan to heave Tony free.

'He's out!' Colette yelled.

The signalman immediately switched the lever to change the points back again so as to send the goods train across onto the other line instead of straight towards the passenger train. In that same moment Tony staggered and lurched, his hurt foot giving way. The goods train was almost upon the two men. All Colette could see was that Tony flew in one direction and Nathan in the other just as the goods train crossed the points and changed lines.

Colette stood transfixed, eyes wide, hands clamped across her open mouth. Then she clattered down the steps and half-ran, half-stumbled to the scene of the incident, dreading what she would find.

Chapter Twenty-Five

Nathan lay face down on the ground beside the track. The goods train had come to a halt, the front half of it snaking around onto the other line, the rest of it still on the line where the platform was. As Colette drew closer, Nathan moved and slowly knelt up. Relief left Colette feeling as though all her strength was about to gush straight out of her body. Her torso sagged forwards but then her strength surged back and buoyed her up – not so much strength as sheer resolve and willpower fuelled by love. Yes, love. If she hadn't known it previously, if she had hidden from the truth before, she knew it now, now and always.

As Nathan stood up, Colette raced into his arms and they clung together.

'I saw you fall,' said Colette, 'just as the goods train came. It looked as if it had struck you. I thought— but you're all right. You're all right,' she repeated, needing to make it even more true.

'I threw myself off the track in the nick of time,' said Nathan, 'and I dropped to the ground. It was the safest thing to do.'

'Thank goodness, thank goodness,' Colette whispered as the tears spilled over.

Then there were people all around them and Colette

eased free, mopping her face with her hanky. This was no time for weakness. A serious incident had occurred.

'Tony . . .' she said.

'Wait here,' Nathan told her. 'I'll go and see.'

'I'll come with you,' she said.

'No,' Nathan said firmly. 'Please, Colette, stay here. If he was struck by the train . . .'

Nathan disappeared and Colette took herself over to the bank at the side of the track. She still struggled to believe what had happened. All that mattered was that Nathan had survived and was safe . . . except that this wasn't all that mattered. She went a few paces up the slope and sat down. All at once she was exhausted and her mind was numb. Over the top of the goods train's wagons she could see the heads of several men on the far side. They were grouped together. One head disappeared, then another, as the men bobbed down. That must be where Tony was. She waited for his head to appear when he stood up, but it didn't.

Tony didn't stand up.

The inside of Colette's own head felt swooshy. She breathed in sharply through her nose and pushed the breath out through pursed lips. She did this several times until her head cleared, though she didn't altogether want it to clear. She didn't want to live through the next part.

Nathan returned. He looked round, spotted her and came up the bank to join her as she pushed herself to her feet. She looked at Nathan. She couldn't speak. All she could do was gaze at him, knowing that her questions were in her eyes.

Nathan said, 'He's alive. He's unconscious but he's still with us. The goods train clipped him and flung him aside.

Goods trains don't travel as fast as passenger trains, and the driver had already applied the brakes.' He bent his head towards her, looking closely into her face, his eyes filled with concern. 'Colette? Did you hear me?'

Colette nodded.

Tony was alive.

It was the middle of the evening before Colette was at last taken to Tony's bedside. She had insisted upon going with him in the ambulance. Nathan had been obliged to assist Miss Stidson with getting the children safely back to Manchester Victoria. He hadn't wanted to part from Colette. She had seen all too clearly in his expression what a wrench it was for him to leave her, but he didn't have a choice. He couldn't abandon Miss Stidson and her class, all the more so after such a traumatic event had taken place.

Colette wasn't entirely sure what had made her so determined to accompany Tony to hospital, but she had been certain it was the right thing to do. She didn't want there to be any kind of link between them, but she had to know what had happened to him. And – and she was his wife and she might be needed.

She had sat on a hard chair in a hospital corridor for several hours, waiting for news to be brought to her, but none came. It didn't seem to matter to her – the length of time, the lack of information. There was a heavy feeling in her stomach. Sometimes her pulse raced but at other times it barely seemed to beat at all and she felt dizzy and cold. Someone told her she was in shock and Colette got confused because the person who said this was a woman but she wasn't in a nurse's uniform. Then it turned out she was a lady doctor and Colette felt stupid for not realising. Disloyal too. Women were capable of doing any job a man could do.

'I don't want to make a fuss,' she had said. 'I'll just stay here. I'll be fine.'

The lady doctor raised her eyebrows but didn't force the issue. She probably had far more pressing cases to deal with. 'Very well, but sing out if your heart speeds up or you feel breathless or your skin goes sweaty. You'll do that, won't you?' She eyed Colette.

Colette nodded obediently.

She stayed put. After some time the police came and talked to her and later some soldiers came and asked the same questions, except that they weren't soldiers exactly. They were the military police.

'We've taken witness statements,' said one officer. 'We've been told Naylor attacked you and that a fellow called Gordon laid into him to give you a chance to escape. Mr Gordon also said that Naylor joined the army as an alternative to being imprisoned for beating you up, but we'll have to check whether that's true.'

'It is,' Colette whispered.

'Why?' asked the other military policeman. 'Why would your husband do this?'

It all felt too complicated to explain. Colette's limbs were heavy with exhaustion and her mind was gradually turning to sludge. Yet there was a hard, bright, painful little corner of her mind that knew precisely what Tony had done and why and what was happening now. She needed to be left alone to take it all in.

Tony had followed her. Spied on her and Nathan. Grabbed her and when she had freed herself, he had chased her. Given the chance, he would have knocked her clean into the middle of next week – and it wouldn't have been for the first time.

At last a nurse came for her and escorted her away, holding up a hand to prevent the police and the military police from following. Colette felt shaky as she went with the nurse, but as Tony's wife it was the right thing for her to do. Every step took her closer to his bedside and all the old feelings came back, the fear, the worry, the inadequacy. She had to remind herself that she was different now. She was stronger, more experienced, grown up.

Tony was in a small room on his own, with a nurse sitting at his bedside. A wave of emotion washed through Colette as she entered the room – sorrow, shock – she didn't know what it was.

'Here, sit down, Mrs Naylor.'

Firm hands thrust her into a chair. She found herself on the opposite side of the bed from the nurse. Colette felt clammy and tingly all over and her mind was sharply focused and oddly distant both at the same time.

'Deep breaths,' said the same voice. It was the nurse who had brought her here. 'Doctor will be here in a while to talk to you.'

'Thank you,' Colette whispered.

The nurse on the other side of the bed gave her a brief smile. 'I'm Nurse Gladwell and I'm here to special Mr Naylor. That means he has a nurse with him all the time.'

Colette looked at Tony in the bed. Unconscious, he lay utterly still with one of his arms on the covers beside him.

The nursing staff liked their patients to look neat. Colette remembered that from her own time in a hospital ward. Tony's other arm was in a sling that held his hand almost on his opposite shoulder.

The lower section of the bedclothes was humped up, draped over a cage beneath which were Tony's legs. Colette gazed at his face, which was so pale that the skin was almost translucent. His cheekbones were a pair of slashes under his closed eyes. There were sharp grazes all down one side of his face. It looked like the skin had been scraped off.

Across the bed, the nurse stirred, catching Colette's eye and by the smallest motion of her head indicating that someone else had entered the room. Colette looked round. It was a doctor, an older man with snow-white hair and black eyebrows above clever eyes, and a thin-lipped mouth.

'Mrs Naylor? I am Mr Salisbury, the consultant.' He made it sound as though he was the only one in the entire hospital. 'Your husband is badly injured, I'm afraid.'

Colette glanced at the sling and the shape made by the cage. Tony had been struck by a train. It was a wonder he was still alive. Then she thought of Matt Franklin and the injuries he had sustained. Yet he was expected to recover.

Would Tony? Would she as his wife be expected to take care of him? How could she refuse? They might be estranged but it wasn't an estrangement Tony had ever recognised or acknowledged in any degree. Whatever their differences, would she have to return to him to nurse him through his convalescence? It sounded like the decent thing to do – but only to the end of his recuperation and not a moment longer, she vowed to herself. Not a single moment longer. Her heart dipped inside her chest. Would nursing Tony at home be her punishment for daring to find happiness elsewhere? And what if— what if he didn't get better? What if he needed to be cared for long-term? Surely no one could expect that of her.

Tony could.

'Do you understand, Mrs Naylor?' Mr Salisbury asked.

Colette jerked her chin in his direction. 'What? I'm sorry, sir. I wasn't . . . My mind wandered for a moment.'

'For rather more than a moment, I'd say.' Mr Salisbury spoke with a kind of heavy patience that made him sound distinctly impatient. 'Is there perhaps a man you can call on to be here with you? I'm sure a man would take things in better.'

Colette bridled. 'I don't need anybody, thank you, sir. My attention slipped, that's all. This has come as a great shock.'

'Very well. I'll explain to you once more. Your husband was clipped by the train and thrown aside. He has various injuries but the most serious and problematic injury is to his head.'

Colette looked at Tony's face. Yes, that grazing was severe. It looked nasty and raw but it was after all only grazing. It didn't make sense for it to be the worst thing.

'When the train hit him and he was thrown to the ground, he struck the back of his head against the metal line of the track. If a different part of his anatomy – his back, his shoulder – had hit the same place, it would have been a very different story. As it is, there is a significant injury. The back of his skull has filled with blood and that is putting considerable pressure on his brain.'

'Can you do anything about it?' Colette asked.

'We have to wait to see if the blood drains away of its own accord.'

There was silence.

'And if it doesn't . . . ?' Colette asked. He ought to have told her without her having to ask, but maybe he had intended her to have the choice of knowing or not knowing.

'Let us hope it does,' said Mr Salisbury. 'If not, then the damage will be severe.'

'What does that mean?' asked Colette.

'It's best if we wait and see,' Mr Salisbury told her. 'And you should prepare yourself, Mrs Naylor. It might be that your husband . . . Do you understand what I'm saying?'

Colette stared at him. No, she didn't understand. One moment he'd been talking about the possibility of brain damage. Now he seemed to be suggesting . . .

'You should prepare for the worst,' said Mr Salisbury. 'Your husband's condition is very serious.' He waited a moment as if giving her the chance to speak, then he nodded and left the room.

Colette looked beseechingly at the nurse, desperate for more information, but the nurse gave her an apologetic half-smile and looked away. Clearly it wasn't her place to say anything.

The door opened again and the atmosphere rippled with emotion. Turning her head, Colette found herself looking straight at Tony's parents. Their eyes were huge and dark with shock. It was the first time she had ever seen them with similar expressions on their faces. Usually Mr Naylor looked stern and unyielding and frankly pleased with himself while Bunty did her best to make herself invisible. But today, here, now, in this situation, Mr Naylor the bully and Bunty the mouse were made equal. They were parents in shock and distress.

'These are Mr Naylor's mother and father,' the nurse who had showed them in said to Nurse Gladwell.

Mr Naylor shook his head, his shoulders slumping. 'My God,' he said breathlessly. 'My God, I didn't really believe it until this moment.'

'Oh, Tony,' Bunty whispered, her eyes filling. 'My sweet boy.'

Colette stood up. 'Here,' she said to Bunty, 'take my seat. Please,' she added, moving aside.

But it was Mr Naylor who came forward. He didn't sit but stood in front of the chair, leaning down.

'Not too close, if you please,' said Nurse Gladwell. She stood up and offered her seat to Bunty. 'Come and sit beside him.'

Wobbling, Bunty made it to the chair and dropped onto it. She gazed at her son. On the other side of the bed, Mr Naylor cleared his throat loudly. These two people loved Tony so much. Colette was glad for their sakes and for Tony's that they were here.

Mr Naylor turned to glare at her. 'What's she doing here?' he demanded of Nurse Gladwell. Then, before the nurse could speak, he said to Colette, 'What's this story we were told? The police said Tony was hit by a train somewhere near here. He told me he was going to follow you, keep tabs on you, see what was what with you and the new boyfriend. The police said the two of them got into a fight.'

'Tony came after me,' said Colette. 'I had to run away.'

'And led him into the path of a train,' said Mr Naylor.

'No!' Colette exclaimed. 'Of course not.'

'It should be you lying there, not him,' Mr Naylor said loudly.

'Mr Naylor, your son is very poorly,' said Nurse Gladwell. 'Please keep your voice down. He needs peace and quiet.'

'Get her out of here,' said Mr Naylor, indicating Colette with a brutish jerk of his chin, 'and I'll have no further reason to raise my voice. It's her fault that this has happened. Carrying on with her fancy man while my son was doing his duty fighting for King and country.'

The door had stood open all this time. Now a young doctor appeared.

'What the devil's going on in here? You can be heard at the other end of the corridor.'

'It's her,' said Mr Naylor. 'She shouldn't be here. She has no right.'

Colette heard a sort of gurgle from Tony and Nurse Gladwell stepped forward.

'Doctor.' Her voice was low and urgent. She put a hand on Bunty's shoulder. 'Please move aside, Mrs Naylor.'

'What's happening?' Mr Naylor demanded.

The doctor was beside Tony now. 'Send for Mr Salisbury,' he instructed Nurse Gladwell. 'If the family would wait outside, please.'

Colette gathered Bunty around the shoulders and led her out, only to have her arm more or less hit away by Mr Naylor, but he didn't offer his wife any comfort. The three of them stood there. Colette didn't want to cause trouble but she had the distinct feeling that she was standing her ground.

Mr Salisbury swept past them into the room and the door shut behind him.

After a few minutes he came out into the corridor.

He addressed Colette. 'Mrs Naylor—'

'I'm the next of kin,' said Mr Naylor. 'She's just the nasty piece who went off with another man. Tell me, please, not her.'

Mr Salisbury remained unruffled. He looked at Colette and Bunty before addressing his remarks to Mr Naylor.

'I'm very sorry to tell you—'

Bunty uttered a cry and Colette caught her as she fell, or tried to, but somehow they both ended up in a heap on the floor, with Bunty in Colette's arms and Colette holding her as tightly as she could while she crooned and murmured.

One of the military policemen drove Colette home to Manchester. There had been no question of the Naylors being asked to take her. Mr Naylor would very likely have exploded had the suggestion been put to him. The journey took ages in the blackout, the motor using headlights that were both shielded and dipped. Colette sat in silence most of the way. The sensation of shock had returned and her head swam with it. She pulled herself together to provide directions for the final part of the journey.

At last she was home again. Mrs Grayson gave the driver a hot drink and a meat-paste sandwich before he set off again while Mrs Cooper settled Colette in a corner of the sofa, where she managed to sit in a normal fashion even though she felt like curling up in a ball. The military policeman had given the news to the two ladies so there was no need for Colette to explain.

Dot sat beside Colette and took her hand. Colette's brain seemed to be working very slowly and it took her a moment to register that Dot shouldn't be here. Then she realised that of course Dot was here. Dear Dot had come to lend her support – as had Fay, Cordelia and Emily. Margaret was upstairs, turning down Colette's bed.

'Word got back to Manchester Victoria pretty sharpish about the incident on the tracks,' said Dot, 'and those of us as were able to come round here this evening knew right away that we wanted to be here when you eventually came home.'

Colette let Dot's words sink in. She looked at her friends, seeing the concern in their expressions. From somewhere in the swirling murk of her thoughts, she seized on something important.

'Nathan. Does he know about Tony . . . ?'

'We have no way of knowing that,' said Cordelia.

Fay crouched down beside the arm of the sofa. Colette turned to look at her. She found herself admiring Fay's gorgeous deep-red hair and her fine-boned face. Why were her thoughts wandering in this way?

'There's nothing we can do about Nathan,' Fay said. Her hazel eyes looked deep into Colette's and Colette found herself focusing on the tiny gold flecks in Fay's. 'In a situation like this, where there's been a terrific shock, what we do is concentrate on the person who needs our help and kindness. That's you, in case you didn't realise,' she added with a smile.

Now Emily was kneeling in front of her. 'Fay's right. We all want to look after you.'

And it was the sight of Emily that started to bring Colette out of the depths of her shock. She had felt protective towards

Emily ever since Raymond had changed his mind and broken off their romance and she didn't want to make this situation worse for her. She sat up straight.

'Thank you,' she said. 'Thank you all for being here. I . . .' She shook her head. 'It's strange. I can clearly picture everything that happened and yet I'm struggling to believe it.'

'That's natural,' said Fay.

Margaret came into the room. Colette heard her ask quietly, 'How's she doing?'

'I'm in one piece,' said Colette. 'You do know, don't you, about Tony?'

'Aye, chick,' said Dot. 'We all know. We know he's gone.'

'Of course you do,' said Colette. She hauled her thoughts together. 'I'm sorry. I'm not making much sense.'

Mrs Grayson entered the room. 'The military man has gone on his way. I'll fill the kettle again. Come and get the cups out for me, Emily.'

Soon they were all sipping tea.

'This is what we do,' said Fay. 'We drink tea. I don't know why it helps, but it does. We drank tea during and after the air raids. When someone receives a telegram, we cram into their house and drink tea with them. And we drink tea with a friend whom we can only help by being with her and showing that we care.'

'Nicely put,' murmured Mrs Cooper.

'This must be what it was like for Persephone after the explosion when Matt was taken to hospital,' said Colette. It was easier to think about Persephone than about herself . . . about Tony. 'I can't seem to pin my thoughts down.'

'You've had a big shock,' said Cordelia. 'A series of

shocks. Tony turning up at that station and attacking you, and then Nathan taking him on. We heard about that business with the points, and Nathan staying with Tony to free him even though the goods train was bearing down on them.'

'And on top of all that, Tony died in hospital,' Dot added.

'You must feel as though you've lived a dozen lifetimes since it all started,' said Margaret.

A long sigh shivered its way up from Colette's lungs and out through her parted lips. 'I've been afraid of Tony for such a long time. I was afraid of him even before I knew that I was. I thought I was anxious; I thought I was desperate to be the perfect wife – and I was both of those things, but underneath I was afraid. It was fear that made me anxious and desperate. Even when I ran away and lived as Betsy Cooper, I never shook off the fear. Even when Tony was sent off to join the army . . .'

'You won't have to be afraid any more after this,' said Fay.

'That must be a relief,' said Dot.

Colette frowned. 'It hasn't sunk in yet. None of it has.'

'It'll take time, chuck,' said Mrs Cooper.

'When it does sink in,' said Colette, 'will I be glad? Glad that he's dead, I mean. And if I am, will that make me a bad person?'

Chapter Twenty-Six

Persephone was shocked to her core by the news of Tony's death. Even though it wasn't a buffet evening, she and the others automatically made their way there, needing to be together. Colette wasn't there but the rest of them were.

'The thought of him following Colette and accosting her sends chills all through me,' said Margaret, shuddering. 'He must have been mad.'

They all looked at one another. Persephone sensed they were all thinking the same thing. It was just a question of which of them was going to utter the words. Often it was Dot who stepped in at such a moment but today Persephone did.

'It's shocking, of course, that he has died as a result of his injuries,' she said, 'but – but, well, if someone had to die, then I don't mind saying I would much rather it was Tony than Colette or Nathan.'

'Agreed,' said Fay. 'From the sound of it, it could just as easily have been Nathan who got clipped by the goods train. In fact, he was jolly brave to stay on the track trying to help Tony release his foot from the points while the goods train was coming. No one would have blamed him for saving his own skin.'

'He's a hero,' said Emily. Then she smiled at Persephone. 'Like your Matt.'

'When are you seeing him next?' asked Dot.

'Tomorrow,' said Persephone. 'They're letting me work split shifts most days so I can go there for afternoon visiting.'

'Give him our best,' said Dot.

'I will,' Persephone promised.

The next day, when she was on her way to see Matt, she consciously pushed aside all thoughts of Tony Naylor. She didn't want to be upset or angry at what he had done when she saw Matt. The doctors had said it was important to be calm in his presence and as relaxed as possible. He had no memory whatsoever of the explosion. He could recall uncoupling the safe wagons at the station but nothing at all of what had taken place after that.

Persephone arrived in good time for afternoon visiting. Some people lingered outside the ward, waiting for the doors to be opened by Sister. Persephone stood to one side, feeling grateful all over again that Matt had survived and was going to get better. Tony's death had reminded her of how lucky Matt was. She had so much to be grateful for.

She looked around as fresh footsteps approached the waiting group. It was Mrs Franklin, her face drawn with worry and fatigue, but with quiet resolution in the set of her shoulders and the angle of her chin. She wore a headscarf over her salt-and-pepper hair.

It was the first time Persephone had seen her since the explosion. It wasn't easy having Matt in hospital away from Manchester and it couldn't be straightforward for his family to visit him. Persephone was well aware that she wasn't Mrs Franklin's favourite person but this was no time to worry about that. She went straight down the corridor to meet her.

'Mrs Franklin, I'm so very sorry about what's happened to Matt. You must have been beside yourself when you heard.'

Mrs Franklin jerked her chin as if to dodge Persephone's words, then her eyes fixed on Persephone's face. 'Yes, it's been one heck of a worry – and for you too,' she added.

Persephone hadn't expected that. She decided not to read anything into it. It must be the emotion of the moment speaking rather than Mrs Franklin's true feelings. She knew Matt's mother didn't approve of her.

'I expect you'd like to see Matt on your own, Mrs Franklin,' Persephone said. 'I can return to work for now and come back here tomorrow. It would be easy enough for me to do, honestly.' It wouldn't but she would manage it.

Mrs Franklin appeared to consider how to reply. 'It's good of you to offer. I appreciate it.'

With a smile and a nod, together with the heavy disappointment of not seeing her darling Matt today, Persephone started to walk away.

'But I think,' Mrs Franklin went on and Persephone turned around, 'that Matt would enjoy seeing the pair of us together. He knows – you both know – that I have my reservations about the two of you seeing one another, but after what's happened that seems like very small fry now. It would mean a lot to Matt if we went in together to see him.'

'Yes, it would,' Persephone agreed.

'Let's do that, then,' Mrs Franklin said in a voice that declared the matter to be settled once and for all. She seemed to be about to turn away but didn't. She frowned and a dent appeared in her cheek as if she was biting it on the inside, but then she shook off the appearance of uncertainty and gave Persephone a firm nod. 'I want to thank you.'

'Whatever for?' asked Persephone.

'For what you did on the night of the explosion.'

'Me? I didn't do anything. It was all Matt and Mr Gibson. They did everything. They were so brave, both of them.'

'I know that,' said Mrs Franklin. 'I'm talking about what you did after the explosion. I've been told you went racing from the station to find Matt.'

'Of course I did,' said Persephone. It seemed so obvious to her.

'There's no "of course" about it,' Mrs Franklin replied. 'It was a mad and dangerous thing for you to do. There might have been further explosions. You might have given your life.'

'I didn't think about it in those terms,' said Persephone. 'I didn't think about it at all. I just wanted to get to Matt.'

'Yes, I can see that and that's why I want to thank you,' said Mrs Franklin. 'Your one and only thought was for him, to go to him and take care of him. I know he was unconscious when you found him, and obviously he has survived, but supposing he hadn't. Supposing he had died, out there in the middle of all that wreckage.' She gave a little gasp and her eyes shone with unshed tears. 'He wouldn't have died alone.'

Persephone, who had been brought up to be able to make conversation with anybody at all in any circumstances, had no idea what to say.

'It means a great deal to me, it means everything to me,' said Mrs Franklin, 'that you were there that night, that with no thought for your own safety, you went to my son's side. I'll never forget that.' She gave Persephone another nod and this one, instead of firm and determined, was grateful and approving. 'Thank you. Thank you with all my heart.'

The ward doors opened and the other visitors started to walk through. Persephone deliberately didn't look into the ward. She didn't move. She appreciated Mrs Franklin's words more than she could say, but she still didn't want to take anything for granted.

Mrs Franklin aimed a smile at her. 'Let's go in, shall we?'

Together, they walked along the ward to the small room at the other end, where Matt was. He looked up and smiled as they walked in.

'I thought it was going to be just me,' said his mother, 'but look who I found waiting outside. How are you feeling, Matt?'

'Fine, thanks,' Matt said, just as Persephone had known he would.

They chatted for a while. Matt didn't want to talk about himself, claiming there was nothing to talk about when all he did was lie still inside his plaster casts all day long. He was eager to hear about the outside world.

Presently a white-coated doctor came in. He was a tall, thin man with shadows under his dark eyes. He stopped when he saw Matt's visitors.

'I was hoping it would be your father this afternoon,' he said to Matt.

'This is my mother, Mrs Franklin, and my girlfriend, Miss Trehearn-Hobbs,' said Matt.

The doctor nodded to them, saying, 'Dr Fieldhouse.' He

barely looked at the two women. To Matt he said, 'Is your father due this evening? Or tomorrow?'

Matt answered the question with one of his own. 'Why?'

'I have to update you on your situation and – well, you may need someone to talk to afterwards. Better to have a man for that.'

The doctor's words had sent a shiver of fear through Persephone. What was wrong with Matt? She was annoyed too by the suggestion that only men were fit to hear bad news.

Evidently Mrs Franklin had a similar response. 'I'm not going to drop down in a dead faint, if that's what you mean.'

Matt spoke up. 'My father can't get here until the day after tomorrow. He's a police sergeant and he works shifts. I'd like to be told whatever it is now, please, and I'm happy for my mother and Persephone to hear it too.'

But Dr Fieldhouse was adamant. 'I'll tell you on your own, if you like, Mr Franklin, but I require the ladies to wait outside.'

Persephone gave a small gasp of outrage mingled with a sharp concern for Matt. She wanted – no, she needed to be here with him while this news was delivered. She wanted to support him and help him through whatever was coming. The thought of Matt, who had already gone through so much, now facing bad news brought a tiny tremor to her limbs. She braced herself against it. It wouldn't do to display any weakness in front of Dr Fieldhouse. She would hate herself for ever if she reinforced his prejudice against women.

Persephone and Mrs Franklin had no choice but to go outside and submit to having the door shut behind them. They looked at one another but didn't say anything. From here, any words would be heard by people at this end of the general ward.

After a few minutes, during which Persephone's stomach tied itself in knots, the door opened and Dr Fieldhouse came out.

'Ladies,' he murmured in brief acknowledgement as he went on his way.

They returned to Matt's bedside. He didn't look at them as they joined him and even if she hadn't known it already, that would have told Persephone that something bad had happened. Matt looked pale – well, he had looked pale before, but now there was a sort of underlying greyness to his skin. When he glanced up and met their eyes, he looked shaken.

'What is it?' Persephone whispered.

Matt started to speak, then had to clear his throat. He blew out a big breath and started again.

'It's to do with my recovery,' he said in a tight, controlled voice. 'I'm going to make a good recovery,' he added quickly, looking at his mother. 'There's no need to worry about that. It's just that . . .'

'What, Matt?' Mrs Franklin asked softly, her eyes full of love and concern for her son.

Persephone understood how Matt's mother felt because she felt the same, desperate for answers yet not wanting to push Matt into saying what was too hard to say.

Matt nodded, as if making a decision. 'It's going to be a very good recovery but not a complete one. To put it bluntly, if I return to the railways, it won't be as a fireman. It's my shoulder – one of my shoulders. It's not just the bones. It's the muscles as well. It's going to have permanently restricted movement. In other words, no more shovelling coal for me.'

'Oh, Matt,' said Persephone. He loved his work. He *was* his work.

'So I've got no choice,' Matt went on as if she hadn't spoken. He tilted his head right back and stared at the ceiling. 'I can't return to my job.'

'It's a great shame,' Mrs Franklin said with tears in her eyes, 'but it could have been so much worse.'

'You don't need to explain that to me, Mum,' said Matt. 'I know all that.'

'Your work as a fireman means the world to you,' Persephone acknowledged softly. 'You gave up a lot to join the railways and that was the right thing for you to do. I admire you for that. I have done from the start. Mr Gibson admired you too. Could you possibly see yourself in another role in LMS? I'm sure they'd bend over backwards to accommodate you. After what you did—'

'Don't,' said Matt. 'Stop trying to make it right. I'm sorry,' he added at once. 'I don't mean to snap, but it's too soon for that sort of talk. I'm still trying to take in what I've been told.'

Persephone tried again. 'It's such a lot for you to lose. You and dear Mr Gibson were so brave and he paid for his courage with his life. Now it turns out you're going to pay a price for it too.'

'That's what Dr Fieldhouse said.'

'Is it?' asked Persephone, gently prodding for more.

'Not exactly. What he said was, "You should be grateful, Franklin. The other fellow lost his life and all you're going to lose is your job." And I *am* grateful to be alive, I am. And I'll feel bad about Mr Gibson until the day I die. But being told to be grateful because I've "only" lost the job that meant the world to me is hard. And if that makes me sound selfish or like a spoiled brat, then I'm sorry, but losing my job is still a loss. When they talked about a good recovery, I thought . . . well, I didn't think this.'

The split shift had made the day extra long, but it had been more than worth it to have seen Matt and to have been there when he received his serious news. Persephone hoped she could find a way to give him the support he needed as he came to terms with this major change to his life. On her way home, she walked briskly alongside the old brick wall that surrounded the grounds of Darley Court until she arrived at the wide gateway inside which stood the gatekeeper's lodge. To either side of the long drive, the old gardens were now laid out for crops on the rota system that Miss Brown oversaw. Persephone started up the drive towards the handsome mansion, which was clearly visible, its many windows criss-crossed with anti-blast tape and the porte cochère, the grand drive-through porch, protruding from the front of the building. In days of yore horse-drawn carriages had pulled up beneath its shelter so that visitors could descend untroubled by wind or rain.

Instead of going up the wide flight of stone steps to enter through the grand front entrance, Persephone veered off and headed around to the rear of the building, pausing to drop into the stables to see the faithful old horses who worked on the land. They snuffled at her hands and she laughed and showed an empty palm.

'Sorry, no treats today. I'll bring you a bit of carrot before you settle down for the night.'

She went in through the kitchen door. Mrs Mitchell looked round from the saucepans she was tending on the vast range.

'How's Matt?' the housekeeper asked at once. 'Did you see him?'

'He's doing well, thanks,' said Persephone, 'but he's just found out that there's permanent damage to one of his shoulders that means there's no question of his being able to return to his old job.'

'That's a shame,' said Mrs Mitchell, 'but it can't come as a total surprise, surely, after what happened.'

'I'm afraid it has,' Persephone told her. 'The doctors have been very pleased with him so far and he thought that meant a full recovery.'

'Has he been told about t'other fellow yet?' Mrs Mitchell asked. 'The driver.'

'Yes. He feels very bad about that. He can't understand how he survived when poor Mr Gibson perished.'

'It might just as easily have been the other way round,' Mrs Mitchell observed. 'It could have been Driver Gibson asking how come he was still alive when his young fireman had died.'

'It's a lot for Matt to take in,' said Persephone.

'Of course it is,' said Mrs Mitchell, 'but he'll get to grips with it. He just needs a bit of time.'

'He'll have plenty of that while he's in hospital,' said Persephone. 'They're talking about bringing him to Manchester so he can recuperate here, closer to home and his family.'

'If he's well enough to be moved, that's a good sign.'

Persephone smiled. A different doctor had come to Matt's room towards the end of visiting time to deliver this piece of news and Mrs Franklin had shed tears of gratitude and relief. Persephone had been glad to be there to share the special moment.

'It's something to look forward to,' she said now.

'I've got some other good news for you.' Mrs Mitchell smiled. 'You've got a visitor.'

'Who? I'm not expecting anybody.' She assumed it must be one of her chums.

But Mrs Mitchell said, 'Your sister. Miss Brown received a telegram asking if she could beg a room for a couple of nights and she got here an hour ago. I've put her in the same bedroom as last time.' As Persephone headed for the stairs up into the main house, Mrs Mitchell added, 'I think you'll find her in the sitting room with Miss Brown.'

A minute later Persephone hurried into the small sitting room, where the golden-edged light of evening poured generously through the windows undeterred by the anti-blast tape, and lending brightness to the colourful cushions on the sofa and the chairs. Miss Brown and Iphigenia looked round as the door opened. Iphigenia started to get up but Miss Brown rose to her feet with a speed and fluidity that belied her age.

'Good evening, Persephone,' she said. 'I'll leave you girls to it. It's a pleasure to have you here again, Mrs McLean Grey. I hope you will stay as long as it suits.'

'You're very kind,' Iphigenia told her hostess, 'and all the more so after the way I foisted myself onto you. Thank you for everything.'

The two sisters waited for Miss Brown to leave the room. Persephone hovered politely by the door to close it behind her, then Iphigenia jumped up from her place and they hugged one another.

'What are you doing here?' Persephone asked as they sat side by side on the sofa. 'Not that I want to sound ungracious. It's wonderful to see you, but something of a surprise.'

'You didn't really expect me to stay away, did you?' asked Iphigenia. 'Not with Matt in hospital. He and the driver were so brave. You must feel very proud as well as quite shattered with shock.'

'You've summed it up perfectly,' Persephone told her with a smile. 'You could be a writer with that kind of insight.'

'No fear,' Iphigenia retorted. 'Now tell me, how is he?'

Persephone described Matt's injuries, seeing how her sister's eyes clouded with anxiety and concern. She explained about Matt's shoulder.

Iphigenia's response was similar to that of Matt's mother and Mrs Mitchell.

'Really, he's astoundingly lucky to get off so lightly.'

'You know that and I know that, but just now it's a lot for Matt to accept. He loves his job – loved it, I should say. It's not going to be easy for him to part with it. But on a happier note, they were talking only this afternoon about bringing him back to Manchester to complete his recovery here.'

'It's truly extraordinary,' said Iphigenia. 'The other chap gets killed outright, yet Matt is going to be right as ninepence eventually. Maybe not quite as good as new, but pretty darned close.' She took Persephone's hand. 'And how are you, little sister?'

'There's nothing wrong with me,' Persephone answered dismissively. 'My only concern is for Matt. It's so good of you to come.'

'I wanted to,' said Iphigenia. 'What Matt and Driver Gibson did was the last word in courage. They saved a great many lives that night.' She paused before saying something Persephone had sensed but hadn't dared put into words even inside her head. 'What they did transcended all barriers, all the ideas and rules we have about class and education. Those two men are the equal of anyone in the land. There is talk of George Crosses, you know.'

'I'd like to see Mr Gibson awarded one posthumously,' said Persephone. 'It would mean a lot to his family.'

'Something to be proud of for ever,' said Iphigenia.

'Do you think . . . ?' Persephone started to say but the words trailed away. She started again. She needed to ask this. 'Do you think it will make Ma and Pa look at Matt with new eyes?'

'They already do,' Iphigenia said at once. 'They're deeply impressed. But if you imagine it makes him son-in-law material, don't fool yourself. They're impressed but they're not *that* impressed.'

'I thought so.' Persephone stifled a sigh. 'Anyway, Matt and I both know what we have is temporary.'

'Oh, sweetie, the look in your eyes when you say that.'

'Let's not talk about it,' said Persephone. 'It really doesn't help.'

'Then let me tell you something else.' Iphigenia leaned closer. 'Something *very* secret. David took me for a spin in his Cessna. He called it going for a spin but really he wanted me to see the south coast. I've been so frightfully worried about Hugo, you see, with him being I know not where, and David wanted to make me feel better.'

'What's on the south coast?' Persephone asked, but she could already guess.

'We flew all the way to Southampton and back along the coast,' said Iphigenia, 'and we saw the fleet, Persephone, and calling it "the fleet" doesn't give you any idea of the size of what has been amassed and got ready. My goodness, all those vessels! David didn't say a word about it but he wanted me to see so that I'd know that wherever Hugo is and whatever he's engaged in, help is on the way, if you know what I mean. They're getting ready for it right now, right this minute – the invasion of Europe. It's been hoped for and talked about for so long and now it's going to happen. And just as David wanted me to know, I wanted you to, because all the munitions trains are a part of what's happening all along the south coast. I don't know how many munitions trains Matt and Mr Gibson drove, but every single one of them counted. That's what you must remember whenever you think of the dreadful night of the explosion. Those two men weren't heroes just for that one night. They played their part time after time – they and all the other train drivers and firemen and guards who delivered munitions. They all contributed to the coming invasion. One day we'll be able to say they all helped to win the war.'

Chapter Twenty-Seven

Colette was dreading the inquest. Every time she pictured it, her breathing accelerated and the knot of anxiety that had taken up residence inside her stomach tightened. Cordelia had explained to her that the coroner wouldn't be interested solely in the cause of death but would want to understand the circumstances of what had taken place too.

'Do you think they'll want to drag up the case that took place in the magistrates' court?' Colette asked her friends. She bit her lip, scared and dismayed. 'That made me look bad and I don't want to be put through that again.'

'Whatever happens, you know we'll all stand by you,' said Alison.

'All the bad things that happened were Tony's fault, not yours,' Emily said loyally.

'Honest to God, I could murder that solicitor Tony employed to represent him,' said Dot. 'He was too clever by half. He turned everything on its head.'

'You deserved a lot better than that,' said Cordelia. She had been one of those who had attended the court hearing with Colette to support her.

Colette remembered Cordelia being called unexpectedly into the witness box by Mr Jeremy Wagstaff, Tony's solicitor, who had cleverly manipulated her into saying that Colette's friends had always considered Tony to be a devoted husband, if over-protective, when they first knew them as a couple. 'We thought her lucky to have such a loving husband,' was what he had led Cordelia to say – and then he hadn't given her the chance to explain how they had later changed their minds. Was Cordelia thinking of that too? Mr Wagstaff had indeed turned Cordelia's intended meaning on its head.

'I don't see why the magistrate's case should come up at the inquest,' Persephone said thoughtfully. 'An inquest looks into the whys and wherefores of a death.'

'Some might say the court case was entirely relevant,' Cordelia replied. 'The coroner will want to know about Tony's state of mind and that means he'll have to be told about Tony and Colette's marriage.'

'And their separation,' Margaret finished in a solemn voice.

'Even if Tony refused to recognise it as such,' Colette added. 'Goodness, doesn't that make me look bad? The wife who left when her husband wanted her to stay. Is it selfish of me to wonder about the possible impact on myself and the way others will see me?'

'Not at all,' the others were quick to assure her.

'Then there's Mr Naylor and the letter he wrote to Tony telling him you were seeing another man,' said Fay. 'That's part of what happened. It explains why Tony followed you and accosted you.'

'When Mr Wagstaff made it sound in the magistrates' court as if what Tony did to me was actually all my own fault because I'd pushed him beyond what a reasonable man might be expected to endure,' said Colette, 'that was bad enough. I can't bear to think that the incident at the station and Tony's death will be made out to be my fault as well – and not just mine,' she added as her heart dealt a thump of panic. 'I dread to think what this could do to Nathan's reputation.'

'But he was a hero,' said Alison.

'Definitely,' Margaret concurred. 'He could have left Tony stuck in the points and saved himself but he stayed and tried to pull Tony free.'

'He only leaped aside at the last moment,' said Emily.

Colette shut her eyes, re-living that terrifying moment when it had seemed that Nathan could well have been struck by the loco leading the goods wagons. 'I wouldn't wish what happened to Tony on anybody,' she said softly, 'but the idea of it happening to Nathan—' She couldn't finish the sentence.

'Aye, chick, we know,' said Dot. 'We understand.'

'Is it right that the inquest is going to be held in Chester?' Joan asked. 'I would have thought it would take place here in Manchester. This is where Tony lived.'

'An inquest is generally held in the jurisdiction where the person dies,' said Cordelia.

'Tony's father did try to have it moved over here to Manchester,' Colette told her friends. 'These things can be done, apparently, but the coroner declined. He said there was no need for it.'

'I imagine there's a lot of red tape involved if you move an inquest from one coroner's area to another,' said Fay.

'Not to mention that the authorities very likely wish to

hold the inquest as soon as possible and get everything wrapped up,' said Cordelia. 'The story of a soldier doing what Tony did isn't something that they will want to be published far and wide.'

'They'll want to hush it up, you mean?' Emily asked.

'I don't think that coroners lend themselves to hushing things up,' said Cordelia, 'but I imagine there is a wish to have this matter dealt with promptly.'

Dot reached over and laid her hand on Colette's. 'It goes without saying that, shifts permitting, as many of us as can will come with you, chick. We don't want you to have to face this alone.'

'Thank you.' Colette was deeply touched, though not surprised.

'Miss Brown has offered to accompany you as well,' Persephone added.

'Miss Brown has?' Joan asked.

'Given the reason why Tony was at that station in the first place,' said Persephone, 'she says that it wouldn't hurt for Colette to have a person of some consequence by her side. It won't sway the findings of the inquest, of course, but it will show that Colette is in highly respectable company and therefore may be supposed to be equally respectable. I'm sorry,' she added, addressing Colette directly. 'I don't mean to make it sound as though there is anything untoward about you.'

'Don't apologise,' said Colette. 'I know exactly what you mean.'

'It's the way of the world,' said Dot. 'Appearances are everything.'

'It's very good of Miss Brown,' said Colette, 'and I'm grateful for her support.'

'She's happy to help,' said Persephone.

Emotion rose inside Colette. Having her friends stand by her meant everything – and not just them but Miss Brown also. That would make a real difference. Miss Brown was an important person and even though she wouldn't be on her own patch, her presence would count for something. Anyone who intended to look with disapproval upon Colette would think again when they saw whom she was with. Dot was right: it was the way of the world.

Colette wasn't just concerned for herself when she thought about the inquest. She was worried on Nathan's behalf too. One bright evening, he came over to Wilton Close and they went for a walk on the meadows, strolling along beside a hedgerow in which early traveller's joy, tempted out by recent warmth, twined its long stems and clung on, its buds waiting to open up and display its scented flowers of greenish-white. A wild honeysuckle also lived in the hedge.

'It won't be long now before it flowers,' said Nathan. 'We'll have to come here again in June and July to watch the moths. The honeysuckle's scent is strongest in the evening and it attracts them.'

Something inside Colette relaxed. Not that she had doubted for a single moment that she and Nathan would still be together as a couple after the inquest but hearing him speak of the future even in such a minor way gave her courage and confidence.

'It's not just myself I'm concerned about,' she told him when they inevitably started talking about the imminent inquest. 'I worry for you too. I hate to think of you being identified as the man who got involved with another man's wife. That's how plenty of people will see it and they'll conveniently forget what Tony did to me. What is reported at the inquest could end up damaging your reputation, not to mention the hurt it would cause to your family.'

'I'd be lying if I said I hadn't thought of it,' Nathan told her. 'I haven't told my family about you yet and this isn't exactly the most desirable way for them to find out.'

Colette hesitated before asking, 'Had you better tell them before the inquest?'

'I gave that some thought but I decided against it,' said Nathan. 'I don't want to be pushed into telling them. This is our relationship and we have to proceed with it in the way that seems right to us – and that doesn't include telling my daughter and sister-in-law because I've been forced into a corner and had the choice taken away from me. You and I were there that day because of acting as railway chaperones to Miss Stidson's class. That's what we have to remember.' He huffed a sigh. 'I go through all that in my mind and then I feel guilty because it might seem as if I'm denying our relationship and that's the very last thing I want to do, Colette. You know that, don't you?'

'Of course,' she answered. 'You're a good man, a good father. You want to protect your daughter from all this nastiness and so do I. I know what it is to be the subject of gossip and speculation. The most important part of this whole situation is to protect Evie from that.'

'And my sister-in-law,' Nathan added. 'I don't want this to be her first knowledge of you.'

Nathan's wish not to tell his family about Colette yet was part of their joint decision to take things slowly. It had suited both of them to do so, not just for their own different and individual reasons but also because each of them understood the other's wishes and point of view.

'It's difficult for me to keep quiet about our relationship,' Nathan said, 'because frankly I feel like shouting it from the rooftops. You're the best thing to happen to me in a long time. Don't ever doubt that. But Dorcas is very protective of Evie – we both are – and it is essential that when I tell her about you, she feels that what I'm doing is certain and right, not just because of your own situation but because – well, to be frank, because of the age difference. I don't want to appear to be a foolish middle-aged man who has had his head turned by a pretty girl.'

Colette didn't feel she could demur at being called a pretty girl because it might seem like fishing for compliments, but she could say, her voice ringing with sincerity, 'No one could ever think of you as a foolish man.'

He smiled at her. 'I certainly hope not. Meeting and getting to know you has given me a second chance that I never thought I'd have and never looked for. When Lilian passed away, I expected to spend the rest of my life alone. Some men would have looked for a second wife simply because they needed one, but Lilian's sister stepped in to look after my household and help me bring up Evie, so I never had to think in those terms, which was a great blessing because I loved Lilian dearly. But now, with you, I have another chance of a loving relationship and I appreciate it more than I have the words to express. I want everything to be perfect for us, Colette.'

'So do I,' she whispered, 'but we have to get the inquest out of the way before we can think about that. And we have to hope that the inquest doesn't cast a shadow of scandal over us.'

'I hate to say it, my darling, but it will be for the best if we arrive at the inquest separately and sit in different parts of the room. I feel bad saying it.'

'You mustn't feel bad,' Colette said at once. 'It's the right thing to do. We have to be discreet and turning up together would be plain brazen. I want Tony's inquest to be a respectful occasion, not a sensational one. Then afterwards I'll be free to move on.'

Chapter Twenty-Eight

Matt had been brought by ambulance to Manchester Royal Infirmary to continue his weeks of recovery. He was allowed no visitors on that day. Knowing his parents would be anxious to see him in the evening on the following day, Persephone rushed to take advantage of afternoon visiting, thanking her lucky stars that she had time before her next shift started.

Matt was on his own in a small room at the far end of a long ward. When she first walked in and set eyes on him, Persephone felt ridiculously disappointed because he looked exactly the same as the last time she had seen him. Her foolish heart had duped her, telling her that if he was well enough to be transferred, then he must have improved noticeably, but she realised now that it was her own deep longing for his recovery that had planted this idea in her head.

She went straight to his side, asking, 'How are you? How was the journey?'

Matt's eyes softened at the sight of her and his lips formed the boyish smile she loved so much. 'You wouldn't think that lying in the back of an ambulance would take much effort but I felt pretty rough by the time I was installed here. I felt as if I'd been called upon to tackle the twelve labours of Hercules all rolled into one. But they gave me some knockout drops to see me through the night and I'm fine today.'

Persephone quirked an eyebrow. 'Fine?'

That smile again. 'A lot finer than yesterday. Believe me, lying immobile inside masses of plaster of Paris is going to be much easier now I'm back in Manchester. It's lifted my spirits no end.'

'Good,' said Persephone.

'I just wish . . .'

There was no need for him to finish. Persephone knew exactly what he meant.

'I know,' she said quietly. 'I wish it too. Everyone does.'

'I don't understand why I survived while Mr Gibson didn't,' Matt said. He had said it many times and Persephone knew he would say it many more before he began to learn to live with it.

'There's no answer to that,' she told him. 'There's just luck and gratitude and . . . guilt.'

'He was such a decent, hard-working man,' said Matt.

'He was,' said Persephone. 'I count myself lucky to have known him. You have lost your closest colleague and he was also a friend to you. That would be hard for anybody in any circumstances, but so much more complicated for you to come to terms with. Mr Gibson gave his life to save I don't know how many other people and,' she gently reminded him, 'you might easily have done the same.'

'I was unbelievably fortunate to escape with just a few broken bones,' said Matt.

'You have suffered a lot more than broken bones,' said

Persephone. 'Part of what you have suffered and what you continue to suffer is the loss of Mr Gibson. It is a loss that will stay with you for a long time after your bones have knitted back together again. And then there's the damage to your poor shoulder and the thought of not going back to your job. It's a difficult thing for you to have to accept. It changes the rest of your working life.'

'I'm lucky still to have a working life,' said Matt.

'You are,' Persephone agreed, 'but that doesn't mean that losing your job is something to be shrugged off lightly.'

'A good thing too,' Matt answered with a smile, 'because henceforth shrugging isn't going to be my forte.'

Persephone's heart lifted. 'I'm glad to hear you joking about it.' She hesitated before asking, 'Do you think you're coming to terms with it?'

'Not so much coming to terms as getting to grips,' said Matt. 'I'm determined to make the best of my life, which probably sounds very positive and even admirable, but the truth is that I can't for the life of me imagine what I'm going to do. I suppose they'll find me a suitable railway post, though of course it won't be a physical sort of job. But I'll have to get used to it and make the best of it, though I know there's nothing that will ever engage me the way being a fireman does . . . did. But that's defeatist talk.'

'No, it isn't. It's the simple truth.'

'You want the truth? I would leave my fireman job without a backward glance if it would bring Mr Gibson back. That's the truth.'

'I know you would,' Persephone told him. 'I know that men are supposed to keep their troubles and their pain bottled up inside and that it's bad form to make an unseemly fuss, but if you ever want to talk, I'll be here to listen and I'll do my best to understand everything from your point of view.'

Her heart felt all set to crack open as she uttered the words. She meant them, every single one of them, but she was also aware that she and Matt were now coming to the end of their time together. She couldn't forget Iphigenia's description of the forces amassed all along the south coast. That meant the invasion of Europe was imminent. The war would still go on for months yet, but there was no question that the end was in sight and when that happened . . .

When it happened, she and Matt would no longer be together for her to support him through his lingering grief for the fallen colleague whom he had liked and admired so much.

A new voice chimed in. 'Is there room for another at the bedside?'

'Miss Brown!' Persephone exclaimed. 'What are you doing here?'

'First things first,' Miss Brown said briskly. 'Are you going to do the honours, Persephone?'

Persephone felt a momentary shame. She loved Matt with all her heart and Miss Brown also meant the world to her, yet there had never been the possibility of introductions. Whenever Matt had come to the Darley Court estate, Persephone had always taken him to the old gatekeeper's lodge, where the land girls lived. There had never been any question of asking him up to the big house. Persephone couldn't have done that any more than she could have invited him home to Meyrick House. It simply wouldn't have been the right thing to do. Miss Brown wasn't a snob, far from it, but it would have been deeply inappropriate for her to allow Matt under her roof when she had Persephone living there with her. It would have put Miss Brown in an awkward position with Persephone's parents.

'Miss Brown,' Persephone began, 'may I present Matt Franklin. Matt, this is Miss Brown of Darley Court.'

'How do you do, Miss Brown?' said Matt. 'I'm sorry I can't get up.'

'I think that can be forgiven under the circumstances,' replied Miss Brown. 'I'm very pleased to meet you. It is an honour to make the acquaintance of a man who showed such selfless courage and may I offer my sincere condolences on the death of your colleague? I imagine you worked alongside one another for some years.'

'Yes, we did.' Matt's voice thickened with emotion.

'I'm glad to catch the two of you together,' said Miss Brown, 'because I have something important to say to you.'

'To us?' Persephone asked in surprise.

'Yes.' Miss Brown looked at Persephone and then at Matt over the rims of her spectacles. It was a familiar habit, one she often used for the purpose of intimidating her listeners. 'I wish to discuss the future of Darley Court with you.' She made it sound as though this was the most natural thing possible. 'Darley Court and its estate were the property of the Darley family for many years. There used to be a title and there were generations of baronets. The last one was Sir Henry Darley, who died in an accident early this century. After him there were no more male heirs and so the title died with him while I, as the nearest relative and indeed the only relative, came into the property.' Miss Brown smiled wryly. 'I was a grave disappointment to the neighbourhood. The widowed Lady Darley was a great beauty whereas I . . .' Miss Brown shrugged. 'I was the grand old age of thirty-five when I inherited, which was held to be considerably older back then than it is today, and the general view was that the estate had passed into the hands of a middle-aged spinster and what a rotten shame that was.'

'They all underestimated you,' said Persephone.

'They did indeed. Of course, I was indeed a middle-aged spinster, but I had no intention of conforming to expectations, especially when those expectations were so low and so very unflattering to me. I ran the estate myself from the beginning and that took the world by surprise, I can tell you. But now I'm well into my seventies and I've been thinking on and off for years what to do with the estate after I'm gone.'

'I don't even want to think about you not being here any more,' Persephone said with a shiver.

'Nonsense,' said Miss Brown. 'It's my responsibility to consider the future.'

'I imagine everything will be left to a relative,' said Persephone.

'There is nobody left now on the Darley side,' said Miss Brown. 'I do have relatives on my other side who would probably love to be left a grand house and its grounds, but they aren't going to get their hands on it.'

'Then what shall you do with it?' Matt asked. 'And why are Persephone and I part of this conversation? It's difficult to believe you're in need of our advice.'

'Not your advice, no,' said Miss Brown, 'but your cooperation. Now listen. I believe the world is going to be a different place after the war and big old estates like Darley Court will have to adapt if they are to find a place for themselves. It won't be enough for Darley Court to be a grand house with just me rattling around in it. It has to have a new purpose.'

'There's the farmland,' said Persephone. 'There will always be the income that generates.'

'Yes, there are the farms, but I'm not talking about them,' said Miss Brown. 'I'm talking about turning the house into something useful. It has been used for meetings and for training purposes by the various Civil Defence organisations all through the war and that has worked very well. Do you remember the beginning of the war, Persephone, when we had to put the house to bed? All the good stuff had to be packed up in straw and put in boxes and crates and stored in the cellars for safety.'

Persephone laughed. 'All those labels,' she recalled. 'All those lists of inventory.' She turned to Matt. 'That was what I did before I worked on the railways: I put Darley Court to bed for the duration. That was the official name for it: putting the house to bed. And we took in some of the minor collections from Manchester Museum and stored them in our cellars for safety too, as well as other private collections.'

'Darley Court has played its part in the war effort,' said Miss Brown, 'and in the future I want it to play its part in peacetime too. It has had generations of being a handsome place that local people could catch a glimpse of through the front gates as they went by. Many of those local people would have been employed there. But that won't be enough after the war, d'you see? Ordinary men haven't died in their tens of thousands, their hundreds of thousands, so that the wealthy can go back to living off the fat of the land. I want to see a fairer society.'

'How does Darley Court fit in?' Matt asked her, intrigued. 'Are you going to turn it into a school?'

'No, that wouldn't work because it would have to be a private school and I want Darley Court to be of benefit to the local community. I'm wondering about setting aside some land to build prefabs on, but mainly I'm making plans for Darley Court itself to be a college along the lines of the Mechanics' Institutes, where the working man could get an education in the evenings. But I want Darley Court to be for women as well and I want the courses available to be more than simply vocational. I want to offer the chance of education for its own sake, the chance to learn about literature, music and the arts simply to expand the mind and bring joy to the soul.'

'I think that is an excellent idea,' said Matt.

Miss Brown looked at him. 'Persephone has told me how you gave up the chance of a grammar school education in order to join the railways, so I'm not surprised you can see the merit of what I propose to do. Furthermore, there's another idea I've been mulling over for quite some time. It stems from the time when your friend Mrs Naylor came to stay with us, Persephone. It seems obvious to me that there will be a great many upset marriages after the war. The divorce rate is expected to rise alarmingly. I don't have definite ideas at present because it all requires a lot more thinking about, but I wonder if we can possibly offer places to a few young women at a time who find themselves in need of sanctuary because of the hand life has dealt them – as was the case with your friend.'

'Oh, *yes*,' Persephone breathed. 'I think there will be a need for that.'

'Good,' said Miss Brown in her usual brisk way. 'Then you'll be happy to stay at Darley Court after the war and help me to run the place, won't you? You'll still have ample time to devote to your writing. And after I'm gone, you can take over.'

'Take over?' Persephone's voice emerged almost as a squeak.

'I'm not leaving the estate to you in my will,' said Miss Brown. 'The death duties would be crippling and goodness knows how much of the old place you'd have to sell off to pay them. No, I'm going to turn the Darley estate into a foundation or a trust and I'm going to smother it in covenants so no one in the future can go back on any of my intentions – one of which is that when I pop my clogs, you will be in charge. Don't look so shocked. You're eminently capable and I know I can trust you. It will mean, of course,' she added casually, 'that you will have to live there permanently.'

Persephone stared. 'Live at Darley Court?'

'Why not? You've already been there for several years.' Having determined Persephone's future, Miss Brown looked at Matt. 'What are your intentions, if I might enquire? Mrs Mitchell told me about the damage to your shoulder and the impact this will have on your future. I was sorry to hear it.'

'Thank you,' Matt murmured. 'I haven't heard anything yet, but there's the possibility of LMS finding me a suitable post, though maybe they won't be able to, in which case I'll have to leave altogether.'

Miss Brown nodded. 'Those were my thoughts on the subject too. I imagine it won't be easy for you to step down from your current job. Persephone has always prattled on about how much you love it and how skilled at it you are. Nevertheless, I suppose you'll take your new situation on the chin. You are a hero, young man. You faced the most severe of tests of character and you did not shirk your duty. I admire you. If Persephone will agree to work at Darley Court after the war and then take the reins after my death, then you, Mr Franklin – or Matt, if I may – have all the personal qualities of the person I would hope to be by her side and share the role with her.' She laughed at their expressions. 'You both appear confounded. Well, I suppose I have taken you by surprise. Think over what I've said. I'm offering each of you a position and a home. You can let me know your answers when you're ready.'

Chapter Twenty-Nine

Colette arrived in Chester for the inquest flanked by Miss Brown and Mrs Cooper, with other friends bringing up the rear – Alison, Joan, Cordelia, Margaret and Dot. They were shown into a spacious room with rows of chairs for witnesses and the general public. The seats all faced the coroner's desk at the front. Over to one side was a lectern where the witnesses would stand one at a time to answer the coroner's questions and give their evidence.

Miss Brown led the way decisively into a line of chairs a couple of rows from the front on the right-hand side.

'Thank you for not marching up to the front,' Colette whispered as they sat down and she put her handbag on the floor beside her seat.

'That wouldn't be your style, my dear,' Miss Brown replied. 'Nor is it mine, for that matter. As the widow of the deceased, you are entitled to a place at the front, but I think a little discretion is advisable.'

Colette nodded her agreement. She had already spied Mr Naylor and Bunty in the front row on the other side. Well, what had she expected? Where else would Mr Naylor sit other than in prime position? To him, that was his God-given place.

Colette heard others walk in but she didn't look round.

She knew the stationmaster would be here and so would the village policeman, as well as at least one member of the military police. The driver of the goods train and the driver of the passenger train that had been awaiting its turn would be called upon to give evidence, as would the signalman and somebody from the hospital, presumably Mr Salisbury . . . and Nathan. Had he arrived? Colette longed to turn around and seek his gaze but didn't want anyone to observe their emotional connection. Besides, she had no desire whatsoever to see if members of the press were present.

An elderly clerk entered through a door behind the coroner's desk. He had a piece of paper in his hand and he stood for a few moments, looking at the people in the seats. As Colette watched, he approached Mr Naylor and Bunty in the front row and spoke quietly to them but if he had intended thereby to be discreet, the effect failed miserably when Mr Naylor said in a loud voice, 'Yes, I am Mr Naylor.'

The clerk made a mark on his paper and walked down the aisle separating the two sections of seating. Presumably he was identifying the various men. After a minute or two he walked along the empty row in front of Colette, stopping halfway along and letting his gaze roam across the faces of Colette and her companions.

'Mrs Naylor?' he asked quietly.

'This is Mrs Naylor,' said Miss Brown and the clerk marked her off on his list.

As the clock struck the hour, the coroner walked in and took his place behind the desk. He was a well-built man who carried himself with confidence but not arrogance; Mr Naylor might learn a thing or two from him about how to appear to best advantage. He introduced himself as Mr Chilcot and made the formal announcement that the death of Anthony Roland Naylor had been opened.

'Often,' he explained gravely, 'the opening of the inquest is a formality to release the body for burial and the inquest itself is postponed to a later date, but on this occasion there will be no postponement. The witnesses will be heard and the matter will be concluded.' He looked round. 'I believe Mr Salisbury is present.'

Mr Salisbury rose from his place and came forward to stand behind the lectern. He swore the oath, then explained who he was and described Tony's injuries and the cause of his death. Mr Chilcot asked some questions, then thanked him and asked him to remain in the room in case there should be further questions that might spring from the nature of the incident that had caused the injuries. Mr Salisbury returned to his seat, looking not best pleased.

'I intend to go through the events in chronological order so that the record will show a clear account of what took place,' said Mr Chilcot. 'This may mean that a witness might be called upon to give evidence twice so as to give the proper flow to the narrative.' He consulted his papers, then looked round the room once more. 'Miss Veronica Stidson, please.'

Miss Stidson took the oath and stood up straight, looking nervous as she prepared herself to answer the coroner's questions.

'Miss Stidson, you took your class to visit their old friends, I understand. Is this correct?'

'Yes, sir. I was assisted by two railway chaperones, Mr Gordon and Mrs Naylor.'

'Mrs Naylor being the widow of the deceased?' Mr Chilcot spoke to the clerk, who nodded.

Prompted by Mr Chilcot, Miss Stidson started to describe what had taken place at the end of the day trip in the waiting room on the station platform. Mr Naylor surged to his feet.

'I protest! She has missed out the most important bit. Those two might supposed to have been chaperones but really they're a pair of lovebirds.'

As a gasp ran round the room, Colette's face and ears became impossibly hot.

Mr Chilcot raised his voice. 'Who are you, sir? You cannot interfere with the proceedings like this.'

'I am Anthony Naylor, the father of the deceased.'

'Ah. I see. May I express my sincere condolences. Nevertheless, you must behave in accordance with the expectations and requirements of the coroners' court, Mr Naylor. If you fail to do so, I will be obliged to ask you to remove yourself.'

'But, sir, you have to understand why my son was there in the first place. His wife was carrying on behind his back—'

'That's enough, sir.' Mr Chilcot spoke sharply. 'I repeat, if you intend to remain in my court, Mr Naylor, you must restrain your feelings. Will you agree to do that – or should I ask the clerk to show you out?'

Mr Naylor sat down heavily, anger and resentment on display for all to see in the set of his shoulders. Beside him, Bunty hunched a little but then sat up straight once more. Colette felt a pang of sympathy. She knew what it was to have to behave according to somebody else's expectations.

Mr Chilcot addressed his witness. 'Please continue, Miss Stidson.'

The teacher looked across at Mr Naylor and then at Mr Chilcot. 'What that gentleman said was quite wrong, sir,' she announced. 'Mr Gordon and Mrs Naylor were completely professional in their attitude and their conduct at all times. It was the second time I'd had them as chaperones for my class and if they'd behaved in the way that the gentleman suggested, I wouldn't have asked for them the second time, would I? They were a great help to me on both occasions. They did far more than they strictly speaking needed to. They helped with the children all day and there was absolutely nothing lovey-dovey going on.'

'Thank you for clarifying that, Miss Stidson,' said the coroner. 'Let us say no more on that particular subject.'

He spoke in a tone of finality. Colette poured silent blessings on Miss Stidson's head for speaking up as she had. Not only that but she had said her piece with a dignity that had made Mr Naylor's outburst appear worse.

Miss Stidson described the scene in the waiting room when she had walked in on Tony and Colette, after which Mr Chilcot called the other witnesses one by one to put together a full picture of all the events in order. Colette expected him to start by calling Nathan but instead he began with the others. The stationmaster described seeing the two men in a tussle on the platform, then sending for the village bobby and the two of them racing down the side of the track because that was where the fight had moved to. The signalman explained what had happened when Tony had got his foot caught when the points moved and the driver of the waiting passenger train described watching in horror as the man he now knew to be Mr Gordon attempted to free the trapped man as the goods train approached.

'Mr Gordon stayed until the last possible moment,' he said. 'The goods train was almost on top of them, then the points opened and Mr Gordon shoved Mr Naylor one way while he jumped for his life the other way.'

Pride in Nathan's courage made Colette breathe in what seemed to be not air so much as pure satisfaction, but at the same time she couldn't suppress a shudder at the thought of the risk Nathan had taken.

Mr Chilcot had got the men to give their evidence piecemeal so as to put the events together in order, but he hadn't called for Nathan at all. Now it was Nathan's turn and before he started, Mr Chilcot spoke to the listening court.

'I have left Mr Gordon until last as his seems to me to be the most important evidence and I wanted to have everything else out in the open first in order that Mr Gordon's evidence can be heard in the knowledge of what has already been stated.' He addressed Nathan. 'Before you begin, sir, I have an important question that I must ask because of the unfortunate interruption we had earlier on. When Mr Naylor appeared on the platform, manhandling Mrs Naylor, did you know who he was?'

'I had never seen him before,' said Nathan, 'but I soon guessed. I read about Mr Naylor's violence in the newspaper some time ago.'

'And why specifically did you intervene?' asked Mr Chilcot.

'The first thing I saw was when he pulled Mrs Naylor out of the waiting room onto the platform,' said Nathan. 'Mrs Naylor staggered, though she didn't lose her balance and fall. He still had hold of her and appeared to be threatening her. I saw her try to free herself but he held on. Then she managed to hit him. When I intervened, it was to protect Mrs Naylor. I believe any man would have done the same.'

Mr Chilcot nodded, apparently satisfied. He then asked Nathan to describe what had happened next. Nathan went through the whole account quietly and accurately, with Mr Chilcot putting in a question here and there, though mainly he left Nathan to relate his account. Nathan was accustomed to writing reports and putting together information so he made a competent and convincing witness.

When he had finished, Mr Chilcot thanked him and dismissed him. On the front row Mr Naylor stirred and Colette worried that there might be another eruption but he restrained himself. There was silence for some moments while Mr Chilcot made notes. When he lifted his head, his expression was thoughtful. He frowned, evidently considering something.

Finally he said, 'I had hoped to avoid this. In general I try to avoid having female witnesses if possible, though I have to say that Miss Stidson made a very good witness. But after the outburst earlier by the father of the deceased, I now wish to hear from the widow of the deceased. Mrs Naylor, if you please.'

Colette's skin went clammy. She wanted to look around at her friends to see their concern and support but was afraid that to do so might make her look weak and unreliable.

Standing, she moved along the row to the aisle and went to the lectern, feeling as if this wasn't really happening to her. Her voice shook as she took the oath. What was Mr Chilcot going to make her say?

'Mrs Naylor, please can you describe for the court the circumstances in which your late husband joined the army.'

Colette directed her gaze at the coroner and kept it there. Even though she was determined not to look at him, she was horribly aware of Mr Naylor's narrow-eyed glare.

Her heart thumped as she said, 'Tony beat me up so badly that I had to spend some days in hospital.'

'Was there any question as to who had attacked you?' Mr Chilcot asked.

Colette shook her head.

'Please answer in words, Mrs Naylor.'

'He admitted it. He never tried to pretend otherwise.'

'And how did Mr Naylor come to join the army?' Mr Chilcot asked, something in his tone telling Colette that he knew the answer already.

That gave her the courage to lift her chin and say clearly, 'The matter went to court and he was found guilty, sir. The magistrate gave him a choice. He could either serve a prison sentence or join up. He chose to do the latter.'

'Thank you, Mrs Naylor,' said Mr Chilcot. 'That will be all.'

Colette clasped the sides of the lectern as Mr Naylor came to his feet again.

'Is that it?' Mr Naylor demanded. 'Ask her about that man she's got in tow.'

'That is enough!' Mr Chilcot's voice held scorn as he

addressed Mr Naylor. 'Sit down, sir.' He pinned his gaze on Mr Naylor as he waited to be obeyed. 'If you persist in this, sir, all you will achieve is to make it plain to the world – even plainer, I might say – precisely what sort of husband your son was.'

Colette was ready to sink through the floor. There was nothing worse than having your dirty linen washed in public. It was something Mother had always dreaded and she had passed on that dread to Colette. Mother had all but died of shame when the truth about her husband's debts had come out after his death. And what must this feel like to Bunty? Poor, dear Bunty.

Mr Chilcot looked at Colette as if he was surprised to find her still at the lectern. She let go of it and returned to her place. It took all her willpower to keep her head up, though she didn't look anybody in the eye.

Miss Brown patted her hand when she sat down. Sat down? Collapsed onto her chair, more like.

'That has gone in your favour,' Miss Brown whispered. 'The coroner clearly isn't going to take any nonsense from your brute of a father-in-law about the way you conduct your life.'

Colette was too shaken to feel glad and frankly she was too scared. She wouldn't dare take anything for granted or put words into Mr Chilcot's mouth.

Mr Chilcot brought proceedings formally to a close and said he would return at half past two to deliver the verdict.

'So we have even longer to wait,' Alison murmured as if the coroner was keeping them dangling on purpose.

Miss Brown led the way outside and crossed the road to

a hotel, where she asked for tables to be pushed together so that her whole party could be seated with one another.

'It's a bit like being with Persephone,' Joan whispered to Colette. 'You know what she's like, all smiles and charm and everyone falls over themselves to do as she asks.'

'Except that Miss Brown achieves it simply by making it clear she expects everyone to cooperate,' Colette whispered back.

'Are you suggesting I'm lacking in charm?' came Miss Brown's voice. 'I may be elderly but I'm not deaf.'

They all sat down and menus were brought. Colette felt too wound up to eat but it was easier to choose a simple meal and make inroads into it than to try to avoid having to consume anything. She knew her friends wouldn't let her get away with that.

Afterwards they lingered as long as they decently could over cups of tea and then had a short walk around in the sunshine, but Colette was anxious to return to the courtroom. They filed back in and resumed their seats as before. Soon others began to return. Mr Naylor marched up the central aisle looking to neither left nor right and took his place. Bunty followed. He didn't escort her, didn't hold her arm or make sure she was comfortably settled. He just left her to come after him, taking for granted that she would do as he required.

'Good grief,' muttered Miss Brown. 'Even a dog would be allowed to walk beside him.'

Colette sat waiting for the whole process to be over and hoping, hoping, hoping that Mr Chilcot would say nothing in his summing-up about her and Nathan.

At last it was time for the inquest to resume. The door behind the desk opened and Mr Chilcot appeared and took his place. He looked around the room at the assembled people and gave a nod that seemed to encompass everybody.

After some preliminary remarks he repeated the main details of what had happened before Tony had been struck by the goods train as it crossed the points and changed onto the new line.

'I would like to make it clear that Mr Henderson, the signalman, having opened the points so as to enable Mr Naylor to be freed, then had no option but to close the points once more in order to enable the goods train to cross the line. If he had failed to do this, then the goods train would have stayed on the original line and driven straight into the waiting passenger train. When the goods train went over the points and clipped Mr Naylor, this was an unavoidable event. Furthermore, Mr Foxton, the driver of the goods train, had seen the commotion taking place on the track ahead of his train and was applying the brakes at the time of the incident. Again, no blame or responsibility may be attached to him. I also wish to commend the courage of Mr Gordon, who when Mr Naylor found his foot trapped in the points, stayed with Mr Naylor and made every effort to free him – at no inconsiderable risk to his own life, I may say. In the moments it took for the points to be opened and immediately closed again, Mr Gordon pushed Mr Naylor clear before saving himself.'

Mr Chilcot had referred several times to his notes while he delivered this speech. Now he paused in order to look at everyone again.

'I would not normally do this, but I feel it would be

advisable for me to explain the difference between an accidental death and death by misadventure.' He didn't look straight at Tony's father as he said this but his gaze passed over him in a meaningful way that left no room for doubt. 'At an inquest, an accident is deemed to be a particular event that leads to a death. The accident could not be foreseen and was neither intended nor expected. Death by misadventure, on the other hand, means that the deceased played a part in what happened. He or she did something, took a risk, that caused the accident to happen. In this case there can be no doubt that the conduct of Mr Naylor was the direct cause of what happened and therefore I pass a verdict of death by misadventure.'

Colette almost slumped in relief, though she was aware of her friends around her all sitting up straighter. From behind, a hand squeezed her shoulder and she glanced round to see Dot.

'There, chick. It's over.'

Mr Chilcot left the room. Colette reached down to pick up her handbag, aware of her companions also preparing to leave. Just as Colette stood up, the elderly clerk who had checked that everyone was present before the inquest opened now approached her, holding out an envelope.

'Mrs Naylor, these are the papers you will need.'

'The papers?' Colette asked.

'In order for the funeral to go ahead,' the clerk explained. 'You will need to give this envelope to the undertaker. It contains the necessary permission for him to remove the body and take it to Manchester. You must also wait for the death certificate to be written. I assume you will hold the funeral service in Manchester?'

Colette stared. She hadn't given that particular matter a single thought. She had focused solely on the inquest and what was going to be said in public.

'You may give all that to me.' Mr Naylor twitched the envelope out of the clerk's hands. 'I will make all the arrangements for *my son's* funeral.'

The clerk gave Mr Naylor a hard look, then he lifted a finger to attract the attention of the policeman who had given evidence and who was still at the back of the room.

'Constable! Your assistance, if you please.'

Mr Naylor gave a snort of disgust and handed back the envelope, but the clerk wasn't going to let the matter go.

'Constable, will you kindly stand by in case this gentleman tries again to take possession of these official documents.'

'Those documents should by rights be handed to me,' snapped Mr Naylor.

'The widow of the deceased is the next of kin,' replied the clerk.

Mr Naylor glared at Colette. 'We both know how deeply inappropriate it would be for you to organise the funeral. You don't deserve that honour.'

'You don't need to engage in this conversation, dear,' Miss Brown told Colette. 'Take the envelope and matters can be sorted out later. If you'll excuse us, Mr Naylor,' she finished in her crispest voice.

'Wait,' Colette said softly. 'Mr Naylor is right. It ought to be Tony's parents who organise his funeral.'

'Ha!' Mr Naylor exclaimed. 'I should think so too. And I will need the death certificate.'

'No,' Miss Brown stated firmly. 'Mrs Naylor has to have that. She is the widow and there may be occasions when she has to prove her status.'

'I'll take it for now,' said Mr Naylor, 'and I'll let Colette have it afterwards.'

'No,' said Colette. 'I want the certificate.'

'You foolish girl,' said Mr Naylor. 'Don't you understand that I need it? How else do you imagine I can organise the funeral?'

'I will arrange for you to have a copy each,' said the clerk, 'if you will kindly wait here for a few minutes.'

He disappeared. Mr Naylor was about to withdraw from Colette and her companions when Colette stopped him.

'I am happy for you to make all the funeral arrangements,' she told him, 'but there is one condition.'

'A condition?' he sneered. 'I've heard it all now. Who d'you think you are?'

Colette lifted her chin. 'I want to be informed of when the funeral is to take place.'

'Over my dead body. You don't deserve any part in it.'

'I married Tony when I was eighteen. It wasn't a good marriage, but . . .' Colette paused. 'I ought to be there. I won't intrude. I won't sit at the front. I'll sit right at the back. In fact, I might not set foot inside at all. I might stand outside. I don't know. But I want to know when the funeral is to take place so that I can be there . . . at the end of my marriage.'

'*What?*' Mr Naylor exclaimed. 'What sort of dramatic drivel is this?'

'That's the condition,' said Colette. 'If you won't agree to it, then I'll take the papers and arrange the funeral myself – and I really don't want to do that.' She tried to send her mother-in-law a reassuring look but Mr Naylor was in the way.

He glowered at her, obviously reluctant to agree to her demand, but if he wanted control of Tony's funeral then he would have no choice. He pressed his lips together so hard they all but disappeared, but at last he nodded.

'Very well – against my better judgement.'

'Thank you,' said Colette. 'I'll write down my address so you can let me have the details.'

'Colette, are you sure about this?' Cordelia asked quietly, drawing her aside. 'About giving Mr Naylor your address?'

'The reason I wanted to keep it secret before was so he couldn't pass it on to Tony,' said Colette.

'More to the point, are you sure about handing over the funeral arrangements?' asked Miss Brown. 'He was your husband, when all is said and done.'

'It's the right thing to do,' Colette answered. 'Too many people know our story for it to be appropriate for me to be the chief mourner. I'd rather take a back seat. People can make of that what they will. It will be easier for Tony's mother if his father and I aren't at loggerheads. Easier!' she exclaimed, tears suddenly welling up. 'She's going to bury her son, her only child. There's nothing easy about that.'

Soon the clerk returned with the two death certificates and he gave them one each. Mr Naylor took the envelope as well, immediately turning away and marching down the aisle between the rows of chairs. He went so quickly that he left Bunty behind, gathering her handbag and looking upset. Without planning what to do, Colette followed them out, snaking her way between the other people who were now in the central aisle.

She caught up with them outside – or rather, she caught up with Bunty, who hadn't yet managed to catch up with her husband.

'I'm so very sorry for everything you've been put through,' Colette said softly but urgently. She knew she wouldn't get long to say this. She clasped Bunty's hands, holding on when Bunty, startled, jerked backwards. 'You don't have to stay with him, you know. You'll always have a home with me, I promise.'

A series of emotions flashed across Bunty's countenance – shock, confusion, embarrassment – and then a blankness. She shook her head and when she started to back away, Colette had no choice but to let go of her hands.

'I don't know what you mean,' said Bunty.

And she hurried on her way.

Chapter Thirty

Arriving with her friends at Chester Station after the inquest to return to Manchester, Alison asked a porter which platform they needed and then ushered the others towards the ticket barrier. The train was already alongside the platform and they gathered around one of the open doors. As Colette was about to climb aboard, she looked back down the platform and stopped. Following her gaze, Alison saw Nathan, himself about to board. He nodded, though whether his gesture was for all of them or just for Colette, Alison couldn't say.

Colette climbed onto the train and soon they were all seated, though not together because there were already plenty of passengers so they had to find places wherever they could. Alison thought about Colette and Nathan sitting in different parts of the train, maintaining appearances. She was grateful life was straightforward for her and Joel. She hoped things would in due course become equally straightforward for Colette and Nathan now the inquest was over and Colette was free.

When they reached Manchester Victoria, no one suggested going into the buffet. It had been a long day.

'Quite honestly,' said Colette, 'all I want is to go home and put my feet up.'

'I can't say I blame you, chick,' said Dot, 'and I know Mrs Grayson will have prepared a nice meal for you to come home to. A good rest is what you need – aye, and a good think an' all. It's a lot to take in.'

Colette thanked them all for standing by her and shook hands warmly with Miss Brown. Alison was impressed that the owner of Darley Court had lent her presence to the occasion. It made her realise once again how her life, indeed all their lives, had expanded through developing friendships with people from other walks of life.

'Let's go and catch our buses,' said Joan.

'Personally, I shall travel home by taxi,' said Miss Brown. 'I'll drop off Mrs Cooper, Mrs Naylor and Miss Thomas at Wilton Close on the way. We should be able to squeeze one more into the taxi-cab.' She looked at Alison. 'Mrs Maitland? We'll be going via Seymour Grove.'

'Thanks,' said Alison, 'but please take Joan – Mrs Hubble. Then she can collect Max from Wilton Close.'

The group separated. Dot, Cordelia and Alison walked to the bus stop. Dot got on one bus, Cordelia and Alison on another.

'What a day,' said Cordelia. 'Let's hope Colette can put it behind her and make a fresh start.'

'She deserves that,' said Alison.

'She does indeed,' Cordelia agreed.

Alison alighted at Seymour Grove and went home. Like Colette, she felt like putting her feet up but she had fish pasties to prepare for tea before that.

She hadn't been home long before she was summoned to the front door by a peremptory rat-a-tat-tat on the knocker, followed by a second equally imperious knock before she could reach the door.

'Keep your hair on,' she muttered as she went down the hallway.

Opening the door, she saw Mr Platt, the rent man. He was a paunchy individual with full cheeks and pads of flesh beneath his dark eyes.

'Hello, Mr Platt,' said Alison as he raised his trilby to her. 'Is there something I can help you with? It's not your day for our road.'

'No, it isn't. I've come to deliver this into your hands.' Mr Platt held out a letter. 'It's your notice to quit the house.'

'*What?*' Alison exclaimed. 'You can't do that. Why?'

'You aren't entitled to be here, that's why. The rent book is in the name of Mr Anthony Naylor and his father has informed me of his sad demise, so you've got to go.'

'That's outrageous,' Alison objected. 'We've always paid our rent in full on the day it's due. We're good tenants. You should just change the name on the rent book to my husband's – Dr Joel Maitland.' She placed a slight emphasis on Joel's title.

'That's not possible,' Mr Platt replied. 'I've already got new tenants lined up. In fact, I brought them here to look around the house earlier on.'

'You did *what*?' Alison demanded. 'You came into our house while we were both out – without our permission—'

'I don't require your permission. It's not your property. It belongs to the landlord.'

'And does he know what you're doing?' Alison asked. 'Is this his idea?'

'Mr Commons is a busy man,' said Mr Platt. 'He trusts me to deal with the rents.'

'Oh aye? And does he trust you to throw out respectable tenants for no good reason?'

'Now then, there's no call to make a palaver out of this,' said Mr Platt. 'I'll tell you what I'll do. Even though your husband isn't the rent-book holder, I'll allow you to stop on for two weeks to give you time to make other arrangements. I can't say fairer than that.'

'Well, I can!' Alison shot back. 'There's no reason whatsoever to ask us to leave. We've been here since Christmas and you haven't minded. You can't pretend you didn't know Mrs Naylor had gone for good. After all this time, you must have known she wouldn't be coming back.'

'Mr Naylor assured me—' Mr Platt began.

'Mr Naylor?' Alison frowned. 'Did Tony Naylor write to you?'

'No, no. His father, Mr Anthony Naylor, wanted me to leave things be regarding this house, ready for his son to return to after the war. He was certain that the young Mrs Naylor would see sense and return to her home.'

'Wait a minute,' said Alison as something slipped into place in her mind. 'It was you, wasn't it? You were the one who told Mr Naylor senior that we'd moved in and Colette had gone. That was you, wasn't it?'

Her lips twisted in disgust. Right back at the beginning of the year when she had told Colette about her father-in-law turning up on the doorstep, Colette had wondered who had spilled the beans. Now the truth had come to light.

'Why shouldn't I inform Mr Naylor senior?' said Mr Platt.

'It was only right that he should know. He has his son's— he *had* his son's best interests at heart, no one more so.'

Something else slipped into place. Alison narrowed her eyes.

'Was it Mr Naylor who told you to come here and serve notice on us?'

'What if he did?' asked Mr Platt, unrepentant. 'He's entitled.' He laughed scornfully. 'After the way Colette Naylor behaved, upsetting her loving husband to the point where he lost his rag and gave her a bit of a slap—'

'A bit of a slap?' Alison repeated angrily. 'She ended up in hospital. In hospital!'

'I'm not going to argue with you, Mrs Maitland.' Mr Platt spoke in a long-suffering tone as if Alison were the one at fault. 'Just hand the letter to your husband, that's all.' She half-expected him to say, 'There's a good girl.'

'You're doing this as a favour to Tony's father, aren't you?' Alison challenged him. 'I'll report you to Mr Commons for this.'

'Be my guest.' Above the pads of flesh Mr Platt's eyes were beady and pleased. 'I already told you: he leaves everything to me. If I've got new tenants lined up, and I have, then that's good enough for him.'

'My husband and I are good tenants,' Alison pointed out again. She was starting to feel desperate. They couldn't lose their home, they just couldn't, but this man had the power to make it happen. 'Doesn't that count for anything?'

Mr Platt looked as if he might be considering the matter, but then he said, 'Not in this instance, no,' and it was obvious he'd just been keeping her dangling.

'Why would Mr Naylor want to get rid of me and my husband anyway?' Alison asked. 'He doesn't even know us.'

'You don't matter two hoots, Mrs Maitland,' Mr Platt told her. 'This is to make sure that young Mrs Naylor can't come back.'

As Alison's mouth dropped open in shock, a new voice chimed in.

'What's going on here, then?'

Alison looked beyond the rent man and saw Mrs Summers, the woman who had been disparaging about Colette in the butcher's queue that time. Her presence was the very last thing Alison needed. Mrs Summers would just love the idea of its being impossible for Colette to return to the house over the road from her daughter, Mrs Nuttall. She would probably offer to help Alison with the packing.

'It's nothing, Mrs Summers,' Alison said firmly, wishing the woman would stop noseying and go on her way.

'Did I hear summat about Mrs Naylor coming back?' Mrs Summers asked, nothing if not forthright.

'No,' Mr Platt replied. 'You heard something about her definitely *not* coming back.'

'Well, I can't say I'm sorry,' said Mrs Summers.

'And are you also not sorry that the way this is happening is by me and my husband being chucked out so Mr Platt can install a new family and put someone else's name on the rent book?' said Alison. 'But who cares about that as long as the disgraceful Mrs Naylor can never come back, eh? Happy now, are you?'

Mrs Summers turned her steely gaze on the rent man.

'What's this about, Herbert Platt? Come on, I'm waiting. Tell me what's going on.'

'Get about your business, Mavis Summers,' Mr Platt ordered. 'This is nowt to do with you.'

'Oh aye? Well, I'm making it my business.'

'It's like I said,' Alison put in. 'As a favour to Tony Naylor's father, Mr Platt is serving notice on my husband and me, and he's just admitted it's so that Colette Naylor can't come back here.'

Mrs Summers rounded on Mr Platt. 'That's typical of you, that is, Herbert Platt. I remember you from school and you always were a slimy, two-faced piece of dirt.'

'Hey, look here—' Mr Platt exclaimed.

'No, you look here, *Herbert*. You'd do anything to get well in with someone you think is better than you and you always admired Anthony Naylor, didn't you? Well, let me tell you summat. I might have been in the same class as you, but my hubby was in the same class as Gerard Commons – aye, your boss, Mr Gerard Commons. He might have done well for himself and gone up in the world, but he's never forgotten his roots and if my hubby went to him, he'd listen. He's very soft on widows, is Mr Commons, and he wouldn't be best pleased to know you were taking the home off one.'

'But I'm not. She doesn't live here any more.'

'Maybe not, but Mr Commons would want her to have the choice. He'd want her to be able to come back if that was what she wanted and you know it as well as I do. So should I tell my hubby to get himself round to Mr Commons's house?'

'You wouldn't—'

'I jolly well would and I flaming well will if you don't put a stop to this,' snapped Mrs Summers. 'Go and fetch your rent book,' she ordered Alison, 'so that Mr Platt can change the name on it to your husband's – and then he's going to go and change the name in the record book in the office an' all. You hang on to that letter he gave you, love, because you'll need that to show to Mr Commons if old Herbert here conveniently forgets to do all the paperwork.'

Alison quickly fetched the rent book and watched as Mr Platt, muttering darkly, crossed out Tony's name.

'And it's Mr Maitland, isn't it?' he asked.

'Doctor,' Mrs Summers said before Alison could.

'Dr Joel Maitland,' said Alison.

'Here you are, Mrs Maitland.' Shaking his head and not meeting Alison's eyes, Mr Platt handed over the amended rent book. 'I'll wish you a good day.'

As he marched off, Alison gazed at Joel's name on the rent book, then looked up to smile warmly at Mrs Summers. 'Thank you. I don't know what I'd have done without your help. Ended up homeless, probably.'

'My pleasure, love,' said Mrs Summers.

'It was especially good of you, because I know what you think of Mrs Naylor.'

Mrs Summers snorted. 'I didn't do it for her benefit. She's gone and I hope she stays gone. Good riddance. This means she can't come back.'

'But – what you said about Mr Commons and widows—'

'So what? That was true,' said Mrs Summers, 'but I only said it to force Herbert Platt to back down and make him hand over the house to you and your hubby. Blackmail, you might call it. I like having you over the road from our Becky. Having a doctor in the street is special. It raises the tone. It's respectable. It's not every street that has a doctor in it. It's more than respectable. Having a doctor here is proper posh.'

Alison forgot everything she had ever been taught about being polite to her elders. 'Is it really?' she asked in a dangerously quiet voice. 'Even if that doctor thinks well of Colette Naylor? Doesn't that reduce his standing in your eyes? Because I'll tell you something: to my eyes, that makes him a better person and it makes me love and respect him all the more. He's kind and understanding and he doesn't follow the herd when it comes to forming his opinions.'

It looked as if Mrs Summers was about to retort, but Alison didn't let her get a word in.

'When he looks at Colette Naylor, he sees a good-hearted, gentle, trusting person who had the bad luck to be married to a rotter who trampled all over her. And because she was strong enough to survive that experience, the good housewives of Seymour Grove see her as brazen and a poor excuse for a wife. Well, the housewives can think what they want, but just bear in mind that Dr Joel Maitland holds Mrs Naylor in high regard – so put *that* in your pipe and smoke it.'

Chapter Thirty-One

Now that the inquest was over, Persephone couldn't stop thinking about Miss Brown's plans for the future of Darley Court – and she, Persephone Trehearn-Hobbs, had been chosen to play an important part. She was deeply flattered and proud. It was no small thing that Miss Brown, whom she looked up to so much, should have so much faith in her. That she should also want Matt to be involved in running Darley Court was utterly wonderful. If Persephone was thrilled by the offer Miss Brown had made to her, she was overwhelmed with happiness that the same offer had been made to Matt.

Although Miss Brown had told her to think about it, Persephone had known right from the start that she didn't need the time to do that. She loved Darley Court and welcomed the chance to remain there. Moreover, being in the position to contribute to its future in the post-war world would be a marvellous opportunity, filled with interest, challenge and promise. She definitely didn't want to go back to her old home and her old life with her parents, much as she loved and respected them. The daughter of a titled, landed family was of no use to anybody if she didn't get married and Persephone couldn't see herself doing that if she couldn't have Matt. Her mother's plan for her left her stone cold.

That thought made her realise something else about Miss Brown's plans . . . or was she kidding herself? She wanted to talk it over. Actually, what she really wanted would be for Matt to bring up the subject, but she knew he wouldn't. It was up to her.

Her work commitments meant that she wouldn't be free to see him tomorrow so she would have to wait until the day after. It was tempting to raise the matter with Miss Brown just to see if this was part of her intention, but Persephone recognised the importance of discussing it with Matt before anybody else. It was a subject just for the pair of them. They hadn't been able to discuss it after Miss Brown's hospital visit, because Persephone had had to hurry off to work.

When she went to see him, his expression brightened as it always did whenever he saw her, but after that his manner included an element of reserve that was most unlike him. She never sat at his bedside because with his being largely immobile thanks to his legs being encased in plaster, it seemed better to stand beside him so he could see her clearly without having to strain. She held his hand as he asked her how her work was going and they talked about the most recent war news about Monte Cassino and the continuing fighting in that region. Persephone was considering how to lead the conversation around to what she wanted to discuss, especially given the time limit imposed by hospital visiting, when Matt broached the subject.

'I expect you've hardly slept for thinking about Miss Brown's kind offer for you to help her run Darley Court and eventually take it over.'

'Something like that,' said Persephone.

'I can't think of anybody who could make a better fist of it than you,' Matt assured her.

'Thank you, kind sir,' she answered. 'And what about you? Do you see yourself also helping run the place?'

'It sounds very interesting, of course,' said Matt, 'and I applaud Miss Brown for her vision, but whether it's right for me is another matter.'

Oh cripes, this wasn't getting them to where Persephone wanted them to be. There was nothing for it but to lay her cards on the table. She fiddled with her wristwatch, feeling apprehensive. What if Matt didn't want what she wanted? Or what if he did but he didn't think it would be right?

'I think Miss Brown has given me the chance of rather more than just a job,' she said. 'Darley Court is going to be my home as well. Yours too,' she added, 'if you take her up on her suggestion.'

'I'm pleased to know that you'll have something fulfilling and worthwhile to do,' said Matt. 'I'm sure you'll do it very well.'

'I certainly intend to,' said Persephone. She had another stab at saying what she really meant. 'What Miss Brown has offered me is more than a home and a position.'

She looked at Matt. Would he help her out by saying what the 'more' was? Or did he not see it?

'It's a home worthy of my parents' station in life so they can't possibly object,' said Persephone. 'It also provides me with a job, which means I'll have my independence.'

Again she paused. Did he really not understand what she was getting at? Or maybe he did know or could guess but it wasn't what he wanted to hear. Could it be that happy-for-now suited him down to the ground and he didn't dream of happy-ever-after?

Well, Persephone dreamed of it, by the stars she did, and she intended to make herself crystal clear on the subject. It was the only way. If things didn't turn out as she hoped with all her heart they would, it wouldn't be because of any misunderstanding or lack of clarity.

'I want you to see what this means for us. Us, Matt. For you and me.'

Matt looked at her and she couldn't read what was in his eyes.

'What does it mean?' he asked.

'Miss Brown doesn't just want me at Darley Court. She wants you too. You have your own place there. Your knowledge and experience form part of her vision for Darley Court's future. My sister said that what you did the night of the explosion transcended all the usual social norms and boundaries and she was right. That act of heroism lifted you up alongside the greatest in the land in a way that has nothing to do with money or titles or tracing the family ancestry back to William the Conqueror. And now Miss Brown has given you the chance to live in Darley Court and be a part of it. Not in a posh way, but in a modern, forward-thinking way that will make your family proud but won't make them feel you've risen above them.'

Still Matt said nothing.

'For me it offers the chance of living my own life without having to fit in with all the old ideas, but in such a way that my family can accept it because they understand places like Darley Court. When I was in London, my mother talked about what life will be like in the grand old houses when the war is over. Some of what she said was plain wrong – like wanting me to marry into an old family.' Ah, was that a flicker of reaction in Matt's eyes? About time too. 'But some of what she said was spot on. Things are going to be different. Upkeep will be an important question for these old places. That's where Miss Brown has been so clever. She knows things won't all go back to the way they were. She knows she must find a new purpose for Darley Court and you and I can both be a part of that.'

'Is that what you meant about what this means for us?'

'Yes, but I meant more than that.' Here it came, the moment when she finally found out whether her future held the one thing she longed for more than any other. 'I meant that we can have our own place in the world, where we aren't bound by the usual social conventions and restrictions. We never talk about us, Matt. We can't afford to. We can't allow ourselves that luxury because of our different family backgrounds, so all we have is happy-for-now. Darley Court gives us the chance of happy-ever-after. That's what I want for us. The question is, what do you want?'

As she held her breath, Matt pressed his lips together and turned his face away from hers. Persephone's heart dipped so hard that she felt it would never come back to the surface, but when Matt looked at her again, his eyes were bright with emotion.

'Of course it's what I want,' he said, his voice husky. 'It's what I've dreamed of all along, but I knew we couldn't have it. I never thought . . . never imagined . . . I've been dreading having to say goodbye to you and having to live the rest of my life without you. It was pure torture listening to Miss Brown's plans and knowing she wants me to be part of them, but also knowing that I couldn't, because of our social differences. And now you're saying that you want us to be together beyond the end of the war.'

'Are you truly interested in the work Miss Brown has offered?' Persephone asked. 'I know that being a fireman will always be your first love, but might the work at Darley Court honestly satisfy you?'

'I've been lying here thinking about this major change in my life, no longer being physically fit to do the job I love. That's a considerable blow, to say the least. I'm sure that LMS would have tried to accommodate me elsewhere in the system, but I wouldn't have wanted an office-bound job with them. But this idea of Miss Brown's is something that truly has appeal for me. It has made something inside me wake up and take notice . . . But I thought I couldn't accept it because it wouldn't be right, it would be presumptuous, to insert myself into your new life.'

'Not presumptuous,' Persephone whispered. 'Just right. Perfect.'

'Are you sure this is really what you want, Persephone?' Matt asked seriously.

'More than anything,' she answered. 'In fact, I'll tell you how much I want it – I'll show you how much. Wait a moment.'

'I'm not going anywhere,' he said lightly.

Looking round, Persephone picked up the circular shaving-mirror that a nurse held for him each morning as he shaved lying up against his pillows. She pushed the mirror into his hands and feeling nervous and elated but also strangely calm because of the sheer rightness of what she was doing, she sank onto one knee beside the bed.

'The mirror is so you can see exactly what I'm doing because you can't lean over. If you're in any doubt, I've gone down on one knee. Well, one of us has to and I'll be waiting for weeks if I leave it up to you. Besides, this is a leap year and that means I'm entitled to do this. I'm entitled to tell you that I love you with all my heart, Matt Franklin. I also like you and admire you and have the greatest respect for you. And I'm entitled to ask . . . will you marry me?'

'Stand up,' said Matt.

'You haven't answered me yet.'

'All I can see is the top of your head and I don't want to do this through the mirror.'

Persephone obliged. She stood beside this man she loved so much and hoped . . . hoped . . .

'The answer is yes,' said Matt. 'We'll live together at Darley Court and face whatever we have to face, but the main thing is that we'll face it together. Three cheers for Miss Brown for making it possible.'

'Three cheers for me for taking advantage of the leap year,' Persephone replied.

'This has given me another reason to get better,' said Matt. 'As soon as I'm able, I'll be the one who goes down on one knee and pops the question.'

'Does that mean we aren't engaged yet?' Persephone asked, disappointment hitting her.

'Oh, we're definitely engaged,' said Matt. 'What will your family say? Are you sure you want to go against them?'

'I wish it didn't mean having to do that,' said Persephone, 'but you and I know that, socially speaking, we're flying in the face of every rule and convention there is. I would dearly love to receive my parents' blessing,' she added, closing her eyes against a sudden yearning, 'but I know I won't receive it.'

'And you're sure about choosing me?'

'A hundred per cent.' She gave a laugh. 'One thousand per cent!'

'The end of the war is coming,' said Matt, 'and we're going to help Miss Brown take Darley Court into the new post-war world. I like Miss Brown's plans. I like the way she'll be giving ordinary people the chance to be part of Darley Court. I like the thought of different parts of society coming together. There will be plenty who never understand it the way we do, but Darley Court is going to bring us together and make me good enough for you.'

'It'll make us good enough for one another,' Persephone corrected him gently, her heart soaring.

'And if we're good enough for one another, I intend to prove it by proposing to you when I can get down on one knee and do it properly. Now there's equality for you,' Matt added, his boyish smile lighting up his handsome face. 'A couple proposing to one another. That's a good start to the rest of our lives, isn't it?'

Chapter Thirty-Two

Persephone and Matt had decided that Matt would tell his parents their news when they came to evening visiting. Persephone had to wait outside in the corridor because only two people were allowed in at a time, the sole exception being if a patient was on his or her deathbed. Persephone sat on a wooden chair, itching to be a fly on the wall.

After some time the ward doors opened and Sergeant Michael Franklin appeared. Persephone came to her feet as she scanned his face. He saw her and his face broke out into a beaming smile.

'My dear girl.' He came towards her, hands outstretched to receive hers. 'Matt has told us the news about the engagement.'

'You look pleased,' said Persephone, urgently wanting him to be but at the same time determined not to take anything for granted.

'Matt explained to us about living and working at Darley Court as well,' said Sergeant Franklin. 'It's unconventional, to say the least, but I can see how that makes it possible for the two of you to be together.'

That was reassuring in so far as it went, but the original question remained.

'You haven't said if you're pleased,' Persephone prompted.

'After everything he has been through, I want my son to be happy. Having to give up his job on the railways was a huge blow for him – and for me and the family too. We know how much it meant to him. But Miss Brown has offered him a future. Not the future he expected to have, but a good one and one that will keep him busy. That's important to a man, especially a clever one like Matt. It will also enable him to be with you. I freely admit that it will take me a while to get used to that, you being an Honourable an' all, but I know how dearly Matt loves you.'

'He's the right man for me,' Persephone assured him. 'No one else could ever measure up. We're in tune with one another. I've spent the past year dreading having to part with him when the war finally comes to an end.'

'Matt said more or less the same things about you,' said Sergeant Franklin.

'So you're pleased?' Persephone asked, more confidently now.

'I'm surprised. I'm taken aback,' Sergeant Franklin said honestly. 'I'm also deeply grateful to know that my son has a future he can look forward to. As for that future including you . . . My dear girl, my dear daughter-in-law-to-be, I'm holding your hands in mine and I'm smiling. Does that answer your question?'

Leaving Sergeant Franklin seated on the wooden chair, Persephone pushed open the doors and walked along the ward. She would gladly have let Sergeant Franklin return to his son's bedside but he'd told her that Matt's mother had asked for her presence. Persephone experienced a twinge of anxiety as she entered the small room. Yes, she and Mrs Franklin had seen eye to eye over Matt's situation since the accident, but before that Mrs Franklin had disapproved of Persephone. Even though it had touched Mrs Franklin's heart to know that Persephone had run to find her injured son after the explosion, and that if Matt had died, he wouldn't have died alone, Persephone had no idea how important that was compared to a whole year of profound reservations.

Mrs Franklin stood at the bedside holding Matt's hand. Persephone went to stand across from her. Matt's arm on this side was still in the sling that held it in place across his chest almost up to his opposite shoulder.

Matt smiled at Persephone. 'Has Dad spoken to you?'

'Yes,' she said, smiling back at him. 'He was very kind.'

'Of course he was,' said Matt. 'He can see how our lives together will work.' He looked at his mother. 'What about you, Mum? Are you going to be kind to Persephone as well? I won't be pleased if you've asked her in here so you can play merry heck.'

'Language,' Mrs Franklin said automatically. She looked from Matt to Persephone and back to Matt. 'I've never been happy about this relationship because it seemed doomed to end in broken hearts.' Addressing Persephone she said, 'I could see all too clearly how deeply my son loves you and I felt scared for him. I hated to think of him getting hurt but it seemed inevitable and I blamed you for getting involved with him in the first place. I thought you should have known better, you being who you are.'

'I'm a big boy,' said Matt. 'I make my own choices.'

'Well, it never seemed like the right choice to me,' his mother replied. 'I always wanted a nice, ordinary girl for you.'

'From our own rank of life, you mean,' said Matt.

'Yes,' Mrs Franklin said immediately. 'That's precisely what I mean and I make no apology for it. But then Persephone came along and . . .' She sighed. 'I could see how very much she mattered to you, but then there was the business with the article to do with good manners between the different classes. It looked as though Persephone had come into our home and used our family for research purposes. That gave me a reason to resent her on a personal level.'

'Mum, if you want to say bad things about Persephone,' said Matt, 'I think you ought to leave. Persephone is my future wife and I won't listen meekly while you criticise her.'

'Don't you see?' asked Mrs Franklin. 'I'm trying to get it all out in the open. That means admitting to how I've felt over the past year and why I felt that way.' She dropped her chin to her chest as if she was ashamed, but after a moment she raised it again. 'Persephone, I accused you of using our family, but when Matt kept on bringing you to our house and I came to know you better, I realised deep down that I'd been wrong and you weren't that sort of person, but I couldn't bring myself to admit it. That's always been a fault of mine. Even when you wanted to do that article about the home where Peggy works, I made a jibe about it.'

'I remember,' said Persephone. 'You said, "Going to use us again, are you?" You made your position very clear.' She remembered the words because they had hurt.

'It was all tied up with being convinced that you and Matt oughtn't to be together,' said Mrs Franklin. 'A girl with a title getting together with a Franklin. I never heard the like. I was angry with you because Matt loves you so much and I knew it was going to end up with him being dreadfully upset.'

'That was then,' said Matt. 'What about now?'

'Persephone was there when you could have got killed,' said Mrs Franklin. 'She raced to find you and that means more to me than I can say. There might have been a second explosion, but she didn't think of herself or her own safety. She thought only of you. It made me see how much she loves you, Matt – and that made me worry even more about the future. I had visions of the pair of you eloping and ending up desperately unhappy because of your different backgrounds. What sort of life could you have given Persephone when you were a railway fireman? And what kind of wife would she have made for an ordinary man?'

'We have a good future ahead of us now,' Persephone said quietly.

'I can see that and I'm grateful for it for both your sakes,' said Mrs Franklin. 'I know Matt would never be truly happy with anybody but you and now the two of you have a way to be together. It won't be all plain sailing. You'll still have a title and he'll still be an ordinary man and there will be plenty of folk who won't like that at all. But,' and here she drew in a breath and released it, 'I won't be one of them. I'll be proud to think of the two of you working together at Darley Court – and I'll be happy and grateful to know that Matt is married to the only girl for him.'

'Thanks, Mum,' Matt whispered.

'Thank you,' said Persephone.

'And if you'd like to have it, you can borrow my engagement ring,' said Mrs Franklin. 'It isn't anything special compared to the sort of jewellery you must have seen all your life, Persephone, but it might do for now, just until Matt is better and can go to the jeweller's.'

Mrs Franklin held out a ring and offered it to Persephone, who took it, feeling overwhelmed by the generous gesture. It was a simple gold band with a small yellow stone.

'It's a citrine,' said Mrs Franklin. 'It's just a semi-precious stone. That's all Matt's dad could afford but I've always loved it.'

'It's so pretty,' said Persephone.

'As I said, it's not what you're used to, but I hope it might do for the time being. If you want to wear it, you're welcome – and it comes with my blessing.'

'Thank you,' Persephone said sincerely.

'Are you both forgetting something – or someone?' Matt asked. 'Let me have the ring, Persephone. Thanks. Now then, hold out your left hand.' He looked up at her, his eyes shining with love. 'Persephone Trehearn-Hobbs, will you marry me and make me the happiest man alive?'

Too full of emotion to speak, Persephone simply nodded, watching through a mist of tears as Matt slid the ring onto her finger.

Chapter Thirty-Three

The Allies at Anzio had now linked up with those in the south of Italy. The news was good, to say the least. In fact, it felt positively inspiring, yet Colette had to force herself to concentrate. She couldn't help but be aware of the general air of expectation around her as everyone waited and hoped for the beginning of the great push against Hitler, but quite honestly she was still shocked about what had happened in her own life. She felt as if she was still coming to terms with it all and she was surprised at what an effort it took. Her whole adult life had been spent either under Tony's thumb or else fearing the influence and effect he could still have on her future. Now she was free – but at what cost? It was a good thing, the best possible thing, to be free once and for all and yet – and yet – Tony had paid the ultimate price.

'But if he hadn't died,' Cordelia said gently, 'you'd be in a worse position now, because goodness knows what troubles you'd have ended up facing.'

Some of Colette's friends had come round to Wilton Close – 'To spend a bit of time together,' Fay had said as if it was nothing special, but Colette was perfectly well aware that they wanted to help her through this difficult spell. They wanted to give her the chance to talk things over in a private environment and feel able to say things that couldn't be said in the buffet for fear of being overheard.

'I know,' she said to Cordelia, 'but it seems wrong to be glad that he died. Not exactly Christian.'

'Aye, chick, but what he did to you weren't exactly Christian either,' Dot pointed out.

'Besides,' Alison added, 'you aren't glad. You're far too good and generous a person to be glad of it, but perhaps you can be grateful that your life is going to be straightforward from now on.'

'Goodness knows, if anyone deserves that, you do,' Joan said. 'You've had to go through so much. I'd like to see you get your happy ending. We all would.'

'Grateful,' said Colette. 'Yes. That's how I see it. Tony's death has set me free and I'm grateful not to have to live in fear any more.'

'I'm a great believer in counting your blessings,' said Dot, 'and you've been given a whopper of a blessing.'

'I feel awful for Tony's parents,' Colette told her friends, 'especially his mother.'

'Of course you do, chuck,' said Mrs Cooper.

'They've not only lost him,' said Fay, 'but they've also had to face up to some painful truths. There were plenty of witnesses to what happened at the station and they all put Tony firmly in the wrong.'

'And so they should,' Emily said stoutly and Colette smiled affectionately. She had helped the younger girl last year and now Emily was feeling protective towards her. 'After everything that Tony did over the years, it was high time he was publicly seen for what he was. If anyone thinks I'm being harsh, then I'm sorry but that's how I feel.'

'We all want to support Colette,' said Dot. 'That's what we've wanted ever since we finally found out the truth about Tony.'

Emotion welled up inside Colette and she had to blink back tears. She wasn't alone in having suffered at Tony's hands. In the end she'd had to escape from him by making it appear that she'd been blown to smithereens in the blast from a bomb and then she had run away to London. But this had also meant that the dear friends who meant so much to her had believed her to be dead and they had all grieved for her. That was more suffering to be laid at Tony's door, as was the way he had subsequently kept her from the others after he had tracked her down and forced her to return home with him, leaving her new life in London behind.

But the main thing now was that she was free. Sometimes her heart would pitter-patter in sheer elation, then at other times the realisation would leave her feeling stunned. It would take time for her to get to grips with this new reality.

Alison had told her about Mr Naylor's act of malice in trying to wrest the house from her and Joel purely to ensure that Colette would never have the chance to return.

'You don't mind that the house is mine and Joel's now, do you?' Alison had asked.

'Of course not.' Colette had been happy to reassure her friend. 'I can't think of anything better. Honestly, nothing would have made me go back there. It's nice to know that Mr Commons is sympathetic towards widows, but that's as far as my interest goes. Even if Mr Commons turned up on the doorstep at Wilton Close and said I could keep the house and have it transferred from Tony's name to mine, I wouldn't do it.'

'Even though you're a lodger in a house that has to be handed back to its real owners after the war?'

'Even though,' Colette had said and she meant it. 'The kind of security I've found through living in Wilton Close is far more important than the security that comes from having your name on the rent book.'

Afterwards Colette had thought more about what Mr Naylor had tried to do and it shocked her. It was so petty and nasty. It was beneath him. Yet he had done it and it showed him up for the sort of man he really was.

And that was not his only act of pettiness. Having waited some days to hear from him when Tony's funeral was to take place, Colette finally realised that maybe he wasn't going to let her know after all.

'I don't like thinking ill of someone,' she told Mrs Cooper, 'but I'm now questioning whether he ever intended to tell me. I shall have to go round to their house and ask.'

'I'll come with you,' Mrs Cooper offered at once.

'Bless you, you're so kind,' Colette said appreciatively, 'but there's really no need. I can manage on my own. In fact, I'd rather.'

'If you say so, chuck.' Mrs Cooper sounded uncertain.

Truth be told, Colette felt uncertain herself. She didn't want to see Mr Naylor again, let alone have to confront him, but if she was right and he didn't intend to share the date and time with her, she wasn't going to let him get away with it. It was a matter of self-respect.

When she went to the Naylors' house, it was Bunty as usual who answered the door.

Colette smiled at her. 'May I come in?'

'Who is it?' came Mr Naylor's voice from inside the house – again, as usual.

'I don't know why he doesn't answer the door himself if he wants to know,' Colette muttered.

Bunty gave Colette a nervous look before calling, 'It's Colette,' whereupon Mr Naylor practically sprang into the hall and inserted himself in front of her in the doorway.

'Oh, it's you,' he said.

'I've come to ask after the funeral arrangements,' Colette said clearly.

'Have you indeed?' He sounded altogether too pleased with himself, especially considering the subject under discussion.

'May I come inside?' Colette asked. 'This isn't something for the front step.'

'There's no need for you to come inside,' replied Mr Naylor, 'because there are no details to give you. We've had the funeral – and you weren't present. End of conversation.'

'But – we agreed,' Colette began, shocked. 'I would never have let you have those papers if I'd known. When did it take place?'

'Goodbye. Don't come here again.' Mr Naylor stared down at her as if he expected her to slink away with her tail between her legs.

Colette stared back at him, too shocked and upset to be angry, though she knew that anger was what Mr Naylor deserved.

He made a move. He was going to shut the door in her face. Bunty appeared at his side – no, not beside him. She was still behind him, as she often was, but she had moved to the side so she could see Colette.

Sorry, she mouthed. That was what Colette expected her to say – except that it couldn't be *Sorry*, because there were too many syllables. Then Colette realised. Not *Sorry*.

Southern Cemetery.

Colette asked Mrs Cooper to go with her to the cemetery and after a little thought she asked Margaret as well.

'I know it's an odd sort of request,' she said.

'No, it isn't,' said Margaret. 'Not if you want a friend beside you.'

'You don't think I'm mad to want to visit Tony's grave? It will only be this once. It's because of being cheated out of attending the funeral.'

'If it's what you want to do, then it isn't mad,' said Margaret.

'It's a way of bringing things to an end,' said Colette. 'Well, a sort of end. I shan't ever forget what he did to me or how I lived in fear.'

They caught the bus along Barlow Moor Road, getting off near the big gates inside which was the cemetery's office building. Colette had been feeling unsettled on the way here but the atmosphere of the cemetery reached out to her, embracing her in its peacefulness.

'Shall I ask in the office?' Margaret offered.

'Let's all go in,' said Colette.

She had brought her copy of Tony's death certificate with

her in case she had to prove a legitimate interest, but it wasn't necessary. The clerk, a smartly-dressed lady with a sympathetic manner, looked through the most recent pages of the current ledger and shook her head.

'There has been no recent burial in the name of Anthony Roland Naylor,' she informed them.

'Are you sure?' asked Colette, though she could see that the lady was.

'I've looked through twice,' said the clerk. 'Have you tried the crematorium?'

Leaving the cemetery's grounds, they walked along the road to the crematorium and again asked in the office. This time it was a gentleman who helped them. He checked the records and then returned to the wooden counter to speak to them in a low voice, confirming that the cremation had indeed taken place.

For some reason, the words hit Colette hard and it must have shown in her face because Mrs Cooper spoke up.

'This lady was expecting to be informed when the ceremony was going to happen,' she said without explaining who Colette was.

'That is not the responsibility of the crematorium staff,' said the clerk. 'It is up to the family to let mourners know.'

Family!

'Were there many people, do you know?' Margaret asked.

A lady-clerk came forward to join her colleague at the counter. 'I was here that day and I can tell you that only the late Mr Naylor's parents were present. They . . .' She hesitated.

'What is it?' asked Colette. 'Please tell me. I – I was Mr Naylor's wife.'

Both clerks had been trained too well to express shock or maybe they were used to dealing with all sorts of family feuds and upsets in their line of work and this was nothing new.

'They did not want to have his ashes returned to them,' said the lady-clerk, 'and so I can show you where his ashes were scattered, if you would like to pay your respects.'

'Yes, please,' Colette whispered, though she wasn't sure that 'respects' was the right word.

'Let me take you to our garden of remembrance,' said the lady. 'If you go back out the way you came, I'll meet you outside.'

She appeared through a different outer door and led them around the back of the low office building and behind one of the chapels into a sort of quadrangle with a large lawn down the centre, flanked by pretty flowerbeds. So accustomed were Colette's eyes to seeing vegetable patches instead of flowers that the sight of colourful blooms, mainly early roses, startled her for a moment before her heart reached out in acceptance of the quiet loveliness of the garden.

'If you look along the front of the flowerbeds,' said the clerk as she led them onto the lawn, 'you'll see that the months of the year have been marked out. When a family does not wish to receive the ashes of the deceased, we scatter the ashes across the part of the lawn dedicated to that month.'

Margaret picked her feet up as if she might be standing on something she shouldn't step on.

'Some of the ashes get taken by the breeze,' said the clerk, 'but mainly they are taken into the earth. Would you like me to show you where May is?'

'No, thank you,' said Colette. 'Would you mind if we sat on that bench for a while?'

The clerk gave her a sympathetic look. 'That's what it's there for. Take as long as you like.'

The three of them sat in a row in the shadow of one of the chapels.

After a while Mrs Cooper said, 'Are you sure you don't want to walk along to the May part of the lawn?'

Colette drew in a deep breath. 'No, I don't, thank you. I'm just . . .' Tears welled and she swallowed. 'I'm just enjoying the sense of peace. That's the one thing I never had with Tony. A sense of peace.'

Later that day Colette sat with Nathan in his little office at Victoria Station. It was early in the evening and Mrs Lister had clocked off for the day. As far as anybody who glanced through the office window was concerned, it was a meeting between colleagues, one on either side of the desk.

She told him about the visit to the crematorium. 'It makes me admire you all the more. I appreciate how very lucky I am to have an honourable man by my side, not just because of the life I lived with Tony but also because of the way his father prevented me from attending the funeral service.'

'That was an unspeakably shabby thing to do,' he agreed, 'especially since you could have insisted upon making the arrangements yourself, as was your right as the widow and the next of kin.'

There was such love and compassion in Nathan's eyes

that it was all Colette could do to restrain herself from reaching across to take his hand.

'I'm looking forward to being by your side openly,' he told her.

'So am I,' Colette concurred with a sigh. 'I don't care for the pretence. On the other hand, I do enjoy the feeling of privacy.'

'Have you given any thought to the amount of time you need to go by before we can be together officially?'

'That's not an easy question,' said Colette. 'The traditional time for a widow or widower is a year, but I'm not the ordinary sort of widow. Besides, I don't think I could wait that long.'

'I don't believe you owe Tony's memory that sort of respect,' said Nathan, 'but I do believe that you owe it to yourself. You have to do what feels right for you. Part of that means taking into account the way your conduct will be perceived by other people.'

'There's also Evie to think about – and your sister-in-law,' said Colette. 'I don't want to upset them in any way. A gap after Tony's death is probably a good thing from that point of view.'

'We'll work it out,' said Nathan. 'The most important thing is that from now on, you're safe. Tony can never hurt you again.'

'And we have our own future to look forward to,' Colette said happily.

'You deserve it,' Nathan told her. 'You're the bravest, loveliest, kindest person I know and I feel proud and amazed and happy that you've chosen me to spend your life with.

We might have to bide our time but I promise you that I will do everything I can to make what comes afterwards perfect for you.'

Persephone was more grateful than she could express for Matt's parents' supportive response to the news of their engagement and she loved Mrs Franklin's citrine ring. It was a bit big for her but that didn't matter. All that mattered was that Mrs Franklin had changed her attitude towards Persephone and the ring was a symbol of that. It was a simple ring of a type that nobody in her family would ever have looked twice at, but Persephone wore it with pride.

She was well aware that a significant portion of Sergeant and Mrs Franklin's acceptance of the engagement lay in her and Matt's joint future working at Darley Court, but that was completely understandable and Persephone didn't mind at all. Indeed, the only reason she and Matt had a joint future was because of Miss Brown's generosity and vision.

She couldn't hope for her own family to view the matter in the same way. Tempting as it was to tell Iphigenia first, it was important to do things in the correct manner and that meant speaking to her parents. Fortunately for her, Pa worked in London in the War Office while Ma held the fort in Sussex, which gave Persephone the opportunity to dodge talking to her father directly. She would let Ma tell him.

Persephone had to put through three telephone calls to Meyrick House before she finally caught her mother. She sat in Miss Brown's office, where the black telephone stood on the corner of the large mahogany desk inlaid with dark-green leather. Dawkins, their dear old butler, answered the telephone each time and Persephone pictured him wearing his Home Guard khaki.

At last he informed her that Lady Trehearn-Hobbs was at home and went to fetch her. After a time, Ma picked up the receiver.

'This is unexpected, Persephone,' was Ma's no-nonsense greeting.

'It shouldn't be,' Persephone answered mildly. 'I've rung before. I'm sure Dawkins will have told you.'

'Of course he has. Don't be obtuse. I merely mean to say that I don't expect to hear from you via the telephone. We write letters.'

'I've got something important to tell you,' said Persephone.

'Have you decided to acquiesce to the plan to find you a suitable family to marry into? That would be a great relief.'

'I'm engaged, Ma. Matt and I are engaged . . . Ma? Are you still there?'

'Of course I'm still here,' said Ma. 'You cannot engage yourself to that fireman, Persephone.'

'I already have,' Persephone replied. 'Before you say anything else, please listen. Our future has been sorted out.'

She explained about Miss Brown's plans for Darley Court, then waited, barely able to breathe.

Finally Ma said, 'Do you mean to tell me that Miss Brown has had a hand in this? Miss *Brown*? But we sent you to Darley Court—'

'—to keep me safe from the bombings down south,' said Persephone. 'Now Miss Brown wants me to stay for keeps.'

'And you think this means you can marry your fireman?'

'He isn't a fireman any longer, Ma,' said Persephone. 'He's going to make a good recovery from the injuries he sustained, but not a complete one. He can't return to his job.'

'I sympathise with that,' Ma said matter-of-factly. 'I really do. He was outstandingly brave and so was Driver Gibson.'

Was it foolish to take heart from the fact that Ma knew Mr Gibson's name?

'Surely you don't begrudge Matt a good job and a home at Darley Court?' Persephone asked.

'Child, if I could shower him with medals and honours, I would because he deserves them, but I have no wish to shower him with my daughter's hand in marriage. Your father will say the same.'

'I'm sorry to hear that,' Persephone whispered.

'What was that? Speak up.'

'I said I'm sorry to hear that, Ma, though I'm not surprised.' She adopted her mother's habitually forthright tone and perhaps it was that which made Ma soften a little.

'Oh, child, I just hope you aren't making the most ghastly mistake.'

'I'm not,' said Persephone, 'though I don't expect you and Pa to think so.'

'You do realise this will close the doors to your old social circle,' said Ma.

'Matt and I will create our own circle,' said Persephone. 'If there's one thing the war has taught me, Ma, it's that other circles may be different to ours but they're every bit as worthwhile – and a lot more welcoming.'

After speaking to Ma, telling Iphigenia ought to have been a breeze. In one way it was, because Iphigenia was thrilled to know that Persephone and Matt were going to achieve the happy ending they had long despaired of, but after that her doubts set in – well, maybe not doubts exactly but her worries for them and their future.

'I know how much you love him,' said Iphigenia, her voice sounding tinny through the telephone line, 'and it broke my heart when I thought of you losing one another at the end of the war.'

Persephone gripped the telephone receiver more tightly. 'But . . . ?'

'Oh, sweetie, you know all the buts. You don't need me to lay them out before you. What I will say is this: I don't know Matt but I do know you and I'm sure that if anybody can make this arrangement work, you can.'

'It's not an arrangement. It's our future, our married lives.'

'I know. I used the wrong word.'

'But thank you for the vote of confidence,' said Persephone.

'One thing I can promise you,' Iphigenia went on. 'Hugo and I shan't cut you and Matt off, no matter what anyone else does. We'll come and visit you at Darley Court.'

'Will you really?' Persephone asked, feeling buoyed up.

Iphigenia laughed. 'You won't be able to get rid of us.'

'I like the sound of that,' said Persephone.

There was a pause on the other end of the line before Iphigenia added, 'Give Ma and Pa time to settle down. They're not the sort to disown you for evermore. Pa will huff and puff but I know how much he admires what Matt did on the night of the explosion.'

'I'm glad to hear that,' said Persephone. 'Will you do something for me? Tell Grandmama that the plan to marry me off to a penniless lord has been ditched and she can leave her money to whomsoever she chooses.'

Iphigenia laughed in pure delight. 'Don't forget she was a Gaiety Girl a very long time ago, so you aren't the first member of the family to make a marriage that is less than conventional. Another thing for you to remember, little sister: I am a wonderful source of glorious wedding dresses.'

'I think we'll probably aim for something quiet in the registry office,' said Persephone.

A movement close by made her glance around and there was Mrs Mitchell. She gestured in the general direction of the front hall.

'I'm expecting visitors and I think they've just arrived,' Persephone told her sister.

They said goodbye and Persephone hurried to greet her friends in the grand entrance hall beneath the vaulted ceiling. Opposite the front door was the staircase, which led up to a square half-landing with an arched alcove containing a statue of Aphrodite. From either side of the half-landing, stairs swept up to the galleried landing.

Emily, Joan, Alison, Fay, Margaret and Colette had all piled inside together, their cheeks prettily flushed from cycling. No sooner had Persephone got them all settled in the small sitting room than the rest arrived. Cordelia had hired a taxi and had picked up Mrs Cooper and Mrs Grayson from Wilton Close and then gone to Withington to fetch Dot.

Dot gave Persephone an approving nod. 'You look a lot brighter than you did the last time we saw you here in this room shortly after Matt was injured.'

'I'm feeling much brighter,' Persephone said with a laugh. 'In fact, I'm unbelievably happy.'

'Matt must be doing well,' said Cordelia.

That made Persephone sober up. 'Actually, he had a major disappointment. He's been told that one of his shoulders has sustained a permanent injury and he won't be able to carry on as a railway fireman.' She held up her hands to stop the cries of sympathy and distress. 'Please don't worry. Yes, it's rotten for him but there is another change ahead. Miss Brown, otherwise known as my fairy godmother, has waved her magic wand and offered Matt and me positions here at Darley Court after the war.'

While her friends listened in astonishment and growing delight, she described Miss Brown's plans for the future. The others were intrigued and asked masses of questions. At last Persephone waved the questions aside. She couldn't wait any longer to share her other piece of news.

'There's more,' she told her friends.

'More?' Fay asked. 'As if all this isn't enough.'

Persephone held out her left hand. There was a moment of silence and then she was greeted by cries of pleasure.

'You're engaged,' said Alison. 'When did this happen?'

'Let me see the ring,' said Joan.

'It's Matt's mother's engagement ring,' Persephone

explained. 'She's letting me borrow it until Matt and I can choose our own.'

'That's kind of her,' said Mrs Cooper.

'And it's been made possible because you'll be living and working here in Darley Court,' said Cordelia. 'Miss Brown has provided you both with independence so you can make a new place for yourselves in the world.'

'Congratulations,' said Emily and the others echoed her sentiment.

'Thank you,' said Persephone.

'Best of all,' said Margaret, 'you and Matt have found a way to be together.'

'I've got another "best of all" to add to that,' said Dot and everyone turned to her. 'Best of all, our Persephone won't be heading off down south to her old home and her family after the war. She'll still be here with us.'

'My Manchester family,' said Persephone, happiness filling her to the brim.

Chapter Thirty-Four

As she cycled home from Darley Court, Alison couldn't wait to tell Joel the news about Persephone and Matt. Arriving at their house, she dismounted and started pushing her bicycle up the side passage towards the garden shed. Hearing her, Joel came outside and took the bike by the handlebar.

'Let me,' he offered. 'You go in and put your feet up.'

It was all Alison could do not to blurt out the news there and then, but she surrendered the bicycle and went indoors. Hanging up her outdoor things, she was glad to drop into an armchair.

'Tired?' Joel asked when he came in a minute later. Sitting down, he smiled at her.

Alison laughed. 'It's somewhat further from Darley Court to here than it is to Wilton Close, but I enjoyed the ride. I had something special to think about all the way home. You'll never guess what it is.'

'Then I shan't try, but I can see it's something you care about,' said Joel. 'I can tell by the way your eyes are sparkling.'

Alison took half a moment to be pleased at the thought of her eyes sparkling and her husband noticing, then she launched into what she had to say, her heart lifting at the sight of Joel's pleasure.

'So Miss Brown's plans for Darley Court have enabled Matt and Persephone to look forward to a future together,' Joel said.

'They can get married,' said Alison. 'No one ever imagined that could happen.'

'Even so,' said Joel, a note of caution in his tone, 'it won't necessarily be entirely straightforward. There will always be those who think they have no business being together, not coming from such different backgrounds. There will be talk.'

'That's no reason to prevent them from marrying,' Alison said at once. After a moment's reflection she added, 'To be honest, Persephone's family will in all likelihood be in that group. Not her sister, of course, the one who lent me that beautiful silk evening gown to be my wedding dress, but her parents will, and presumably other relatives as well. That isn't going to be easy.'

Joel nodded in agreement. 'She's got brothers, hasn't she? I wonder what they'll make of it. I hope they stand by her.'

'And I hope the General and Lady Trehearn-Hobbs come round,' Alison added with feeling.

Leaving his armchair, Joel came to kneel in front of her and clasped her hands. 'Let's be happy for them and leave the future to take care of itself. They know the social upset their marriage is going to cause and they've decided not to let it stop them. Three cheers for them,' he finished with a grin.

Alison smiled, buoyed up by his attitude with its mixture of optimism and common sense. He was right, of course. Persephone and Matt were well aware of what they were doing and that included the possibility of having to face unpleasantness, but they would face it together and that was what mattered. Alison knew the importance of having Joel by her side and was happy to think of Persephone having Matt to rely on not just for the duration of the war but for always.

Leaning forward, she dropped a kiss on Joel's mouth.

'What was that for?' he asked.

'I'd never have met you if it hadn't been for the war,' she told him. 'Joan wouldn't have met Bob, and Mabel wouldn't have met Harry. Colette wouldn't have met Nathan.'

'And Persephone definitely wouldn't have met Matt,' Joel finished.

'All those wartime romances,' said Alison. 'But it hasn't been happiness all the way. Without the war, Emily would never have met Raymond and he wouldn't have broken her heart. Poor Emily. I do so hope she'll meet somebody else.'

'She will one day,' said Joel. 'She's young.' He laughed at himself. 'Hark at me. I sound quite the middle-aged parent.'

'It means a lot to me that you like my friends,' said Alison.

'It's clear how much you all mean to one another,' answered Joel. 'I like seeing how you all look after one another. That's always important but even more so in wartime.'

'It isn't just a handful of marriages the war has brought about for us,' said Alison. 'It brought us together as a group in the first place. We've seen one another through a lot of ups and downs and now we know we're going to be friends for the rest of our lives.'

'Talking of the rest of our lives . . .' said Joel.

'Yes?' Alison asked.

'And also what I said about sounding like a middle-aged parent.'

Alison frowned and smiled at the same time, not catching his drift but drawn in by the warmth in his eyes and his voice.

'I've been thinking,' Joel told her, 'and now seems like as good a time as any to say it. I know we said we wanted time to ourselves before we start our family, and that's still fine as far as I'm concerned, but I want you to know that when you feel ready to have a baby, that decision will make me very happy.'

Surprise fluttered inside Alison, making her catch her breath, and not just surprise. Excitement too.

'This is sooner than we were thinking of,' said Joel, 'and the last thing I want to do is push you into it before it's the right time for you. All I'm saying is that when the time comes for me to be a dad, I can't think of anything better than for the two of us to be parents.'

'I had no idea you were thinking this way,' said Alison. 'Is it because of Alec? And everything Lydia has lost?'

'I can't honestly say whether that is part of the way I feel,' Joel admitted. 'It might have had a bearing on it, of course, because Alec's death has affected all of us. All I can tell you is how I feel. What's going on in here,' and he touched his chest, 'is my deep love for you and my appreciation of the life we have together. Those feelings aren't new, of course, but now they have an extra feeling alongside them, a new awareness of us as a couple and the family we're going to have one day. We have so much to give our children. Not just materially, thanks to my professional position, but also the love we have to offer.'

Alison tingled with anticipation. She knew Joel was right. He was going to make a wonderful father. Having lost his brother when they were just boys would give him an extra appreciation of parenthood.

'Are you trying to talk me into it?' she asked, half-teasing. Right then, loving him as she did, admiring him as she did, she would have agreed to anything.

'No, I swear,' Joel replied. 'The time has to be right for both of us, not just for me. All I'm saying is that when you want us to start our family, don't feel shy of saying so and don't wonder whether I'll agree, because I'm telling you now that the answer will be an emphatic yes.'

Yesterday had seen the beginning of June. This evening, Friday, some of the friends met in the buffet to chat together before the weekend.

'Just think,' Cordelia remarked to Alison. 'If you had kept to your original wedding plans, this would have been your wedding month.'

'When we got engaged, I couldn't think of anything better than being a summer bride,' said Alison, 'but now I can't imagine anything more special than getting married on Christmas Eve.'

'It was all perfect,' Emily recalled dreamily. 'You in that beautiful dove-grey dress with the long fur cloak to keep out the cold, and all those Christmas trees at the reception.'

'Not to mention all the toys everyone had made for the

local children and the kids who were spending Christmas in hospital,' Margaret added.

For a while they reminisced about Alison's Christmas wedding and she was only too happy to join in, but on the edge of her mind was the knowledge of the real reason why the wedding date had been brought forward from this June to last December. As long as she lived, she would never forget being told – not asked, not requested, but honest-to-goodness instructed – by Mr Samuels and Mr Mortimer that she wasn't permitted to have a summer wedding because it would be too much of a distraction.

And now she fully understood the reason why. She had thought she understood when she'd been told, but she hadn't really. It was the sort of thing you couldn't completely comprehend until you had lived through it – and now she had, or rather she was still living through it, organising the travel of the special trains ferrying men, ammunition and equipment to the invasion marshalling centres along the south coast. Since shortly before the middle of May, the transporting of the stores and heavy equipment had been under way. Someone had nicknamed it the Tarpaulin Armada because everything had to be shrouded beneath covers so that nobody could tell what was being moved around the country.

Ordinary passengers were accustomed to trains being longer in wartime so presumably they didn't think twice if they saw one that was unusually extensive. Special codes were the order of the day – X for Cardiff, A for Tilbury and so forth. The onward travel operators knew the codes by heart and they also grasped the importance of keeping them utterly secret, because if they should fall into enemy hands . . .

Alison thought too of the innocent-looking rural station Mr Samuels had taken her to see last year. Beside it had been a small siding and beyond that a field, where work was being carried out to extend the siding. Beyond that was a wood . . . and in there, between felled trees, were two long lengths of railway track that headed into a vast open space with yet more sidings and an array of buildings, all tucked away in secret.

Now whispers occasionally reached the onward travel office of hidden lengths of sidings long enough to house two thousand or more wagons, and once-sleepy stations on the south coast that, thanks to their hidden expansion, might see as many as thirty thousand wagons passing through during the course of this momentous year. As for what had to be transported: vehicles, gun turrets, spare engines, medical equipment, tanks – yes, and what a devil they were to move from A to B; all kinds of special arrangements had to be put in place – army blankets, kitbags, canned foods . . . the list was endless. Then there were the pontoons, which Alison had never heard of before except as the name of a card game, but which she now knew were flat-bottomed boats that were used for constructing floating bridges. Even telegraph poles and cranes had to be transported, as well as massive quantities of fuel and oil in what were known in the onward travel office as the 'jerrycan specials'.

It was extraordinary to think of and the most amazing thing of all was that it was ordinary railway workers who were organising it, and Alison was one of them. Part of her wanted to shout it from the rooftops, but of course she knew that was just her being daft and she didn't really mean it.

She understood as thoroughly as anybody the importance of secrecy.

Oh, but wouldn't it be grand to tell Joel and watch his face light up with pride? She would be permitted to tell him one day but not until after the war.

And would she also tell their children? Knowing that Joel was ready to become a father had taken her by surprise – but it was a good surprise, not a bad one. A very good one indeed. She vowed to think hard about her own hopes and wishes in that direction, but not yet, not until the invasion of Europe was well under way.

Even so, she couldn't block the thought from her mind and didn't want to. She had seen the adoration Joan and Bob felt towards their little Max, and she had listened time after time to Lydia's disappointment at her lack of a honeymoon baby. Not that Joan's experience or Lydia's provided reasons for her to make the decision herself, but they were bound to affect her way of thinking.

And Lydia – what would Lydia think if Alison and Joel announced there was a baby on the way? Would she be thrilled – or distraught? Would she remember all the times she had urged Alison to get her family started and be happy for them – or would her own lost marriage leave her in despair? But if it was the right thing for Alison and Joel, then they couldn't put it off to spare Lydia's feelings, which might sound harsh but it was true.

Alison worked on Saturday and was due to meet Mum in her dinner break, so she tried to thrust all thoughts of babies out of her mind in case Mum saw it written all over her. Wouldn't Mum love that! She had accepted, albeit unwillingly, that Alison and Joel had decided to put off starting their family, but if she thought for one moment that their choice was perhaps under review, there would be no stopping her.

In the event, however, Mum had heard from Lydia only that morning and so that was where all her attention was focused. She was still deeply concerned and worried about her younger daughter, though she had accepted Lydia's chosen path.

Mum was already at a table and had placed an order for two different meals when Alison hurried into the British Restaurant, giving Alison the choice of which she preferred: curried cod or vegetable casserole followed by either ginger pudding or steamed date pudding.

'Lydia has been told what her job is going to be,' said Mum.

'Don't keep me in suspense,' said Alison.

'She's going to be a meteorological observer,' said Mum.

'That sounds interesting,' said Alison. 'A lot more interesting than being a shipping clerk. How long does the training take?'

'Six weeks,' said Mum, 'and she has to go to Chelsea for it,' she added, her voice rising in pitch. 'In fact, she'll be arriving there tomorrow.'

'What's wrong with that?' asked Alison. 'I expect she'll be glad to escape from the training camp.'

'*Chelsea*,' said Mum. 'London. What about this new blitz that's going on? I take it you've heard of that?' she asked with asperity.

Alison chose to ignore the sarcasm, knowing what a

worrier Mum was where her daughters were concerned. 'That's a worry,' she acknowledged in a steady voice, 'but it's not as though Lydia has never been in an air raid before. Everyone knows what to do. Beyond that, it's a matter of luck.'

'Really, Alison,' said Mum, 'I've never subscribed to the "If it has your name written on it" school of thought. This is Lydia we're talking about.'

'And I want her to be safe every bit as much as you do,' said Alison, 'but there's nothing to be gained by getting into a flap about it.'

'I am not in a flap,' Mum said indignantly. 'Honestly, can't I express my concern for my daughter without you jumping down my throat? You're as bad as your father.'

Alison smiled to herself. She liked being compared to Dad.

'Will she be in Chelsea just for the training period?' she asked Mum.

'Yes, and there's no knowing where she'll be posted after that. She could be sent anywhere.'

Alison nodded. 'They have weather observers at every aerodrome, so yes, it could be anywhere.' Putting down her knife and fork, she reached across and laid her hand gently over Mum's. 'I know how worried you are, but this is what Lydia wants. If it helps her to get through the worst time of her life, then it's up to us to be positive about it.'

'I know,' said Mum. 'It's everyone's duty to be strong and make the best of things. That's the attitude that has brought us this far.' She smiled ruefully. 'I know I make a fuss sometimes but it's because I love you two girls so very much. You're my world and that's all there is to it. That's what happens when you become a mother. A whole new section of your heart opens up – and so does a new section of your worry-box.'

Alison was on duty on Sunday night and Monday night. Walking home from the bus stop shortly after eight o'clock on Tuesday morning, she was bewildered to see Joel come hurrying out of their house, leaving the front door open. As he ran up the road towards her, Alison went hot and cold all over. All she could think of was Lydia, newly arrived in Chelsea to start her training, being killed in an air raid. Dread rolled through her and she stopped dead, then all at once she took off and raced down the street to meet Joel. At some point along the way she registered that the look on his face wasn't shock or grief or concern for her – it was excitement.

Practically skidding to a halt, he caught hold of her arms.

'It's started,' he exclaimed. 'It's happening – it's happening right now.'

'What?' she asked, though she knew immediately without waiting to be told. It was what everyone had hoped for, waited for, longed for.

'The liberation of Europe has begun,' said Joel. 'Come home. We need to listen to the wireless.'

'Has it been on the BBC news?' Alison asked as they hastened down the street to their house.

'Yes and no,' Joel answered. 'There has been no official word as yet, but the BBC has reported what the German news is saying.'

As they hurried towards their house, the postman intercepted them.

'Have you heard?' he asked. 'Mrs Nuttall across the way from you has just told me.'

'Yes,' said Joel. 'We're on our way home now to see if there's any more news.'

They hadn't been indoors long before Joel had to get ready to go to work.

'I wish I didn't have to go,' he said, which was something Alison had never heard him say before. 'Today of all days, we ought to be together. This is a day for the history books.'

'I know,' Alison agreed. 'I feel the same but you have to go. Your patients are relying on you. Have you eaten breakfast?'

A little later, when Joel was ready to set off, he enveloped Alison in a warm embrace, holding her close to his heart. She clung to him, not wanting to be parted. This was a pivotal day of deep significance. Joel kissed her, held her close once more and then went on his way.

Alison flitted about, too wide awake to settle down and sleep even though she'd been up all night. She kept returning to the wireless, anxious not to miss the crucial announcement. Shortly after half past nine, the official confirmation came. John Snagge, his voice composed and authoritative, informed the nation that 'D-Day has come. Early this morning, the Allies began the assault on the north-western face of Hitler's European fortress.'

Even though she had known what she was going to hear, Alison's breath caught in her throat in a great gasp as if she was profoundly shocked. After so long at war, after the air raids and the shortages, the rationing and the dreaded telegrams, the heaps of rubble and the long lists of the dead, this day had finally come.

She put on her things and went out, not to go shopping but just to be with other people, to share the news and the hope, the sense of longing and purpose. There was some excitement, yes, but mainly the atmosphere was one of gravity and of letting the news sink in gradually. They all understood, every single one of them, what this day meant and how important it was to the future of the world.

Joel wouldn't be home until the early hours of Wednesday morning so Alison decided to go over to Wilton Close for the evening. She didn't want to be alone. Mrs Nuttall across the road had invited her to spend the evening with her family but although she appreciated the kind offer, Alison felt the need to be with those she knew best, the ones with whom she had lived through the war side by side.

There had been occasions when the group of friends had gravitated towards the station buffet even when they didn't have an arrangement to do so, but a need to be in one another's company at an important time had drawn them all there. Now it seemed the same thing had happened again, because when Alison walked into the front room in Wilton Close, she found she was by no means the only visitor.

Cordelia's family was there, her husband as well as Emily.

'I'm sure everyone in the country is glued to their wireless sets this evening,' said Cordelia. 'I'll admit it was a wrench to leave the house but Wilton Close isn't far and we wanted to share this momentous occasion.'

Alison nodded. 'It's important to be together.'

'It's been important all through the war,' said Cordelia. 'Is Joel with you?'

'He's at work,' said Alison.

'And you didn't want to be on your own,' said Margaret. 'I don't blame you.'

Joan, Bob and Joan's grandmother were there too, not to mention Brizo the dog.

'Max is staying overnight with Bob's parents,' said Joan, 'so that we could go out for our wedding anniversary, but then this happened.'

'It isn't our actual anniversary today,' said Bob, 'but this is the only day when I've got the evening off.'

'I'm glad you chose to come here,' said Mrs Cooper. 'You an' all, Mrs Foster. You're very welcome.'

'Thank you, Mrs Cooper,' replied Mrs Foster. 'I nearly didn't come because I'm not one of your circle, but then Bob said, "This isn't a day for sitting in splendid isolation," and he's right, so here I am.'

'Aye,' said Dot, who was here with her grandson. 'I didn't want to be alone either.'

'You wouldn't have been, Nan,' Jimmy replied. 'You'd have had me with you.'

'You know what I mean, lad,' Dot replied, tousling his hair. 'This is a special evening, summat for you to remember all your life. I want you to remember sharing these moments with your nan and her friends.'

'And Brizo,' Jimmy added, sliding an arm around the dog.

Bob smiled. 'Brizo has never forgotten how you got us to rescue him, Jimmy.'

'Where's Mr Green tonight?' Joan asked Dot.

'On ARP duty,' Dot answered. 'And our Sheila is on the night-shift, which is how come I've got Jimmy. Our Pammy wanted to be with her parents, so that's where she and Jenny are. Me and Jimmy could have gone an' all, but, well, I wanted to be with my wartime friends. It seemed right.'

'I can appreciate that,' Fay agreed. 'I had the same feeling.'

The doorbell rang and Mrs Grayson went to answer it, returning with Mr Darrell, Margaret's father.

'I hope it's in order for me to invite myself round,' he said.

'Of course it is,' said Mrs Cooper.

'We were all just agreeing that coming here felt like the right thing to do,' Fay told Mr Darrell.

'In my case,' he replied, 'my boy is overseas and my older girl and her little ones are away in the country, so I wanted to be with Margaret.'

'That's entirely understandable,' said Cordelia.

Alison looked around the room. They were all here – no, wait.

'Is Persephone working tonight?' she asked.

'She's visiting Matt,' said Colette. 'I imagine they'll be thinking of all those munitions trains Matt was on, and how those were a part of what is happening now across the Channel.'

Alison noticed that Cordelia's husband wore a red carnation and a white carnation tied with a sliver of blue ribbon on the lapel of his jacket.

'That's a very patriotic buttonhole,' she commented.

'I wish I could take the credit for it,' said Cordelia with a smile.

'All the florists in town were selling them today,' said Mr Masters.

'I'm not surprised,' said Mrs Grayson.

'It's been a funny old day in town,' went on Mr Masters. 'I had to leave the office once or twice to go to appointments and there were people standing in shop doorways where the wireless was playing inside. Bus drivers and lorry drivers leaned out of their cab windows asking for the latest news and the moment the evening papers appeared on the streets, huge queues formed at all the news-stands.'

'I'm glad you're all here so we can listen to the King together,' said Mrs Cooper.

Emily looked at the clock on the mantelpiece. 'He's making his address at nine o'clock.'

'I'm surprised by how sombre I feel,' said Colette. 'I had expected today to feel more exciting. We've looked forward to it and yearned for it for such a long time.'

'We all feel like that,' said Alison.

'It's because we know what a massive undertaking it is,' said Margaret.

'And there is bound to be huge loss of life,' said Mrs Cooper.

As nine o'clock approached, they all fell silent while they waited for His Majesty to make his address. The King, speaking with his customary quiet sincerity, referred to the Battle of Britain when 'our nation and Empire stood alone against an overwhelming enemy . . .' before speaking of what now lay ahead and he called upon everyone to unite in prayer as what he dubbed 'the great crusade' commenced.

'God save the King,' Colette whispered at the close of the speech and the others echoed her words.

'And God save the troops as well,' Margaret added, her fingers brushing the dainty silver W necklace she wore in honour of her brother William. The others had bought it for her when she had changed her surname in honour of her mother.

Mrs Cooper looked at Cordelia. 'Do you remember the toast you gave at the end of Joan and Bob's wedding day, after they'd gone off on the train and us four mothers-of-the-bride had a cuppa together?'

'I do, actually,' said Cordelia. 'It was: to family and friends. No, not friends – friendship. I remember it because of something that Dot – I mean Mrs Green – said about friendship running deeper than she'd ever imagined and it was thanks to us doing our war work.'

'Fancy you remembering that,' Dot remarked.

'Aye,' chimed in Mrs Grayson, 'and you also said that friends can become a kind of family.'

'That's us,' said Mrs Cooper. 'Friends brought together by the war. Today that feels extra special.'

'Not just brought together by the war,' said Alison, 'but by the railways.'

She looked around the room at her friends. One day she would be allowed to tell them about the huge number of onward travel operations that had taken place all over the kingdom – not for her own glory, not because she wanted to be congratulated and admired for her own small part in it, but so that they could share her pride in the railway network and the many members of railway staff who had worked tirelessly together to make D-Day possible. Her heart filled with gratitude, hope and a sense of the enormity of the occasion.

Emerging from her thoughts, she realised everyone was listening to Colette.

'. . . it's true that friends can become family,' said Colette. 'My friends have certainly become mine.' She gave Mrs Cooper the warmest of smiles.

'We should also remember the ones we've lost,' said Mrs Grayson.

'Aye, that's true,' said Dot. 'Little Lizzie.'

Colette looked at Mrs Foster and Joan. 'And Letitia.'

'And Alec,' Margaret said to Alison. 'None of us knew him apart from you, but we know Lydia and your parents. Your family's loss matters to all of us.'

Alison nodded. On this evening of all evenings, she had needed to hear that.

'They died in the course of their duty,' said Mrs Foster. 'We must take what comfort we can from that.'

Jimmy piped up. 'They died in the cause of freedom.' When everyone looked at him, he added, 'We had an extra assembly this afternoon and that's what our headmaster said.'

'He was right,' said Emily.

'I think we need to raise our teacups in a toast,' said Mrs Cooper, 'just like we did after Joan and Bob's wedding reception.' She looked expectantly at the guests filling her front room.

'I don't think we can do better than the toast we had last time,' said Mrs Grayson. 'Family and friendship.'

'And the railways!' Alison said quickly, before anybody could echo the words. 'Working for LMS brought us together and made us into a family, made us friends for life.'

If only she could say, 'D-Day couldn't have happened without the railways'; but the words were there in her heart.

'Family, friendship and the railways,' said Dot.

They all raised their cups and mugs as they repeated, 'Family, friendship and the railways.'

'And victory,' said Jimmy.

'And victory,' was the sincere echo all around the room.

Dear Readers,

One feature of being an author is that you have no idea of the circumstances in which your book will be read. For example, I heard from one reader who told me that she started reading the Railway Girls series because of losing her nana, who had been a lover of sagas. On Nana's bookshelf were the early Railway Girls books and her granddaughter started reading them so as to feel close to her darling nana. After a while, the characters crept into her heart and she found herself reading the stories not just for Nana's sake but also because she was eager to find out what happened next. I was very touched to hear this, and I'm sure you are too.

When Colette first became a viewpoint character back in book four, *Christmas with the Railway Girls*, I soon found that her plot had struck a deeply personal chord with many readers. As her story has unfolded, I have heard from various women who have told me about their marriages to their own 'Tony', and how they escaped. 'Escaped' is the word they all use. I have also heard from mothers whose daughters were married to a Tony and, as with Colette in the early days, no one else had any idea. I am honoured that these women feel that Colette's story is true to life.

I hope you enjoyed reading *Springtime with the Railway Girls*. I derived a lot of pleasure from writing it. The characters all mean a great deal to me and I love exploring their lives and relationships – and I love having all my readers along for the ride. As you know, female friendship is the most important aspect of the stories and I hope you regard Dot, Joan, Colette and the rest as your friends.

Much love,

Maisie xx

CHOREOGRAPHING THE ACTION

As you may have seen in the acknowledgements, my husband Kevin gets the credit for planning the action sequence that takes place at the country station. You might be surprised by how much work and preparation goes into one of these action sequences. For instance, back in book four, *Christmas with the Railway Girls*, there was an incident involving a set of railway wagons that ran unchecked down a hill, causing what might have ended up as a fatal accident. On the page, it took just a few lines in Chapter Six to describe what happened but, before that, Kevin worked out the necessary gradient of the hill and how many wagons there needed to be, so as to ensure that what I wanted to describe could really have happened.

In *Springtime with the Railway Girls*, the country station sequence took far longer – and many more diagrams – to work out than any previous action sequence in the series, because there were so many elements to take into consideration. How long was the station platform and how far from the end of the platform was the signal-box? Where exactly on the railway line did the passenger train wait? It had to obscure the signalman's view of the railway tracks where the incident was about to happen (which is why, having got to the signal-box and spoken to the signalman, Colette then goes down a couple of steps so she can see clearly what is taking place). How fast was the goods train travelling, given that it was going to switch from one line to another on the points?

Every time Kevin came up with a way of making the events unfold the way I needed them to, I'd say, 'It can't happen that way because Colette wouldn't be able to see that bit happening – and if she can't see it, then the reader can't either.'

And Kevin would calmly go back to the drawing board . . .

BIBLIOGRAPHY

As always, I am indebted to the authors of a variety of books that have helped me in my writing. If you have seen previous bibliographies of mine, you may recall that there are some books I refer to again and again. Here, I am going to mention some titles that haven't appeared in previous lists.

Jerry White's ***The Battle of London 1939–45: Endurance, Heroism and Frailty Under Fire*** (Vintage, 2023) helped Iphigenia write her letter to Persephone.

Anne de Courcy's ***Debs at War 1939–1945: How Wartime Changed Their Lives*** (Weidenfeld & Nicolson, 2005) guided Persephone through her trip to London and also gave Iphigenia the opportunity to fly in a Cessna over the south coast.

The Illustrated London News: Great Events of the 20th Century (Guild Publishing, 1989) was one of the sources I consulted for battles and other events overseas. Another was **Rodney Castleden's** ***Harrap's Book of British Dates: A Comprehensive Chronological Dictionary of British Dates From Prehistoric Times to the Present Day*** (Harrap Books, 1991).

The Handbook of British Dates For Students of English History, edited by C. R. Cheney (Royal Historical Society, 1978), is a book I have turned to throughout the series. Using this has meant I always know what day of the week it is in the story.

And if you want to know the details of the role the railways played in wartime, including how they supported the D-Day invasion, I strongly recommend ***Steaming to Victory: How Britain's Railways Won the War* by Michael Williams** (Arrow, 2013). In this book you can also read about Driver Ben Gimbert and Fireman Jim Nightall, whose extraordinary heroism saved the market town of Soham when their munitions train caught fire.

Acknowledgements

Usually I start my acknowledgements by thanking the editorial team, but this time I'm putting my husband Kevin first. He has choreographed various railway incidents in the course of the series, but none has ever required as much time and discussion or as many diagrams as the one that takes place at the country station in this story.

I am grateful to everyone at Penguin Random House who worked on this book, especially Katie Loughnane and Rose Waddilove. If you love the cover, that's because Emma Grey Gelder is such a talented designer.

Thanks to book bloggers Julie Barham, Karen Mace, Yvonne Gill and Zoe Morton; and also to Jen Gilroy, Jane Cable, Beverley Hopper and Catherine Boardman.

SIGN UP TO OUR SAGA NEWSLETTER

Penny Street

The home of heart-warming reads

Welcome to **Penny Street**, your **number one stop for emotional and heartfelt historical reads**. Meet casts of characters you'll never forget, memories you'll treasure as your own, and places that will forever stay with you long after the last page.

Join our online **community** bringing you the latest book deals, competitions and new saga series releases.

You can also find extra content, talk to your favourite authors and share your discoveries with other saga fans on Facebook.

Join today by visiting
www.penguin.co.uk/pennystreet

Follow us on Facebook
www.facebook.com/welcometopennystreet

Penny Street
the home of heart warming reads